Praise for *The Double Happi...*

'Katie Rivers is a heroine for . Coming from the most unlikely ⌣ ui the New Mexico desert, this ballerina in ...sues her destiny with a passion that is both admirable and reckless. This sweeping family saga, set against the background of the Vietnam War, takes the reader from the rural Southwest to the New York City of Katie's dreams, to the Yukon wilderness and back again, as a young girl and her family strive for resolution and confront their special demons. *The Double Happiness Company* is a wonderful story and a cautionary tale that will stay with readers long after they have set this compelling book down.'
—ROSANNA SERAVALLI, *Professor of Ballet, Purchase College, State University of New York*

'This is a wonderful book! It's true to life and captures the thoughts and feelings of a dancer struggling with her family and career, present and past. And, as good dancing does, it will stir your memories and lift you up.'
—FINIS JHUNG, *Master Teacher, former Principal Dancer, Harkness Ballet*

'Wonderful writing and a beautiful, unique novel.'
—ROGER LEVY, *author of* Icarus

'A heart-rending tale.'
—CHRISTIAN HOLDER, *former Principal Dancer, City Center Joffrey Ballet*

Also by Anne Aylor

No Angel Hotel

'Anne Aylor's *No Angel Hotel* . . . is a finely crafted and moving exploration of the youthful pain and the lasting passion of love.'
—*Washington Post Book World*

'The multi-talented Anne Aylor (she is also a professional dancer) has produced a novel of spellbinding intensity . . . Written in brief, ephemeral passages as if a more prolonged focus would scorch the page, this is an exhilarating first novel.'
—*Yorkshire Post*

'With a spare elegance that lives up to her publisher's comparison—with the romances of Jean Rhys—Aylor's first novel presents a passionate, gloomy story of abandoned innocence and abused love.'
—*Kirkus Reviews*

About the author

Born in the USA, Anne Aylor is the author of *No Angel Hotel* which was published by HarperCollins and St Martin's Press. In 2008 she was shortlisted for the Bridport Prize with her short story, 'The Speed of Dark'. She has danced with the Oakland Ballet and currently teaches ballet at Morley College, London. She worked in postwar Bosnia at the Pavarotti Music Centre where she taught ballet and treated those affected by the war with acupuncture. She is the founder of Anne Aylor Creative Writing Courses.

ANNE AYLOR

The Double Happiness Company

BareBone
Books

The Double Happiness Company
ANNE AYLOR

First published by BareBone Books in 2011
46 Beversbrook Road
London N19 4QH
www.barebonebooks.com

© Anne Aylor 2011

The right of Anne Aylor to be identified as author of this work has been asserted in accordance with the Copyright, Designs and Patents Act 1988

All characters and events in this publication, other than those clearly in the public domain, are fictitious and any resemblance to real persons, living or dead, is purely coincidental.

The chapter 'The Double Happiness Company' has previously been broadcast on BBC Radio 3.

Designed and typeset by word-design.co.uk
Printed in Great Britain by Imprint Digital
ISBN 978-0-9566725-0-6

for
ALICE ROSS

&

in memory of
GERALDINE GODFREY
(1922 – 2004)

CONTENTS

Fortuna, 1977 1

El Paso, 1967. 23

El Paso, 1969. 51

Fortuna, 1971 135

New York, 1971 191

Whitehorse, 1977 253

Fortuna, 1977 257

FORTUNA, 1977

Home is so sad. It stays as it was left,
Shaped to the comfort of the last to go
As if to win them back.

PHILIP LARKIN

In her old bedroom is a trunk her mother has labeled KATIE'S PRECIOUS THINGS. Inside this box of relics is a photograph of her at thirteen. She is on the back porch wearing the costume her father ordered from New York because no store in a thousand miles had anything like this pink-and-purple tutu with sequined fruit stitched to the strap.

Her eyes are closed against the glare of the sun. There is a tiara in her hair and a look of rapture on her face. On her feet are a pair of Nicolini pointe shoes. Balancing on tiptoe, her satin feet stab the boards of the patio, legs snapped together as tightly as scissors. She remembers what her brother said when this picture was taken: 'If Martians got hold of this, they'd think earthlings only had one foot.'

In the fading Polaroid she is smiling, her barbed-wire teeth just visible. Her arms are flung over her head. Her skinny legs echo the shadows of the grape arbor whose slender beams crisscross in rhomboids behind her. In contrast to the potato-white house which is her backdrop, she is wearing a cloud of damson net. In this tutu she is a ballerina, the Sugar Plum Fairy who lives in the Land of the Sweets.

This picture was taken when she was on a mission to become the greatest dancer the world had ever known. When she was alone at home, she'd secretly put on her mother's make-up and fake fur coat. Nobody knew she swanned around her bedroom pretending to be Anna Pavlova. If she had admitted this to anyone, they would only have laughed. Fortuna was a border town full of farmers and cowboys, not so many years away from Apache massacres, Billy the Kid and the law of the gun.

She traces her finger around the picture's stiff edges. Her father must have taken this. She would never have posed with such abandon in front of her mother, who drove her to her weekly lessons but never approved of the stage as a career. 'Ballet is nice for little girls,' she liked to say, 'otherwise it's as useful as a tit on a boar hog.'

The photo is drenched in sunlight. It exposes every hollow, muscle, bone. At the time it was taken she wouldn't have seen her adolescent gawkiness. She is not Katie Scarlett Rivers. She is Katerina Gorbanyevskaya, the name on the back of the photo, written in Russian letters so no one can tease her.

At twenty-five, what strikes her most about this picture is, although she is alone, she is supremely happy. Happier than anyone in the sad, curtained house behind her because she is doing what she was born to do. Dance.

3

Homecoming queen

WELCOME TO FORTUNA, NEW MEXICO • 10,154 FRIENDLY PEOPLE AND A FEW SOREHEADS.

They had driven an hour to reach this bullet-pocked sign in the desert. The car sailed past the rusted square of metal, heading toward jagged mountains that looked like a dragon's back against the sky. Yucca and creosote gave way to scattered buildings hugging the highway. Apache Motel. Sands Motel. Sierra Ice and Water.

At the Tortugas Diner a neon turtle poked its head out of its shell, alternating with *TRANSMISSIONS REPAIRED*. Katie sat in the back seat of the Lincoln: silent, preoccupied, as she watched her childhood landscape slide past.

Before the railroad tracks was a weathered board with a huge pink hand. *CRYSTAL BALL & TEA-LEAF READINGS • TAROT CARDS.* She stared at the faded palm, remembering what Orbalee had told her. *You will be the healer. You will be brother and sister, daughter and son.*

Her father looked at her in the rearview mirror. 'You all right back there, Katie? You look like you've seen a ghost.'

'These hives are driving me crazy.'

'How many of those suckers you got?'

She heard her mother give his leg a little slap. 'Haywood, I'll never get you polished.'

'About forty, Daddy.'

'When we get home,' he said, 'I'll give you some cream to take the fire out.'

'Show me how bad they are, sugar,' her mother said. 'You've been scratching like a mangy dog ever since you got off the plane.'

Katie reluctantly held out a welt-covered arm.

'Ye gods, sugar,' her mother said. 'You've made yourself bleed.'

Katie fell against the back seat. With each second they were getting closer to home. What had made her think she could do this? She scratched the hives that had suddenly appeared at the airport, tiny volcano-shaped wheals that hadn't bothered her for years.

They were nearing Mesquite Street and she prayed the old star would be up. It had sat on the top of their house every Christmas for as long as she could remember. Her father had cut the huge star out of plywood, drilled holes around the edges and screwed in strings of blue lights. Having not been home for six years, Katie was afraid the tradition had been abandoned but, from a block away, she was relieved to see it on the ridge of their roof, throwing out a cold, clean light.

Her father pulled into the driveway. 'Honey, you go in the house with Momma. I'll take your bags to your room.'

She waited for her mother to unlock the side entrance. She expected her dog to be in the den, barking like crazy, but Burrito was nowhere to be seen. 'Has something happened to Burrito you haven't told me about?'

Her mother nodded toward the kitchen. 'She's probably in there. She's been deaf as a post the last few years.'

Burrito was curled up in her bed. Katie knelt to pet her, upset the old dachshund wasn't shimmying and shaking to welcome her back.

Her mother unbuttoned her coat. 'She's hardly got any teeth left. I told Daddy he should try and make her a pair of doggy dentures.'

Katie scooped the miniature dachshund into her arms. Burrito felt smaller, bonier. It was like hugging her mother at the airport.

'You're miles away, sugar.'

'What?'

'I just said Burrito yelps whenever she eats. The vet says there's nothing we can do except give her puppy food to flop her gums around.' Her mother tied a Christmas apron over her dress. 'Leave that hound alone for a minute. You should be walking around to see what's new in here.'

Katie shuffled around the kitchen, the dog in her arms. Everything looked exactly the same. The room was decorated with the holiday gewgaws her mother had used for over twenty years. A gumdrop tree spearing a few forlorn pieces of candy, a sleigh with tiny packages pulled by wire reindeer, a ruby-robed chorister with a smashed face. Once there'd been a whole choir. Katie stared at the lone papier-mâché figurine, then forced herself to look at the dining table, heartbroken to see only three chairs around it when there had always been four.

'Well?' her mother said.

Katie twirled around, not wanting her mother to see her face. 'You have a new stove.'

'Right.'

'New carpet?'

'One more.'

She nuzzled Burrito as she glanced at the open shelves of canned goods, now covered with a beaded curtain. 'I don't remember that.'

'Isn't it pretty?' her mother said. 'It picks up the colors of the kitchen and it's so much nicer to look at than old tin cans. Who wants to have Vienna sausages staring you in the face every time you walk in?'

Katie brushed her hand against the orange translucent beads. They started to hula and click.

'I showed Berma Langstrom my new curtain and she had the gall to say they have these in cathouses. Without batting an eye I said, "Berma, how'd you know what they have in cathouses?"' Her mother grinned triumphantly. 'Want me to fix you something to eat or did they tank you up on the plane?'

'I'd love a coffee.'

Her mother filled the kettle and put it on the stove to boil. 'How's your knee?'

Katie looked up, nervous her mother would ask something she'd have to lie about. 'Fine. Why?'

'You were limping when you came off the plane. I thought you might have hurt it again.'

'My corns have been giving me trouble lately.'

'I've been going to a new podiatrist. He's real good. I can make an appointment with Dr Bouchard tomorrow.'

'That'd be great if he's got room.' She lowered Burrito into her bed and straightened up to feel her mother's hands clapped over her eyes. 'What's going on?'

'You'll find out soon enough. Start walking.'

Her mother guided her into the living room. Before lifting her hands she shouted, 'Surprise, sugar, surprise!'

Red, white and blue streamers crisscrossed the ceiling. Above the couch was a banner with gym-sized letters: WELCOME HOME,

KATIE SCARLETT! She knew it must have taken her mother hours to put up these decorations, but she couldn't thank her. If she said one word, she'd start crying and wouldn't be able to stop.

Her mother stepped in front of her, her brow furrowed with disappointment. 'You haven't said anything.'

Out of the corner of her eye, she saw her father duck into his room. Now she knew why he hadn't joined them. He didn't want to be around when she saw those streamers that looked like a soldier's homecoming.

Find something else to talk about, Katie told herself. Find something else. She turned to the corner of the room where the Christmas tree had always been. A small pink artificial tree replaced the ceiling-high fir they'd had when she and Rhett were growing up.

The kettle started to whistle. She was grateful for the opportunity to run into the kitchen to turn it off.

Her mother called after her, 'I want to hear all about your plans for the wedding. We've got a hundred things to organize before August rolls around.'

Katie leaned around the door. 'I'd like to hit the sack if you don't mind.'

'But you just got here, sugar.'

'I know, but I'm feeling really bushed.'

'What about your coffee?'

'With all these hives, the caffeine might keep me awake.'

Her mother picked up the rippled knit blanket draped over the couch. She looked hurt. 'It's cold tonight. Take this African to bed with you. Just make sure to say good night to Daddy. You know how much he dotes on you.'

Katie opened her bedroom door, shocked to see the oyster-white walls were now the color of cotton candy. Nothing else had changed: the Nutcracker doll was still screaming on the vanity, the paint-by-number ballerina still leaned over to tie the ribbons on her shoes. On the curtains, plump Degas dancers balanced on their pudgy legs. Katie walked over to finger the flimsy cloth. Her mother had made them for her tenth birthday from dress material too thin for floor-length curtains. Unlined, unweighted, they hung uneasily, let in too much desert light.

Her eyes skipped around the pink box of her childhood. Propped against the mirror was a souvenir program with a picture of Katie dressed as a puppet. Standing next to her was Madame Feodorova in a magician's cape and jeweled turban.

You were a fool, Katya, to throw away a brilliant career.

Katie laughed at herself for imagining a picture could talk.

You can't do it anymore, can you?

'I don't have to prove anything to you.'

Then do the 'Russian Dance'. It's your chance to show me you were right and I was wrong.

Katie jerked open her closet, crammed from floor to ceiling with boxes and clothes. She tried to slide her mother's dresses back to see what was behind them, but the rack was so full it was impossible to move the hangers. She struggled with the tightly-packed clothes until she found her old records behind a lime-green evening gown.

She flicked through them until she found *Petrouchka*. She slid it out of its cover. Knowing exactly the band she wanted, she put the record on the turntable and sat on the end of the bed. Stravinsky's music filled the room. Her head drooped as her feet snapped upward, legs jerking, arms swinging, as if her limbs were controlled by strings. To the accelerating music she twisted from side to side, a marionette magically brought to life. She leaned backward and lifted both feet off the floor, crossing and beating her heels in the air.

Madame Feodorova glared at her from the cover of the souvenir program. *You're off the beat, Katya. Faster!*

Once this tempo would have been easy for her but, after only seven bars, she was lagging behind.

One, two, three, four, five, six, seven, eight. One, two, three, four, five, six—

She was so intent on keeping up with the music that it took her a few seconds to realize a fist was beating time on the other side of her door.

'What's that awful noise, Katie Scarlett?'

She jumped off the bed and lurched toward the stereo. 'Nothing, Momma.'

'It's that horrible *Patricia*, isn't it?'

Katie lifted the needle arm, returned it to its cradle.

'Daddy's found your hive cream.'

'I'll get it later, Mom.'

'You'll get it now so you can stop that durn dancing and get some sleep.'

Through the crack in her father's door she saw him doing the crossword. She knocked three times.

'Charge,' he said. 'What your Momma does so well with my Visa card.'

Hanging on the wall behind him were her baby pictures and smiling portraits of her parents' younger selves. She searched them, desperately hoping to see a photo of Rhett. Not a single one.

Her father waved a tube of ointment. 'There was so much junk in the medicine cabinet I almost didn't find it.' He handed her the cream. 'This cortisone should give you some relief.'

She leaned down to kiss his forehead. 'Thanks, Daddy. I could sure do with some of that tonight.'

He pinched the fused cartilage at the top of her ear, something he used to do with her brother. Her father liked to say the genetic quirk the three of them shared was how he could tell which kids were his. 'It's a shame Wieslaw couldn't come home with you. It would have been nice to meet him before the big day.'

'He's working over Christmas. He couldn't get away.'

'Mom and I are so thrilled for you, honey.' He paused for a long time and she knew it was because he was struggling not to cry. 'Katie.'

'Yeah?'

'It sure is good to have you home.'

'It's good to be home,' she said. 'Night, night.'

In her bedroom a portable television flickered in the dark. The station had stopped broadcasting hours ago. The screen was filled with snow. She turned up the sound of the static, hoping it would help her fall asleep.

She clawed the greasy hives covering her body. The more she scratched, the more they itched. The ointment her father had given her was years out of date. At least a dozen more welts had erupted as she'd tiptoed around the house with a flashlight, trying to discover some evidence of Rhett. She'd found nothing. No balsa airplanes, no books on astronauts, no photographs.

She took her father's bent postcard out of her purse. *Looking forward to your arrival a week from tomorrow. I've been marking off the calendar. When I passed the train trestle in Cloudcroft the other day, I thought of you and your first horseback ride. Those were some of our happiest days, Katie, and we did not even know it.*

She fell on the bedspread and pulled a pillow over her face. At the airport her father had been the one who'd cried. He'd stood at the front of the crowd, waving like a man who was drowning. He'd swung his arms, making Xs in the air, while her mother had stood behind him, dry eyed as a cigar-store Indian.

Marrying a Polack

'Sleep well, sugar?'

Her mother was in the doorway, her face shiny with Vaseline. From the way she stood, hands on hips, shoulders hunched, Katie guessed her mother's back was hurting. Seeing her so stooped made Katie sad. Her mother was only fifty-six, but looked older because of her silver hair and premature dowager's hump.

Katie lifted her arms, stretched. 'Like a log.' But she was lying. All night she'd had the same terrifying dream. She was spinning, falling, then jackknifing up in bed before she smashed into the ground.

Her mother reached under her night hat to take out some curlers. 'I always slept well my first evening back home. I felt like a little girl again with all the old, familiar smells.' Her face softened and, for a second, Katie thought she looked almost young again.

'I managed to make an eleven o'clock appointment with Dr Bouchard. We need to be out of here in an hour.'

'Thanks for booking that. I appreciate it.'

'Careful how you kiss me.' Her mother bent down to offer her cheek. 'I'm all greased up. Your mouth might just go shooting off into the middle of next week.'

Katie smiled and gave her a peck.

'We need to start making plans for your wedding when we get back from the doctor's. I've got a long list of what we need to discuss.'

'I don't want you to worry about anything, Momma. Wieslaw and I have everything under control.'

'You'll need me to book the church and the minister and the florist—'

'We're not getting married in Fortuna.'

Her mother's head jerked backward. 'Why ever not?'

'Because all our friends are back east.'

'But the First Baptist is so lovely and Reverend Bridgewater would do such a good service—'

'Wieslaw and I don't want to get married in a church. We were talking about having it in a field.'

'A field?'

'Being surrounded by wild flowers instead of fussy bouquets. We think it's kind of romantic.'

Her mother looked horrified and embarrassed at the same time. She pointed at Katie's gown. 'I see you found your nightie.'

The last letter she'd received from her mother had inventoried what she didn't need to pack. *Housecoat, houseshoes, hair dryer, nightgown, underwear (I bought you a days-of-the-week panty set for Christmas). You won't need shampoo or sanitary towels either. I've got a drawer full of samples I've saved over the years. I'm letting you know ahead of time so you'll have more room in your suitcase for what you want to take back.*

Her mother started to rub the gown's fabric, a cloth heaven stamped with gold planets and shooting stars. 'Remember this nightgown, sugar?'

Katie shook her head, but she was lying.

Her mother reached up to push away the hair falling across Katie's eyes. 'Remember me telling you these were fairy locks? When you were little, you asked why your hair was tangled when you woke up. I told you the fairies liked to dance in it while you were asleep.'

Katie pictured the matchboxes her mother had pasted together as a place to store their cobweb gowns. She remembered the chest covered with scraps of brocade, tiny moonstones from a broken necklace for handles. As a child, that fairy chest had been her most prized possession.

Her mother stroked a handful of split ends. 'It's time you got a new hair style. You look like some old dog no one can be bothered to comb out.'

'I have to have it long to dance.'

'You could chop your hair off and wear a wig on stage. You'd look pretty in a pageboy.'

'I hate to tell you, Momma, but pageboys went out in the Sixties.'

'I'll never understand what long hair has to do with ballet. You don't dance with your hair.'

'Long hair is a dancer's trademark.'

'Hooey,' her mother said, flicking her hand. 'If you want to keep that fiancé of yours, you should go to the beauty shop every week like I do. Not let it hang down your back like some old squaw.'

'It's 1977, Momma. Women don't have to be slaves to curlers anymore.'

'I'll bet Weeslaw—'

'Vee-ess-suave,' she said gently. 'Poles pronounce their W's as V's. V for Victor, S for sugar, then Suave like the home permanent.'
'I'll bet he wouldn't be impressed if you turned up at LaGuardia dressed like an Indian. I nearly died when you got off the plane wearing a buckskin jacket and skirt. I don't want Daddy's patients thinking I have a child who dresses like it's Halloween.'
Katie stared out the window. She hadn't come back home to fight.
'You haven't said a thing yet about your room,' her mother said. 'Don't you notice anything different in here?'
'I loved pink when I was little, but it's a color you kind of grow out of.'
Her mother jammed her hands on her hips. 'No matter how hard I try, Katie Scarlett, I can't do anything to please you.'
'I do appreciate what you've done,' she said, hooking an arm around her mother's. 'But I'm almost twenty-six. I've changed. I've grown up.'
'All you've grown is away.'
'Please, let's not argue, Momma. Okay?'
Her father poked his head around the door. He was holding Burrito. 'Morning, ladies. Mind if we join you?'
Katie gratefully waved him inside. He was wearing a burgundy-colored robe embroidered with a gold dragon. She was amazed to see him wear silk: so impractical, so luxurious, so unlike anything else he had ever owned. He put Burrito in her arms and leaned down to kiss them, Katie first.
'You should come home more often,' her mother said. 'Your father doesn't kiss me when you're not around.'
'Now, Momma,' he said. 'Stop exaggerating.'
'I am not your Momma,' she said, 'and I am not exaggerating.' She picked up a music box on the chest of drawers and cranked the key. Two ceramic lovebirds jerked into action, twirling around each other to the theme from *Love Story*. No one said anything as the music wound down.
To end the awkward silence Katie said, 'I've been trying to figure out what's different about your hair, Daddy.'
'That's his "dry look",' her mother said. 'People think I've got myself a new boyfriend ever since he threw away his Wildroot Hair Oil.'
Her father said, 'Why don't you tell Katie the funny thing that happened at Kiwanis last week?'

Her mother stubbornly shook her head.

'Come on, Lo,' he said, patting her hand. 'Nobody tells it better than you.'

Her mother's face relaxed. Katie knew it was that 'Lo' that did it. He hardly ever called her that.

'It was Pancake Day at Kiwanis Club,' her mother said, 'and Hay was sitting on the dais with the other members of the board. Kaki Davenport, who just got divorced, leaned over to me all googly-eyed and said, "Lola, who's that good-looking Italian up there?" And I told her, "Kaki, that's no good-looking Italian. That's my husband without his Wildroot Hair Oil."'

They all laughed, her father the loudest.

'Hey, Katie,' he said, 'ever since you told us you were going to be Mrs Borkowski, I've been saving up my Polish jokes.'

'Daddy, you know I don't like redneck humor.'

'Be a sport. Once you've married that Polack, I won't be able to tell them.'

She sighed, but it was all part of their game. Her reluctant straight man to his corny comic. 'Go ahead.'

'Why did the Polish chicken cross the road?'

'I don't know.'

'To ask Colonel Sanders for political asylum.'

'Daddy, that's terrible.'

'How can you tell the bride at a Polish wedding?'

Katie shook her head.

'She's the one with the braided armpits.' He watched her pained reaction and slapped his thigh.

'*Padre*, that's racist.'

'At least we try to talk,' her mother said. 'You've hardly said a word since you've come in the door.'

He put a hand on his wife's arm. 'Don't, Lola—'

'Don't you "don't" me. I'm dying to hear about her wedding plans and she hasn't said three words that I haven't pulled out of her like teeth. She's like someone else I know.' She jerked her pajama top and flounced out the door.

Puzzled, Katie looked at her father. 'Didn't she know I was kidding?'

'Your mother's just tired, honey. She's been so excited you were coming she hasn't slept. Then she put her back out decorating the living room. I told her the streamers weren't a good idea, but she put them up anyway. I tried to tell her you can't be turned into a substitute for—'

Your brother. That's what he was about to say, but the dead could never be mentioned. Her parents had stripped the house of anything to remind them of him. The only thing Katie had managed to find was the marble collection she and Rhett had hidden years ago. Before her parents were awake, she'd gone to the back yard to dig it up. She'd brushed the dirt off the jar and held it up to the sun, a dusty cathedral of stained glass filled with cat's-eyes, agates, peewees and boulders.

The Rockettes or something like that

Her mother drove down Main Street, four lanes empty of traffic. Fortuna was a ghost town compared to the shove and push of New York City: no one on the empty sidewalks, no honking, no screams of sirens.

Her mother tapped a nail on the windshield. 'We've got a skyscraper now. That's where Dr Bouchard's office is.'

Katie shaded her eyes as she squinted at the ten-story building glittering in the distance. The sun's reflection in the copper-colored windows was blinding.

'If you need some sunglasses, sugar, there's an old pair of yours in the glove compartment.'

Katie rummaged through the stack of maps until she found some wraparound shades. A little thrill ran through her. Rhett's glasses. It made her feel good to wear something that had belonged to her brother, something that had somehow survived.

'You could have driven yourself to this appointment if you hadn't let your driver's license expire.'

'You don't need to drive in New York.' Katie stared at the huge silver igloo they were passing. The weather-beaten sign said TOMMY'S ROLLER RINK. This Quonset hut was where she'd first danced the hokey cokey, puppy-loved boys flying past on skates.

'One day you'll get tired of all that crime and lousy weather and come back home where you belong.'

'I know you find it hard to believe, Mom, but I like New York.'

'I don't know how anyone can like New York.'

'Lots of people live there.'

Her mother tossed her head. 'Lots of people live in Communist China. That doesn't mean they like it.'

'Did I write you about the Bulgarian ballet teacher I heard at a dance seminar last month? Her real name was listed in the program as "I Topolova".' Katie started to laugh. Her mother didn't.

'Why don't you give up that old ballet? Do something useful with your life for a change.'

'I read that Native Americans used beaver teeth for knife blades.'
'Don't change the subject, young lady. It's time you got some letters behind your name.'
'Mom, I didn't come home to be lectured.'
'You were a straight-A student. You could have gotten into Oxford if only you'd—'
Katie began to recite.

'Twas brillig, and the slithy toves
Did gyre and gimble in the wabe;
All mimsy were the borogoves,
And the mome raths outgrabe.

'Ballet is a short career,' her mother said, speaking over her. 'You'll need something to fall back on when you stop dancing. You can't depend on a man to look after you. Weeslaw might leave you. He might die.'
Katie glared at the liver spots on the back of her mother's hand. 'Wieslaw is twenty-eight. Odds are he's not going to die any time soon.'
Her mother's knuckles whitened as she tightened her grip on the steering wheel. 'You'd never have gone to New York if it hadn't been for that old ballet.'
Katie started to recite again, louder than before.

"Beware the Jabberwock, my son!
The jaws that bite, the claws that catch!
Beware the Jubjub bird, and shun
The frumious Bandersnatch!"

Katie wandered around the waiting room, the walls covered with Dr Bouchard's impressions of the desert. The podiatrist's landscapes were variations on a theme: the local mountain range that formed the tail end of the Rockies. The canvases were encrusted with undiluted colors: ultramarine blue, madder red, chrome yellow. They were all for sale.
Her mother glanced up from her *Readers' Digest*. 'Aren't Dr Bouchard's pictures gorgeous? If you see one you like, I can buy it for you and Weeslaw as a wedding present. I'll bet he hasn't seen any paintings like these in New York.'

The consulting-room door swung open. 'Morning, Mrs Rivers. This must be the daughter you've told me so much about.'

'Sure is.' Her mother stood up, beaming, and motioned Katie to go forward. 'My daughter was just admiring your beautiful pictures.'

The podiatrist shook her hand. 'Glad you like my work, Miss Rivers. I've developed some new brush strokes to represent the amazing light out west.'

'My daughter's always going to exhibitions in New York, aren't you, sugar?'

Dr Bouchard pointed at her feet. 'Must have bought those shoes in the Big Apple. Sure don't see Swede footwear like that around here.'

Her mother blushed. 'I don't know why she wore those. They make her look like the boy who stuck his finger in a dike.'

'If you'd like to step into my office, Miss Rivers, I can have a look at your feet.'

In the treatment room he asked her to go behind a screen to remove her shoes and tights. She peeled off her pantyhose and shoved them in her purse.

'I'm impressed you wear clogs,' he said as she came out. 'The human foot was designed to be splayed, not squeezed in pointy footwear.' He pointed at his leather chair. It was like the one in her father's dental office, except the controls were at the base. 'Have a pew.'

She sat down, shivering after she placed the soles of her feet on the cold metal.

He examined one foot, then the other. 'You've got some of the worst calluses I've ever seen, young lady.'

She stared at her yellow corns, deformed nails. Her toes were definitely the ugliest part of her. 'I was a—' she started to say, then remembered her mother on the other side of the flimsy-looking wall. 'I'm a dancer.'

As far as her parents knew, she was a soloist with American Ballet Theater. Whenever they suggested she come to Fortuna for a visit, she'd tell them she was touring, rehearsing, performing. The same lies she'd been spinning for years because she couldn't face seeing them while she was fat.

Dr Bouchard said, 'Your mother mentioned something about you being in New York City with some ballet company. The Rockettes or something like that.'

She smiled, picturing herself high kicking in a line. 'Something like that.'

He rubbed his thumb across her toes. 'How much do you want off?'

'What do you mean?'

'You won't be able to dance on your toes anymore if I shave off most of your calluses. You'd get blisters.'

She studied her feet; they had thickened skin the color of cheese rinds. 'Shave the calluses off. All of them.' She blurted it out before she had a chance to change her mind.

He must have seen how upset she was because he asked, 'You're sure?'

'I'm retiring from the stage, but I haven't told my mother yet. I'd appreciate if you didn't say anything. It's kind of complicated.'

'Your secret's safe with me,' he said and winked. He took some cotton balls and soaked them in liquid. 'I'm going to rub salicylic acid over the thickened areas to make it easier to remove the dead skin.' He looked up. 'So what's it like to be back in Fortuna?'

She stared at one of his oils, taking time to consider her answer. 'It's like returning to a strange land.'

With a small brush he started to paint her toes red: not the nails, the flesh. 'Think you'll ever come back home to live?'

She scratched a clump of hives on her neck. 'Took me too long to get out.'

'Hard to keep 'em down on the farm once they've seen Paree.'

'With that accent,' she said, 'you're not from around here.'

'I was born in New England so I like it out here. Not too many people and lots of good weather.' He picked up a scalpel and started to remove the leathery skin on the ball of her foot.

'How long have you been painting?' she asked.

'I didn't take it up seriously till I came out west. The light's different here. It's whiter. More intense. Every time I try to capture that clean bright light, it just about breaks my heart.'

She studied one of his sun-drenched landscapes as he worked. In the background, the familiar jagged pipes of the Organ Mountains. In the foreground, an arroyo dotted with scrub. She had never belonged here. She had always been a misfit, a cuckoo egg in her parents' nest. The best thing about the desert was leaving on that long blue highway that headed out of town.

'Well,' Dr Bouchard said, wiping the blade on a swab, 'that about does it.'

The tray was filled with pared skin, some flakes Mercurochrome red and others the color of church wax. She looked at her baby-smooth feet, wanting to laugh and cry at the same time.

The podiatrist washed his hands and cracked open the consulting-room door. 'She's ready for you, Mrs Rivers.'

Katie pointed at the tray and whispered, 'Can I keep the skin?'

They walked across the parking lot, the soles of her clogs clanging on the concrete. Her mother asked, 'How do your feet feel now?'

She cradled the small cardboard box that Dr Bouchard had given her. 'Light,' she said.

On the drive home her mother kept glancing at the box, but didn't ask what was inside until they were on the front porch. 'What have you got in there, sugar?'

When she heard what it was, her mother made a face as if she were about to throw up. 'Ye gods, Katie. Why did you go and do a fool thing like that? I'll never be able to look Dr Bouchard in the face again.'

Katie went straight to her bedroom, locked the door and started to lift things out of her trunk. Tubes of old lipstick and greasepaint. A stencil with a dozen eyebrow patterns. Chignons. An arm cast sliced down the middle like a razor clam. A pair of *pointe* shoes with suede on the tips. Artificial flowers. Pink leg warmers. A plug-in make-up mirror with a dozen small lights around the sides.

She lifted out a padded album. The scrapbook's leaves were heavy with glue and old paper, bound with cord so you could rearrange your history: add to, or subtract from, your life. She opened the emerald-green album bulging with souvenir programs, recital photographs and newspaper clippings. On the first page was an article from the *Fortuna Sun-News*.

> **Dec 15, 1967.** For ten of her fifteen years, Katie Rivers has been a student at Carmel McCleary's School of The Dance. Her dedication to the art of ballet has finally paid off.

EL PASO, 1967

Dance comes from the muscles,
the sinews, the gut and the soul.

MERCE CUNNINGHAM

Acrobat of God

From a block away she could see the pole sign against the turquoise sky. *FEODOROVA'S BALLET ACADEMY • SCHOLARSHIP AUDITION 10.30 TODAY.* Katie tipped up her bifocals to take a final glance in the rearview mirror. She'd spent the last hour pinning and repinning her hair, until she looked like Margot Fonteyn. She felt like a real ballerina, except for her batwing glasses. She wished she could take them off for the audition, but without them she could only see a few inches in front of her face.

Her mother swung the Thunderbird into the parking lot and plucked her handbag off the seat. 'I don't know why I let you talk me into this.'

'The paper said Madame Feodorova has students in companies all over the world. The New York City Ballet, the San Francisco Ballet, the Royal—'

'Danish Ballet.' Her mother slammed the door. 'It's a waste of gas to drive a hundred miles to throw your legs in the air.'

Katie got out of the car, her synthetic ermine cape pulled around her. She'd ridden all the way from home, dressed in ballet shoes and the new plum-colored tutu her father had bought just for this audition. 'Not if I win the scholarship,' she said.

'Sugar, it's dangerous to want things as badly as you do.'

'Why?'

'Because a little hope is a dangerous thing.'

'Then you don't have to worry,' she said. 'I don't have a little hope. I have a lot. This is the opportunity I've been waiting for my whole life.'

Her mother sighed. 'Katie Scarlett, that's just what I mean. There'll be stiff competition in there. Especially if that Madame is as good as the newspaper says she is.'

Katie started to *bourrée* across the blacktop, bending and straightening her knees in tiny traveling steps as she floated across the parking lot. 'You should be glad you drove me to El Paso. I'm doing all the ironing for six months. Cross my heart and hope to die.'

She opened the lobby door, swirled off her cape and was shocked to hear loud giggles. Girls in chiffon skirts and matching leotards were pointing at her bare legs. They were wearing not one, but two pairs of tights. Pink ones covered with black ones, the heels and toes of the outer pair cut away so they could be worn over their *pointe* shoes like spats. Katie quickly ducked through the lobby to reach the observation window. The ones with corkscrew hairdos and skirts must be Madame's students. So what if they had laughed at her? This audition is what is important, she thought. I'm not going to let those girls psyche me out.

The studio was full of identically-dressed baby ballerinas who looked about eight. A woman in a knee-length net skirt and pink cummerbund swooped from one young girl to the next. Katie knew it had to be Madame Feodorova; she looked like a dancer in a Degas painting with her velvet choker and layered tulle skirt. Madame moved around the room, prodding bent knees, rounding awkward arms. Each little girl she spoke to held herself better, turned faster, balanced twice as long.

Katie pressed her nose against the window. It was as if Madame Feodorova was a sorceress who could make her students do anything she wanted. She magically sent whatever they needed to know into their muscles and bones.

Madame started to demonstrate a sequence with two running steps and a *grand jeté*. Though she didn't jump very high, she seemed weightless, hovering in the air like a sylphide in a cloud of net.

The little girls formed a line in the corner. Madame banged out the tempo with a stick as the children danced across the room to a Chopin waltz. Katie watched enviously as a girl with carnations encircling her bun performed the combination better than anyone. She was halfway across the studio when Madame shouted, 'Alejandra, throw your leg into high *grand battement*.'

Madame stopped the music to show her how to brush the floor with her leading foot and push with the second to get more elevation. She motioned the little girl back to the corner. The pianist started to play; the girl repeated the step. This time she did a perfect splits, her body momentarily suspended in mid-air.

Katie could do difficult turns and jumps but, after ten years of study, she didn't look remotely like that little girl with carnations in her hair.

Now she realized it was because Carmel rarely gave corrections. She sat on a stool next to the record player, calling out steps as her students pranced and flitted across the floor.

She heard her mother saying, 'What's wrong, Katie? You're shaking like a betsy bug.'

She couldn't take her eyes off the window. Even though the carnation girl looked half her age, she had twice as much technique.

Her mother's voice got shriller. 'Look at me when I'm talking to you, Katie Scarlett.'

She whispered, praying her mother would take the hint to lower her voice, stop saying her stupid *Gone With the Wind* name. 'I need some flowers.'

'Fla-ow-ers? What kind of fla-ow-ers?' Her mother's Tennessee drawl seemed to hang in the lobby air like a strong cologne.

'I need some cloth carnations for my hair.'

Her mother stared at the line of jumping girls. 'You don't need flowers to dance.'

'There's still time for you to go to that Woolworths we passed. Please, Momma.'

'I've got a drawer full of flowers at home. I'm not going to waste good money buying any more.'

Katie nervously tightened the strap of sports elastic that kept her glasses from flying off. 'I just know I won't win the scholarship unless I have some flowers in my hair.'

'Not having any isn't going to make an ounce of difference. Even a cockeyed fool can see these girls are better than you.'

Her eyes started to fill. She knew what her mother said was true. As Carmel's best pupil, it had never occurred to Katie that she might fail. She pulled her cape around her and hurried toward the changing room to somehow make herself look like one of Madame's students.

'Where are you going?' her mother called after her.

She didn't answer.

Katie stared into the dressing-room mirror with a sinking heart. Droopy tutu. Goosepimply legs. A snood that looked like she had a cow pie on the nape of her neck. She unpinned the heavy net to try and scrape her hair into a corkscrew; the trouble was she didn't know how. She combed her hair into a ponytail, thinking that would be a start.

She was trying to figure out how to make her hairdo look less old fashioned when a Mexican girl came into the dressing room. At least she won't be any competition, Katie thought. She's at least twenty pounds overweight.

The girl wiggled into a purple leotard and turned to face the mirror. Katie watched her put her hands on her chubby thighs. The girl started to cry, her eyes flicking back and forth from her own reflection to Katie's. Sniffling, the girl tugged down the legs of her leotard.

'Nervous about the audition?' Katie asked.

'I didn't know we was supposed to wear tights.'

'Me neither. But you're welcome to borrow these.' Katie took two pairs of pink leg warmers out of her bag and gave the girl a set. 'They'll hide your calves.'

'*Gracias.*' The girl smiled as if she'd given her a handful of diamonds. '*Mil gracias.*'

Outside, the sound of clapping. The beginners' class was over and the audition was about to start. Katie frantically looped and twisted her hair before jamming in some bobby pins. She grabbed her dance bag and headed for the door. 'Good luck,' she said over her shoulder.

The Mexican girl said, 'You too.'

Katie rushed out of the dressing room in time to watch the little girls troop out and the chiffon-skirted dancers go in. Even though she looked ridiculous in her recital tutu and bare thighs, Katie knew Madame Feodorova would spot her talent. She had to. If she didn't, she'd have to go back to Carmel McCleary's School of The Dance.

As Katie stepped inside the studio, the first thing that hit her was the smell. Rank, like puma piss at the El Paso Zoo. She sniffed again, shocked to realize the stink must have been made by the beginners. She knew professional dancers sweated buckets, not eight year olds.

The girls in chiffon skirts lined up behind a tray filled with whitish powder. It must be a rosin box; at Carmel's they used wet sponges so they wouldn't slip on her waxed floor. One by one, the dancers stepped into the wooden tray, crushing the crystals of pine sap until they were a coarse dust. Katie pretended she knew what she was doing, confidently pawing the soles of her slippers. She walked to the back of the studio and was horrified to see she was the only one who'd left a trail of sticky powder.

Madame rapped the floor with a stick. 'Students auditioning up here, please.'

She thought Madame would ask them for their names. Instead, the pianist handed them a number stenciled on a square of cloth and two safety pins to attach it to their chests. Katie glanced down at the figure she'd been given. Five. She knew her number was a good omen. It looked like a Russian letter, a capital B.

Madame said, 'If you are serious about ballet, you must surrender to the discipline necessary to make an instrument of your body. Do not question what is asked of you. You have come from other schools who do not have my standards. You must aspire to perfection. You must have a vision of perfection, even though you never achieve it.' She rapped the floor twice. 'Find yourselves a place and we start.'

Katie squeezed onto a barre opposite the wall of mirrors and made the sign of the cross. Ever since her mother had bought her a biography of Anna Pavlova for her eighth birthday, she had believed that to dance beautifully was something holy, a gift given by God.

Madame stepped up to a barre, her net skirt swaying gently from side to side as she put her heels together and forced her feet into a straight line. Katie copied her, placing her feet along a single narrow floorboard so that each foot was turned out 90 degrees. She looked down at her perfect first position. Carmel didn't make her stand like that.

'We do,' Madame said, and demonstrated the *plié* combination she wanted them to perform.

Katie prayed to the icon she'd hidden inside her ballet bag. Dear Virgin of Vladimir, help me. Help me to dance better than I've ever danced in my life.

Lola waved on the lobby side of the window. Seeing the reflection of her blurred hand, it looked like she was waving goodbye. Don't be ridiculous, she thought. Katie's not leaving. She'll have a bad audition if she sees you out here crying.

Lola watched the ballet teacher walk around the room, making notes about the girls with numbers pinned to their leotards. She knew

Katie didn't have a hope in Hades of winning this scholarship. Ever since that article in the *Fortuna Sun-News* had come out a month ago, Lola had been trying to prepare her for the worst.

Madame banged the floor like a majorette. Lola didn't like the look of her: huge false eyelashes, tomato-red lipstick, blue eye shadow applied as subtly as house paint. The woman reminded her of the whorehouse madam in *Gone With the Wind*.

Lola sat down when the girls started dancing; she didn't want to make Katie more nervous than she already was. Last night she'd gone into her daughter's room and found her muttering to a square of wood.

'What is that thing you're holding?'

Katie didn't answer, her face a pout.

'Answer me when I'm talking to you or I won't drive you to the audition tomorrow.'

Her daughter looked at her defiantly. 'An icon.'

Lola grabbed the pine block coated in varnish so thick it looked like it had been dipped in honey. 'Where'd you get this?'

'I made it.'

'Why?'

'So I could I pray to it.'

'And what do you pray for? To become a ballerina like that stupid Pavlova?'

'She's the greatest female dancer the world has ever seen.'

'I should never have bought you that durn book. Only a lunatic would refuse an operation to save their life.'

'Pavlova didn't want to live if she couldn't dance.'

'I've never heard such bull in all my life.'

'Go ahead, Momma. Make fun of me. That's why I never tell you anything anymore.'

That was where it had ended. Katie's angry words flapping in the air like drying laundry. It frightened Lola that her daughter had faith in an icon, that she had secrets. Katie had been so tightlipped the past few months Lola was convinced she had a boyfriend. Lola had picked the lock on her diary, only to discover that her daughter was devoting her life to becoming the next *prima ballerina assoluta*. That was the only reason she'd agreed to take her here today, to nip that crazy idea in the bud.

Lola heard thumping and asked a Mexican-looking woman standing in front of the window what they were doing. Lola had seen her there since the start of the audition, chewing off her lipstick. The woman turned her head only long enough to answer. 'They are jumping in their toe shoes.'
'Sounds like a herd of elephants.' Lola joined her at the observation window. 'Which girl is yours?'
The Mexican woman looked as proud as if she were dancing herself. 'Mercedes is number nine. Which one belongs to you?'
'The one in a tutu.'
The woman looked around the room. 'Now I no see her.'
Lola tilted up her bifocals and spotted Katie at the rear of the crowded studio, bent over, panting like a hound dog who's been chasing a coon.

Katie straightened up, completely winded. For the first time ever, sweat was stinging her eyes and her tutu bodice was soaked. Madame clapped and started to mark the next set of steps with her hands.

'We do *sissonne tombé, pas de bourrée, glissade derrière sans changé, assemblé* over. Reverse other side and repeat. Three *sautés fouettés* like so.' She indicated a jump on the left leg, one on the right and another on the left. 'Lower from arabesque to *pointe tendu derrière*. Close right front.' She picked up her stick and banged the floor. '*Préparation: un, deux, trois—*'

They were halfway through the combination when Madame stopped the music. 'You in the back. Tutu girl. From the beginning. Alone.'

Katie was panic-stricken at the thought of having to dance by herself, but she got into fifth position. Blessed Virgin of Vladimir, she prayed, help me to bring beauty into the world.

She hadn't even started when Madame put her hand up. 'Sloppy. Turn out more. Fifth is sacred position, source of all ballet technique.' She demonstrated a perfect fifth, her feet aligned so that her front foot hid her back.

Katie copied her, maneuvering her legs into position.

'Begin.'

The music started. Katie had only danced four counts when Madame stopped her again. '*Non, non, non*. Push from ball of the foot in *glissade*, then stay in the air. Again.'

Her legs were shaking from exhaustion and fear, but she repeated the combination, determined to do it as Madame had asked.

'Keep your back up. Don't look at the floor. Open your arms like you're giving away a bouquet of flowers.' When she had finished Madame said, 'Again. With more *plié* and less schmaltz.'

Katie didn't know what schmaltz was, or what she was doing wrong, but she wanted to make the combination look as effortless as the carnation girl. Katie deepened her *plié*. She jumped higher than she ever had before. She caught her reflection in the mirror, suspended in mid-air, one arm up like a wing. It looked like she was flying.

'Better,' Madame said. 'But still not good enough.'

Katie felt her cheeks get hot when she saw the chiffon-skirted girls eyeing her.

Madame turned to the class. 'Ballet is the most impermanent art. It leaves nothing behind. No paintings, no poems, no sculptures. Enjoy it, *mes petites,* for the thrill of being alive.'

The audition over, she hung back, watching Madame Feodorova make notes on her clipboard. Katie took off her *pointe* shoes and went over some of the steps they'd done, hoping that Madame would look up and tell her the scholarship was hers. Blessed Virgin, please let Madame take me. I'll do anything to win. Anything. Just make her take me.

The Mexican girl came over to where she was practicing to hand back the leg warmers. 'I bet you win the scholarship,' she said.

Katie shook her head. 'I was terrible compared to those girls in skirts.'

The Mexican girl hit her chest. 'But you dance with *corazón.* With heart. And your pirouettes. You do triples easy.'

Madame Feodorova looked up. 'The audition is over. Leave the studio, please.'

Katie could hardly make her legs move. All those hours of practicing and praying to the Virgin had been useless. Useless. There was not another good ballet school for five hundred miles.

She was shuffling toward the door when she heard Madame's voice behind her. 'Number 5, come back here, please.'

Katie turned around. Madame was patting the bench beside her, but Katie was afraid that she was seeing a mirage.

'What is your name, *golubchik?*'

Katie could hardly breathe, but she somehow managed to stammer out her name.

'Is that your mother outside?'

Katie nodded.

'Tell her to come in.'

Waving wildly, she signaled to her mother who was standing in front of the observation window, her purse welded to her stomach.

The door swung open. Her mother stepped into the room. 'It stinks to high heaven in here.'

Katie wanted to curl up in embarrassment, but Madame stood and elegantly extended her hand.

'That is the perfume of hard work, Mrs . . . ?'

'Rivers.' Her mother hesitantly took the fingers she was being offered. It looked like she was uncertain what to do, shake Madame's hand or kiss it.

'Yekaterina Feodorova.'

Her mother's eyes narrowed. 'I've never met a Russian before.'

Madame fluttered her lashes. 'I am French by passport, but Russian is my first language. After the Revolution, my mother was an *émigrée* in Paris.'

'Why did you call me in here?'

'I want to discuss your daughter. She can't sustain her placing and her feet, they are hopeless.'

Katie felt as if Madame had reached inside her chest and plucked out her heart.

'Come on, sugar,' her mother said. 'Let's not waste any more of this woman's valuable time.'

'You misunderstand me, Mrs Rivers. I'm offering your daughter a scholarship.'

'What?' Katie blurted out.

'It's true,' Madame said, putting a hand on her shoulder. 'I would like to train you.'

'If she's so bad,' her mother said, 'then why are you offering to take her on?'

'She is from a *plié* parlor, but she has something special. Something that can't be taught.'

'I'm afraid you're going to have to speak plain English,' her mother said. 'I'm American.'

'Her problem is technique. For her to dance properly, I will have to take her apart and put her back together again.'

'That won't be possible,' her mother said. 'We live fifty miles away.'

Madame drew a short line in the air with her finger. 'In America, fifty miles is nothing.'

'It may be nothing to you,' her mother said, 'but I have better things to do than be a chauffeur.'

'She is your daughter, *non?*'

'Of course she's my daughter.'

'Then you want the very best for her?'

Her mother looked like she'd been asked a trick question. 'Of course I do.'

'Your daughter's feet are a catastrophe. Something must be done quickly or she will never have a ballet career. Take off your shoes so I can show your mother what I mean.' Madame took a tube out of her bag, unscrewed the top and coated Katie's insteps with foundation. 'Stand in first position.'

Katie forced her feet into a perfect first, one foot pointing east and the other west.

'Mrs Rivers, when did your daughter begin training?'

'When she was five.'

Madame pointed to the make-up on the floor left by her feet. 'See how her arches have fallen? Early overforcing of the turnout causes tendons in the foot to become overstretched. That makes her feet weak. Children shouldn't train seriously until they are eight. Katya has completely flat feet whereas you,' she pointed to her mother's arch, 'have a high instep.'

Madame wiped the floor with a tissue and placed it on the bench. 'There are so-called teachers who know nothing about the art of ballet. They are amateurs who produce amateurs. Girls who might become dancers are taught badly and their feet are ruined forever. How old is your daughter?'

'Fifteen.'

'Sixteen in January,' Katie said.

'There's not much time.'

Her mother raised her eyebrows. 'For what?'

'A dancer's career is short. It takes eight years to train a student for the stage. Your daughter has many bad habits that need to be erased.

With hard work, it might be possible for her to join a company in two years' time.'

'Her father and I don't want her to join a company. Katie's a straight-A student. We want her to go to college.'

'Anyone who pays for college in this country can go, Mrs Rivers. Dancers are what Martha Graham called "acrobats of God".' Madame tapped the elastic strap that secured Katie's glasses. 'Your daughter will need contact lenses. No glasses on stage unless they are part of a costume. When she performs, we can't have her falling into the orchestra pit. Also she will need to wear simple make-up to class.'

'When I was growing up,' her mother said, 'women who wore make-up in the daytime were considered fast.'

'It's important for a dancer to be made up. To dance beautifully, we must be beautiful.' Madame opened a zippered bag. *'Ma petite,* take off your glasses and close your eyes.'

Madame brushed on green eye shadow and caked Katie's lashes with mascara. 'Another time I will show you how to do your hair.' She picked up something furry and started to rouge her cheeks.

'What in the devil is that?' her mother asked.

'A rabbit's-foot brush. Dancers are superstitious. We need all the luck we can get.'

Madame applied lipstick, then pulled Katie's tutu high over her hipbones. '*Voilà.* Now you have legs growing out of your ears.'

Katie slid her glasses back on. It was like a young ballerina had slipped inside the mirror and was staring at her in disbelief.

'Beautiful, *non?* We dancers spend our lives in front of the mirror creating beauty. We can't afford to look like cooks.'

Her mother curled her lip. 'Come on, sugar. I've got to get home to make dinner.'

'Just a little more time, Mrs Rivers.' Madame put a hand on Katie's shoulder. *'Ma petite,* do you have any sisters?'

'Only a younger brother.'

'How will you feel when you see him eating waffles and syrup and candy bars and you can't have any because you must watch your weight?'

'I'll give up anything if it means I'll be a dancer.'

Madame put her hands around Katie's waist, her thumb and middle fingers almost touching. 'Boys will be lifting you over their heads with

one hand. You'll need to stay thin as a pencil.'
Katie nodded.
'From today, you must commit yourself totally to the dance. Everything else must take second place. You must give up boyfriends, college, sports. You must work until your muscles scream, until your *pointe* shoes are wet with blood.'
'Ye gods,' her mother said. 'I thought ballet was supposed to be beautiful.'
'It is, Mrs Rivers. But it is an illusion built on enormous personal sacrifice.'
Madame turned to face Katie. 'I promise nothing but hard work. Come back Monday at five thirty for company class. You'll be on a one-year trial. If your feet don't improve or you get too tall, you'll be asked to go. However if you progress, your scholarship will be renewed. I am no fortuneteller, *golubchik*, but there is a Russian saying: "No one can hide the sun with their fingers."'

On the drive back to Fortuna, every time Lola tried to make conversation, her daughter gazed out the window. By the time they got home, Lola had had enough. She threw her purse on the dinette table and grabbed some potatoes from the vegetable rack. 'Who does that durn Madame think she is, trying to make me feel like a hick?'
'She wasn't doing that, Momma.'
Lola stared at herself in the mirror above the sink: limp hair, lipstickless lips. 'Oh yes she was. All that crap about ballerinas not looking like cooks.'
'Madame Feodorova was only showing me how to make up for class.'
Lola turned around to see her daughter doing ballet exercises holding onto the back of a chair. 'I saw how she stood, Katie. She was making fun of my humpback.'
'That's the way real dancers hold themselves.'
Lola ran water over the potatoes and started to scrub off the dirt. 'Carmel doesn't look like that.'
'She's a cotton farmer.'
'Carmel may farm cotton, but she's taken you to two ballet conventions in Dallas and wouldn't accept a dime.'
'But now I need a better teacher, Momma. Someone who can turn me into a ballerina.'

'There are thousands of girls from Nutt, New Mexico, to Bald Knob, Arkansas, who want the same thing. What makes you think you're so special?'
Katie pulled a thigh against her cheek. 'Madame Feodorova said I have the potential to be a professional dancer.'
'She was sizing you up like a piece of meat. She reminded me of the alligators in the fountain at San Jacinto Plaza.'
'Don't be silly, Momma.'
'I can see she's already got your hopes sky high. Even if you do study with that woman, it doesn't mean a durn thing. If you don't come up to scratch, she'll drop you like a hot potato.' Lola let go of the King Edward she was cleaning. It boomed as it bounced in the metal sink.
Her daughter flung a chair onto the floor. 'You love spoiling everything, don't you? You always expect the worst because your life didn't turn out the way you wanted it to!'
Lola felt her eyes tearing up so she began batting her eyelids. 'Your daughter must get contacts. She must wear war paint so she looks like a little Jezebel.'
'Stop making fun of me!'
'She must dance till her shoes are filled with blood.'
'Stop it!'
'We must look beautiful to be beautiful. We must make beauty when we dance.' Lola leaned against the Frigidaire, cocking her leg like she'd seen her daughter do a thousand times.
Katie started to snicker, then they both burst out laughing. Lola had glimpsed herself in the mirror. She looked like she was peeing against the refrigerator.
'I'm sorry for shouting at you, Momma, but I don't want anything to spoil today. I've never been so happy in all my life!'
'Don't go counting your chickens before they've hatched. Your father might not let you take this scholarship. El Paso's a two-hour round trip.'
'He will,' her daughter said triumphantly. 'Daddy knows how much I want to dance.'
It was true. Katie had always been able to twist Haywood around her little finger. If she asked him for some stardust, he'd do anything in his power to try and get it for her.

THE DOUBLE HAPPINESS COMPANY

'Just you wait,' Katie said. 'I'll be a great ballerina like Pavlova. One day I might even dance at the Maryinsky Theater in St Petersburg!'
Her daughter picked up the overturned chair and motioned for her to sit down. Lola lowered herself onto it as her daughter took a bow, one hand swooping to the linoleum as if picking up a bouquet. 'This is my only chance to become a dancer and I have to take it.'
'That's what you hope, sugar. I had dreams once too of being a schoolteacher with a fur coat and a different color pair of patent-leather shoes for every day of the week. Then your Daddy came along with his wavy hair and football shoulders. I was sure of what I wanted too once, but life got in the way.'
'I won't let anything get in the way. I'll be a famous ballerina and tour the world and make thousands of people happy!'
The way Katie was standing, looking so gangly and wide-eyed, reminded Lola of the way new calves did after they were born. Her father would keep them in the barn the first few days and when he let them out for the first time, they would gallop at full speed into a barbed-wire fence at the end of the paddock. Bleeding, they would stagger onto their spindly legs and do the same thing all over again. She begged him to stop the calves from hurting themselves. *I can't do that, Lola Mae. The calves will have to learn what they can and can't do without any help from me.*
Lola stared at her daughter's thickened lashes. 'Wash that goop off now.'
'Please let me keep it on till Daddy comes home.'
'I said wash your face. You look like you've got mold on your eyelids.'
When Katie didn't move, Lola nudged her.
'Just a little longer.'
'I won't have you look like a dance-hall girl.'
Lola was determined that her daughter would have all the advantages she'd been denied growing up. Katie would have art and ballet and piano lessons. She would go to college. She'd graduate *magna cum laude* and be awarded a Rhodes scholarship. She would be a doctor, a scientist, a simultaneous translator at the United Nations. Her daughter was not going on the stage to parade around in public with hardly any clothes on.
She shooed her daughter toward the bathroom. Katie danced off, waving her arms like a swan.

37

Weirdnik in a tutu

'Know how the West was won?'

Katie looked up from studying French conjugations. Her father didn't talk much on the drive to El Paso, especially when he picked her up straight from work.

'John Wayne,' her brother said from the front seat. He was rolling a model plane along the dashboard, using it as a runway.

'Windmills and heliographs,' her father said. 'A windmill pumped water when people couldn't homestead near a river and the Army used heliographs to flash messages from the top of one mountain to another.'

'Who cares?' Rhett said. 'I'd rather be riding my Kawasaki.'

'In that desert out there,' her father said, 'Geronimo gave the army the slip for almost thirty years. He and his little band dodged thousands of soldiers because they knew every canyon and watering hole, but technology got them in the end.'

Katie said, 'They didn't have technology back then.'

'Course they did,' her father said. 'When the Army figured out how to use Morse code with mirrors, they could send messages up to sixty miles away. It was all over for the poor Apaches when they started using the sun as a telegraph.'

She looked at the dashboard clock. Five to five. Time to wrap her toes so her skin wouldn't get blistered from *pointe* work. By the time she'd made ten little mummies with surgical tape, she saw Christ the King on top of the mountain. Her heart lifted to see that huge limestone statue. The enormous outstretched arms seemed to gather her up and throw her skywards. It was at this point in the journey that her heart started to accelerate. From *El Cristo Rey* to Madame's studio was fifteen miles, her signal to change out of school clothes into her leotard and tights.

Under the football blanket her brother had nicknamed 'the dressing room', she gave thanks for *The Nutcracker* parts Madame had given her: a maid and one of the Snowflakes in Act I and a member of the corps de ballet in 'Waltz of the Flowers'. The maid only appeared for a few bars in the opening scene, but Katie had checked out a book on Stanislavski to learn how to make the role convincing.

She was wondering what to give the maid as an objective when the radio snapped on. She started to struggle out of her school clothes, half-listening to the evening news.

> *The world's first human heart transplant was performed today in Cape Town by cardiologist Dr Christiaan Barnard. The operation, which lasted nine hours, required a team of thirty surgeons to replace the heart of Louis Washkansky, a fifty-year-old with—*

'It's like science fiction,' she heard her father say. 'Who'd ever have thought something like that was possible? A woman's heart in a man.'

> *Protests around the country have continued after President Johnson's announcement of new bombing raids over Hanoi. Police in Berkeley, California, have arrested over twenty students who staged a sit-in protest on campus. A professor, who asked not to be identified, said that outside agitators were behind this latest—*

Her father switched the radio off. 'If the damn hippies are protesting in California, other places are going to pop.'

'What's wrong with hippies?' she heard her brother ask.

'Commie chickenshits. They ought to ship them to Siberia. See how they like it over there if they're not prepared to fight.'

Rhett asked, 'Anyone in our family ever die in a war?'

'Your Great-granddaddy Rivers was killed at Gettysburg.'

Katie was wiggling into her leotard when she noticed a hand lifting a corner of the blanket. She slapped her brother's fingers away. 'Get out, you little creep.'

'Taller than you are.'

She poked her head out. 'Daddy, tell Rhett to leave me alone. I've got to get ready for class.'

'Only little girls go to ballet lessons,' Rhett said. 'You're the only fifteen-year-old weirdnik in a tutu.'

'You're the weirdnik,' she said, ducking under the blanket. 'You thought you could fly to the moon in a cardboard box.'

'When I was ten.'

She felt a thump on her back. 'That hurt, Rhett. Cut it out.'

'You two knock it off,' her father said. 'I've been on my feet since eight this morning.'

'I don't know why I have to come along,' Rhett said. 'It's her rehearsal, not mine.'

'Your mother's visiting her sister,' her father said. 'You can't be at home by yourself, buckeroo.'

Katie threw off the blanket. 'Change places with me, Rhett. I need the mirror.'

She and her brother climbed over the seat in opposite directions.

'What time do you think you'll finish tonight?' her father asked.

'Ten thirty or eleven.'

'Why so late?' Rhett asked.

'We're doing a complete run-through.' She clipped on her new rhinestone earrings and turned her head in the mirror, admiring their sparkle and flash. 'Thought any more about me moving to El Paso, Daddy?'

Her father glanced out the side window, drumming his fingers on the steering wheel. Ever since she won the scholarship, she'd been begging him to let her move to Texas. 'It's really important to take daily classes with Madame, not just three times a week.'

'You're too young to move away from home.'

She twisted her hair tight against her skull and started to shove in a handful of bobby pins. 'Only fifty miles, Daddy.'

'Fifty miles is five-O too many.'

'Look at all the driving you and Mom have to do.'

'I like being on the road,' her father said. 'Makes me feel like I'm going somewhere.'

'Mom hates it,' she said.

'So do I,' her brother said. 'It's not fair I have to tag after my weirdnik sister.'

'If you let me move,' she said, 'Rhett could stay at home and you wouldn't have to miss golf anymore. I could live with the Hieberts and come home at weekends.'

'Who are the Hieberts?'

She felt like clapping her hands. For her father to even ask who they were meant he hadn't ruled out the idea. 'She and her husband live around the corner from the studio. Rosalia has been Madame's pianist for years. Madame's already talked to them and they said they'd love to have me live in their daughter's old room.'

Her father shook his head. 'I don't know, sister.'

'Please, Daddy. It would be the perfect solution. I'd be living with a family. Rosalia's really nice. She's from Naples.' Katie took off her glasses. Her new contact lenses hurt like crazy; they made her eyes water the whole time she wore them, but she was increasing the wearing time by a half hour a day so she'd be able to perform in *The Nutcracker*. 'You couldn't learn to be a dentist on the farm. You had to go to Memphis. I'm training for my career just like you trained for yours. I've just had to start earlier. At least think about it, Daddy?'

At a quarter past midnight they pulled into their driveway. Her father and brother went straight to bed, but Katie wanted to practice before putting on her pajamas.

In addition to taking the company class, Madame had told her today that she needed to study with the beginners. *Time is running out, Katya. You are seven years behind girls your own age. Practice does not make perfect. It makes permanent. Blame that* plié *parlor for all the mistakes you have to unlearn.*

Among the eight-year-olds she would be a giant, but she didn't feel humiliated to have to start all over again. She was grateful to have been given the chance. That was why she had to leave Fortuna. She would never have a professional career if she didn't.

She stuffed a towel at the bottom of her door, dressed as if Madame's eyes were still on her. Hair scraped back, earrings glittering, spat tights, chiffon skirt. Behind her was a picture of Maria Taglioni. She had put it up to inspire her daily practice. Madame had told her that the Italian ballerina trained so hard that, at the end of class, she would collapse in a faint. Her teacher would dress her in street clothes and have her driven home, unconscious, in a hansom cab. *That,* golubchik, *is how hard you must work if you want to dance. You must practice day and night to catch up with the others.*

With her teacher's voice in her ears, she put a barre record on the stereo, the volume low. She did half- and full-knee bends, holding onto a chair to gently warm up her legs in preparation for the more strenuous exercises that followed. Her favorite was *battement tendu* because it was the foundation of all ballet technique. She stood in a perfect fifth and slid her front foot away from her supporting leg. Going through the ball of her foot, she stretched it as far as she could, pointing her toes until she could see all the muscles in her leg. Without stopping, or losing contact with the floor, she slid it back, caressing the planks as if her foot were a hand.

Eight *tendus* to the front, eight to the side, eight to the back, eight to the side, then repeating the whole combination with the other leg. After countless ones she'd practiced on her own the last three months, she was finally learning how to play her body like an instrument, finally beginning to look like a real dancer.

Her muscles were already aching when her right calf went into spasm. She grunted as she hobbled around the room. *To be a dancer, Katya, you must have a high threshold of pain, otherwise you never will become an acrobat of God.*

She stood on a thick book and lowered her heels until they touched the floor. Up and down, up and down, lengthening the contracted muscles until the cramp was gone and she was able to finish off her practice with jumps.

She set herself a goal of a sixty-four *entrechats quatres*. She rose into the air, pointing her feet strongly and pulling up her knees. At the height of each jump, she beat her feet at the last possible moment before landing in fifth position. She pushed off the floor, again and again, changing her breathing and the depth of her *plié* to increase her elevation. Students at the Imperial Ballet School in St Petersburg used to have jumping competitions into the hundreds. Sixty-four was nothing.

She collapsed on the bed when she'd reached her goal. She gave herself a minute to recover her breath as she mooned over the pictures of Nureyev on her bedroom walls: Rudi in class, Rudi performing. One day—one day if she worked hard enough—she would dance the role of Giselle with the best male dancer in the world.

She did sixty-four more *entrechats quatres,* trying to do each one more cleanly, more sustained than the last. She stared at her bouncing reflection. Her lungs were burning and her legs aching, but when she got it right, it was like magic. When she managed to hover long enough, she appeared to defeat gravity and, for that split second, it was like she was standing in thin air.

Deer broken

Before they left for the Pancake Dinner, Lola knew she had lost. Once Haywood made up his mind about something, he rarely changed it. She picked up a tube of Tangee lipstick and threw it into her purse.
'Katie does not need to move to El Paso. She can commute like she's been doing the past three months.'
Her husband pretended he was looking for something in his sock drawer.
'Haywood, are you listening to me? I said our daughter does not need to study ballet six days a week.'
'I've enrolled Katie at Coronado High, Momma. She starts tomorrow.'
'Then she can get unenrolled.'
'I promised her that she could move and I'm not going back on my word.' He looked at the clock. 'It's six twenty. I have to be at the Copper Kettle in fifteen minutes.'
She shoved the barbecue apron she'd ironed at him. 'If you'd put your foot down, we wouldn't be in this damn mess.'
'Pipe down, Lola,' he said. 'The kids'll hear.'
She dropped her voice. 'You should never have agreed to let her go without talking to me first.'
'You were with your sister in Memphis. You had other things on your plate.'
Lola didn't want to be reminded that Delta was sick. Really sick. Her sister's cancer was something she preferred not to think about.
Haywood picked up his chef's hat. 'We need to hit the road.'
'We should be here for Katie's last evening, not at some durn Kiwanis Club event.'
'The Pancake Dinner was fixed months ago. I'm President.'
'You could have found a way out if you'd wanted to.'
'It's the club's biggest fundraiser. We need every hand on deck.'
Lola marched toward the porch. The car was the best place for

this argument because she and Hay would have to look straight ahead and not at each other.

Inside the Thunderbird, Katie's boxes were stacked high in the back seat. Seeing them made Lola want to scream and cry at the same time. She had gone into Katie's bedroom this afternoon while she was washing her hair. In her daughter's wallet she'd found photographs of Pavlova, Burrito, Haywood and Rhett, but not one of her own mother.

Her husband put the key in the ignition. 'Tell her you've changed your mind,' she said to the windshield.

'You sound like a broken record.'

'You don't say that when Katie goes on about something.'

Haywood put his arm on the seat to back out. 'She's exceptionally gifted. You've said yourself, Lo, that when she's on stage you can't look at anyone else.'

'She's gifted getting out of you what she damn well wants. She wasn't supposed to take ballet seriously. She only went because Edith Kallman talked me into carpooling so that Marilyn could dance.'

'That is not the point.' He jammed the car into reverse.

'We wouldn't be in this mess if Edith had driven Marilyn instead of roping me in.'

'Don't you want Katie to be happy, Momma?'

'You don't seem to give a damn that I'm not.'

'You think I'm happy?' he said.

'You've got a good career because I put you through school. You'd still be on Pea Ridge looking up a mule's butt hole if it wasn't for me.'

They were at the traffic lights now, the engine idling. Haywood hit the steering wheel. 'I guess you'd like to be bent over people's mouths all day. I guess you'd like to hear people bitch about their dentures not fitting.'

'Better than all the damn housework I have to do.' She heard her voice rise. 'I had dreams once too, Haywood. They bit the dust. All I'm qualified to do is keep house.'

'Katie needs to have her chance. You don't want her dreams to get sidetracked too.'

'You're just scared she'll hate you if you don't let her go.'

'This argument's going round in circles, Momma.'

The car behind honked. The light had changed and neither of them had noticed.

'Be a man. Tell her you've changed your mind.'

'She'll always hold it against us if we make her stay in Fortuna.'

'Don't be such a damn coward, Haywood.'

Her husband put his foot on the accelerator. She glanced at his knuckles. He was squeezing the steering wheel like he was about to rip it off.

'Goddamn it to hell, Lola. For once in your fucking life, keep your fucking mouth shut!'

In her whole life she'd never been sworn at like that. Lola bit her lip and stared down the dark ruler of the highway. It was straighter than anything she had experienced in forty-seven years of life. To Katie, everything was so simple, but Lola knew it was the curving roads that make up a life. Roads that take you to destinations you haven't bargained for, chicken-scratch roads that aren't even marked on the map.

Haywood gunned the car down Main Street. He was going faster than the speed limit, but for once she didn't tell him off.

They screeched into the Copper Kettle's parking lot. He lifted his chef's hat off the boxes in the back. 'Ever since Katie won the scholarship, you two have been fighting. No wonder she can't wait to leave home.'

She watched him get out of the car, pull on his puffy white hat, tie his apron on over his clothes. She got out and slung her purse at him. 'Son of a bitch!' she screamed. There wasn't anyone to hear her and, besides, she was worn out. Worn out trying to hold her family together while her husband was tearing it apart.

Haywood disappeared into the kitchen to make batter. Lola went to the bathroom and locked herself into a cubicle. She was supposed to be setting tables, but she was too upset. She didn't want her daughter to move away and yet she was powerless to stop it.

She sat on the toilet seat, head in her hands. She had always wanted to be close to Katie, but there had always been a wall between them and that wall was her husband. She knew Hay didn't want Katie to move to El Paso, but he was scared of losing her love. For years, he'd been protecting her instead of teaching her to be tough.

The first time she remembered him being lily-livered was when Katie was two. Lola had driven out to a friend's farm to pick Haywood up after a deer hunt. Two huge stags were hanging in the barn, suspended by their hind legs. Katie saw them and became hysterical. 'Deer broke-ed, Daddy! Kiss deer and make better!'

Instead of Haywood telling her they were going to put their deer in the freezer to be eaten, he made her take Katie inside while he tied it to the hood. On the ride home, Lola drove while he sat with Katie in his lap, trying to cover her eyes, both of them crying to beat the band.

When it came to the goodbyes

Lola was shocked to see the Hieberts' neighborhood. Most of the yards on the street looked uncared for. The Hieberts' house was immaculate with freshly-painted shutters and manicured bushes, but the properties on either side had more dirt than grass. One even had a rusty refrigerator sitting in the driveway like hillbillies lived there.

Katie ran up the path, her ballet bag banging against her cape. Lola forced herself to smile as she watched Rosalia hug Katie as if she were her mother.

'Welcome,' Mr Hiebert said as she and Haywood came up the steps. 'Welcome.'

Mr Hiebert was a portly man with a shaggy salt-and-pepper beard. She'd met him a few times at the studio when he'd come to pick up Rosalia from work. Even though he couldn't have been more than five eleven, he towered over his wife who only came up to his armpit.

Hay went toward them, hand outstretched. 'I'm Haywood Rivers. I understand you've already met my wife.'

Mr Hiebert said, 'Come in out of the cold.'

In the living room, Lola was shocked to see a large painting over the fireplace of a woman with uncombed hair and a bosom bursting out of her blouse. A prostitute with rounded breasts pressed together like two ostrich eggs. As she stared at the picture, she became aware that Rosalia was talking to her.

'I take Katie to her room and show her where things are.'

Lola stood up. 'I'll come too.'

'No thanks,' Katie said, waving her down.

Lola bit her lip as she watched her daughter and Rosalia disappear into a corridor.

Mr Hiebert pointed to a sideboard lined with bottles. 'What can I get you folks to drink?'

Lola said, 'Coke.'

Haywood said, 'I'll have a Coke too, but mix mine with Johnny Walker.'

'Sure thing. Ice and lemon in your Coke, Lola?'
'Just ice, Mr Hiebert. Thank you.'
'Call me Jack.'
Her husband said, 'Jack, that's some picture you've got up over the fireplace.'
'That's a Frans Hals reproduction. I love it.'
Haywood said, 'I sure can see why.'
Mr Hiebert left the room and Lola whispered, 'You're drinking to upset me, Haywood.'
'I'm drinking because I'm upset.'
'You'll get a migraine and I'll have to drive home in all the durn traffic.'
'I'm having one whiskey and Coke, Momma.'
'You're a Baptist. You're not supposed to drink.' She was about to give him a piece of her mind when she heard footsteps.
Mr Hiebert came in with a tray and glasses. 'Coke's on the left, Johnny's on the right.'
Hay reached for his drink. 'Thanks, Jack.'
Lola took her Coke, but not before shooting her husband a look.
'*Salute*,' Mr Hiebert said, raising his tumbler.
'Cheers,' her husband said back.
She watched as Hay tipped too much liquor into his mouth.
'I've got a joke for you,' her husband said after a long silence.
'Let rip,' Mr Hiebert said.
'A man and his wife were having some marital problems so they were giving each other the silent treatment. A couple of days went by because neither of them wanted to be the first to speak. Then he had to leave town on business and wanted his wife to wake him up.'
Lola sipped her Coke, watching Mr Hiebert glance at the TV playing quietly in the corner. Walter Cronkite delivering more bad news about Vietnam.
'The guy wrote, "Honey, I'd appreciate if you'd wake me at 5.00 AM," and left the note where his wife would see it. The next morning he looks at the clock and it's after nine. He's about to yell at her when he sees a piece of paper next to his pillow. "It's 5.00 AM. Wake up."'
Mr Hiebert laughed, his belly shaking. 'Men aren't equipped for contests like that.'

Her husband saw Mr Hiebert glancing at the screen. 'What's your take on the Tet Offensive?'

'I'd say it's a big mess.'

Katie came into the room and ran straight out the door to get the rest of her things. She didn't even look in Lola's direction.

'There's no way we're going to win this war,' Mr Hiebert was saying. 'I'm retired Army and I've heard top brass admit there's no way we can win. The French were thrown out and we'll be thrown out too. It's only a matter of time. The tragedy is a whole lot of people have died and will continue to die for no good reason.'

Haywood said, 'I thought you were a communist when I saw you. The beard and sandals give you away.'

Lola guessed her husband was joking because he was half-smiling, but she wanted to disappear through the floor. There are things you don't say in someone else's house, even when your daughter is moving away from home and you're all torn up inside.

When it came to the goodbyes, Haywood pretended he wasn't crying. He jingled his change so loudly Lola couldn't hear what Mr Hiebert was saying. She knew Haywood didn't realize what he was doing so she placed a hand over his pocket to get him to stop. He turned away to wipe his cheek, but kept on jingling.

Katie was crying too because when saw her father crying, she put on a pair of sunglasses, even though they were inside the house. Lola witnessed it all, trying to push away the jealousy that squeezed her heart. She's always loved him more than me, she thought. Ever since she was a baby. In the parent sweepstakes I'll always be the runner-up.

His chin quivering, she watched Haywood take Katie into his arms, but when it was Lola's turn to say goodbye, she couldn't. She was frozen. Lola knew that if she did she wouldn't be able to let go.

Katie gave her a look like she was the most cold-blooded mother on earth.

Lola wanted to say, Just because I'm not carrying on like your father doesn't mean I don't love you, that I'm not upset. I've spent a lifetime hiding my heartbreak. I've just learned to put my hurt where other people can't see it.

EL PASO, 1969

In composing the music, I had in my mind a distinct picture of a puppet, suddenly endowed with life.

IGOR STRAVINSKY

Petrouchka

Madame was going through lighting cues with the stage manager when Katie heard the marionettes' theater being rolled in. She wanted to jump up and down when she saw its Cyrillic gold letters and midnight-blue curtain. The set painters had made it look like the original in the 1911 Ballets Russes production.

Madame walked around the life-sized Punch-and-Judy theater, testing to see if the wheels worked smoothly, if the curtain got stuck, if there were any splinters that might injure the dancers. She clapped her hands, satisfied everything was in working order. 'Puppets, let's see it in action. Scene 1.'

The company gathered on stage and took their places for the start of the tech rehearsal. Along with the two other marionettes, Katie stepped inside the plywood booth. She hung from the padded arm supports, head drooping to one side, feet inches off the floor. Unlike Britt Bromilow, who played the Ballerina Doll, and Quintus Harrell, who was the Blackamoor, she was only an understudy. Petrouchka would be danced by Gary Chryst from the City Center Joffrey Ballet. Katie was his stand-in until his arrival from New York. She had been taught the role because she was the fastest study in the company.

Madame called out, 'First electrics off, please, and sidelights on. Close the booth curtain. Corps de ballet, get ready to move the puppet theater downstage.'

A drum roll from the rehearsal record and the booth was pushed from the back of the stage to its new position. The curtain flew open. From her slumped position, Katie twitched upright as if a bolt of lightning had struck her sawdust body. Her puppet feet snapped upward, legs jerking, arms swinging, feet turned in. To the music of the 'Russian Dance', she jigged her legs and arms in time with the Ballerina and the Moor. Almost immediately, Madame stopped the record.

'Puppet theater position is fine. Spike marks, please, then move the booth to where Petrouchka is chased in Scene 4.'

A stagehand put strips of fluorescent tape on the floor and the marionettes' theater was pushed upstage. The puppets ducked behind the curtain and Madame clapped her hands to begin.

Katie ran out of the little theater, chased by the jealous Blackamoor. To Stravinsky's wild arpeggios, she zigzagged around the stage, trying to escape the Moor swinging his prop sword. She felt herself grabbed by her leotard as Quintus spun her three times and struck her with a plywood scimitar. Her arms shot upward and she fell, fatally wounded, to the floor. To the squeaks of piccolos, she lifted her head and let it sink down. She touched her mittened hand to her lips as she lay dying. With jerky, tender movements she sent her last kiss to the Ballerina Doll.

Members of the corps de ballet surrounded her, blocking the audience's view as she stood and ran up the steps to the top of the little theater to hide on its roof. Madame, playing the Magician, raised a large doll dressed in a costume like Petrouchka's. She shook the dummy violently to prove to the crowd that the sawdust dribbling out of it was not blood. A murder had not been committed, only two puppets entertaining them with a mock fight.

The Magician was dragging the dummy toward the booth to hang it up for the night when Petrouchka's ghost popped up on the roof of the little theater. He taunted his cruel master with wildly waving arms and then collapsed over the top, Petrouchka's death indicated by two trumpets clashing in different keys.

'Terrible!' Madame shouted after Petrouchka had fallen forward. But when the music stopped, Katie was relieved to hear the stagehands clapping.

Lola squinted in the rearview at the motorist behind her. She hated driving on the freeway, hemmed in by cars doing seventy miles an hour. With her poor eyesight, cars whizzing past on all sides made her as nervous as a cat in a roomful of rocking chairs.

Every Saturday for the past two years, she had forced herself to brave the city traffic so Katie could spend weekends at home. Fighting the urge to speed up, Lola shouted at the man tailgating her, 'One car length for every ten miles an hour. Haven't you heard of defensive driving?'

She shot him a look in the rearview mirror, catching sight of the molasses-brown wig on a styrofoam head in the back seat. Her own hair used to be that color, but since Rhett had been giving her trouble, her hair had gone gray as a steel pipe.

For the last six months, Rhett had become unmanageable. He'd grown his hair down to his shoulders. He spent hours assembling model airplanes instead of doing his homework. He ignored his ten o'clock curfew and when she'd grounded him for rolling in at one in the morning, he'd smashed his fist through the den door.

Four days ago she'd been called in to see Rhett's principal. Remembering that awful meeting she felt her face flush. Soon as she'd gone into Mr van der Dool's office he'd started to chew her out, saying that Rhett had been responsible for some band members hanging moons on the bus. She asked him what was wrong with a few decorations. Surely he should be pleased that Rhett showed some school spirit. Then Mr van der Dool took a photograph out of his drawer, a Polaroid of three pairs of bare buttocks flattened against a bus window. *I was told your son was the ringleader. If he ever tries something like this again, he'll be suspended. Have I made myself clear?*

Haywood had had the gall to laugh when she'd told him. 'If exposing his butt in a school-bus window is the worst thing he gets up to, Momma, we should thank our lucky stars.'

She held out a leather belt. 'We didn't raise him to behave like that. You'll have to beat some sense into him.'

'You and Willie van der Dool are making too much of a schoolboy prank. Everybody's got a butt, Momma, and everyone's seen one.'

'If you don't punish him, we're going to have a juvenile delinquent on our hands.'

'You were the one who named him. You should have expected trouble.'

She snapped the belt. 'At least Rhett Butler had gumption!'

'It was a joke, Momma. Loosen up.'

'That boy has no respect for authority. He's going to end up in jail if we're not careful.'

'I'm not horsewhipping Rhett because of a little innocent fun.'

'Then no mattress mambo for you, bud.'

Haywood had stormed out of the room when she'd said that, so she decided to do something more drastic, something to let him know she meant business. That night she left a note in red ink on his pillow.

You haven't done a durn thing to punish Rhett for mooning so I'm taking over his room. Rhett will have to sleep on the Hide-A-Bed in the den until he learns to do what he's told. You will sleep by yourself until you teach that boy to straighten up and fly right.

She'd always gone along with Haywood's all-too-frequent urges, afraid that if she didn't, her good-looking husband would find another woman to satisfy himself with. But this time was different. She had no choice but to put her foot down. Sex was the only bargaining tool she had.

As downtown El Paso flashed past, Lola was looking forward to picking up her daughter even more than usual. Haywood hadn't said a word to her since their fight, but tonight he'd start talking to her again. He had left a note this morning to say he didn't want Katie to know they'd been fighting. That suited her down to the ground because she wasn't about to apologize. She had nothing to apologize about.

Lola pulled into the Hieberts' driveway. She was getting out of the car when she remembered the wig. Her hair looked like the devil because she'd had to cancel her dye-and-set to see Mr van der Dool. She grabbed the wig and jammed it on her head as she walked up the sidewalk. With one hand she rang the bell; with the other she tugged her wig into place. There was no answer, but she could hear noise trying to pass itself off as music.

Both the screen and the front door were unlocked. She walked through the living room toward Katie's bedroom. A horrible smell led the way. She fanned the air as a terrible thought crossed her mind. 'Katie Scarlett,' she said, bursting into her room, 'are you smoking marijuana?'

Her daughter laughed. 'That's patchouli incense.'

'Rosalia should keep the front door locked. I could have been a rapist.'

Katie's foot tapped the floor, her head bobbing up and down. It was the same ugly music she'd been playing every weekend for the last few months. Lola stared at her daughter, jerking and weaving as she packed. Usually when Lola picked her up, Katie looked sad, but this afternoon she was grinning from ear to ear. 'What's up, sugar?'

'What makes you ask?'

'You're either higher than a kite or lower than a snake's belt buckle on a wagon ride.'

Katie grabbed her hands and spun her around. 'I've never been so happy in all my life!'

Lola let go to adjust her wig that had slipped over one eye. 'Hold your horses, sugar. I can't see a thing.'

'I wasn't going to tell you and Daddy till tonight, but I've been given my first lead. I'm dancing the title role in *Petrouchka*!' Her daughter threw her arms to the sides and twirled around the room. 'Madame told me after the tech rehearsal. She's so pleased with what I've done she's canceled the guest artist. I'm dancing Petrouchka instead of Gary Chryst!'

'You're replacing someone called Gary?'

'One of the best dancers in New York.'

'She's too cheap to pay a guest artist so you can dance the part for free.'

'You don't understand, Momma. Petrouchka is one of the greatest roles ever choreographed.'

'If it's so great, why isn't Gary doing it?'

'Because I can jump like a man.'

'That can't be healthy for a woman's organs.'

Katie stood on tiptoe and took a stagey pose: arms above her head like they were an oval frame. 'Madame said *Petrouchka* was the Ballets Russes most influential production.'

'You need to eat more,' Lola said. 'You're starting to look like a clarinet. A woman is supposed to have curves. It's no wonder you've never been on a date.'

'Why can't you just be happy for me, Momma? And I don't want to date. I want to dance.'

Lola wished she could act excited about her new part, but she couldn't. 'You're meant for better things than strutting around in a spotlight.'

Katie started throwing *pointe* shoes into her suitcase. 'I wish I was staying here this weekend. Rosalia would make my favorite dinner and Jack would open a bottle of Spumante. We'd pretend it was champagne and celebrate all evening because I've been made principal dancer.'

Katie continued to pack in silence for the next few minutes. Lola decided to walk over to a miniature theater on the dresser to try and make her talk. 'Where'd you buy this from?'

'I built it.'

'You did?'

'Daddy's been helping me.'

Lola fingered the hollyhock-red curtains hemmed in neat, tiny stitches.

So that's what Haywood had been doing with the jigsaw. 'How'd you find the time to do this with all your rehearsals and homework?'
'I make time for the things I love.'
Lola slid back the velveteen folds. In front of the painted backdrop with a merry-go-round were cardboard carnival booths and a little theater. 'What's this supposed to be?'
'The Butter Week Fair from *Petrouchka*.'
'Looks pretty old timey with those long dresses and top hats.'
'It's set in the 1830s.'
Lola picked up the star-cloaked figure next to the little theater. 'Who's this?'
'The Magician,' Katie said. 'He does tricks to get customers to come to his Punch and Judy show.' She pointed to three marionettes. 'That's the Blackamoor, the Ballerina Doll and Petrouchka. At the beginning of the ballet they're hanging by their armpits in this booth.'
Lola pointed at the black-faced figure dressed in green. 'Why does he have a nicer costume than you?'
'Because the Magician hates Petrouchka. He likes the Blackamoor, but beats Petrouchka every chance he gets.' Katie turned a knob at the side of the theater and another painted backdrop unrolled in front of the first: a bare, black room with a portrait of the Magician in the center of the wall and two devils painted on the door.
'When the puppet show is over,' Katie said, 'the Magician humiliates Petrouchka by pushing the Ballerina Doll into his room. Petrouchka's madly in love with her, but she doesn't love him because he scares her. He's skinny and ugly and she's in love with the handsome Blackamoor.'
'I thought you said they were puppets.'
'They are.'
'These theatrical fairy tales are idiotic.'
'People come to the theater to escape reality, Momma. To forget their problems and their boring lives. It takes great acting to convince an audience that a puppet has feelings and dreams, particularly when you can't move your face because you're playing a doll.'
'Phooey.' Lola adjusted her wig. 'Are you ready, sugar? I've got to get home to cook dinner.'
Katie suddenly started to dance. Her feet were pigeon-toed and her

head drooped. She pretended to beat the walls with her fists, then began jumping like she was deranged.

Lola covered her eyes. 'I thought Madame Fedora said ballet was supposed to be beautiful.'

'Ballet is beautiful and it's Feodorova, Momma.'

'How much are the tickets for this crazy show?'

'Five dollars.'

'I sure wouldn't go if you weren't in it. There's enough unhappiness in the world without having to pay to see a heartsick doll go berserk.'

Katie stared at the Saturday traffic, upset her mother couldn't understand her excitement. Two hours since she'd heard the news and her heart was still racing. She wanted to roll down the window and scream at every passing car, I'm dancing Petrouchka with the El Paso Civic Ballet!

Her mother pulled off her wig. 'Put this on the stand for me, sugar. My head's hot.'

Katie stretched the curls over the styrofoam head and put it in her lap. She spread her fingers wide so her hands were like two pink starfish. *Every part of a dancer has to become as expressive as the face.* She started doing the hand exercises Madame had given her, waving them like a stage hypnotist lulling someone to sleep.

Her mother eyed her in the rearview mirror. 'Put your mitts down, Katie. You're making me nervous.'

'Madame's mother was a member of the Ballets Russes. Sophie Feodorova was Diaghilev's first choice for the Ballerina Doll, but then Tamara Karsavina—'

'You'll have to be quiet till I get out of El Paso. I have to concentrate or we'll have a wreck.'

Katie watched the landmarks fly past: the Franklin Mountains, Hotel Cortez, *El Cristo Rey*. She was happy to say nothing, already looking forward to Sunday night. Going back to Madame's to dance, dance, dance.

Her mother raked her fingers through her flattened hair. 'Fedora's working you like a slave driver. Every weekend you come home worn to a frazzle.'

Katie stared at her mother's shoes: silver lamé with rockets she'd sewn on to celebrate last summer's moon landing. 'Opening night is the eighteenth of December. I've got a lot to improve on in the next few weeks. A dancer can't ever work hard enough.'

'You never say that about helping me in the house.'

Katie looked at her mother and felt a rush of pity. Seeing her in that faded polka-dot smock she thought, I'm not going to end up like you. Having babies that wreck your figure and rushing home to make a man pork chops.

'You should be enjoying your youth,' her mother was saying, 'not cooped up in some smelly ballet studio. You need to do something useful with your life, not have your head stuck up some cloud.'

But Katie wasn't listening. She was staring at an old billboard on the outskirts of her hometown, a discolored picture of crystal ball being held by a disembodied hand. *ORBALEE, CLAIRVOYANT AND HEALER • 100% RESULTS GUARANTEED TO MAKE YOU A WINNER • 1149 PICACHO BOULEVARD • FORTUNA*

Even though she'd passed that billboard hundreds of times, she had never really paid any attention to it. She wrote down the address on the inside of her arm, then restarted her finger exercises. 'There's something else I didn't tell you. On opening night Madame is flying in Enrique Martínez to see me perform.'

'What the heck are you talking about now, Katie?'

'He's the ballet master at ABT, the biggest company in the country. Madame says that if Enrique likes me, he'll invite me to join American Ballet Theater after I finish high school!'

Her mother's chin jutted out. 'Young lady, you are going to college whether you like it or not. I'm not going to let you throw your life away. Living out of a suitcase is like being in a circus without the elephant crap.'

Katie grabbed the styrofoam stand and squeezed the neck so hard her ring made a dent. It wasn't worth another argument. Not today. It was five months until she graduated. She would only have to put up with her mother's nagging a little longer.

A visit to Orbalee

Katie looked over her shoulder as she rolled her bike out of the garden shed. She wanted to slip away before dinner, not answer questions about where she was going. She pumped up the wilted tires of the Schwinn, then did a *grand battement* over the seat. Aiming the handlebars like a gun, she pedaled down Mesquite Street, singing at the top of her lungs.

She turned west onto Picacho Boulevard, passing the municipal tennis courts and swimming pool, its blue bottom littered with dead leaves. She flew past Cactus Motor Company, Zozo's Food Mart, the A&W Root Beer stand. Across the railroad tracks were adobe houses, small and down-at-heel compared to the brick homes in her part of town, but many of them had Christmas lights glowing on the porch or spiraled around a bush in the yard.

She had no trouble finding the address advertised on the billboard. A big pink hand faced the sidewalk on an A-frame sign. *ORBALEE, CLAIRVOYANT AND HEALER • CRYSTAL BALL • PALM & TEA-LEAF READINGS • TAROT CARDS*

She flipped down the kickstand. She'd never been to a fortuneteller before. She was both excited and scared. A couple of times her brother had wanted her to fool around with a ouija board, but she had no desire to contact the dead. To have her palms read didn't seem so spooky or dangerous.

She stared at the mounds and the dotted lines curving like roads on a map. Head Line. Heart Line. The Mounts of Mars and Venus. She was trying to figure out what they meant when the front door opened. A large woman in a broomstick skirt and concho belt stepped out. 'Can I help you, honey?'

Katie pointed nervously at the painted hand. 'I'd like to have my fortune told.'

'Then you've come to the right place.' The woman waved her toward the house.

'How much is it?' Katie asked as she scraped the toe of her shoe on the sidewalk. She hoped it wasn't more than the six dollars she'd wadded in her sock. Money she'd saved by skipping school lunches for a month.

'It's three dollars for the first reading. Another two fifty if you want more than one.'

Her heart was racing as she followed the fortuneteller inside. Katie looked down and noticed that Orbalee was wearing basketball sneakers. She'd never seen someone with gray hair wearing high-tops before.

The living room didn't look so different from other people's houses except for a coffee table covered with crystals in different sizes, colors and shapes. Orbalee lit a candle and held some dried leaves in the flame before placing them in an upturned shell. A fragrance began to perfume the room.

'What's that you're burning?' Katie asked.

'White sage, honey.' She gestured toward a table and invited her to sit. 'Grows only in the high desert. So what is it you want?'

'I'd like my palms read. I've just been told some incredible news and I want to find out if it's—'

'Slow dow, slow down.' Orbalee put up her hand. 'Just your name for the time being.'

'Katerina Gorbanyevskaya.'

Orbalee put on the half-moon glasses resting on her chest. 'What's your real name, honey? You don't want to jinx your fortune with a lie.'

It was the first time she had ever admitted her stage name to a grown-up. She looked in her lap, ashamed. 'Katie Rivers.'

'That's more like it. Which hand do you write with?'

'My right. Why?'

'If you're a north paw, the left hand shows what traits of character you're born with. The right what you'll make of your gifts in this lifetime.'

Orbalee cupped Katie's hand with her own and started to study it. She turned it, palm up, palm down. She bent Katie's thumb backwards, stroked her little finger upward. 'What a Mercury.'

'Pardon?'

The fortuneteller looked up. 'You have what we call psychic hands, the hands of a visionary. You're a dreamer lost in your own world.'

Katie smiled to herself, thinking her mother would agree with that part of the prediction.

'You tend to be impractical. You need to tether yourself to the grounding energy of the earth.' Orbalee traced a line in the middle of her palm that ended under her ring finger. 'There's a lot of creativity in this hand, but you're going to go through a long period of indecision. Your emotional energy will be scattered for a long time.'

'But I'm very decisive,' Katie said.

'Maybe now, honey. We're talking the future.' Orbalee picked up her other hand. 'I see a lot of heart-ache around the age of eighteen.'

'Where do you see that?'

The fortuneteller pointed to a line that ended near the base of her index finger. 'This break is something life-changing. These healing lines here show me this incident will direct you toward your true purpose.'

'What break?' Katie frantically searched her open hand. Her eighteenth birthday was next month. 'I don't see any break.'

'There.'

Katie turned her palm toward the candle. She immediately felt sick; it was there, just as the fortuneteller had said. 'Is there anything I can do about it?'

'I suggest you buy a quartz crystal with a termination at one end.'

'Why would I need that?'

'To the Ancients, crystals were frozen light. They deflect bad energy.' Orbalee leaned closer to study the markings on her palm, then placed her hand on the table.

'Why did you stop?' Katie said. 'Did you see something bad?'

'There's nothing more I can divine from your hands, honey. What about a tea-leaf reading?'

She guessed that Orbalee was trying to get more money out of her. Even though she didn't want to hear any more, her debut was in two weeks and she needed to hear something good before she left. 'Okay,' she said.

'I'll prepare a cup.'

Orbalee left the room and Katie's stomach began to somersault. She was remembering the story Madame Feodorova had told her about a fortuneteller her mother had seen in 1916. On New Year's Eve the ballerina Kschessinskaya threw a ball in St Petersburg and employed a clairvoyant to tell her guests' fortunes. The gypsy told everyone the same thing, whether they were a Grand Duke, *coryphée* or Hussar. 'Make your preparations well because your world will soon disappear.'

Several guests complained about getting the same prediction so Kschessinskaya turned the old gypsy out in the snow. In less than a year, Lenin was addressing crowds from the balcony of Kschessinskaya's house and Madame's mother, who had been a guest at the party, was an *émigrée* in Paris with nothing but an icon she'd smuggled out of Russia in a loaf of bread.

Orbalee came back into the room, carrying a teapot in one hand and a cup and saucer in the other. When she put them on the table, Katie could see the tidemarks of old fortunes staining the inside of the cup.

'Drink that, honey. Leave about half a teaspoon, then take the handle in your left hand and swirl it three times clockwise. Turn the cup upside down and concentrate very hard.'

Katie did what she was told. Orbalee lifted the cup and swiveled it in one direction, then another.

'Near the bottom is a ring which signifies marriage. The letter W indicates a union with someone whose name begins with that letter. This big spider halfway down indicates a large gift of money that will come to you when you need it most.'

Katie felt like fanning her face with relief. That was more like it.

Orbalee pointed to the pattern near the top. 'This dragon indicates sudden change. And this comet symbolizes bad luck. It's on the rim which means this change will happen very soon.'

'That can't be.' She leaned over the cup to see for herself.

'There's the body, honey, and there's the tail.'

'Maybe it doesn't mean that,' Katie said.

Orbalee shrugged. 'The leaves say what they say. This clover signifies prosperity and happiness, but it's near the bottom so that's some time in the future. Are there any questions you want to ask me, honey? We're almost at the end of our time.'

Comet, bad luck, happiness a long way in the future. Katie was so upset she couldn't think of anything to say.

Orbalee lit more silver-gray leaves before lifting a crystal ball from its stand. 'We ask that I might be a channel for the Master who will give the advice that is needed at this time.' She stared into the cloudy glass and started to speak in an unearthly voice. 'You will lose everything. You will lose nothing. You will be gone with the wind. You will be the healer. You will be brother and sister, daughter and son.

Remember well our counsel and heed the prophesies of the stars.'

Katie got on her bike, crying so hard the lines in the middle of the road joined in a blur. There was no way she'd tempt fate by riding home and having an accident. The only thing she could do was pretend she'd had a flat.

She pushed her bicycle to a phone booth across the street. She uncapped the back tire and pushed in the valve to release the air. When the tire was half its diameter, she fished a dime out of her shoe and fed the warm coin into the slot. She stared at the palm in front of Orbalee's house, waiting for someone to answer. Let it be Rhett, she prayed. Please let it be Rhett.

He picked up on the tenth ring.

'Hey, it's me,' she said. 'I ran over a nail on my bike . . . Yeah. My back tire is flatter than a tortilla. Could you pick me up? . . . Great. That's great. I'm at the Texaco station on the corner of Picacho and Valley Drive.'

Rhett squatted on the sidewalk to examine the flat. 'Puncture, huh?'

She nodded.

He said, 'Cap's gone.'

'Crazy what people'll steal these days.'

He lifted the bicycle into the pickup. 'Thought you said you ran over a nail.'

'Thought I did.'

He was turning the key in the ignition when she put a hand on his arm. 'How about a drive?'

'You're on,' he said. 'Mom's really bent tonight.' He pulled away from the curb, squealing rubber.

She glanced behind her at the fortuneteller's sign. She wanted one thing right now: to get as far away as possible from that big pink hand.

Rhett turned into the parking lot of the Frontier Coffee Shop. She'd never liked going there because it was full of stuffed animals. In their living room was a stag's head her father had shot. It had hung on the wall so long she hardly saw it, but when she was eating, the severed heads of buffalo, moose and elk were more than she could bear. She started to ask Rhett to take her somewhere else, then decided it would only make him mad.

They walked past a pimply kid in a band jacket sitting at the counter. 'Hey, Mooner,' she heard behind her. 'Who's the groovy-looking chick?'

She turned around and saw the same kid hunkered down, hands around his glasses, as Rhett jabbed his middle finger in his face.

'That's my sister, Doak. Shut your face unless you want this rammed down your throat.'

'Okay, okay,' he said. 'I get the message.'

'You better, you scurvy rat fink.'

Rhett led her toward a table at the back. Compared to the huge seats of the other booths, where her brother chose to sit was a lovers' cubbyhole.

She asked, 'Who's that guy back there?'

'Some asshole.' Rhett had his back to the wall, glaring at the kid in the band jacket. 'Want anything to eat?'

In a glass case were uncut pies with handwritten labels: *PECAN, BLACK BOTTOM, COCONUT CREAM.* She caught the mournful eyes of the buffalo. 'Not hungry,' she said.

'This place has the best pies in town.'

'I want to lose a couple of pounds.'

'You're scrawny enough.'

'I've got a big performance coming up. Stage lights add five pounds.'

A waitress came toward their table holding a pad. *GENOBA* was embroidered in red curlicues on her uniform. She had a lined face and platinum-white hair pinned across the top of her head like a pioneer. The waitress turned to Katie, lifting the skinny pencil jutting above her ear. 'What will ya have tonight, hon?'

'Black coffee, please.'

'Make that two,' Rhett said. 'And a piece of your black-bottom pie.'

'Okeydokey.'

The waitress smiled and headed in the direction of the kitchen. Katie picked up the sugar dispenser and sprinkled a miniature beach along the table edge. *You will be gone with the wind.* What did that mean? Had Orbalee somehow seen her stupid middle name in the crystal ball?

'What's up with you, sis?'

'Nothing.'

'You've been nervous as hell ever since I picked you up.'

She drew KATERINA in the crystals. 'I am not.'

'Don't give me that.' He flicked the sugar. 'You don't make messes. You're so tidy it makes me sick.'

Genoba returned to their table with Rhett's pie and a steaming coffee pot. Her eyebrows lifted when she saw the sugar beach, but she didn't say a word. She put the plate on the table and filled their mugs. 'Can I get you kids anything else?'

Katie wrapped her fingers around the cup. She was embarrassed she'd made work for an old lady to clean up. 'No thanks. Just the bill, please.'

The waitress scribbled one, put it in front of Rhett and turned to a couple waiting to be seated.

Her brother ate his dessert while Katie secretly studied her palms. She was trying to remember exactly what Orbalee had said about the crystal with a termination at one end and why she needed one.

Her brother licked chocolate off his fork. 'Why'd you fake a flat?'

She felt her cheeks get hot. She blew on her coffee and didn't answer.

'Don't shit me, Katie. There was no nail. You let the air out so someone would come and pick you up.'

She lifted his plate and swept the loose sugar into it. Though she was afraid he'd laugh at her, she felt too depressed to lie. 'I was scared to ride home in case I had a wreck.'

'What made you think that?'

'This premonition I had.'

'You're upset because of something Orbalee told you.'

He said that and she burst into tears.

He pulled a napkin out of the dispenser and held it out to her. 'Katie, Katie,' he said, shaking his head. 'I didn't think you were such a coconut.'

She dabbed her eyes. 'Madame gave me the lead in *Petrouchka* today. I was so happy until I had my palms read.'

'What'd you see Orbalee for if you had such good news?'

'I thought she'd tell me I was about to join American Ballet Theater. Not that I'd have seven years of bad luck.'

Her brother started to laugh.

'It's not funny, Rhett.'

'I don't know why you're so worked up. If she didn't say a few creepy things, people wouldn't think they got their money's worth.'
'How do you know about her?'
'The guys in the band go to her for a laugh.'
'You've been?' she asked.
'It was a blast and a half.'
'What'd she say?'
'It was all baloney.'

Katie knew that, despite what her brother just said, she had to be careful the next few weeks. And then it hit her what she needed to do. She would ask her icon to intercede with God. She kissed the tips of her fingers and reached into her coat pocket. If the Virgin of Vladimir could stop Mongol hordes from attacking Moscow, surely she could stop any bad luck coming Katie's way.

Feeling more optimistic, she stroked the varnished wood. 'Rhett, I will have a piece of pie after all, only can you pay? I was so upset I gave Orbalee all my money and didn't wait for change.'

Her brother perched on the hood of the truck, mouth open, like he wanted to drink the sky. 'Nanatasis said that's Long Sash, what we call Orion, and that group over there are the Seven Dancing Girls.'

Katie loved the Indian names for things. She knew trees were Standing People and rocks were Stone People and animals were the Four-Leggeds, but her grandmother had never told her the Cherokee names for the constellations.

Rhett pointed to the Big Dipper. 'That's Great Bear.'

She leaned out the side window. 'It's late. Mom'll hit the roof.' They were in the desert and it would take them at least twenty minutes to drive back.

'You were the one who wanted to stay out tonight, Katie.'

'It's two hours since you picked me up. *Madre'll* be on the warpath.'

'She already is. She's been threatening to send me to the Roswell Military Institute.'

'What for?'

'None of your beeswax.'

She glanced at the dashboard clock. 'Come on, Rhett. We need to go.'

He leaned over the hood and spat. 'Always been Little Miss Goody

Two Shoes, haven't you? Always toeing the line. No wonder *madre* doesn't have a clue what a real teenager is like.'

'All I asked was for you to drive me home.'

'"Your sister never gets into trouble. Not once have I ever had to go to the principal's office because of some fool thing she's done." You're the freak, Katie. You can't even drive by yourself. You still have your learner's permit.'

'I haven't had time to take the test. My career comes first.'

'I know all about your fucking career. Dad and I sat in the car till midnight waiting for your *Nutcracker* rehearsals to be over. Did it ever cross your mind you're a selfish bitch as far as your career is concerned?'

Katie felt as if he'd slapped her. She wanted to say, It's not my fault Madame's school is in El Paso, but her brother wouldn't care about that. 'Tell me more about what Nanatasis said about the stars.'

'You were never interested. You always had your head in a ballet book.'

'Show me some more Cherokee constellations.'

He jammed his hands in his pockets, shook his head.

'Pretty please. With sugar on top?'

'Why should I waste my breath on you?'

She got out of the truck to stand beside him. 'Because I'm proud we're quarter Indian and I want to find out more about my heritage.'

He took his hand out of his jacket and pointed above Picacho Peak. 'That one's the Rattlesnake. The North Star is the one that doesn't travel. Nanna said Great Spirit put it there for the Two-Leggeds so that we'd always be able to find our way.'

'Know what stars remind me of?' she said. 'The candles in front of my icon when I close my eyes almost shut.'

'Stars don't have to be anything other than what they are.'

'Come on, Rhett. We've done enough stargazing for one night.'

'Look, Katie!' Her brother pointed at a streaking ball of light. 'You see the tail on that shooting star?'

She swallowed. 'Is that the same as a comet?'

'Pretty much.'

'What do you think it means?' she asked.

'Nothing.'

'Orbalee told me comets were unlucky.'

'Maybe in the old days,' he said. 'Before they could be explained.'

She was certain the shooting star was one of the tea-leaf omens. She put her hand in her pocket, squeezed her eyes shut and started to stroke her icon. Mighty protectress of the sorrowful, chaste Mother of God, helper of the afflicted, shelter of the universe. Blessed Virgin, I'm begging you to please turn away any bad luck this comet may have brought like you did with Tamerlane's armies.

'You okay?' Rhett asked, taking her elbow. 'You were swaying like you were about to faint.'

'Haven't eaten anything except pie all day. I'm starving.' She pulled some leaves off the nearest creosote bush and crushed them in her fingers. 'Once I get out of here,' she said, 'I'm never coming back.'

'Don't say that, Katie. New Mexico is where you were born.'

'I've never belonged here. You said yourself I'm a misfit.'

Her brother threw himself on the ground. Arms crossed, he rolled like a hyena, sending up plumes of dust. He turned wildly, first in one direction, then another, making a pattern on the ground.

'What on earth are you doing?' she said, coughing.

He just kept rolling.

L'acteur le plus grand du monde

'Dancers, this is your chance to make the history of ballet come to life.' Madame was standing in the auditorium with a clipboard, still dressed in the Magician's star-covered robe and white beard, giving first dress-rehearsal notes.

Katie hunched over to take another panting breath. Six hours of class and rehearsal. Weeks of immersing herself in the role of a puppet with a human soul. She was half dead from exhaustion, but more alive than she'd ever felt in her life.

'Inhabit your characters,' Madame was saying. 'Make the audience believe you're a drunken coachman or conceited aristocrat. In the crowd scenes some of you look like you're buying hot dogs at a baseball game.'

The stage manager shouted from the wings, 'Ghost lights in thirty minutes, Yekaterina. Let these kids go. It's after midnight. We need to lock up.'

Madame glanced at the auditorium clock and lowered her clipboard. 'That's all for now, company. I will give you the rest of your notes tomorrow. Go home and get some sleep.'

The crowd from the Butter Week Fair drifted offstage, scattering the plastic snow that had fallen in the last scene: grooms, nursemaids and beggars, the performing bear with its trainer, Lenten masqueraders with their grotesque papier-mâché heads.

After the third run-through, Katie's lungs were burning and her leg muscles felt like Jell-O. She was too tired to move so she watched the Ballerina Doll sit on the apron to remove her shoes and the lambs' wool padding stuck to her tights. Britt limped toward the wings with the Blackamoor, holding her bloodstained shoes by the ribbons.

'Katya,' Madame called out, her voice echoing in the empty auditorium, 'I want you to stay behind to rehearse.'

Katie saw the Ballerina Doll and the Blackamoor, staring at her and whispering. Britt and Quintus were jealous. She'd seen it in their eyes.

Madame said, 'I'm not happy with your conception of the part.'

Katie squinted into the darkened auditorium. She felt sick.

Opening night was only a week away.

'*Petrouchka* is not just about cruelty and death. It's about resurrection. Hope overcoming despair. The audience shouldn't have to buy a program to know that.' Madame ripped off her beard and looked up. 'Backdrop, Scene 2,' she shouted.

High above the stage the flyman called back, 'Never gonna let us go home, are you?'

'Not until it's right.'

'Heads up,' he said. 'Fly coming in. Heads up.'

The backdrop lowered into place as Katie removed a mitten to coat the inside of her mouth with Vaseline. Dancers weren't supposed to drink while they were performing. Petroleum jelly would seal moisture inside her mouth.

Madame put on the record. 'You know what Nureyev said about performing? "Every step must be sprayed with your blood."' She clapped her hands. 'The whole of Scene 2. *Du sang.*'

Katie took her place upstage in a black room with a portrait of the Magician peering down from the wall. Pretending to have been kicked into her cell, Katie fell, face down. She lifted her body and flopped forward like a rag doll. Trembling, she looked over her shoulder at the painting of the Magician.

'More fear,' Madame shouted. 'Let me see in your eyes you're terrified of your master.'

Katie fisted her hands and shook them at the picture. She mimed being kicked in the back. She covered her face with her hands, put them to her heart and drew them away from her chest as if they were attached to a puppeteer's strings.

'Stop,' Madame shouted. 'This is rubbish. Complete rubbish.' Madame brushed her own face as if she were wiping away a tear. She struck the back of her neck with her fists. Her eyes flashed with hatred as she pretended to be kicked. She twisted from side to side as she tried to comfort herself with sawdust arms.

Katie's skin rose in goosebumps. She'd seen Madame do this before when she was teaching her the part, but never with this intensity. She felt as if she were watching Nijinsky's ghost.

'You must be lifelike, yet never human. Natural, yet stiff like a doll. After Sarah Bernhardt saw Nijinsky dance this role she said, *"J'ai peur,*

j'ai peur, car je vois l'acteur le plus grand du monde.'"
Madame put on the rehearsal record and Katie began the sequence again. She whirled in a series of pirouettes, trying to break through the walls of her cell. Her movements became more demented, desperate. She spun wildly to the discordant music.

'More ecstasy when the Ballerina Doll comes into your room,' Madame shouted. 'From your hands to your feet. Let your soul speak with your whole body. You must be in communication with the geniuses who made this ballet. Fokine, Stravinsky and, above all, Nijinsky.'

Katie jigged and jumped, wildly windmilling her arms to the percussive piano and strings.

'When the Ballerina leaves, you want to stop her so you jump after her. Don't look where you have to land. Look with your legs.'

Katie bounded across the stage, gasping for breath, arching her back so that her soft leather boots hit her head.

'Why are you holding back?' Madame stopped the music. 'Push your feet into the floor and breathe out as you straighten your knees. Again. Three *sauts de l'ange* across the stage.'

Katie walked into position as Madame put on the music. She inhaled as she bent her knees. Ribs heaving, sweat dripping into her eyes, she tried to convey Petrouchka's desperation by hurling her body toward the painted doors. Between her second and third jump, she heard Madame shout, 'Defy gravity!'

On her last jump she landed, not on two feet, but on one. Her right knee collapsed, her leg twisted backward like a chicken's wing. She lay on the floor, screaming.

A stagehand dropped his broom and knelt over her as she heard someone run up the stage steps. 'I'll call an ambulance,' he said.

'You will call nothing.'

Madame stood over her wearing the Magician's robes. She knelt down to pull Katie's leg out from behind her. She felt Madame push up her pantaloons to inspect her right knee.

'Get up and walk.'

'I can't, Madame.' She was sobbing.

'You must.'

'Something snapped,' the stagehand said. 'It sounded like a gun shot.' She felt Madame's hands run up and down her knee. 'Nothing's broken.'

'That kid needs a doctor.'

'You are not paid to give medical advice. You are a stagehand.' Madame picked up his broom and threw it at him. 'Get rid of that snow.' She felt Madame tapping her face with her finger. 'Enrique Martínez is coming to audition you. You can't let your knee get stiff.' Katie forced herself to sit up and look at her injured leg. It was unrecognizable as a knee. It had ballooned into something else.

Madame said, 'Do you want to dance Petrouchka or lay there crying?'

'I can't get up.'

Madame pulled her to her feet. 'You'll never be a ballerina if you let a little pain defeat you.'

Madame draped one of Katie's arms around her neck and made her hop to the wings. 'Put your hands on the barre. There's nothing wrong that *pliés* won't cure.'

With tears running down her face, she tried to bend her knee, but it was useless. It was only then she noticed the record was still playing the happy music of the Butter Week Fair.

'*Demi plié,*' Madame said. 'Command your body to obey you. *Demi plié*. Brave girls can stand a little death.'

Jack Hiebert was called to the theater to drive her home. She had to sit in the back seat of his Chevrolet, her leg sideways, because her knee was so swollen it wouldn't bend.

Rosalia was standing on the porch when they pulled into the driveway. She saw her crying and said, 'I'm calling the doctor.'

'No!' Katie said, wiping her face. 'It's just a little sprain.'

They helped her out of the car and up the three steps of the porch, Jack on one side and Rosalia on the other. Katie caught a glimpse of herself in the living-room mirror as she hopped past. She'd had no time to take off her make-up. Staring back at her was Petrouchka. Putty-colored cheeks, twisted mouth, a faded eyebrow flying off into space.

Jack helped her onto the couch and gave her some aspirin. All she could think about was opening night and Enrique Martínez flying in from New York to audition her.

Rosalia left the room and came back with a jar of horse liniment and a sweater. 'I do something we do in Italy.' She cut a sleeve off the old jumper and coated Katie's knee with smelly yellow cream, winding the tube of wool around the joint before securing it with a safety pin. Before Rosalia had started, Katie's knee looked like it had mumps. Now the wool made her leg look even more swollen, which made her start crying all over again.

Rosalia stroked her arm. 'Try to sleep with your leg propped against the wall. It will help with the swelling. Jack will give you some cognac. In the morning you need to see a doctor.'

'No!'

'But we are your guardians—'

'Madame said I didn't need a doctor. Promise me! You both have to promise you won't tell my parents!'

Rosalia turned to Jack. She looked worried, but when her husband started to nod, Rosalia nodded too.

Every hour Katie got up and tried to walk around her room, desperate to see if there had been any improvement. There wasn't.

During the night she had a strange dream. She was limping down a dark street, dragging her leg behind her. Painted on a sign outside a tailor's shop was *ANY REPAIR UNDERTAKEN. SATISFACTION GUARANTEED.* Inside, a man was cross-legged on a table, working by candlelight. She tried the door, but it was locked. She banged on the window. The tailor came to the door and asked what she wanted. She uncovered her leg, hidden by the red sleeve of a sweater, only to see that it had been turned into a piece of wood.

The moon of Islam

The schoolroom clock said it was a quarter past three. Terrified of being knocked over, Katie was still sitting at her desk, waiting until the crowd in the hall had thinned. At half past she struggled into the corridor, relieved to see only two stragglers stuffing books into their lockers.

She walked in the direction of the entrance, only it wasn't really a walk because only her left leg could manage that. She hobbled through the doors etched with rearing stallions and headed toward the bus stop. She was wondering if, by some miracle, she might somehow be able to take class tonight. She'd tried yesterday, but had to stop during the first exercise. Madame had been furious when she'd left the studio. *Come back to the barre, Katya, or I won't let you dance Petrouchka!*

She kept her eyes glued to the cracked sidewalk so her clumsy leg wouldn't make her trip. As she inched along, a familiar pair of silver shoes came into her line of vision. Moon-landing shoes with rockets on the vamp.

'I told the Hieberts not to tell you! I made them promise!'

'Sugar, they had to tell us.' Her mother reached up to dry her face with her hand. 'Rosalia called and said you'd hurt yourself. I'm taking you now to see a doctor. To find out what's wrong with your leg.'

'But I can't see a doctor, Momma, I can't! I'm dancing Petrouchka next week!'

Her mother opened her purse and handed her a tissue. 'Daddy spent all morning on the phone finding the best orthopedic man in El Paso. Every doctor in Fortuna gave him the same name. Dr Berlinghieri was appointed the official surgeon to the US ski team.' She tapped her watch. 'Daddy's made an appointment at his office in half an hour.'

The doctor was standing behind his desk when she limped in. Katie was surprised that he had a carnation in the buttonhole of his lapel. She'd never seen a man wear a flower before.

'Dr Berlinghieri.' He shook hands, first with her and then with her mother. 'Please have a seat.' He pulled a stool in front of Katie's chair.

'You'll be more comfortable with your foot on this.'
She noticed him studying her as she lifted her stiff leg with both hands.
'Ever hear of *RICE*?'
'Paddies?' she said.
He shook his head. 'Standard management for joint injuries. Rest it. Ice it. Compress it. Elevate it. You do any of those things?'
'I elevated it.'
'Your father told me you fell two days ago. Is that right?'
She nodded.
The doctor clicked his pen. 'Want to tell me what happened?'
Katie cleared her throat, hoping she wouldn't cry. 'I'd been rehearsing all evening for a ballet performance. I was doing some big jumps and my knee buckled when I landed.'
'Pretend your arm's your leg and show me.'
She wrenched her right fist behind her back like a policeman restraining a criminal.
Dr Berlinghieri motioned to the paper-covered couch. 'If you'd like to lie down, I'll examine you.'
She was on her back and then her side as he tugged, twisted and pushed her leg. The examination seemed to last for hours. Most of what he was doing made her want to leap off the couch, but she managed not to faint. Or scream.
'That injury's worse than a lot of skiing accidents.'
Her mother looked worried. 'What's wrong?'
'Knees are complicated joints. You can never be a hundred percent sure until you get inside. You can sit up now, young lady.'
He washed his hands and picked up a plastic knee from a display cabinet of demonstration bones. He bent it so she could see inside. 'From the range of movement, it appears that you've ruptured your anterior cruciate ligament, or ACL, which is here, and torn the medial cartilage, which is here.'
Katie looked at the stringy band his pen was pointing to and then at a C-shaped pad between the two big bones of the model.
'The swelling is due to torn cartilage and the escape of blood from your ACL. I can't repair the ligament. That damage is permanent, but I can remove the cartilage you've mashed up.'
He turned the plastic knee so she could see better. 'Between the big

bones of the leg, fibrocartilage acts as a shock-absorber. These two inflexible pads are called menisci. They're crescent-shaped like the moon of Islam and prevent the femur and tibia from rubbing together.'

Katie only half took in what he was saying. She was struggling to imagine what the inside of her knee looked like with one of its moons mashed up.

'The knee is subjected to too much stress in ballet to have loose bodies floating around. Removing them will prevent your knee from locking.'

He picked up a roll of LifeSavers on his desk and peeled the wrapper. She thought he was going to offer her one, but he crushed the butterscotch ring with a small hammer and inserted several pieces into the model joint until it jammed.

'That's what a torn meniscus can do during strenuous activity. A knee lock causes further damage to the joint so it's something you'll want to avoid.'

'Does that mean . . . an operation?' Katie asked.

He took a letter opener and started to gouge out the broken candy. 'If you stop dancing, young lady, then no. You could be a wife and mother on that leg and not have surgery.'

'But I don't want to be a wife and mother,' she said. 'I want to be a dancer.'

The surgeon removed his glasses. 'When I was your age, I thought I wanted to be an opera singer. My father told me I was going to be a doctor. I fought him for a few years and then realized he had my best interests at heart. Now I have the best of both worlds. I'm an orthopedic surgeon and a soloist in the El Paso Civic Opera.' He returned his glasses to the end of his nose and smiled at her mother.

Katie began to speak slowly, as if she were using a language he did not understand. 'All I've ever wanted to do my whole life is dance. That's what I was born to do.'

'In that case, you'll need a meniscectomy.'

Katie looked at the knee model for a long time. 'What will you do?'

He picked up a pen and pointed at the plastic joint. 'An incision is made on the inside of the knee to remove any damaged cartilage. That will leave a three-inch zipper scar. There's a hospital stay of a few days, followed by physiotherapy to build up the quadriceps and restore a full range of movement.' He returned the pen to his clipboard and leaned back in his chair. 'I'll have my secretary book you into Hotel Dieu for surgery tomorrow.'

Katie was starting to feel hopeful until he suddenly stopped smiling.

'What I can't promise,' he said, 'is that you won't continue to reinjure yourself. Your cruciate ligament has been overstretched like an old rubber band. Your knee will always be unstable. It won't hurt, but it will be prone to reinjury.'

She wanted to scream, It isn't fair, God. It isn't fair! She looked at the floor and wiped away a tear sliding down her cheek.

Her mother asked, 'Are there any risks in this operation?'

'Any surgical procedure carries a degree of risk. In a meniscectomy, there's a possibility your daughter might have a stiff leg for the rest of her life.'

Katie noticed that he didn't look at her when he said that. He was busy digging the crushed candy out of the plastic joint. 'You mean I could be a cripple,' she said.

'If you want to dance, young lady, I'm afraid that's the risk you'll have to run.'

Her mother opened the back door of the Thunderbird and helped her to maneuver her leg out of the car. 'I don't know why you have to see Madame Fedora right now.'

'I'm booked into Hotel Dieu tomorrow. I have to tell her to get someone else to dance my part.'

As she headed up the sidewalk, she heard a car door open and her mother call out, 'Katie, the doctor said you shouldn't be walking.'

'Stay in the car.'

Madame was at the front of the studio, watching the closing scene of the Butter Week Fair. One by one, gypsies, wet nurses and coachmen stopped dancing as Katie made her way to the bench at the front, dragging her leg.

'Why aren't you here rehearsing?'

Madame spoke so softly that Katie had to struggle to hear. 'But you know why.' She pointed at her grotesquely swollen leg.

Madame Feodorova sniffed. 'It's five days until opening night, Katya. You're standing, aren't you? You're walking. Then you can dance.'

'But the doctor says I have to have the cartilage in my knee removed if I want to dance.'

'So you'd believe a butcher before you'd believe me?'

'No, Madame, but I've been told I need an operation.'

'Surgeons are knife-happy. They don't care what happens to you. They only want your money. Your body knows what to do to heal itself.'

'Please don't confuse me, Madame. I'm already scared.'

'Russians have a saying, Katya. "Don't go into the forest if you're afraid of wolves."'

'But I don't have a choice if I want to dance.'

'You do have a choice, Katya. If you have an operation, I forbid you to set foot in this studio again.'

Falling stars

Katie limped to the entrance of Coronado High. Her mother was to arrive at two thirty to drive her to the hospital. She'd been let out of class early and was alone in the lobby, except for three sorority sisters decorating the Christmas tree. Janet Fisketjon, Susan van Haslen and Barbie Lundgren ignored her, even though all of them were in her English class.

Standing next to the huge tree, the Varsity cheerleaders looked like life-sized dolls with their bouffant hair combed into perfect shoulder-length flips. They wore identical wool jackets, the name of their sorority in gold letters across their backs. *GNATSUM* looked like a Latin word, but it was only the Coronado mascot spelled backward.

The cheerleaders were giggling about the film everyone was talking about. *The Graduate* had been released a few years ago, but had only just arrived in El Paso. Katie edged closer to hear what they were saying. She'd seen the billboards of Dustin Hoffman staring at an unseen woman pulling on a black stocking.

The sorority sisters were talking about Benjamin being seduced by Mrs Robinson. Barbie was saying, 'Know what my father said after we saw *The Graduate*? "No wonder our kids have no morals if this filth is what Hollywood is churning out."'

Then they all laughed. They had the same laugh, like real sisters.

Katie's eyes drifted from their frosty-pink lips to the hems of their miniskirts. She fisted her hand around the strap of her purse, wanting to swing it at them. Although those sniggering girls didn't need them, they all had perfect knees.

A nun wearing a white cap shaped like an origami swan led the way to Katie's room. Behind her was her mother carrying a pot of poinsettias and an overnight case. Katie brought up the rear. By the time she had hobbled to the end of the corridor, the nun had taken her mother into the room and was already heading back to the elevator.

Katie found her mother frowning at a religious painting. 'I wish your doctor wasn't Italian.'

Katie threw her purse on the bed. 'What's that got to do with anything?'
'Because he picked a hospital run by the durn Pope. No one but a Catholic is happy to see a crucifixion.' Her mother eased the large frame to one side and bowed out her cheeks in exasperation. 'They'd notice if we took it down. The roses on the wallpaper behind it are brighter than the rest of the room.'

Her mother tapped her foot like she was trying to figure out what to do, then marched into the bathroom and returned with a stack of towels. Katie watched her drape as much of the painting as she could. Any other time she would have been embarrassed by what her mother was doing, but she was too depressed to care. By the time her mother had finished, the only part of the picture that was visible were rocks, the hem of Mary Magdalene's robe and the sandaled feet of some soldiers.

'There,' her mother said. 'No one can get well with blood and gore staring them in the face, especially at Christmas time.'

Her mother opened the overnight case and took out what looked like a red-and-gold flannel shirt. She removed the pins and cardboard and a nightgown fluttered loose.

Katie felt like throwing up. The material was covered with comets.

'Look what I bought for your operation, sugar. Isn't it gorgeous?'

Katie's legs started to shake. *Remember well our counsel and heed the prophesies of the stars.*

'Put it on, sugar,' her mother said. 'Let's see how it fits.'

'I'd rather not.'

'But I just bought it.'

'I'll wear the hospital one.'

Her mother rubbed the material. 'This is warm flannel. Not some backless doofunkey that leaves your fanny whistling in the wind.'

'I told you I don't want it.'

'Katie, this is all I've brought for you to wear. They won't give you a surgical gown until tomorrow.'

'I'll wear a sheet.'

Her mother tried to push the gown into her hands. Katie couldn't tell her that Orbalee had seen a comet in her tea leaves. Terrified the gown might jinx her operation, she dumped it on the floor.

Lola picked the gown up, folded it, put it at the foot of the bed. If it had been any other time, she would have yelled at Katie for behaving so ungraciously.

She opened her purse and took out the papier-mâché choirboys she'd wrapped in newsprint. Every Advent since Katie had been a child, they'd sat on the shelf in the kitchen, their mouths open like hungry young birds. She arranged the dozen choirboys on the nightstand and placed the pot of poinsettias in front of the mirror so the reflection made it look like twice as many choristers, twice as many blossoms. She wanted to make Katie's room as cheerful as possible because of what the doctor had told her this morning. *Bone surgery's no picnic, Mrs Rivers. A meniscectomy feels like an amputation. It's a long, painful recovery and your daughter's going to go through hell for a few weeks.* Better that she doesn't know, Lola thought. Better she's in the dark before she goes under the knife.

She arranged the fruit for her daughter she'd brought from home. 'Apples, tangerines and bananas. In the nightstand are the leg warmers you've been knitting. I brought one of my music boxes as a treat.' She put it on the bedside table, pleased she'd made the room look so cheerful. 'Daddy and Rhett will be wanting their dinner. Anything you want before I go?'

Katie mumbled, 'A good knee.'

Lola looked at her daughter slumped on the bed and slid her handbag over her arm. *A good knee.* Her saying that almost broke her heart. If it were possible, she would have gladly taken on Katie's pain rather than see her suffering like this. 'I'd better be going, sugar. The sun's on its way down. I'm afraid to drive alone after dark.'

'You've got nothing to be afraid about. After tomorrow I might be a cripple!'

Lola clutched her purse. 'I'll be here, sweet pea, when you wake up from the anesthetic.' She stood in the doorway wanting to say, I love you. I'm afraid for you. I pray your surgery will turn out all right. She waved, desperately wanting her daughter to wave back. When she didn't, Lola reopened the suitcase.

Katie had always wanted a screaming nut doll so when Lola had seen one in a department store window, she'd browbeaten the manager into letting her buy it, even though the nutcracker wasn't for sale. She had planned to give it to her tomorrow, but her daughter was so down-in-the-mouth she needed some cheering up now. Lola lifted the ugly doll out of its bed of tissue paper and raised the lever to open its mouth. Her daughter glanced at it and turned her face to the wall.

'Aren't you going to say anything about your surprise?'

Katie curled into a ball. Lola put the nutcracker on the nightstand and backed out the door. Her heels clacked as she walked, and then ran, the length of the hall.

A stain shaped like Antarctica

'The hospital just called and said that Katie's surgery might have to be postponed.' Haywood threw his briefcase onto a chair. Eight twenty. Bone tired. Two hours late for dinner because of Mrs Montoya's root canal. 'What in the devil for?'

'Because a consent form hasn't been signed.'

'Why didn't you sign it when you were down there?'

'I signed everything they gave me, Haywood.'

'You didn't sign everything if there's a paper left to sign.'

His wife folded her arms across her stomach. 'It's not my fault they forgot to give me some damn piece of paper. You'll have to go to El Paso. I have trouble seeing after dark.'

He opened the refrigerator, took out a carton of milk and tipped it to his mouth.

'Stop guzzling that milk, Haywood, and get your butt in that truck. We can't have Katie wait another day for surgery when she's scared half to death.'

'I just got in the door, Lola. I'm pooped. Can't you go?'

'I've been to El Paso already today. Besides, I've got to be at the hospital early tomorrow before her surgery. I'm not about to drive at night and have a wreck.'

He stared at the tendons framing his wife's neck. She drove all the time after dark when it suited her. 'Goddamn it, Lola,' he said, banging the carton on the table. 'Goddamn it to hell!'

He jerked on his jacket and left without saying goodbye. He gunned the truck down Main Street. After passing the city limits, he pumped the horn on the empty highway for at least a mile.

He got back at a quarter past eleven. Rather than ask Lola to reheat dinner, he made himself a peanut-butter-and-banana sandwich and went straight to his room.

He was in bed doing the crossword when he heard his wife next door. Cry, he thought as he chewed the end of his pencil. You've made your bed. Now you can lie in it. He scratched his cheek with the eraser and concentrated on the next clue, View. Eleven letters. Pressing the newspaper against his thigh, he penciled in *PERSPECTIVE*. 17 Down: Arrogance. *HAUTEUR*.

When he finished the crossword, he could still hear her muffled crying. He stared at the bedroom wall lined with family portraits. Lola smiled at him from the center of the bank of pictures, her face naked without glasses, her hairdo wavy and dark.

That portrait had been made at Ballard's Picture Emporium the day they'd left Tennessee to start a new life. While the car was being serviced, Haywood told her to have her portrait taken because he'd never seen her look so happy. He remembered what she'd said that day. *I want to leave Tennessee so bad, I don't care if we have to live on roast prairie dog.*

The first person they'd sent their new address to was Sam Ballard. His portrait of Lola had hung in every home they'd had since 1950, a time machine that had the power to take him back to when they were young and in love and on the brink of something good.

The room was dark except for the orange night-light plugged in next to the bed. Haywood stood in the brightness of the hallway, looking into Rhett's old room. His wife was lying on the lower bunk, head covered with a pillow, air going in and out of her so fast she was panting. 'You all right, Momma?'

She kept crying.

He sat on the edge of the mattress and lightly touched her shoulder. 'What's the matter, Lo? Tell me what's wrong.'

She left the pillow where it was, her crying softer now, as if she were trying to pull the sound back in. 'I'm scared.'

He lifted the pillow off her face. 'Of what?'

'Katie's operation.'

'What's there to be scared about?'

'That she'll die under the anesthetic.'

'Don't worry about it. Berlinghieri's good. Every surgeon in Fortuna recommended him.'

'Things go wrong, Hay. People go under and never wake up. You read about it all the time in the paper.'

'Katie's strong as an ox. You told me Berlinghieri said she had an athlete's heart, one of the slowest he's ever come across.' He squeezed his wife's shoulder and she started to sniffle again.

'I can't get the way she looked out of my mind. When I left her, she was half crazy with fear.' Lola wiped her face with the back of her hand.

'How was she when you saw her?'

He'd found her clutching her icon, a wet stain on the pillowcase where she must have cried herself to sleep. 'She looked so peaceful, Lo, I didn't want to wake her.' He took a corner of the sheet and started to dry his wife's face.

'You know the screaming nut doll I told you about? I thought it would cheer her up, but she didn't even say thank you.'

'Katie's going through a tough time, Momma. I'm sure she appreciated it. She just couldn't say so.'

'She hasn't even had the operation and she's already acting like she's given up. I'm afraid, Hay. I'm afraid she'll . . .' Her voice trailed off.

'She'll what?'

'Be like my mother.'

'But Nanatasis is fine.'

'Now she is.' Lola leaned over, blindly tapping the carpet. 'You see my glasses anywhere?'

He nudged her pearl frames out of sight with his foot. 'I'd like to look at you without them for once. Smile for me,' he said, tilting her chin until it was at the angle of the portrait in their bedroom.

'What's this all about, Hay?'

He wanted a glimpse of the eighteen-year-old he'd fallen in love with, the girl who'd enjoyed his body and his company and didn't snap at him for every little thing. 'Just smile and don't ask any more questions.' He ran his finger along her undyed hairline. He looked into her eyes and said sadly, 'Lo, what's happened to us?'

Her brow furrowed. She looked afraid, like he was about to give her some bad news. 'What do you mean, Hay?'

'Move over,' he said, 'and let me give you a hug.'

He spooned his body against hers and she felt his breath, hot and insistent, on the back of her neck. It was the first time they'd shared a bed since she'd given him her ultimatum about Rhett. She felt his foot rub hers and she jerked her leg away.

He hit the pillow. 'Momma, I don't understand you at all.'

'What's there to understand? You only want sex.' She stared at the shadows of Rhett's model planes, wheeling and turning on the wall. Since she moved into their son's room, Hay had refused to say one word to her unless it had to do with Katie's operation. He'd watch TV, do the crossword and when it was time for bed, he wouldn't even say goodnight. Thinking he'd come to his senses, she'd put up with his silence but, after a week had passed, she'd taken her plate and eaten in the den. It wasn't the way she wanted to live, but hell, if that's the way he wanted things, he didn't have a monopoly on being mad.

Her husband sighed. The sound was long and deep and drawn out. It reminded Lola of her father's favorite hound whose old legs went out on him. Rather than have to carry Coony home, her father would tie him to the porch while the rest of the pack went hunting. Coony would give her a hangdog look like she was the one who had spoiled his fun. He'd sigh every time she passed to show how miserable he was.

Hay sighed again. Even though she wanted to punish him with some of his own medicine, those sighs tugged on her conscience. She let another minute go by before she forced herself to speak. 'Hay, what are you thinking about?'

'All those dreams we had once.'

'What made you think of that?'

His voice caught a little. 'Your picture on the wall in our bedroom.' The way her hair was combed in that photograph was the way she'd worn it when he'd been in college. That thought led him to remember the single bed they'd slept on during his first year at the University of Tennessee. He bought it in a secondhand store from an old man who'd helped him tie the mattress to the roof of his Ford. A five-dollar bed sunken in the middle, a dark stain shaped like Antarctica on the blue-and-white ticking. Even so, Haywood was proud of that bed because it was the first piece of furniture he'd ever owned.

The unfurnished apartment they'd lived in after the war was a converted chicken shed with a tarpaper roof and poorly-fitted windows that let in the rain and snow. They were so strapped for cash they didn't have anything except two Army sleeping bags, a Primus stove, a few pots and pans and a rickety ironing board. His desk was four planks balanced on a pair of sawhorses. No closet, just some orange crates for their clothes and a battered anglepoise lamp he'd found in a trash can.

He promised himself that, when he had the money, he'd buy Lola a proper bed. She was so good to him, working two jobs to help put him through dental school: at a dress shop during the day and waitressing at night. She never complained about having to drop out of college or their cramped quarters or what they couldn't afford.

The first time she came in from work and saw the bed, he knew it was worth every cent just to see the look on her face. She threw her arms around him and cried to have a real bed, even if it meant there was hardly any room to walk.

She put fresh white sheets on it and said it looked like a banqueting table and later, when they were in it, she took him in her mouth for the first time. In those days, Lola had been timid, still a new bride despite the five years they'd been married, separated for most of that time by four long years of war.

He pressed up against her now, wanting her. Wanting her to remember the single bed where they'd shared so much happiness. Wanting to make up, to make contact. He put his hand on her thigh, but she turned, taking the blankets with her, her back a wall she refused to let him climb.

Room of hope

Lola jumped out of bed and looked at the clock. She'd promised to be with Katie before they took her to the operating theater, but her alarm hadn't gone off. By the time she had thrown on her clothes, driven to El Paso and taken the creaking elevator to the fourth floor, her daughter was gone.

She stared at the indentation where Katie had been lying. The sheet was still warm when she touched it. She ran to the nurses' station to find out if there was a chance she might still see her, but the sister on duty said that Katie was already on her way to the operating theater.

Lola followed the signs to the waiting room on the ground floor, the whole time her stomach doing somersaults. The double doors had a plaque on them in Spanish. *Sala Esperanza*. She remembered enough Latin from high school to know that it meant 'room of hope'. She felt sick she'd arrived too late to see her daughter, but seeing those reassuring words cheered her up a bit.

She picked up a copy of *Better Homes & Gardens* and tried to read an article on decoupage. By the time she returned the magazine to its rack, she still didn't know what it was or how to do it, only that it involved paper, glue and varnish.

She watched a doctor in a surgical gown speak to a crying woman clutching rosary beads. Lola knew she wasn't the only relative terrified about how an operation might turn out.

A nurse had told her that it would be an hour and a half before her daughter came out of recovery so she decided to go somewhere more peaceful to be alone with her thoughts.

'Jingle Bells' was playing in the corridor outside the operating room. Because it was a Catholic hospital, Katie expected to hear something celestial like a Bach Christmas cantata, not the canned sound of Muzak.

The orderly pushed her through two sets of swinging doors. She saw surgical tools laid out on metal trays: tongs, hammers, chisels, scissors. Each one looked like an instrument of torture.

She was hoisted onto a freezing steel table in a backless gown, terrified to be asked by three masked people if it was the right knee they were to sterilize. Her whole body started to shake as she felt rubbing alcohol bathing, then evaporating off her leg.

A few minutes later she heard the anesthetist saying, 'You're going to feel something cold going into your wrist.'

Tears filled her eyes, ran down her temples, dripped into her ears. Above her the anesthetist mumbled.

'Count backward from ten.'

'Ten . . . nine . . . eight—'

The last thing she heard was, 'Are you sure it's the right knee?'

Afterwards, they told her she talked about rabbits.

Lola slipped into Hotel Dieu's darkened chapel. It didn't look, or smell, like her light-filled Baptist church. There were no Apostles smiling from lollipop-colored windows, no empty cross that promised resurrection. Just the gagging stink of incense and gruesome paintings showing Jesus being scourged and crucified.

She sat on a pew to collect her thoughts. She couldn't believe her daughter had found the courage to go through with this operation, Katie who had no courage at all. She was remembering when her daughter was little and had to have rabies injections after being bitten by a neighbor's dog. It had taken three adults to hold Katie down and she'd been terrified of doctors ever since. This operation was the worst thing Katie had ever had to deal with, but it wasn't half as bad as what she'd gone through at the same age.

The year Lola had been seventeen she'd been standing at the stove washing dishes. The firewood had been cut too long and the range door wouldn't shut. Flames licked through the opening, setting her apron, and then the left side of her body, alight. From December until April, she'd been bedridden with second-degree burns. The doctor had come every other day to tweeze off the dead skin while she'd clamped a pillow between her teeth so she wouldn't scream and upset everyone.

Lola took a Kleenex out of her purse and placed it on her head because she hadn't brought a hat. She eased herself onto the prayer railing, laced her fingers and closed her eyes. Dear God, please make everything turn out all right for my daughter. I don't know how she's going to make it through this because the only thing she's ever wanted to do is dance. I never wanted her to, but it doesn't seem fair this had to happen just before her big chance. But I've lived long enough to know the last thing that life is is fair. Please give her the courage of her namesake, Katie Scarlett O'Hara. Amen.

Lola started to get up and knelt again. I forgot the most important part. Operations can go wrong, Lord, so I'm praying to you with all my heart. Please guide the hands of the surgeon and the anesthetist, not only for my daughter, but for all their other patients. Amen.

An elderly Mexican couple entered the chapel just as she was lifting herself off the prayer rail. Both of them made the sign of the cross before lighting a candle in front of a statue of the Virgin Mary. They kissed her pink plaster toes and recited prayers that echoed in the small chapel.

Lola didn't know if it was forbidden for a non-Catholic to enter into their rituals, but she dropped a dime in the offering box and chose a candle. She lit it and pressed it on a tiny spur, glancing over her shoulder to see if the couple had guessed she was an impostor, but they were still praying, their eyes lifted upward. It made Lola think that each prayer said for a loved one must be rubbing against the ceiling, competing for the busy ears of God.

She twiddled her fingers as she stared at the towel-covered crucifixion in her daughter's room. She needed something to do until Katie came back from surgery. She'd been in such a hurry to leave home this morning she'd forgotten her embroidery hoops and yarn.

Lola checked her watch. Over an hour since she'd left the chapel. She paced up and down before lying on the hospital bed. She traced her finger over the repeated Dutch-blue words on the pillow: *HOTEL DIEU HOTEL DIEU HOTEL DIEU*. She opened her purse, put it down again, forgetting why she'd picked it up in the first place. She heard a gurney in the corridor and leaped up as two orderlies wheeled Katie in. 'Her eyes are still closed. Is she all right? Is my daughter all right?'

'She's just been released from recovery.'

'How is she doing?'

'She'll be awake soon.'

They slid her onto the bed and wheeled the gurney out. Lola

listened to it squeaking down the corridor as she squeezed her daughter's hand. Lola studied Katie's face, watched her ribcage going up and down. Lola wished her husband had canceled his patients today in case something went wrong so she wouldn't have to keep watch all by herself.

She was thinking that as Katie started to scream. It was so terrifying that Lola yelped too. She looked for the buzzer and frantically pressed it a half-dozen times. No one came so she ran into the hall. She stopped the first nurse she saw, even though there was tinsel on her white hat and she carried a paper cup covered with reindeer.

'My daughter's just had surgery. She's in 404 and squealing like a stuck pig.'

'I'm off duty, m'am.'

The nurse started to walk away, but Lola cut in front of her, making punch splash on her uniform. 'I don't care if you're off duty or not. You're a nurse and my daughter may be dying.'

The nurse turned her head, pretending to cough, but Lola saw her roll her eyes. Lola felt like slapping her until she saw her head in the direction of her daughter's room.

The nurse was reading her chart when Katie gave another blood-curdling yell. The nurse calmly looked at her dressing and took her temperature and blood pressure. 'Your daughter's vital signs are normal. She's had Demerol which can make some patients agitated. Despite the noise she's making, she's not feeling a thing.'

Lola held a hand over her heart. 'Thank the Lord and Jesus Christ.'

The nurse wiped Katie's face with a cloth, then used it to try and scrub out the berry-dark stain.

'I'm sorry about the punch,' Lola said.

The nurse patted her shoulder. 'It's a tough time of year to have family in the hospital. Why don't you take a nap? After knee surgery, she's going to need you when she wakes up.' The nurse picked up the reindeer cup and pulled the door shut behind her.

Lola dragged a chair to the bed and reached for the music box on the nightstand. On the lid inlaid with different types of fruit wood was a swan. The music box had been a present from a German widow Haywood had been billeted with after the war. She had given it to him in return for his sharing his Army rations and making repairs to her house. She said the music box was a gift for the little girl Haywood said he dreamed of having when he was shipped home.

Katie asked to hear this music box so often when she was little that Lola was afraid she'd wear it out. *Play, Momma, play.* Lola would crank the butterfly key and Katie would leap and twirl around the living room in her petticoat.

Lola wound it up now and put it next to her daughter. She laced Katie's limp fingers into her own, trying to think what the tinkling music reminded her of. The nearest she could get was something Katie had said when she was little. *Mommy, it's the music the fairies dance to.*

Katie moaned and reached for her leg.

'I can't make your knee go back to the way it was, sugar, but I'll do anything in my power to help you. Anything.'

Katie said something and Lola moved closer to hear. It sounded like, 'Don't go in the forest,' then she started mumbling about rabbits.

Lola leaned over the bed to stroke her daughter's face. She couldn't understand how Katie could cry while she was still unconscious until she realized the tears she was wiping away from her daughter's face were her own.

God's Hotel

An orderly came into Katie's room four hours after she'd had surgery. He was holding a pair of crutches. He propped them against the wall and turned back the covers of her bed. 'Ready to get up?'
She squinted at him through her bifocals. She had wanted to start her rehabilitation as soon as possible, but her leg felt like it had been hacked off below the knee. 'You've got the wrong room, mister.'
He leaned over to check the chart hanging at the end of her bed. 'According to this, you're Katie Rivers and I've got orders to get you up.'
'My knee's just been cut open. If you don't believe me, ask my mother when she comes back from the cafeteria.'
The orderly said, 'How tall are you?'
She looked at him, still a little groggy. 'Five seven. Why?'
He spun the wing nuts off one crutch. 'We walk people as soon as possible after surgery. Cuts down on blood clots.'
The orderly adjusted the height and helped her stand. He slid the crutch under her armpit. 'Perfect.' He lowered her to the mattress before making the second one the same length. 'All you do,' he said, 'is move your sticks and operated leg at the same time, followed by your good leg.'
'I can wiggle my ears. Want to see that instead?'
He smiled as he hoisted her bandaged leg off the bed. 'Keep your eyes straight ahead. I'm right beside you.'
Katie stared at her knee, expecting to see blood gush through the snow-white wrappings. The room started to pirouette, the last thing she remembered before the floor met her chin.

Dr Berlinghieri came in dressed in a surgical hat and gown. 'They tell me you were unconscious for a little while, young lady.' He pulled back the blankets to inspect her knee. 'I want you to lift your leg for me.'
It sounded like an insane request, but she was a dancer; her body had been trained to obey her. She tensed her quadriceps as hard as she could. Her right leg trembled, but refused to move.

'You lifted it for me just after the operation,' he said. 'Try again.'

She didn't remember doing that; she must have been coming round from the anesthetic. But if she'd done it before, she was determined to do it again. She pushed her hands into the mattress and struggled to raise her heel clear of the sheet. She tried, again and again, even though she was afraid she'd pass out from the pain. 'I can't,' she said, finally. 'I can't.'

Dr Berlinghieri patted her on the shoulder before handing her a Kleenex. 'Don't worry, Giselle. You'll be kicking your legs up in no time.'

That night her father loped into her room with a smile glued to his lips. 'I've got something for you.' He handed her a small cardboard box.

She opened the lid. On a layer of cotton was a necklace. Hanging from the gold chain was a pea-sized globe of lucite that contained a small seed. 'What it is, Daddy?'

'Read the note, honey.'

She lifted a slip of paper out of the box. '"If ye have the faith as a grain of mustard seed, nothing shall be impossible unto you."' She fingered the tiny sphere, trying not to cry. 'Thanks, Daddy.'

'Want me to put it on for you?'

'Please.'

He undid the clasp and fastened it around her neck. 'That knee of yours up to some exercise?'

She glanced at her throbbing leg. It wasn't, but she wanted to get better so she could dance again.

'Are you sure you should be doing this, Haywood?' her mother said.

'I'm not going to drop her like some damn orderly.'

Katie gritted her teeth as her father slowly, gently, lowered her padded leg to the floor. His arms encircled her as he helped her out of bed and handed her the crutches. 'Berlinghieri told me what happened this morning, honey. From now on, no one's allowed to walk you except me or your physio.'

They headed toward the corridor, pain making her lurch as awkwardly as Frankenstein's monster. During the hundred yards that seemed like a hundred miles, her father had his head tipped down like he was about to say grace. She saw the way people in the hospital looked at them and politely turned away, tears running down both their faces.

'Hey,' he said, 'did you hear the one about the three-legged dog who

went to a saloon? He asked the bartender, "Can you help me out, pardner? I'm looking for the man who shot my paw."'
   She started to sway and he steadied her.
   'You okay? Not feeling like you're going to faint?'
   She shook her head. She was trying to be brave for his sake.
   'Hey, have I told you why blind people don't like sky diving? It scares the hell out of their guide dog.'
   'Has Madame Feodorova called, Daddy?'
   'Not yet, honey.'
   She fell against his shoulder, crying. She hadn't told anyone what Madame had said. That if she had the operation she wouldn't ever let her come back to the studio again.
   'Leg hurting, honey?'
   She nodded.
   'Did you hear about the Polack who froze to death at the drive-in? He went to see *Closed for the Winter*.'
   'Please take me back to bed, Daddy.'
   'Just a little further.'
   In front of the nurses' station he saw a coin. 'Hey,' he said. 'A lucky penny. You lean against the desk while I pick it up.'
   He flipped it over to read the date. 'This was minted the year you were born.' He shined it and dropped it into the pocket of her comet gown. 'It's lucky,' he said. 'Extra lucky.'
   She wanted to ask him if the penny had the power of cancellation, if its magic was powerful enough to wipe out the bad luck of those falling stars.

Hotel Dieu: God's Hotel. She had a private room. She could choose her own menu, multiple-choice meals she ticked a day in advance: roast beef, sloppy joe's, even chicken Kiev. She'd never paid much attention to food, but lying in bed, wondering if she might be lame for the rest of her life, food was the only pleasure she had. Nothing to look forward to but the morphine and the meals. She ate. She slept. She ate. She wanted to sleep for ever.
   Her doctor sang Puccini on his rounds and always wore a boutonniere. Her father made a joke about it. *Every time you see Berlinghieri, he's wearing a carnation. For what he charges, he should be wearing an orchid.*

Lady lay

Katie lifted the hem of her gown and timidly began to explore her bandages. It had been three days since her operation and today was the first time she'd been able to force herself to touch the thigh-high wrapping. She pressed her leg lightly, then more firmly as she probed the thick gauze-and-cotton padding. Her finger touched something that felt like wire. You can't sew skin with metal, she thought. It's impossible. She'd seen dental sutures in her father's office. Stitches had to be catgut which dissolved or waxed thread that was cut and teased out. She was reinspecting the dressing when she was interrupted by a loud wolf whistle.

Standing in the doorway of her room was her best friend from Coronado High. Joe was wearing a pair of hip-hugging bell-bottoms and a paisley shirt she'd never seen before. He was grinning at her exposed legs.

She flipped down the hem of her gown. For two years, Joe Karolak had been asking her out and, for two years, she'd been refusing him. She pulled her hair around her glasses. She felt embarrassed he'd seen her wearing batwings, but another part of her didn't care because she was feeling so awful.

From behind his back he whipped out a red hippopotamus and a box of heart-shaped chocolates. She was flattered he'd cut class to see her, but his unexpected kindness made her cry.

'Hey,' he said. 'Seeing me was supposed to make you happy, not bring on the waterworks.'

'You should go,' she said, wiping her face. 'I'm not feeling so great right now.'

He balanced the hippopotamus on his shoulder and handed her the box. 'And miss seeing the most gorgeous girl at Coronado High in her nightgown? Not on your sweet bippy.'

She smiled as she tried to rip open the cellophane, but her nails were too short.

'Let me do the honors,' he said.

Underneath the wrapping was not Brach's Cherry Cordials or Whitman's Samplers, but expensive Belgian chocolates. He lifted the lid to study the printed sheet inside. 'I don't know what you're having, but I'll have a Lady lait.'

'Very funny, Karolak.'

'What can I tempt you with? Coeur noir, Lady noir, Volupté?'

'Black Lady.'

He picked up the oval of dark chocolate and tried to pop it in her mouth, but she snatched it from his fingers. 'What about Barbie Lundgren?'

'You're the only chick I've met who's been able to resist me.'

She liked Joe, but she'd never wanted to date him. A cheerleader might get turned on by a football player, but the only man she had ever fantasized about was Rudolf Nureyev.

'How'd the surgery go?'

'My doctor said my knee was so screwed up I had to have an extra incision to get all the pieces out.'

He lifted the hippopotamus off his shoulder. 'Really upsets me seeing you laid up like this. I know how much you were looking forward to dancing that puppet ballet.'

Trying not to cry, she picked up another chocolate and stuffed it in her mouth.

'When you get out of here, Rivers, I'll take you to Juarez. The cantinas are a blast.'

'I couldn't care less.'

'It'd do you good to get out in the real world.'

'I don't give a fuck about the real world.' She didn't feel like talking about a trip to a Mexican bar, not when her knee felt like it had been hacked by a machete. 'If you don't mind, I want to rest.' She eased herself back against the pillow and closed her eyes.

Karolak cleared his throat a few times, but she pretended she was asleep. She heard Joe tiptoe across the room a few minutes later and let himself out. The door clicked and she chose two champagne truffles and crammed them both into her mouth.

Her father arrived that night with a *GET WELL* balloon tied to a stick. Her mother cradled a cone of wilted flowers. 'You'll never guess who

these are from,' she said. 'Madame Fedora. Wasn't that nice of her?'
Katie looked at the bouquet and pushed it back at her mother. On opening night Madame would have sent a dozen American Beauty roses with stems of baby's breath, not drooping carnations tied with wrinkled ribbon.

'Madame went to a lot of trouble to send you this bouquet, Katie Scarlett.'

'Where's the card?'

'Hey, sister,' her father said. 'I've got a joke for you. Know what Mrs Santa calls her husband's helpers? Subordinate Clauses.'

Her mother arranged the carnations in a vase and placed them on the dresser with the other dying bouquets. 'Rhett would have come tonight, sugar, but he's got marching band.'

Her mother sat beside the bed, looking through her get-well cards. She picked one up with Einstein on the front. 'Wilmoth? Who's Wilmoth? You've never mentioned her before.'

'She teaches accelerated math.'

'It's not respectful to call a teacher by their first name.'

'She's not my teacher, *madre*. She's my friend. Someone I know from the bus.'

'Did she visit today?' her father asked.

She shook her head. 'She mailed it. It's hard for Wilmoth to get around.'

Her mother's eyes landed on the box in the wastebasket. She lifted the cardboard heart out of the trash. 'Who brought these?'

'Joe Karolak.'

'He must be sweet on you to buy Godiva chocolates.'

'He's not sweet on me,' Katie said. 'His father's rich.'

'When did he come?'

'This morning.'

Her mother said, 'And you've eaten a pound of chocolate? You're not exercising to burn it off.'

Katie stared at the carnations drooping at the end of her bandaged leg. On opening night, of all nights, she didn't want her family or Joe to visit. She'd trade their company for just five minutes with Madame. Five minutes to plead with her to let her come back so she had something to live for again.

'They don't waste any time putting their invoices in around here,' her mother said. 'We've already been billed by the surgeon and the anesthetist. I bet they charge so much because they give half to the durn Catholic church.'

'I'm sorry I'm costing so much,' Katie said.

'Honey,' her father said, 'that's not what Momma meant.'

Her mother drummed her nails on the nightstand. After a long silence she said brightly, 'Daddy and I have a little surprise for you.' She opened her handbag and took out a glossy souvenir program. 'We stopped by the theater on the way here.'

On the front was a color photograph of the Magician taunting Petrouchka in his cell. Knowing it had been taken the night she fell, Katie hurled the program across the room. Howling, she swept her arm across the top of the nightstand, knocking off the pot of poinsettias and the papier-mâché choristers. The last thing she remembered was a nurse sticking a needle in her arm.

She woke up twelve hours later. She looked for the souvenir program, but it was gone. All that was on her bedside table was one ruby-robed choirboy with a mashed-in face.

What kind of pain do you want to talk about?

Every opportunity she got, she moved what she could. Left foot, left leg, fingers, arms, shoulders, head. Before the operation, Berlinghieri had promised she'd be out in a few days and she'd already been here six. She needed to keep moving so her body wouldn't get any weaker.

For as long as she could remember, she had danced. She'd leapt and spun around the living room in a petticoat tutu, chubby arms in unmistakable ballet positions. Those home movies shot long before she'd had ballet lessons were proof that she'd been born a dancer.

Before the orderly came with a wheelchair to take her to physiotherapy, she pointed and flexed her left foot. Up and down, a hundred times. That's how she shut out the moans of the other orthopedic patients, how she kept the muscles of her good leg alive.

The calendar next to the door said DECEMBER 23. Only two weeks ago she and Madame had been at the dressmaker's for a fitting. She pictured herself arriving in her teacher's Citroën and going inside the house filled with costumes. Madame had insisted they were copies of the original 1911 designs, complete with imitation ermine and paste jewels. Having them made in Juarez had saved the Ballet Guild thousands of dollars.

Madame held up Petrouchka's patchwork trousers. 'Try your costume on to see how the fabric moves.'

She pulled on the white blouse with a ruffled collar, followed by the pantaloons made from diamonds of red and yellow silk. She danced through scraps of rainbow-colored fabric, her arms and legs twitching as if they were attached to a puppeteer's strings. She mimed the Magician beating her, throwing her arms in the air to protect her head.

The dressmaker's eyes widened. She crossed herself, mumbling something to Madame in Spanish.

Madame held her hand up. Katie looked at her, surprised she'd been asked to stop.

Madame had the faintest trace of a smile on her lips. '*Golubchik*, you're frightening Mrs Garza. She said to dance like that you must be a witch.'

The orderly rolled her into the physiotherapy room full of old people. The sight of the other patients depressed her. She was the only teenager in the orthopedic ward.

Sitting near the door was a white-haired woman with a frizzy permanent, her gnarled hands resting in a bowl. 'What I want to know,' she said, 'is who invented this hot wax torture.'

The physiotherapist glanced up from massaging an elderly patient. 'Be with you in a minute, Miss Rivers.' He continued to pummel the old man's thigh. 'How's your pain now, Mr Muncrief?'

'What kind of pain do you want me to talk about, son? Sciatic pain? The pain of outliving my friends? What about the pain when my wife dropped dead and I couldn't even tell her goodbye?'

'Mr Muncrief,' the physiotherapist said, 'I'm talking about your leg.'

'If you want the truth, it's the same as when I came in. Maybe worse.'

The physiotherapist ducked under the treatment couch and came out with a pair of shoes. 'Make sure you do up your laces, Mr Muncrief. Wouldn't want you to trip.'

The old man took his time to put his shoes on and tie the laces into a neat bow. Wincing with pain, he shuffled toward her. Every day since she had starting coming to physio, Katie had seen Mr Muncrief here, looking resentful and hopeless. Until now, she had never given his pain a second thought.

'Good luck with your leg,' she said.

He patted her on the arm. 'Looks like you could use some luck yourself in that department.'

The physiotherapist pointed at the parallel bars and held up two hands, fingers open wide. Ten lengths, twice as many as last time.

'You do the distance today,' he said, 'and I'll sign your release papers.'

Katie wanted her knee back. If that meant going up and down the mat a hundred times, she'd do it to get out of here. He helped her up and she moved to the end of the parallel bars, curled her fingers around the waist-high railings.

'Won't be so hard today,' he said.

Gritting her teeth, she pulled herself forward, dragging her stiff leg behind her. She was determined the pain wouldn't break her rhythm. Her knee would get better and Madame would take her back. She had to. Her father had found that lucky penny.

Morphine dreams

Every night she fell off cliffs, down wells, was pushed from speeding trains. Each time just before she hit ground, she woke. Thinking she was about to die, she would jerk up, terrified and half-asleep, trying to figure out where she was. Posters of Nureyev told her she was home. Rudi high above the stage in *Diana and Acteon,* Rudi sweating in class, Rudi dancing his variation in *Flower Festival in Genzano.*

She flipped on her bedside light, her heart still racing. Eleven o'clock. Past time for her pain medication. She threw the purple pills on her tongue and stared at the *pandoro* on the dresser, a mountain-shaped cake Rosalia had made to celebrate her discharge from Hotel Dieu. Rosalia had scooped away the front to create a cave's mouth. Inside were tiny ceramic figurines of Mary, Joseph and the Christ Child. Katie had been so touched the Hieberts had driven a hundred miles to give it to her that she'd put it in her room where she could see it from the bed.

She wanted to delay her morphine dreams so she decided to watch TV till it went off the air. She struggled out of bed to turn on the set. Two men in a gallery were examining some paintings. One was saying to the other, 'I've never seen anything like them. They're surrealistic, visionary. Who's the artist?'

The camera cut to a handsome young man in a wheelchair, a paintbrush gripped between his teeth. The last thing Katie wanted to see on Christmas Eve was a documentary about a cripple, but what stopped her from switching off the set was his look of fierce determination as he painted.

The camera showed the artist's family eating a meal. The artist's father was cutting up his son's meat. 'Our son was paralyzed when he was a teenager. At the time, his social worker was concerned his mother and I weren't taking the news harder. She accused us of refusing to accept our son would be a quadriplegic for the rest of his life. What she didn't understand is that we had God. We had God to help get us through this.'

The camera stayed with the young painter who had a sardonic look on his face. It was his father, not the painter, who had a God. The documentary ended and Katie cried through the credits, cried through 'The Star-Spangled Banner', cried for the gifted young man whose broken body had to be hoisted out of bed every morning like a side of beef. She pulled off a ledge of Rosalia's *pandoro* cake and pushed it into her mouth.

Rhett left the campfire and walked out into the bushes. After half a carton of beer, he needed a wiz. He stared at the bowl of the Big Dipper as his bladder emptied, remembering what his grandmother had told him. *To the Cherokee, that is Yona, the Bear, who has been making his way across the sky since the beginning of time.* Then she pointed to the stars in the handle. *Those are the three Hunters. The one nearest to Yona hit him with an arrow, but the wound wasn't deep so Yona has been running from the Hunters ever since. Yona's wound opens a little every fall. His blood falls to earth and turns the leaves red.*

'Where the fuck are you?' DD's voice sounded loud in the desert silence.

'Taking a leak.'

'Get yourself back here. I've got something for you.'

Of all the bikers Rhett rode with, DD Striker was the maniac. The guy would race on mountain roads with thousand-foot drops, taunt and out run cop cars just for a laugh. His 750cc Triumph Tiger was modded to the max with big-bore high-compression pistons, full race cam, dual amal carbs and upswept open megaphone pipes. The Tiger had so much power in its first two gears that DD could easily loop it and do way over the ton in top gear.

Rhett headed back to the fire where DD was holding out a lumpy roll of paper. 'Have some, Rivers.'

Rhett shook his head.

'Come on, man. Don't be such a candy ass.'

Rhett had tried marijuana a couple of times. It hadn't done anything except make his head spin, but to make DD happy tonight he took the joint. He blew the smoke out as soon as he could, trying not to cough. 'So what are you gonna do with the card?'

DD threw his ponytail over his shoulder. 'Nothing I can do.' He

put his hand out for the joint.
'Sure you can,' Rhett said. He picked up the packet of skins, pulled one out and dropped it into the fire. The thin paper curled to nothing.
'I'm 1-A, Rivers,' he said, 'but I'm no flag-burner.'
'You could hang out in Mexico. On the chopper, you could be across the border in less than an hour.'
DD held out the joint and smiled. 'No can do. Hate refried beans.'
Rhett took another hit and peered up at the sky. Since the last time he had inhaled, the stars seem to have multiplied. 'You're too damn anarchic to be a soldier. The slammer's gotta be better than being shipped to Nam.'
'Gotta go, old buddy.' DD kicked the sand. 'Wouldn't want anyone in this town thinking Dare Devil Striker is a coward.'

Katie was surprised to see her bedroom door swing open at two o'clock on Christmas morning. Rhett came in, his Tony Lamas skidding on the floor. His boots were so big they looked like they were walking him, rather than the other way around.
In slow motion he set his beer on the floor. 'Saw your light.' He patted all his pockets like he was frisking himself, then fished out a church key from his jacket.
'Where have you been?' she asked.
'Honkin' around with DD.'
'Look's like you've had a few too many.'
'Where's your Christmas spirit, Goody Two Shoes?'
She rubbed a guilty hand over her stomach. She'd just eaten a whole *pandoro* cake.
He flicked the stocking hanging at the end of her bed. 'On Dancer, on Prancer, on Vomit and Blitzen.'
She put a finger to her lips. 'You'll wake Mom and Dad.'
He cocked his head as if he were studying her. 'You've been leakin'.'
She tugged at some tufts on her bedspread. For the last two hours, all she'd done was cry and eat cake. 'My contacts have been playing up.'
'Like hell,' he said. 'You got your bifocals on.' He lifted the beer bottle and took a sip. 'You drive around and look at the lights?'
'Didn't want Dad to wreck.'
Rhett looked confused. 'Don't get your drift.'

'The roads are full of potholes. I'd have screamed my head off like I did coming home from the hospital.'
'Knee that bad, huh?'
'Morphine only takes the edge off.'
Rhett belched. The pukey smell drifted toward her. With cake filling her stomach, it made her feel like gagging.
He eased himself onto the floor and looked at her bandaged leg. 'Only a few months till you graduate. What you plan to do afterwards?'
'Dance *Swan Lake*.' She faked a smile. 'And you?'
'All depends on Uncle Sam.'
She stared at her brother. She'd never imagined the war would last long enough for him to be drafted.
'Gets worse,' he said. 'I've been suspended for six weeks. Haven't told *madre y padre* yet.'
'Jesus, Rhett. What'd you do?'
'Remember that dork at the Frontier?'
'The kid on the stool?'
He nodded. 'Doak saw me moon some girls on the band bus. He ratted on me again to the principal.'
'What's that got to do with Uncle Sam?'
'Can't sit my SAT. Fucks my chance for a college deferment.' He rolled onto his back and stared at her. 'Think we should be in Nam?'
'Dad says we have to stop the communists or they'll be over here in our backyard.'
'Great,' Rhett said. 'Let the Cong mow the grass for a change.' He burped again. 'In the desert tonight I heard Nanna talking to me. She was saying that people who die go into the sky and become stars.'
'Why do you think she was saying that?'
'I think it means I'll be drafted. Means I'm gonna die in a rice paddy on the other side of the world.'
He looked so scared that she put a hand on his arm. 'I don't think it means anything. You just had a little too much to drink.'
'I wish I had a crap leg like yours to keep me out of combat.'
She looked at him, not believing what he'd just said. 'Goddamn you,' she said. 'Goddamn you!' She couldn't reach her crutches so she picked up the cardboard Rosalia's cake had been on and threw it. 'Get out. Get the hell out of my room!'

He stumbled toward the door and she jerked the covers over her head. She tried to curl into a ball, small as a baby, but only her good knee could reach her chest.

On Christmas morning the house smelled of turkey. Her mother had put a twenty-pounder in the oven to roast overnight. That turkey had entered her morphine dreams. Just before she woke up, she'd been free falling from a plane, holding a drumstick instead of a rip cord.

Her heart was still banging when her mother appeared in her 'Twelve Days of Christmas' dressing gown with appliquéd swans, milkmaids and twelve drummers drumming around the hem.

'Rise and shine, sugar. We'll be opening presents soon.' Unwinding a curler she walked over to the bed. 'What's this mess?'

Katie looked at the greasy crumbs on the spread as if they'd fallen in the night like a mysterious yellow snow. 'Rhett ate Rosalia's cake.'

'That was supposed to be for you.' Her mother jerked a roller out of her hair. 'Now I'll have to wash this durn bedspread. As if I didn't have enough to do. Where was that stinker last night anyway?'

'Out in the desert with a friend.'

'With one of those hippy bikers no doubt.' Her mother fastened a button, reuniting the turtle doves. 'You get dressed, sugar, and I'll wake Rhett. The way that boy's snoring, you'd think he was sleeping something off.'

The biggest present Katie had ever seen was in front of the Christmas tree. A waist-high gift with four rubber-stoppered feet sticking out of red tissue paper. 'A barre,' she shouted, tearing the covering with her crutch. 'My own barre!' She ran her hand over the plumbing joints and sections of black pipe. 'Where'd you buy it?'

'Group effort,' her father said, pointing at Rhett.

'How'd you know how tall to make it, Daddy?'

'I called Carmel,' he said. 'I bought the pipe and and screwed it all together, but it was your brother's idea.' He put a hand on Rhett's shoulder. 'The buckeroo did all the paint work. Three coats of Japanese black.'

She looked at her brother, feeling guilty she'd pinned the blame on him for the bedspread. 'Thank you,' she said, 'thank you. It's the best present I've ever had.'

Rhett said, 'Try it out.'

She handed him her crutches and put both hands on the barre. She tried to turn out her feet, but pain stabbed her leg, bad enough to make her see stars.

'Hold your horses,' her mother said, grabbing the crutches away from Rhett and handing them back to her. 'That barre's for after your stitches come out.'

Twelfth Night

Katie stood in the lobby of Dr Berlinghieri's office. As the receptionist signed her in, Katie noticed a sprig of holly pinned to her mother's lapel. How could she not have noticed it before?

During the Russian winter, fir and holly branches are brought inside to give the tree spirits warmth. After the fifth of January, they are taken outside so spring will return.

Katie pointed at the waxy leaves. 'Please take that outside.'

'Whatever for, sugar?'

'It's unlucky to have Christmas things around when it's over.'

'I like to make Christmas last as long as I can.'

'But it's the sixth of January. Madame said it's bad luck because spirits live in trees and—'

'I don't want to hear another word about that durn woman.' Her mother picked up the January issue of *Family Circle* and started to read '20 Delicious Recipes For Turkey Leftovers'.

Katie was so worried about the holly that when the nurse called her name, she told her mother to stay in the lobby. The last thing she wanted was for bad luck to be anywhere near her when she had her stitches out.

Dr Berlinghieri was behind his leather-topped desk, a frilly red carnation in his buttonhole. 'How's the patient this morning?'

She cleared her throat, hoping he wouldn't notice her shaking legs. 'How long will it be before I can dance again?' She was staring at his Christmas tree which almost almost touched the ceiling. On its unlucky branches were kite-shaped decorations the Mexicans called *ojos de Dios*. Katie prayed those eyes of God would somehow protect her from angry tree spirits kept inside too long.

He looked over his glasses. 'You'll be throwing passes in no time.'

She forced a smile. 'I'm a ballet dancer, Dr Berlinghieri. Not a quarterback.'

He walked to the sink and turned on the tap. 'You won't be doing any dancing for a while.'

'My muscles lose strength every day I don't practice.'

His hands were a cloud of lather. 'I'll start you off with some exercises to strengthen the quads and gentle bends to help restore mobility.'

She glanced at the tree. 'I have to get my knee back. As soon as possible.'

He dried his hands. 'Hop up so I can have a look at my needlework.'

She lifted herself onto the table and pulled her leg after her. He picked up a pair of oddly-shaped scissors and started to cut the dressing above her ankle. He unwound yards of bandages and padding. She felt queasy to know she'd soon see the wounds of her cut-up knee.

She glanced at the light above the examination table before closing her eyes. She wanted to pretend she was in a stage spotlight, not having a medical procedure.

She felt her leg get cooler as Berlinghieri snipped away the last of the gauze. Finally she heard him say, 'Have a look.'

She didn't recognize the withered leg lying on the couch, but there was something worse that had been hidden by the bandages. Sticking out of her raw scars were four one-inch pieces of wire.

Pic Quik

She faced her new barre like a beginner: head erect, weight forward, stomach pressed upward toward the small of her back. 'Mighty protectress of the sorrowful, chaste Mother of God, helper of the afflicted, shelter of the universe. Blessed Virgin of Vladimir, I pray for a full recovery so I can use my body for the glory of God. Amen.'

She turned on the record player and slowly opened her feet to first position. Pain shot up her leg as the eight-count introduction was played. She and the pianist started together, but two counts into the first bar she was in agony. She gritted her teeth, started over, but her knee refused to move. Trying to get her right leg to bend was like trying to fold mahogany.

She repeated the same piece of music, again and again, struggling to manage the shallowest of *pliés*. Even dosed up with morphine, the pain was unbearable. Half an hour later she lay down and jammed a pillow over her face.

The door rattled. 'Katie Scarlett, what are you doing in there with the door locked?'

She lifted her head from the damp pillowcase. 'I'm practicing, Momma.'

'You only had your stitches out yesterday.'

Katie stopped the record. 'Berlinghieri said I could do some exercises at the barre.'

'You'll tear your poor knee up.'

'He said I could. Cross my heart and hope to die.'

'Then take it easy. I'm off to the Beauty College for a permanent. The cake on the table is defrosting for bridge tonight.'

The front door slammed. Katie pulled off her plastic sweat pants. Since the bandages had been removed, she had avoided looking at her leg. She was upset to see two fiery, smiling scars visible through her tights. Even more shocking was the weight she'd put on. She limped to the bathroom and stood on the scales. A hundred and twenty-eight pounds. Eleven more than when she'd been admitted to Hotel Dieu. She hobbled to the kitchen on her crutches and returned holding a plastic bag. Inside was a cardboard box and a carving knife. She opened the lid and tried to push the blade through the wavy surface of the icing, but the cake was rock hard. She waved her hair dryer over the top until it had defrosted enough to saw a slice. Chocolate icing lipsticked her mouth as she rolled the cake around until it was soft enough to chew. Her teeth were aching by the time she was able to swallow. As soon as she finished, she reached for the knife to hack off another slice. This will be my final treat, she thought. To cheer myself up. At midnight I'll go on a strict diet.

To punish herself for gaining so much weight she forced herself to listen to the whole of *Petrouchka*. By the time the ballet was over, an empty Sara Lee carton sat on the vanity. She flattened the cardboard and lifted her mattress to hide the box. The packaging joined wrappers from a box of Moon Pies and a half-pound bag of M&Ms. She couldn't throw them in the trash; her mother would be sure to find them. All she had to do was crutch it to the Pic Quik store on the corner for a cake to replace the one she'd eaten and her mother would never know the difference.

Cantina El Cairo

Katie was peeking out the Hieberts' living-room window as the convertible pulled up. Joe was driving the Christmas present his father had given him for getting into med school, a red Jaguar with tinted glass and black vinyl top. Before Joe had time to honk, she was heading out the front door on her sticks.

Every day since the winter semester began, Joe had been saying, 'We should go to Juarez. We can hit the marketplace first, then go to a floor show for a few laughs. A couple of cocktails will make you forget your knee for a night.'

If she'd been dancing, she would never have been tempted to accept Joe's offer, but the Hieberts' house felt so empty now when she came home from school. Rosalia played at the studio every night until seven and Jack came back from the bank even later. Going to a cantina had to be better than mooning around the house by herself because she didn't have class or rehearsals to go to anymore.

She limped down the sidewalk in her new midi coat, relieved to see someone in the passenger seat. She'd told Joe she'd go to Mexico on one condition: that he took someone along as chaperone. She opened the door, expecting to see Joe's steady, but it was Coronado High's star quarterback. 'Karolak,' she said. 'What do you think you're up to?'

'What do you mean?'

She waved her crutch at him to get out of the car. 'I want a word with you in private.'

Joe followed her to the side of the house.

'If you think I'm going to Juarez with you and Brad Boonstra, you're nuts.'

'You wanted an escort.'

'I thought you'd bring Barbie Lundgren.'

'And make her jealous?' Joe got down on one knee and put a hand over his heart. '"A thousand times the worse, to want thy light."'

'Get up.' She was flattered he'd memorized some *Romeo and Juliet*, even though it was probably meant for Barbie.

'You don't have to worry about anything,' he said. 'Brad's a perfect gentleman.'

'I've heard what he's like on the football field.'

'I told him you were a real ballerina. He wanted to meet you. He's a jock, but he told me ballet makes him cry sometimes.' Joe walked back to the car and started to take down the top. 'Climb in, babe. You won't forget it.'

Joe locked his elbows as he pushed away from the wheel. 'Ready to hit J-Town, Rivers?'

She was sitting sideways in the back seat of his sports car because she still couldn't bend her knee enough to put her feet on the floor. Her hands were stiff with cold, her leg was aching and her teeth were clicking like castanets because Joe had insisted they drive to Juarez with the top down, even though it was January.

They were on the bridge now, fifteen minutes from the border. For the last half hour, they'd been inching their way toward Mexico, surrounded by laborers and maids who worked in El Paso during the day and returned home at night.

Joe swept his hand across six lanes of gridlock. 'Look at all these taco wagons. They're putting out more pollution than the copper plant.'

'They're poor, Joe,' she said. 'They can't afford a new car every year like your dad.'

'Okay.' Joe raised his hands. 'Cheap shot.'

She looked at the stalled traffic. 'Exactly where is this cantina we're going to?'

'In the Old Town. It has Ladies' Night on Fridays.'

The Jaguar finally reached the checkpoint. The Mexican immigration officer lowered his gaze to read Joe's plates, then waved them into Juarez with a sweep of his hand.

The highway narrowed into dusty boulevards with giant billboards for Mexican garages and dentists, the Pronaf Center, the Plaza de Toros Bullring. Women with Aztec faces stood on street corners holding armfuls of lilies for sale.

A crumpled car with tail fins pulled up beside them at the first set of traffic lights. The driver, hair greased into a ponytail, rolled down his window. '*Yanqui* want to race?'

Joe stared straight ahead as the driver revved his engine.
'Gringo not *hombre* enough?' The driver made his hand into horns.
'You going for it, Karolak?' Brad asked.
'Not in this.'
The lights flipped to green. The Mexican accelerated and immediately swerved into their lane. Joe jammed on his brakes and Katie fell against the front seat, her knee screaming at the violent stop.
Joe leaned on his horn as the driver sped off. 'You okay back there, Rivers?'
She rubbed her leg. 'Think so.'
'That loony tried to get me to smash into his rust bucket.'
Brad turned around. 'That's how you know you're south of the border, Katie. Why everyone in J-Town has a magnetic Jesus on the dash.'

She headed through the narrow aisles of the *mercado* on her crutches, wanting to see everything. Pyramids of tropical fruit. Stacks of vanilla pods and roasted corn. A wooden cart that sold nothing but tiny metal arms, legs, eyes, hearts. Mangy dogs sniffing the ankles of a woman cooking a pig's head in a tray of popping fat.

Near a watermelon stall was an organ grinder with a monkey dressed in a doll-sized *charro* suit. The animal chattered, pulled off his little sombrero and put it on again. She thought it was so cute she threw the monkey a dollar.

Next to the organ grinder was a man in *huarches* who was selling cockatoos, a dozen of them in a filthy cage meant for a pair. While the vendor looked away, Katie wanted to open the wire door, but she was afraid she'd be thrown into a Mexican jail. She only had ten dollars, not enough for a fine or a bribe.

Sad she couldn't free the birds, she struggled to catch up with Joe and Brad, who were at a stall that sold paintings on black velvet: Jesus in acid purple, Marilyn Monroe in lurid green. There was even a psychedelic copy of da Vinci's *The Last Supper*. She pointed at a painting of the former First Lady. 'You can't pass up Jackie O's portrait on velvet,' she teased Joe. 'That's going to be a collector's item one day.'

The large sign said CANTINA EL CAIRO. A neon camel flashed, galloping through dunes of yellow sand. An arrow pointed upstairs.

AMERICAN COCKTAILS • EXOTIC FLOOR SHOW • $ $ $ WELCOME.
She nervously fingered her new shawl covered with embroidered birds. Joe had bought the *rebozo* for her at the market because she'd told him she felt cold. She watched him disappear into the dark of the stairwell, hoping he didn't expect anything in return. She lagged behind on her crutches, inching her way up, holding her breath because the place smelled like a public toilet.

At the top of the staircase there was an open doorway covered with a beaded curtain. She pushed her way through. In the dim light of the cantina it took her a few seconds to find Joe and Brad in a booth in a corner, a palm tree buzzing above their heads. As she limped through a crowd of men, it dawned on her that she was the only female, except for three heavily-made-up waitresses in pageboy wigs.

She sat down and Joe shoved a grubby cardboard list into her hand. 'Bradski and I already ordered. Ladies get two for the price of one.'

In addition to spirits and beer, there were cocktails with names she'd never heard of: Tequila Sunrise, Blue Lagoon, Slow Comfortable Screw Against the Wall with a Kiss. At her parents' house, there'd never been anything stronger than blackberry wine. She tugged Joe's jacket. 'What have you ordered?'

'Mescal.'

'What's that?'

'Tequila with a worm at the bottom of the bottle.'

She made a sour face. 'Yuck. What makes you want to drink bug juice, Karolak?'

'Because it's like rocket fuel.'

Brad cupped the bowl of his glass. 'Make that paint stripper.'

'I want something sweet,' she said.

Brad said, 'Can't beat a Grasshopper for a lady's drink.'

She shook her head. 'Nothing remotely connected with bugs.'

Joe glanced down the menu. 'Here's something you might dig. A White Russian. A few of those and you'll be dancing on the table.'

She said, 'Give me another month, Karolak, and I will.'

A waitress came to their booth in a cheesecloth dress and open-toed sandals. With her tea-colored skin and kohl-rimmed eyes, she looked like an extra in *The Ten Commandants*.

Joe said, 'The lady here wants a White Russian, a brandy for my buddy and another mescal for me.' He threw back his drink and headed toward a saloon-style door with *HOMBRES* painted on it.

Brad said, 'I saw that Russian defector on the *Bell Telephone Hour.* He was like a spaceman the way he could jump.'

'I saw him dance in Houston two years ago,' Katie said. 'He's like a god who came down to earth.'

As she was talking, a half-dozen drunk lettermen crashed through the beaded curtain. They were from Irvin High School because their V-necked sweaters were stitched with rockets.

Brad said, 'Those guys are already hammered.'

The lettermen bunched in front of the stage, whistling for the floor show to start. 'We want *chichis,*' they started shouting. 'We want *chichis.*'

'Is that a cocktail?' Katie asked.

Brad took a sip of brandy. 'What exactly did Joe tell you about this place?'

'That we were going to a floor show for a few laughs.'

Another waitress in a wig walked across the stage and one of the lettermen grabbed her rear as she went past.

Brad ran his finger around the top of his glass. 'Guys like that give gringos a bad name.'

She thought he might be blushing, but with that neon palm tree winking off and on she couldn't be sure.

The waitress came back to their table with their drinks. Katie opened her wallet to pay as Joe slid into their booth. 'Tonight's on me,' he said, waving a fifty-dollar bill. Counting the notes the waitress handed back, he tucked five dollars into the waistband of her miniskirt.

Katie stared at her two drinks on the table and nervously took a sip. She could feel Joe's thigh pressing against hers so she moved her leg away. She didn't like what the mescal was doing to him, but she was surprised how innocent her White Russian tasted. It was almost like drinking milk.

A man in a Mexican wedding shirt walked onto the platform that served as a stage. He bent toward the microphone. *'Bienvenidos, amigos.* I happy to welcome you to our floor show tonight at Cantina El Cairo. Beginning our performance is the beautiful Señorita Josephina, the Tamer of the Bulls.'

The house lights dimmed as he stepped up to a turntable. To a fanfare of Mexican trumpets, a woman appeared on stage in a red flamenco skirt, yellow blouse and sequined bolero. Lit by a single spotlight, she slithered across the platform, a plastic rose clenched between her teeth. She cupped her cantaloupe-sized breasts and a roar went up from the lettermen.

A student shouted, 'Take it off! We gotta have the car back before midnight.'

With a bump and a grind, the rose was the first thing to go.

'*Anda, anda!*' shouted an old man until the stripper stood on the platform wearing nothing but a pair of stilettos and a G-string. She sucked her index finger, then jiggled it between her legs.

Katie glanced from the stripper's hand to Joe's face. She wanted to leave, but she was hemmed in. She kept drinking, trying to blot out what was happening. She glanced at Brad and was relieved to see that he looked as uncomfortable as she felt. She tried to keep her eyes down, hoping that Joe would realize how repulsed she was, but she couldn't help staring, upset to discover that it excited her too.

The stripper's squirming was interrupted by a man dressed in a bull costume. He charged in and pawed the floor, talcum powder snorting from his papier-mâché head. The stripper picked up her skirt and began to use it as a matador's cape, her breasts swinging as she performed a series of passes close to their booth.

Josephina swirled the skirt a few more times before picking up a sword at the back of the stage. She lunged at the snorting bull with the rubber blade. The sword hit its mark and the bull fell to its knees, its glass eyes flashing red. Josephina did a stiff *grand battement* over the animal before bouncing offstage as the lettermen whistled and stamped their feet.

Katie tipped up what was left of her second drink, her feelings a mixture of excitement and shame. 'I need another milkshake,' she said.

Joe yelled at a waitress, 'Another White Russian over here.'

One of the lettermen shouted, 'Hurry up with the circus act.'

Katie saw a fat woman with no pubic hair lower herself onto a trapeze. Mariachi music played as the naked woman swung over them, smiling and kicking her feet.

Who the hell did Joe think she was to bring her here? She wanted to go home but, when she tried to stand, she fell back into the booth. She turned to Joe. 'Room's spinning.'

'No,' he said, smiling. 'You are.'

The way Karolak was staring at her made her feel like she wanted to take a bath. She looked down, trying to focus on the table, but it was fuzzy. 'I don't feel well,' she said.

'I'll order you a coffee.'

'Wanna go home.'

'The floor show's just getting started, Rivers.' She wrapped the bird-covered shawl around her. 'Don't want to see any more.'

'You're a dancer. You see naked women all the time.'

Brad leaned across her, jiggled his upturned hand. 'Give me the keys, Karolak. I'll take her to the car. She looks like she needs some air.'

She punched at her coat, unable to find the sleeves. Brad helped her stand. He held her coat up, guiding her arms in. She felt his hand around her shoulder and, for a moment, she confused him with her father in Hotel Dieu, helping her learn to walk again.

She felt herself weaving on her crutches, dizzy at the sight of the stairs. 'Hold me,' she said.

Brad hooked her crutches over his arm, then swung her up. He carried her down two flights. At the bottom, he handed her the crutches and aimed her in the direction of the car while he ran ahead to unlock it.

'You okay?' he asked once she was inside. His brandy breath was close to her face.

She nodded, leaning forward to see what was causing the ache in her calf. She was sitting in the back, but she couldn't remember getting in. 'Frame's sticking me.'

He lifted the velvet painting, sliding it between the bucket seats.

'I can see why Joe's always talking about you,' Brad said. 'You hold yourself like a ballerina, even on crutches.'

Air, she thought. Need air. She knew if she could put her head out the window she wouldn't throw up.

'I'm sorry about that dive,' he said. 'I told Joe to tell you there were going to be strippers. He said it was a surprise. To take your mind off your leg.'

She reached to roll down the window, but couldn't find the handle. Before she knew it, Brad and Jackie Onassis were splattered with White Russians.

120

Class of 1970

The night before Katie's graduation, Lola sat at the table, her daughter's high-school yearbook and her own lying side by side. Katie's *Hoofbeats* had cost as much as a gold filling and, as far as Lola was concerned, it was worth every penny. Embossed purple stallion on the cover, hundreds of shiny pages, beautiful leather spine. Lola had no idea why Katie had told her not to buy it, why she didn't want to be reminded of her two-and-a-half years at Coronado High.

No one had been generous enough to purchase Lola's copy of the *Log Cabin;* she'd had to buy it herself. Depression dollars were hard to come by and when she'd asked her father for the money he'd said, 'You can't eat an ol' book, Lola Mae. Five dollars will buy seed corn for the back lot.' She'd purchased her yearbook secretly with money she'd earned picking cotton.

The night before she graduated, her mother found it under Lola's bed. Her parents were so angry they refused to come to her graduation. Lola decided that she wasn't going to let their absence sabotage the biggest night of her life. She would be the first Baker in her family to get a high-school diploma. She told herself that her parents had only had four years in a one-room schoolhouse and didn't know any better, but she wasn't going to let them ruin her night of glory.

Lola remembered everything about the night she graduated: ironing her suit on the parlor floor, curling her Indian-straight hair twice. She felt like Joan Crawford in the ensemble her Aunt Lucille had loaned her: the navy-blue shoes and matching patent-leather purse, the rope of seed pearls, the double-breasted paramatta suit with gold buttons. Everything she was wearing had been bought in a Memphis department store, not ordered from Sears and Roebuck.

She walked three miles into town for her commencement and when she got there, she carefully cleaned the dust off her open-toed shoes. For one exhilarating night, Lola Baker had been a scholar, her cap and gown making her more than a poor farmer's daughter. She made a vow to herself that she wasn't going to be like her parents, so beaten down they'd given up hoping for a better life.

Lola let the pages of the *Log Cabin* fly through her fingers, treasuring even the ads: FELTS DRUG COMPANY, PRESCRIPTIONS CAREFULLY COMPOUNDED. JITNEY JUNGLE • QUALITY GROCERIES OUR SPECIALTY. She felt cheated her education had had to end after twelfth grade, but she was proud to have put her husband through college. As a dentist's wife, she would never have to worry about losing everything because of freak storms or a plague of boll weevils.

Thirty years on, Lola still loved to look at photographs of her classmates with their fresh young faces and hair that didn't need a bottle: Anzonetta Bradley, Bubba Dotherow, Vista Smartt. It reminded her of how she'd felt to be eighteen years old and on the threshold of life.

Katie sat on the front row of the bleachers, grateful the ankle-length purple gown disguised how big she really was. She was desperate to leave Coronado High, but the last thing she wanted was to have to parade in front of two thousand people. Since her operation, her scars had healed, but she had ballooned to seventy pounds over her dancing weight.

Every morning she went to school wearing the same few outfits because her size 8 clothes wouldn't fit. She had two pairs of stretch pants she could still squeeze into, but she was always repairing them because the seams split. The only other clothes she could still wear was a tent dress that cut into her armpits and a empire dress covered with cherries.

If her wardrobe wasn't humiliating enough, yesterday the city bus drivers had gone on strike and she'd had to walk two miles to school. Now she had blisters the size of silver dollars at the top of both thighs. She dreaded collecting her diploma: a stadium full of people watching her waddle across the football field like a goose to avoid her suppurating sores.

Lola squinted across the grass and tipped up the frames of her glasses. She couldn't see well so she'd made sure she and Haywood had left Fortuna in plenty of time to get front-row seats. She didn't want to sit any further away than she had to. Not on a night like tonight. She hadn't even seen Katie in her cap and gown yet because the Hieberts had driven her to the ceremony.

Her husband sat beside her, scowling as he leafed through Katie's annual. She wondered what he'd found to be upset about. She couldn't worry about his mood now. She was too interested in watching the class of seniors milling around the bleachers on the other side of the stadium. To her nearsighted eyes, they looked like a huge flock of crows that were getting ready to land.

Katie was standing on the grass, legs apart beneath the pleats of her graduation gown. She was looking for Joe when she saw her mother marching across the field in a purple dress that matched her robe. Katie's heart fell; if that wasn't trouble enough, there was a Polaroid camera strapped around her neck. Katie tipped her mortarboard down to hide her chipmunk cheeks.

'Sugar, let's go to the front of the school.'

'What for?'

'So I can take a photo of you next to the Coronado sign.'

Katie kicked the grass. 'No pictures, *madre*.'

'In a few years you'll want a memento of tonight.'

'No memento. I hated high school. All I've wanted the last two years is to get out.'

Her mother aimed the camera. 'Then I'll take a picture of you here.' Katie jerked her hat off and held it in front of her face. 'No pictures!'

'Stop making such a fuss. That tent helps hide how big you are.'

Not believing how cruel her mother had been, Katie looked over the mortarboard. Her shock was met with a flash of light. Covering her face, she ducked through the crowd. She forgot the pain of her weeping sores and just ran.

Lola started to walk back across the football field. She felt bad she'd upset Katie. She hadn't meant to say what she'd said, but the truth was the truth. Since her daughter's operation, whole boxes of cake mix would disappear, entire loaves of Rainbow Bread, but whenever Lola brought up the subject of weight, Katie would blame it on her metabolism rather than on her mouth.

Last weekend, Lola had found a notebook in Katie's room. Glued inside were ads of women who'd lost weight by eating diet candy to reduce their appetites. The pictures showed the same people twice: enormous women in muumuus next to themselves, a hundred pounds lighter, in low-cut dresses or skimpy swimsuits. Lola had wanted to wave the scrapbook under her daughter's nose and say, All you have to do is to exercise some self-control. I could be twice the size if I didn't make myself leave the table hungry each night.

She felt bad she'd upset her daughter, but Katie was going to have to face the music. She'd have to find another career now that her knee was wrecked. There were plenty of things she could do with her life. Not being able to prance around on tiptoe was no reason to look like a sow being fattened for slaughter.

Haywood peered across the field, trying to see if Katie had come out from under the bleachers. For her to run away like that, Lola must have made a crack about her weight. His wife had never been able to keep what she was thinking quiet. She was reckless in that department. She had a reckless mouth.

He was looking at his daughter's thin, beautiful face in the annual and picturing the full moon it was now. Under her senior picture some jerk had written,

Doughnuts are round
Pancakes are flat
As a sophomore, you were skinny,
As a senior, you're fat.

If he had known which bastard had done that, he'd punch the son of a bitch in the mouth.

His wife sat down on the bleachers as a man was testing a microphone on the podium. A huge fork of lightning illuminated the sky. Haywood counted the seconds until the clap of thunder. One thousand and one. A mile away.

There was another flash, an almost simultaneous crack of thunder. He glanced at the invitation printed on cardboard. *In the event of rain, graduation ceremonies will be held in the gym.* Nudging his wife's arm he stood up. 'There's going to be a downpour. Let's get a head start so we'll have a good seat.'

As Lola tied on her rain hat, Haywood shot off the bleachers like a ruptured duck. 'Slow down,' she called out. 'I don't have stilts for legs.' She hurried to catch up, remembering the first time they'd walked together. Even then she'd had to run.

It had been on Valentine's Day after the Shoe Box Social. She'd spent half the morning making cookies and the other half decorating the shoe box they would be sold in. Like the other girls in Home Ec, she'd written her name on the outside, wondering who would buy her sugar cookies at auction. The boy who did would get to sit with her, knowing he'd helped raise money to buy new baseball uniforms for the school.

When her box had been held up, Haywood had outbid both Dather Strickland and Theron Rust. He'd paid the huge sum of a dollar and a quarter. That was how Lola first found out he'd had a crush on her.

She'd been thrilled to sit in the cafeteria with one of the handsomest boys in McKenzie High: a six-foot-four basketball player with blue-black hair and Indian-dark eyes. Then, Hay had been shy as a spider. The boys who lived in McKenzie were always ribbing him about his hatchet-shaped nose and the way he smelled by the time he'd ridden five miles into town on a horse. After the Social, he'd left his daddy's horse in town and walked her home, resting her red shoe box against his hip, while she'd clung to his arm.

Lola quickened her pace now, trying to keep up, but Haywood was still half a furrow in front of her. She put a hand on top of her rain hat and ran. When she caught up, panting, she reached for his elbow like she'd done the night of the Social, but he jerked it away. 'What's the matter, Hay?'

'You shouldn't have made Katie upset.'

'All I wanted was a picture in her cap and gown.'

'There's a photograph in the yearbook, Momma.'

'Katie needs a graduation picture for the scrapbook I'm making.'

'She hates Coronado High. She's said a hundred times she was never made to feel welcome.'

'How can she hate the place that's given her an education?'

'You could have given the damn picture a miss.'

'If she's so damn sensitive about her weight, why doesn't she stop eating like a pig?'

Her husband didn't say anything, just gave her a look that made her want to shrivel up. 'Why should I pussyfoot around her feelings, Haywood? Nobody bothers to pussyfoot around mine.'

'Because she's the teenager and you're the adult. You're supposed to have more sense.'

She was smarting as she watched him stride off without her. Another tree of lightning illuminated the night sky, followed by a downpour. Lola suddenly found herself surrounded by stampeding seniors, their mortarboards their umbrellas, as they laughed and slipped, running across the field toward the shelter of the gym.

The speeches seemed to last for hours. The principal finally ended his address and started calling out names for the presentation of diplomas. Lola didn't think he'd ever get to the Rs as the seniors kept parading single file, like ants, across the gym.

Katie's name was finally called. Even from where Lola was sitting, she looked big as a house. Her daughter made her way toward the podium and a piercing whistle echoed around the gymnasium. Bored after all the long-winded speeches, the audience began to laugh. Lola wanted to disappear, both for her fat daughter and for herself.

To Lola's surprise, Katie acted as if nothing had happened. She slowly made her way across the floor. Lola had to admit there was something majestic about the way her daughter floated down the aisle. Maybe the thousands of dollars they'd spent on ballet lessons hadn't been a complete waste of money.

Katie sat watching Barbie Lundgren shower her sorority sisters with confetti. Why would Barbie do that just because she'd been handed a stupid diploma with her name in italics?

As the paper fluttered down, Katie saw her mother rush through it, waving a copy of *Hoofbeats* in one hand and a corsage of carnations in the other.

'Congratulations, sugar, congratulations!'

Her father came toward her, his bottom lip quivering. 'We sure are proud of you, sister.'

She separated her blistered legs. 'There's nothing to be proud of, Daddy.'

'Yes there is,' her mother said, handing the annual to her father. 'An A+ average is nothing to be sniffed at.'

Her mother pinned the corsage to her graduation gown and stood back to admire it before opening her purse to take out a black velvet box. 'It's for you,' she said, biting her lip, her front tooth smeared with strawberry lipstick.

Katie stared at the box. When her mother had asked her what she wanted for graduation, she'd told her a set of matching luggage. To own two Samsonite suitcases was the glimmer of hope she would escape to New York with something better than the embarrassing cardboard luggage her parents had bought during the war. A set of 'please-don't-rain' suitcases that nested inside each other like Russian dolls.

'Aren't you going to open it, sugar?' her mother asked.

Katie flipped open the top. Inside the box was a wristwatch. She lifted it out and read the engraving on the back. *To Our Honor Scholar, Love, Mom & Dad.* Below the engraving were more words. *WAFER-THIN, SHOCK-RESISTANT.* At a hundred and eighty-seven pounds she wasn't either of those things. She stared at the curly inscription. 'Thanks. That's a really fantastic gift.'

While her mother was strapping on the Timex, Katie managed to work her mouth into a smile by thinking about the suitcases she'd buy. She'd get a job long enough to earn thirty dollars and if she couldn't earn the money she needed, she'd leave with her clothes in a paper sack. She handed the rolled-up diploma to her father. 'Hold this for me, Daddy. I have to turn in my cap and gown.'

'Wait,' her mother said as Katie started to unbutton her robe. 'Don't give away your beautiful corsage. I'm going to press it in your graduation scrapbook.'

After she'd returned the carnation to its plastic box, Lola became aware of the largest woman she'd ever seen waddling in their direction. Her flowered dress was buttoned down the front with safety pins, her grimy brassiere visible between the gaps of straining fabric. She was wearing clown-red lipstick and her hair was dyed the color of psychedelic carrots. She was gasping from the heat.

Lola was shocked to see Katie put her hand on the woman's pillowy arm. Surely she didn't know this creature wearing thongs to graduation, her toes fat sausages, twice normal size.

Katie said, 'I'm so glad you could come tonight, Wilmoth. Meet my parents, Dr and Mrs Rivers.'

'You've certainly got a daughter to be proud of,' the woman said, panting. 'Graduating tenth in a class of over six hundred.'

Lola smiled politely, edging away from the woman's ammonia smell.

'Doctor,' Wilmoth said, 'you must be disappointed your daughter doesn't want to go to college. If she applied herself to mathematics, she'd have a career for life.'

Haywood put his hand on Katie's shoulder. 'I just want her to be happy.'

Lola said, 'We're still trying to persuade her to apply to Oxford.'

The woman took a thick package out of her purse. 'I've got a little something for you.'

Lola watched Katie tear the newspaper away. *The Complete Fairy Tales and Stories of Hans Christian Andersen.*

'Thank you, Wilmoth. Thanks so much!'

It pained Lola to see that Katie was more thrilled with that child's book than she'd been with her own gift of the watch.

The woman said, 'There's a quotation by Godfrey Hardy in the front.'

'"A mathematician, like a painter or poet is a maker of patterns,"' Katie read. '"If his patterns are more permanent than theirs, it is because they are made with ideas." That's beautiful, Wilmoth.'

'I remember you saying that ballet dancers make patterns in space.'

'Every time I look at this book, I'll think of you.'

Katie disappeared into the woman's arms. Their heads were touching; they could barely reach around each other to hug.

'Whatever you do, Katie, I'm sure you'll do great things.'

The woman patted her daughter's back and started to make her way slowly through the crowd. Lola saw people smirk and gawk as they moved aside to let her pass. 'Who in the devil was that?'

Katie said, 'One of the best teachers in this school.'

Lola's favorite teacher had been Miss Fronie Langford who'd given her extra lessons so she wouldn't have to stay back a year when she'd been burned. Miss Fronie had always looked as neat as a pin in her feminine dresses with high-necked collars. 'That woman's in the wrong profession. She should be a fat lady in a circus.'

Haywood snapped, 'Momma, that's enough.'

'It's true,' Lola said.

'She's a graduate of Stanford, *madre*.'

'She stinks to high heaven. They didn't have teachers like that when I went to high school.'

'Hold this.' Katie gave her mother the book of fairy tales and traded it for her yearbook. 'Joe wants to sign my annual when I turn in my cap and gown.' She took off her robe and started to push her way through the crowd.

'I hope to God Katie doesn't end up like that dugong in a dress.'

'Lay off, Momma,' Haywood said. 'I think you've made enough cracks about weight for one night.'

Katie waddled toward the clothes racks, trying to keep her blisters apart. She stopped for a moment to pull down her new dress. It was too short, but at least it was loose and comfortable, with sleeves as wide as angel's wings.

Joe had invited her to his party and she'd made this lace outfit for tonight. The Simplicity pattern required a six-foot circular tablecloth. The only cutting had been the circle for the neck and two triangles she'd had to remove to stitch up the side seams. Her mother had said she couldn't wear it to graduation because it looked like a whore's nightgown. 'This is the latest fashion, Momma,' she'd said, 'and I'm going to wear it whether you like it or not.'

She saw Joe in the crowd and held up her yearbook so she could stay where she was.

'Congratulations, Rivers,' he shouted.

'Congratulations yourself.'

He moved to hug her and she stiffened. She hated to be touched now that she was fat.

'It's been a great night,' he said, 'except for getting soaked.'

'Who cares about a little rain?' she said. 'We're out of school.'

He took her copy of *Hoofbeats*. 'I've got a minimum of six more years.'

'It's what you want,' she said. 'It'll be worth it to become a doctor.'

'Promise you won't read what I write till the party?'

'Cross my heart and hope to die.'

He took a pen out of his pocket and clicked it. 'Turn around.' He propped the annual against her shoulder blade. If she wasn't so fat, she would have enjoyed the feel of the book pressing against her back as his hand moved across the page.

He slammed the yearbook shut and gave it back to her. 'How are you getting to the motel?'

'My parents are dropping me off.'

'They're not going to hang around, are they?'

She shook her head. 'They're heading home after they drop me off. I'm spending the night at Rosalia's.'

'Ramada Inn on Mesa,' he said. 'Suite 301, third floor.'

'I thought you said it was a pool party.'

'Mom booked the room late. People will have to go downstairs if they want to swim. How are you getting back to Rosalia's?'

'Haven't thought about it.'

'I'll give you a lift. We've got to celebrate, Rivers. I might be in Nam this time next year if they end deferments for med students.'

For the first time tonight, she read the banner above the bleachers. *WE MAY NEVER PASS THIS WAY AGAIN.* The gold letters sewn on the purple cloth had been there since the Senior Prom but, until now, she had never stopped to think what they meant.

Her father turned into the packed Ramada parking lot. 'You don't need to take me to the door,' she said. 'I can find the room myself.'

Her mother said, 'Your father will escort you to the party.'

They circled the motel, trying to find a place to park. Even though there was a space beside a Corvette, her father didn't pull in.

'Daddy,' she said, pointing in the direction they'd just come from. 'You could have gone in there.'

'Didn't you see that "Make Love, Not War" sticker? I'm not parking next to a communist.'

'But it's after ten,' she said, glancing at her watch. 'I'll be late.'

'How are you getting back to Rosalia's?' her mother asked.

'Joe said he'd give me a lift.'

Her mother leaned over the seat and tapped the face of her new watch. 'You be back at the Hieberts before midnight.'

She smiled sweetly. 'I will.' She had no intention of being Cinderella tonight. She was going to have some fun for a change.

On the edge of the lot her father found a space next to a pickup. She grabbed her annual and her aunt's fur coat off the back seat.

Her mother made a face as she pulled on the sealskin. 'I thought you said this was a pool party.'

'It is.'

'So why are you wearing your Aunt Delta's coat?'

She saw the huge swamp coolers sitting on the Ramada's roof. 'Because.'

'Because what?' her mother said.

'Because I hate air conditioning.'

The music was so loud that nobody inside heard the bell, even on the third ring. Her father put an ear to the door and grinned. 'Doesn't sound much like Tchaikovsky.'

'It's the Beatles, Daddy.' She pressed the bell again, her stomach doing flip-flops. She was nervous she wouldn't have the courage to make small talk to anyone except Brad and Joe, but at least she had her aunt's full-length fur to hide in. Her mother had flown back from her sister's funeral last month with a suitcase of Delta's clothes, including the glamorous ballerina coat Katie had coveted as a child.

The door finally cracked open. The Senior Prom King stuck his head out. He glanced at Katie and then at her father. Who's the fat girl and the old guy? was written all over his face.

Katie defiantly lifted her chin. 'I'm a good friend of Karolak's.'

'Suit yourself,' he said, opening the door.

Katie watched her father shift his gaze from a girl in a bikini to the king-sized bed, then to a keg of beer on the dresser. Her father didn't look too happy, but he slipped her ten dollars.

'Here's money for a taxi, honey. In case your friend's too tight to drive.'

'Bye, Daddy,' she said. 'Thanks for the ride.'

She kissed him goodbye and pulled the coat around her as she pushed through couples dancing. A half-dozen bottles were sitting in an ice chest. She lifted one to read the label. Veuve Cliquot. She poured the champagne like she'd seen in the movies. She wasn't sure if she liked the taste, but when she rolled the liquid around her tongue, it felt like tiny stars exploding in her mouth.

She didn't have anyone to dance with so she sat on the end of the bed. The emerald color of the champagne bottle reminded her of the tutu she'd worn on Mexican TV. She pictured herself wearing the hand-embroidered costume from *The Sleeping Beauty*. In it she'd felt like a Fabergé egg: glittering, beautiful. She saw herself on the tips of her satin shoes, doing little hops on *pointe* like a fairy skipping across the forest floor.

The Prom King nudged her. 'Got anything on under that coat, fat girl?'

Burning with shame, she pulled her hair around her face. She pressed her yearbook against her stomach so hard that it hurt. She was praying that Joe would come by and rescue her, but he was probably swimming. She sipped her champagne, delaying the moment before she could face reading what he'd written.

She opened the cover to look for his senior picture. Under it was, *With all my love, Joe Karolak '70'.* Tucked in the back cover she noticed a note on blue paper.

Dear Rivers,

Two and a half years have come and gone so quickly it makes me sad when I think about it. Ever since we've known each other, I've felt very strongly about you even though we've never really dated. I wish we could have had the time to be closer (you know what I mean). Maybe in another time or place we could have had a chance, but ballet is your one love and girls are mine. I hope in the future you'll see the light. My graduation party will be the topper. It will be the first and only night we can spend together.

PS: When I qualify as a doctor, I'll buy you a solid-gold leotard.

She was numbly reading the note again when she heard someone shout over the music, 'Anyone here called Rivers?'

Her heart started to pound. Joe was the only one who called her that. 'Someone called Rivers is to come to the door.'

She threw back the rest of her champagne and pushed her way through teenagers dancing the Funky Chicken. When she got to the entrance, it was her mother, clutching a handbag against her stomach.

'You're coming home now, young lady. Your father didn't have the gumption to come back for you, but I sure do.'

She heard what her mother was saying, but she was more aware of screaming from the pool below and Ringo Starr singing, 'We All Live In a Yellow Submarine'.

'You're leaving right now, Katie Scarlett. You do not belong in a den of hippies and drunks.'

She closed the door on her mother and turned to go back to the party. She was halfway across the room when someone grabbed her coat from behind.

'You'll come with me right now, young lady, or I'll scream bloody murder.'

Katie wasn't going to give in until she saw her mother's fillings. One thing she knew; Lola wasn't one to bluff. Katie frantically looked around the suite, desperate to find Joe, but she couldn't see him anywhere. She didn't want to disappear without saying goodbye, but her mother hadn't given her any choice.

Katie followed her down the concrete walkway to the stairs, hating everything about her mother from her wing-tipped bifocals to the lace on her slip that hung past the hem of her skirt. She hated her strawberry lipstick and stupid purple dress and the cut-glass rhinestone brooch in the shape of a bug. She hated her for dragging her away from the party and, most of all, she hated her for not letting her say goodbye to Joe whom she might never see again.

She leaned against the railing, waiting until her mother reached the ground three floors below. Katie pictured herself jumping over the balcony, flying through the air, her lace dress fluttering. When she landed, it would look like her mother had been crushed by a fat, giant moth.

FORTUNA, 1971

The body never lies.

MARTHA GRAHAM

Slenderella

Lola stood up to clear away the dinner dishes. She lifted her daughter's untouched plate as Katie scraped frozen Slenderella from a can. Scratch, scratch, scratch. The noise made Lola want to scream. 'Why are you eating that junk when you didn't touch your dinner?'
Katie kept digging at the crystals with a spoon.
'If you ate what I cooked instead of that durn diet drink, you'd have managed to lose some weight by now.'
Scratch, scratch, scratch.
'Answer me if you know what's good for you.'
'Slenderella is a balanced diet, *madre*.'
'It's chocolate-flavored water. It costs an arm and a leg and you're still the size of a house.'
Katie muttered something that Lola didn't catch. From the hornet-stung look on her daughter's face, Lola knew it wasn't nice. 'What did you say, young lady?'
'Nothing.'
'You should eat real food, not frozen cow plop.'
Katie slammed her spoon on the table. 'Fried chicken and mashed potatoes and gravy aren't two-hundred-and-fifty calories a serving.'
'You fainted in the shower because that icy crap is the only thing you eat.'
'You should congratulate me for trying to lose weight, *madre*, instead of saying I look like a baby manatee.'
Lola turned toward the sink. Seeing her daughter's naked body this morning had upset her. Lola had found her, unconscious, on the floor of the shower because Katie hadn't eaten anything but Slenderella for three days. 'If you weren't so lazy, you'd help me clear these dishes without being asked.'
'Can't you leave me alone for five seconds?'
'Then do something useful. Get off your fanny and help.'
'Daddy never does any housework.'
'He's a man.'

'Ever hear of women's lib?'

Lola threw a pile of chicken bones into the garbage. 'Daddy puts our food on the table. He's exempt.'

'Rhett doesn't.'

'Your brother disappears when there's work to do.'

'Bingo.'

Lola pointed at her daughter's sequoia-sized thighs, twice the diameter they'd been last year. 'It won't hurt you to do more housework, Slenderella. With those hams, you need the exercise.'

Katie screamed, 'You have to walk thirty-two miles to lose a pound. How many trips to the sink is that?'

Lola drained oil from the frying pan. In the mirror she saw her daughter cut a sliver of pecan pie and cram it in her mouth. 'I don't know why you ate such a tiny slice. You'll only sneak in here when Daddy and I are asleep to finish it off.'

'Does it make you feel good hounding me twenty-four hours a day?'

'I am not hounding you. These crackpot diets will ruin your health.'

Katie shuffled over to the sink and held out an elbow. 'Do you think this is eczema?'

'Don't ask me. Ask that skin doctor. We're paying him enough.'

'One of Daddy's medical books said eczema can break out before a schizophrenic attack.'

Lola looked at the reddened patch of skin. 'What you need is a job to occupy your mind. All you do is watch soap operas all day long.'

'I can't leave the house, Momma. I'm going bald.'

Lola jammed her hands on her hips. 'What on earth are you talking about now?'

Katie lifted her hair and pointed at a patch of bare skin.

Lola leaned against the counter to steady herself. It reminded her of her mother's scalp before they'd taken her away. 'You're not going bald,' she said firmly. 'A well-balanced diet would cure everything.'

'Not my knee,' Katie said.

Lola put the plug in the sink and turned on the hot water. 'Start going to church,' she said. 'You haven't been since Easter.'

'Like God's going to do something.'

Lola picked up the potato masher and savagely started to scrub it. 'You need someone bigger than you are to turn your problems over to.

Daddy and I aren't always going to be around to pick up the pieces.'

In the past six months they'd paid a dermatologist a fortune to treat Katie for acne, styes, boils, seborrhea and hives. Last week she'd taken Katie to see Dr Seaver for the second time in as many days and he'd called Lola into his office to speak to her privately. 'The skin is connected to a patient's state of mind. In my opinion, your daughter is having a nervous breakdown. I'd advise you to take her to a psychiatrist as soon as possible. Katie's psychological problems need to be addressed, more than her dermatological symptoms.'

Lola had wanted to shout at him, What do you know about breakdowns? You didn't specialize in brains at medical school!

She hadn't told her husband what the doctor had said. When they came back from Seaver's office, she'd found Haywood crying because he'd found dozens of candy wrappers stuffed down the side of his Barcalounger.

'Katie's falling apart in front of our eyes, Momma. I don't know what we can do to help her.'

'All she needs to do, Haywood, is pull herself together and stop feeling sorry for herself.'

Lola slung the dishcloth across a plate, remembering what her husband had said. 'Someone who's cracking up can't pull themselves together. They need professional help.'

What she'd wanted to tell him then, but wouldn't, was that Katie wasn't laudanum-crazed like her grandmother, speaking in tongues and answering the door to the preacher with nothing but a poke bonnet on. Lola had never breathed a word to anyone about Nanatasis' stay in an asylum, least of all Haywood. She had never believed her mother was crazy. Nanatasis had tricked everyone into thinking that so she could have a rest from washing and ironing and cooking and chopping wood. But her plan had backfired because after she'd been in a loony bin for six months, not only had she been called a dirty Indian; she was a dirty, mad Indian as far as the community of Macedonia was concerned.

Since her mother had been dragged away in a straitjacket, Lola had believed that people had no right to break down. She'd made a promise to herself that she would never shame her family the way her own mother had done. Each time something terrible had happened, she'd kept her mind and hands busy. She didn't have the time or opportunity to fall apart.

Katie's chair whined across the linoleum.

Lola turned around. 'What are you going to do now?'

'Watch television.'

'I want you in bed after Johnny Carson. Not sneaking around stuffing your face.'

Katie stormed out of the room and Lola reached into the cupboard for the chocolate icing; it wasn't on the shelf where she kept it. 'Katie,' she yelled over the TV, 'have you seen a box of Betty Crocker icing?'

'No!'

'I bought a box today. I have to make fudge for the Potluck Dinner at church.'

'Don't know anything about it, *madre*.'

Lola opened the dishwasher. Under a saucepan was a mixing bowl with flecks of brown icing. 'Katie Scarlett, get in this kitchen right now!'

When her daughter appeared in the doorway, Lola slammed the bowl on the table. 'Who do you think ate the icing that was in here? Rhett? Your father? Or maybe Burrito taught herself to stand on her back legs and use a spoon.'

'I don't know what you're talking about.'

She grabbed her daughter's hand and dragged her in front of the mirror. Katie tried to pull away, but Lola pressed her palms on either side of her head. 'Look at yourself. Just look at yourself. I don't know of anyone on earth who could eat a whole box of icing except a billy goat.'

'Let go of me!'

'I've had it with your sneaking and lying. Open your eyes and look at the glutton you've become!'

'Let go!'

'Just because you'll never be a ballerina doesn't mean you can't do something else.'

'Leave me alone, you stupid bitch!'

'Don't you speak to me like that. And quit that bawling or I'll give you something to bawl about!'

Her daughter kept screaming. Lola pulled her hand back and put her shoulder into it. The flat of her palm against Katie's face sounded like a belly flop from the high dive.

There was silence for a moment, then her daughter started howling again. Lola stared at the red handprint she'd made. Someone had to knock some sense into her. This damn self-pity had to stop.

Seventy-two snails in three minutes

At night she was a traveler: Vienna sausages, Peking duck, Boston baked beans. She ate her way across whole continents without ever leaving her chair. She picked in public and pigged in private, stashed candy bars in the toes of shoes too tight to wear.

She had two dresses: the tablecloth outfit she'd created for graduation and a muumuu she'd made to have something to wear besides pajamas. Since Katie had moved back to Fortuna, her mother had been nagging her to buy new clothes, but purchasing a size 18 wardrobe meant she accepted being fat, that she would never lose enough weight to be able to dance again.

Under her mattress were ten graphs she'd made, one for each month she'd been home. Horizontal lines plotted the days of the month and the vertical ones recorded her weight. Instead of a gentle downward slope to her goal of a hundred and seventeen pounds, the graphs looked like an erratic heartbeat, her weight going up and down as she binged and starved.

She had tried fruit diets, vegetable diets, high-protein diets, even a diabetic diet she'd picked up in her doctor's waiting room, but she always ended up overeating whenever she got upset.

Her peak weight, a hundred and ninety-four, was recorded a month ago when she'd joined Weight Watchers. At the first meeting she'd felt exhilarated. The group leader was a thin, attractive woman. Sharnee had walked behind a screen and brought out a life-size cardboard cutout of an enormous woman in a baglike dress. 'Ladies, five years ago this was me. I was fat my whole life until I joined Weight Watchers. I've turned my life around and I'm here to help you do the same.'

Katie left the church hall with hope, a handbook, menus and a scale for weighing what she ate. After the starvation diets she'd been on the last year, the variety of foods thrilled her. She could treat herself to a pat of butter or two ounces of ice cream. As long as she didn't veer off the type or amount of food permitted, everything was fine. But if she so much as ate a crumb of cake, she'd feel guilty and weak and end up eating the whole thing. At her first weigh-in a week later, she'd put on nine pounds. She stopped going to meetings after that. Now she refused to weigh herself, afraid the scales would top two hundred pounds.

The last few days she'd managed to limit herself to nine cans of Slenderella, but after the humiliation of having been slapped by her mother, all she wanted to do was comfort eat. She looked at her watch. Almost midnight. Her mother had been in bed an hour and Katie was waiting until she was sure she was asleep. The refrigerator was padlocked which meant Katie had to raid something else.

Only a small bathroom separated the chest freezer from her mother's bedroom. Katie opened the lid, praying the hinges wouldn't squeak. Her mother had stopped buying Fudgsicles, ice cream sandwiches and Eskimo Pies months ago, but what she didn't realize was that Katie was slowly eating her way through whatever she could find in the deep freeze.

She held four pieces of bread in front of the foot heater like a giant hand of cards. After eating half a loaf of Rainbow Bread, her mouth felt like Alaska. She had to heat the slices for ten minutes before they could be chewed. She pressed them to see if they'd defrosted enough, then stacked the slices on a plate.

She held a piece of bread over the evening paper to smother a slice with honey. Her mother was always looking for evidence she'd stolen food so she had to be careful about crumbs. As she chewed the sweet, icy dough, her eye caught a news item.

> **Associated Press, Mar 15. Nancy, France.** Marc Quinquadon, the world snail-eating champion, died of indigestion in hospital yesterday after eating 72 snails in 3 minutes.

There are a lot of ways to kill yourself, she thought, but that's another class of death altogether. Anyone can put their head in a gas oven or drop a hair dryer in the bath, but the absurdity of snails was brilliant.

The night she'd driven back from her second Weight Watchers' meeting her parents were at bridge. After the disastrous weigh-in, she decided that if she'd never be a hundred and seventeen pounds again, she'd rather be dead. At the rate she was going, she'd end up like

Wilmoth anyhow. The trouble was there were no buildings in Fortuna high enough to jump out of and she was too strong a swimmer to drown. She didn't like guns. Men were the only ones selfish enough to blow their brains out and leave other people to clean up the mess.

Katie went into her mother's bedroom to find her sleeping pills. In a book about suicide she'd read about a girl who'd swallowed several knives and spoons, nails, window-bolts, a brass cross and a hundred and one pins and still hadn't managed to kill herself.

She counted out twenty-five and swallowed them. Waiting for the Nembutal to knock her out, she pictured herself on the floor, cold and dead, and realized how awful it would be for her parents to come home from bridge and find her body.

That night she had forced her fingers down her throat, promising herself the next time she'd do it right. The next time had to be foolproof and, more importantly, something that looked like an accident. People talked in a small town like Fortuna. She wanted to spare her family the shame of a suicide.

She called all the supermarkets in town, looking for snails: Safeway, Furr's, Piggly Wiggly. No luck, not even with the new delicatessen, Goldfarb's, that had just had its grand opening. No one in Fortuna had a single snail, alive or dead. She went to her bedroom and stuffed herself with coffee cake with freezer burn.

She was trying to figure out what she could eat to kill herself when she had a brilliant idea. How many times had she choked on peanut butter? Not only was it a cheap way to kill herself, it was ironic. Flying into Never-Never Land with a stomach full of Peter Pan Peanut Butter. There was only one catch; she was afraid she'd change her mind and chicken out like she'd done with the sleeping pills.

That left the car. She knew how proud her father was of his new Oldsmobile, but the pickup was a stick shift and she'd only driven automatics. She'd never be able to get that old Ford truck into fifth gear.

Going for a drive, she scrawled on the note she left on the kitchen table. Short and sweet. No goodbye. She didn't want anything to be read into it later.

Lights were coming on in the valley, the sun a fat orange on the horizon. By the time she was out of the city limits, it would almost be dark. It would be easier then; it would be more like going to sleep.

Ahead of her was a green reflector sign: *ANTHONY EXIT 1/2 MILE*. There was an overpass there, the only one between Fortuna and El Paso. The highway was practically deserted. No witnesses. All she had to do was steer toward the concrete buttress and close her eyes.

She neared the exit and pressed the accelerator, felt the power as the car picked up speed, automatically changed gear. Eighty miles an hour, eighty-five, ninety. She felt calm, almost happy. She wouldn't have to worry about her fat body or wrecked knee anymore.

The car left the asphalt, wheels juddering on the soft shoulder. Gravel pinged the hubcaps, seemed to talk. *Don't . . . don't . . . don't.* Then she saw her father's face before her, wet with tears. *For God's sake, stop!*

She was about to steer toward the buttress and found herself pressing the brake pedal instead, pumping it so the car wouldn't spin. The Oldsmobile swerved before skidding to a stop on the far side of the overpass. Sobbing, she stared at her face in the mirror. It looked like a huge white plate.

She turned the car around and drove home, more confused than ever. She didn't know if she'd ever be able to lose weight or if her bad knee would allow her to have a professional career. She didn't know if she'd made the right decision to have the operation or if she should have listened to Madame and never let Berlinghieri near her.

Fatso goes nutzoid

Lola glanced nervously around the Psychology lobby. She didn't see anyone who looked like they could be the undergraduate student she'd talked to on the phone. The girls wandering past all looked like hippies with their parrot-colored clothes and long straight hair.
She glanced at her watch. Three to two. Her appointment was in a few minutes. She wondered if she had time to retouch her lipstick before the girl from Massachusetts arrived.
Lola was digging in the bottom of her bag when she heard someone clear their throat.
'Mrs Baker?'
Lola stiffened at the sound of her maiden name. The same East Coast voice she'd spoken to yesterday, polished as cut glass. She turned around, relieved to see at least one student dressed sensibly. In an ice-white pantsuit the girl looked like someone in a summer catalogue, standing on the deck of a yacht. 'You must be Nancy Chichester.'
'Pleased to meet you.' The girl smiled and extended her hand.
Lola took her fingers nervously, barely holding them as she glanced around to see if she saw anyone she recognized. 'Is there somewhere private we can talk?'
'Of course. Would you like to follow me?'
Miss Chichester led the way to an empty classroom.
Lola was glad she wasn't on display like she'd felt in the lobby. In a small town, having a prominent dentist for a husband meant you couldn't miss a bowel movement without people hearing about it. 'Your ad said you needed to interview fat people so you can get your degree.'
The girl's face flushed red above the whiteness of her suit. 'I wouldn't put it quite that way, Mrs Baker. But, yes, I do need to write up more case studies before I submit my thesis.'
'What do you need to know?'
'You said that Katie doesn't like to leave the house so this will be a preliminary interview before I talk to her.'

'I've got one question before we go any further. Will the people who take part in your survey be anonymous?'

Miss Chichester tucked a lock of blonde hair behind her ear. 'I can assure you that anything said between us now, or with your daughter later, will be held in the strictest confidence. Not even my supervisor will know the identity of those who have agreed to take part.'

Miss Chichester placed a form on top of her clipboard. OVER-EATING SURVEY. Lola could read the heading, even upside down.

'Could you tell me the names your immediate family members, please?'

'There's me, my husband, Haywood, Katie and my son, Rhett.'

'How many times a day does your family eat together?'

'I cook seven days a week.'

'But do you eat meals together?'

'We sit down together three times a day. Or they sit down and I serve them like a waitress.'

'Are mealtimes occasions for conflict?'

Lola eyed Miss Chichester. 'Of course they're not. What are you trying to say?'

'Are there disagreements at the dinner table?'

'Of course not. Nobody says anything.'

'You eat in silence?'

'My family eat as fast as they can so they can run off to watch TV. When are we going to get to the questions about my daughter?'

Miss Chichester scribbled something. 'How old is Katie?'

'Nineteen.'

'And your son?'

'Eighteen.'

'How long has Katie been overweight?'

'A year and a few months.' Lola craned her neck. She saw ADDICTIVE BEHAVIOR written upside down with a big question mark. Lola put her purse on the table between them and took out two photographs. The first was Katie in a tutu, her body skinny as an ice pick. The other was a fat faced senior, peeking over the edge of a mortarboard. She laid them, side by side, for the counselor to see. 'That's what Katie used to look like and this is what she's like now. She just blew up. I have to padlock the refrigerator at night, otherwise she'd eat herself bug-eyed.'

'Do you have any idea why Katie began to overeat?'
'All her life she wanted to be a ballet dancer and then she had a bad knee injury. That's when she started eating like there was no tomorrow.'
As the girl took notes, Lola scooted forward to see what she was writing. Miss Chichester noticed and tipped her clipboard so the form disappeared.
'Fill me in a bit more, Mrs Baker, on your daughter's eating habits.'
'Katie starves herself on Slenderella, then eats things that would make a goat upchuck.'
'For example?'
'I got up in the middle of the night and caught her eating brown sugar and Crisco.'
The girl's chin lifted. 'Vegetable shortening and sugar?'
'Mashed up together. A whole cup of it. "Fatso goes nutzoid".'
Miss Chichester looked flustered. 'Mrs Baker, I'm afraid I'm not following you.'
'That's what my son said after Katie tore up some calendars in a store.'
'Calendars?'
'A policeman came to the house asking for damages. You'll have to ask my daughter what happened. I haven't been able to get a word out of her for two days.'
'Any idea what might have made her destroy them?'
'Katie's always been melodramatic.'
'Could you give me an example?'
'Is all this really important?'
'Actually it is, Mrs Baker.'
Lola was unconvinced, but she couldn't have a policemen turning up at the house again and Haywood finding out. 'Ever since she was little, she's wanted everything to be perfect. Everything has to be just so. I've tried to tell her that there's always going to be a train wreck around the corner and she's got to stop acting like the world's coming to an end just because she hurt her knee.'
'Do you and your daughter have any major disagreements?'
Lola took her glasses off, wiped them and put them on again. She wasn't about to tell a stranger about the arguments and hissy fits that had gone on for months. 'I thought this was supposed to be a survey about overeating.'
'Could you give me a recent example of a difference of opinion

between you and your daughter? I have to fill in all the boxes.'

Lola puffed out her cheeks in exasperation. 'A few days ago, Katie begged me to take her to a psychiatrist. I told her she didn't need one. All she needed to do was get out of the house and stop crying all the time. When she realized I wasn't going to cave in like her father, she locked herself in her room and wailed for three hours.'

'Are you sure it was three hours, Mrs Baker?'

'I know how long it was. It nearly drove me crazy.'

'Do you have any difficulties with your son?'

'Just stick to my daughter's problems and leave my son out of this.'

'It would help me with Katie's case history if you could give me a little family background.'

'Have you read *Gone With the Wind*, Miss Chichester?'

'I've seen the film.'

'I've been telling Katie she needs to be like Scarlett O'Hara. She needs to develop some gumption and stop feeling sorry for herself just because she's lost something she loved.'

'How did she react when you said that?'

Lola flicked her hand. 'She doesn't listen to a word I say. I can't make her go to college. I can't make her get a job. I can't even get her to wash very often. She sits around stinking because she says there's no point doing anything if you have to keep doing it, over and over, for the rest of your life.'

'How does your daughter feel about you coming here to see me?'

Lola glanced at the photographs lying on the table. 'She doesn't know.'

Miss Chichester put her pen down. 'I'm afraid there's no point continuing this conversation.'

'Why not?'

'Because you can't force an interview on someone who hasn't agreed to it. People have to admit they have a problem before they can be asked questions about it.'

'Katie knows she needs help. She asked to see a psychiatrist. Please talk to her, Miss Chichester. My daughter needs someone her own age and sex to talk to, not some nut doctor in a white coat.'

The girl looked at her incomplete form. She was biting her lip.

Lola said, 'Could you come to my house tomorrow at ten thirty? It'd mean the world to me.'

'I'll have to speak to my professor first. If he gives his permission, you'll need to tell your daughter I'm coming. The interview must be held in neutral territory.'

'What do you mean by neutral?'

'Somewhere communal. A sun porch or a living room.'

Lola grabbed her hand. 'I can't thank you enough, Miss Chichester.' She opened her purse and handed the girl a piece of paper she'd written her address and phone number on before she'd left the house. 'If someone was to find out that Katie had almost been arrested, I couldn't raise my chin in this town.'

Lola sat in the chair near the front door, wagging her leg as she waited for Miss Chichester to arrive. Since Lola had told Katie the college student was coming, she'd locked herself in her room and refused to come out.

She jumped up to plump the sofa pillows, straighten the large painting above the couch, watched by the glass eyes of the buck Haywood had shot. She was about to pick up a dog biscuit by the front door when she saw Miss Chichester on the porch. She threw it in her pocket and took a deep breath.

'Come in, come in.' She ushered the college student in and waved her in the direction of the couch. 'Have a seat. I'll be right back.'

She went into the kitchen and returned with a glass of shrimp cocktail. She handed it to Miss Chichester with a silver spoon she'd just polished with Brasso.

The girl looked confused. 'That's very kind of you, Mrs Rivers, but we need to start the survey.'

Lola's eyes met the deer's. 'There's a little problem. Katie will only see you in her room.'

'But that was one of the conditions we agreed on. Neutral territory.'

Lola fished in her apron and held out a bottle of Nembutal. 'Last night I opened what should have been a new prescription and half the pills were gone.'

Miss Chichester read the label and started to back away. 'These are barbiturates. I'm not qualified for this. I'm sorry, Mrs Baker. I have to go.'

Lola grabbed her arm. 'You can't leave. When I asked Katie about my pills, she refused to talk, the same way she did with the calendars.

You've got to help me, Miss Chichester. I'm at the end of my rope and I'm afraid she'll do something stupid like Marilyn Monroe.'

Lola stood behind the counselor as she knocked on her daughter's bedroom door. Burrito started to bark behind it. 'Hush,' Lola shouted. The dog didn't stop so she took the Bonio out of her pocket and slid it under the door.

'Your mother told you I was coming to do an interview, Katie. Would you like to let me in?'

Lola glared at the back of Miss Chichester's hairdo. She wanted to say to her, You can't pander to a teenager. You have to demand she let you in.

Miss Chichester waited a little while before knocking again.

Silence.

Lola crooked her finger for Miss Chichester to follow her into the living room. When they were in front of the deer she whispered, 'Tell her you're a policewoman. That way she'll be forced to cooperate.'

'I can't lie, Mrs Baker. That's no way to earn anyone's trust.'

'This will go on all day and you'll never get one word out of her.'

'This has to be done the way I've been trained or not at all.'

Miss Chichester walked back to the door and knocked again. 'May I come in and talk to you, Katie? I'm doing a psychological survey and I'd like to interview you.'

From behind the door Lola heard, 'My mother sent you here. You're going to come in whether I want you to or not.'

'I'll only come in, Katie, if you want me to.'

Lola looked at Miss Chichester, wanting to slap her into the middle of next week. You think you know more than I do, she wanted to say, and I've been on this planet almost fifty years.

'Really?' she heard her daughter say.

'You have my word.'

Lola was surprised a few seconds later to hear the sound of the handle being turned. The door cracked open an inch.

'Will you leave when I ask?' Katie said. 'Cross your heart?'

Miss Chichester moved her hand like a priest.

'Only for a little while then.'

Miss Chichester stepped into the darkened room and locked the door behind her.

Katie sat on her bed in a housecoat and muumuu, glaring at the stranger with chin-length blonde hair combed into a perfect flip.

'My name's Nancy Chichester. Thanks for letting me see you.'

Katie examined her knees. After faces, that's what she always inspected now when she met strangers.

Miss Chichester put out her hand. Katie didn't take it.

'Mind if I sit down?'

Katie shrugged. She watched Miss Chichester perch on the edge of the vanity stool like a little canary.

'I'm studying psychology at the university. My job is to help people understand why they do what they do so they can learn to alter their behavior. I'm doing my thesis on eating disorders.'

'I told my mother I wanted to see a psychiatrist,' Katie said, 'not a cheerleader.'

Miss Chichester smiled and took out a clipboard. 'Have you talked to anyone about what your life has been like the last year and a half?'

Katie shook her head.

'Almost everyone feels better if they can talk about what's bothering them. Maybe we could start with something small like—'

'What makes you think you can help me anyhow?'

'Because I can see you feel you're beyond help.'

Hot, stupid tears started to roll down her face. Katie tried to wipe them away, but they kept coming.

Miss Chichester said, 'You've got a pretty face under all that hair.'

'You're a liar,' she said. 'I'm fat as shit.'

Lola stomped around the living room, slinging a dust cloth. She wasn't happy that Miss Chichester had refused to tell Katie she was from the police. Her daughter had no business destroying merchandise. Katie needed to be scared a little before taking that eating survey; it might force her to respect other people's property.

Lola reached into her apron for the half-empty bottle of Nembutal. She didn't think for one minute that her daughter had swallowed those sleeping pills. Being fat was no reason to kill yourself. She'd have bet a million dollars that Katie had flushed the pills down the toilet. Now that she wasn't spinning around on her toes, she probably stole them for attention.

The person she was really worried about was Haywood. One of his golfing buddies had dropped dead a month ago and Haywood had been acting strangely ever since. A week before the calendar incident he'd said he was going to do what he damn well pleased. 'I'm fifty-two years old and I'll probably die at sixty-five like my dad and brother. So I'm going to be playing a lot more bridge and golf because that's what makes me happy. I'm under a lot of stress and if you have a problem with the kids, Lola, don't come running to me all the time or you're going to be a widow.'

She felt he was being selfish, but there was heart trouble in the family and he did work like a dog. As he was the breadwinner, she had to respect Haywood's wishes whether she agreed with them or not. One thing she did know. She didn't want to be the one who gave him a heart attack.

She lifted the counselor's untouched dish of shrimp cocktail. The sniffy way Miss Chichester had refused it made her feel as uncomfortable as she'd been in Melba Kincaid's parlor thirty years ago. Lola had been invited to her house as a member of the Shoe Box Social Committee. Melba's father owned a pajama factory and had the biggest house in McKenzie, Tennessee.

Melba handed out fancy glasses filled with shrimp cocktail. It was the first time Lola had eaten seafood; the closest she'd ever come was crawdads. Melba lifted her chin and looked at her with the contempt city people reserved for farmers. *This is what is called an hors d'oeuvre, Lola Mae. I'll bet you don't know what that is. Someone like you doesn't know anything except when to plant cotton.*

That day Lola had made a promise to herself. Even though she'd been born in the country, she'd learn high society's airs and graces and no one, especially a damn Yankee like Miss Chichester, would ever make her feel humiliated like that again.

'Looking at your room, Katie, I'm guessing you've been dancing a long time. How long?'

Katie stared at the floor. She was going to say, Since I was five, but that wasn't strictly true because she hadn't been able to do a barre for months. Her thighs were so fat she couldn't stand in fifth position anymore. 'Crabs get rid of urine through their head.'

'I don't think you want to talk about crabs. I think you want to talk about something else.'

'Like what?'

'Are you tired when you wake up?'

'A cockroach can be headless for nine days before it starves to death.'

'Do you think you might be depressed, Katie?'

She twisted her hair into a rope. 'My mother doesn't believe in depression. I can't be in a state that doesn't exist, can I?'

Miss Chichester sat with her hands folded, studying the bedroom walls papered with Nureyev posters. 'Maybe you'd like to dance how you're feeling.'

Katie stared at the picture above Miss Chichester's head. Nureyev in the role of Prince Albrecht, carrying an armful of lilies to Giselle's grave. Katie looked at his grief-stricken face and wondered how you danced wanting to never wake up again.

'Are you doing any ballet now?'

Katie continued picking at the chenille bedspread. She didn't say anything for three whole minutes; she knew because she was watching her Timex. Are you blind? she wanted to scream. How can I when I'm seventy-four pounds overweight?

'I want to help, Katie, not to pry. I'll go if you don't want to talk to me. I hope things get better for you soon.'

She heard Miss Chichester's shoes heading toward the door. 'My knee was injured before a big performance,' she blurted out. 'My doctor told me I had to have an operation and my ballet teacher said she wouldn't let me study with her anymore if I did.'

'That must have been confusing for you.'

Katie stared at the floor, nodding. She was trembling with the effort of keeping her tears inside.

'Why do you think your teacher didn't want you to have surgery?'

Katie looked into Miss Chichester's eyes for the first time. 'I have no idea.'

Miss Chichester handed her a Kleenex. 'Why don't you tell me when things started to go bad for you?'

'After I hurt my knee, everything just fell apart . . . I think my mother was glad.'

'Why should your mother be glad you hurt yourself? She loves you.'

'She never wanted me to dance. She wanted me to go to college because she had to put my father through school.'

'Tell me how you feel about your mother.'

'You want me to write a book?'

Miss Chichester smiled. 'No. Just tell me how she makes you feel.'

'She puts me down. She never leaves me alone. She nags me twenty-four hours a day.'

'What sort of things does she say?'

'"Stop feeling sorry for yourself. Get a job. You look like a baby manatee. Read Anne Landers if you want to hear about people with real problems."'

'Has it ever occurred to you that by putting on weight you could get back at her?'

Katie stared at Miss Chichester.

'Your body is the only thing that really belongs to you. Your mother can try to control you in other ways, but she can't control your eating.'

Katie looked at her huge thighs. Her mother despised fat people all right. She thought they were weak-willed, a step away from drug addicts.

'Another thing we need to talk about, Katie, is your knee.'

'What about my knee?'

'Your operation was traumatic in more ways than one.'

'You think I fucking don't know that?'

'Being overweight takes you out of ballet. Eating may be your way of dealing with it. Punishing your body for letting you down.'

Katie's shoulders started to shake. She turned away so Miss Chichester couldn't see her face. She cried for what felt like a long time, her palms wet with tears and snot. When she was finally able to stop sobbing, she felt a Kleenex being tucked into her fingers.

Miss Chichester gently cleared her throat and sat down on the vanity stool. 'Your mother said you'd torn up some calendars a few days ago. Maybe you'd like to talk about that.'

She started to wipe her cheeks, her hands. 'What's that got to do with anything?'

'It sounds like it might be an outward expression of what's going on inside.'

She pulled at some tufts on her bedspread. 'My Mom and I had a big fight two days ago.'

'About what?'

'She said she was tired of me sitting around the house all day and locked me out.'

'Locked you out?'

Katie nodded. 'I'd been begging her to take me to a psychiatrist. I was pleading and crying. She kept screaming that I didn't need one. In the middle of our fight I went to get the mail and she locked me out. Wouldn't let me back in. That's when I walked to the joke shop and saw some calendars.'

'What kind of calendars?'

'Nudes.'

'What were nudes doing in the joke shop?'

'It was a calendar of women who must weigh three hundred pounds. They were so huge you couldn't see their pubic hair.'

'Why did you tear them up?'

'I couldn't stand the thought that people would hang them on their wall to laugh at them. I ripped up a stack before the manager caught me. He said if I paid for them, he wouldn't press charges, but I didn't have any money.' She bent over to pick up Burrito who was begging to be lifted.

Katie was stroking her when Miss Chichester asked, 'Have you ever had a boyfriend?'

She shook her head.

'Ever dated?'

'Not really.'

'A pretty girl like you?'

'I didn't want anything to distract me from ballet.'

'You've been comforting yourself with food for the past year and a half. You need to find something else. You need to have some fun.' Miss Chichester turned to look at the posters of Nureyev. She pointed at one where he was wearing a pair of white tights that revealed every curve and bulge. 'Do you ever have erotic dreams?'

Katie felt herself blush. 'Only if I dream about him.'

'He's not around so go see *Butch Cassidy and the Sundance Kid.*'

She was about to ask why when she saw the strip of light under her door broken by shadow. She jabbed at it to get the counselor's attention, furious that her mother was trying to listen.

Miss Chichester put her finger to her lips and tiptoed across the room. When she opened the door, there was a bloodcurdling yell.

'Sorry to have scared you, Mrs Baker. I was just going to the bathroom.'

'Baker?' Katie said. 'Our last name isn't—'

'Hush your mouth, young lady.' Her mother marched into the room with her handbag. 'This session is over, Miss Chichester. My daughter has to be somewhere at twelve o'clock.'

'Would you mind stepping outside until we've finished, Mrs Baker? We were late getting started.'

Her mother pretended she hadn't heard her and opened her purse. She pulled out a checkbook.

'What's that for?' Miss Chichester asked.

'Your trouble.'

'I can't accept money.'

'Oh yes you can,' her mother said, taking out of a pen. 'Gas money.'

While her mother was filling out the check, Miss Chichester scribbled something on a piece of paper and slipped it under her pillow. 'Like I said, Katie, make sure you go see *Butch Cassidy and the—*'

Her mother tapped the face of her watch. 'That's all we have time for. If we ever need you again, I've got your number.'

Her mother showed the counselor out while Katie read Miss Chichester's message. *Give me a bell if U need 2. Here's my number.*

From her bedroom window Katie watched Nancy's car leave and, ten minutes later, her father's truck drive up. She knew her mother wanted the counselor out of the house before he came home for lunch. Like the calendars and pills, Miss Chichester was another big secret.

Buffalo gal

She watched her parents try to polka around the living room, their toes barely visible in the thick shag pile. They had recently taken up a correspondence course in ballroom dancing. They were doing their homework barefoot.

Her father stopped the record while he studied a page of diagrams. He stared at them, his face furrowed in concentration. 'Will you take a look, Katie? They're the squirreliest instructions I've ever seen.'

She studied the arrows and lines: the man's steps indicated by footprints, the woman's by high heels, a pair of isosceles triangles above two tiny dots. 'A polka has two steps and a hop, Daddy, not three. That's where you're going wrong.' She got off the sofa to demonstrate.

He struggled to follow her, stepping on his left foot, sliding his right, hopping, then robotically reversing the pattern.

Her mother stood watching, patting her lacquered bonnet of hair. 'Loosen up, Haywood. You're stiff as a board.'

'One thing at a time, Lola. I have to get the step first.'

Katie watched him as he polkaed around the room. Neither of her parents had natural grace or talent, yet she loved to help them learn their ballroom routines because it was the only dancing she saw anymore.

Her father stopped looking at his feet long enough for her to give him the thumbs up. He beamed with pride.

'Thanks, Katie. I'd never have figured that out. When Momma and I were growing up, we weren't allowed to dance.'

'You're kidding,' she said.

'Nope. The only people who danced in Weakley County were white trash or Negroes.' He took a swipe at her mother's rump. 'Primitive Baptists think dancing is vertical fornication.'

Her mother pretended to slap his arm. 'Watch your mouth, Hay.'

'Whatever you say, boss.' He gave Katie a wink. 'Play the record again. Let's give this polka another spinneroo.'

Katie lowered the needle onto the old 78. A cowboy crooned in a scratchy, familiar voice,

Buffalo Gals, will you come out tonight,
Will you come out tonight, will you come out tonight?
Buffalo Gals, will you come out tonight?
And dance by the light of the moon!

The record was the same one she remembered her parents square dancing to in the Fifties. She pictured them getting ready for the Do-Si-Do Club: her father in his cowboy shirt and bolas tie, greasing his hair with Wildroot Hair Oil; her mother competing for space at the bathroom mirror, her turquoise squaw dress increased a foot in diameter with the addition of a half-dozen net petticoats.

Katie had adored Friday evenings at the Temple of Agriculture. There'd been a live band and caller, cake at intermission and a forest of pant legs and nylon stockings, spinning and reeling above her two-year-old head. She loved to stand by the musicians, copying the grown-ups as they smiled and skipped across the floor. Those nights at the Do-Si-Do Club had been her first dancing lessons. Her first memory of happiness.

Her father started to hum along with the cowboy as he danced around the room. 'Look at me now, sister,' he said, high stepping as he leaned into a turn. 'You've managed to teach an old clodhopper with two left feet.'

She was delighted her father had learned to polka, but wished he'd change the record. She wanted to hear Tchaikovsky, Stravinsky, Prokofiev. Music that gave her goosebumps, that lifted her out of this ordinary family, this ordinary life.

Her parents hopped around, practicing, while she read a ballet brochure Joe Karolak had sent. *Before being considered for an audition at the School of American Ballet, applicants must send two recent photographs in leotards, 5"x 7" or larger.* She enviously traced her hand over the girls' paper-doll-thin bodies. Their hipbones stuck out as sharply as the wing mirrors on Joe's car. If she hadn't been fat, she'd have joined American Ballet Theater a year ago. She needed to get in a company soon or she'd be too old, stuck out in the desert for the rest of her life.

Her father called out, 'How're we doing, sister?'

She looked up as he started to flutter his hands and shimmy his hips. Her mother burst out laughing. 'We're supposed to be practicing the polka, Hay. You're dancing like a colored man.'

Her father grabbed her mother's wrist and spun her around while she tried to protect her hairdo with her free hand. 'I spent three hours at the Beauty College this afternoon to look pretty for you, Hay.'

He twirled her mother out again and she screamed like a girl on a roller coaster. 'Cuttin' up the rug is a helluva lot more fun.'

Katie saw her mother's baggy pink panties under her billowing skirt. She'd hoped to catch a glimpse of the sexy black pair her mother had hidden in her drawer. Katie coveted the see-through triangle of cobweb lace that had never been worn, so different from the dumpy panties her mother bought her, the day of the week embroidered above the leg.

Her father spun her mother toward him like a yo-yo, then out again. She slapped down her ballooning skirt with her free hand.

'Quit dragging your axle, Momma, and cut loose for a change.'

'Stop,' her mother said, grabbing her side. 'I've got a stitch.' She stooped over, hands on knees, to catch her breath.

The way her father was staring down her mother's cleavage reminded Katie of Joe.

'Haywood, behave yourself.'

He made a monkey face and moved behind her to give her a squeeze. For a second—one second—Katie felt a stab of jealousy. No man had ever held her like that, except on stage and that was only pretend. Joe had tried a couple of times, but she'd always pushed him away because he and Barbie Lundgren were going steady.

Her father started to rumba, rolling his hips in a way that Katie had never seen before. She thought of Joe's card hidden under her mattress. *Went to see the New York City Ballet at Lincoln Center. In this Japanese number one of the women practically screwed her partner on stage. She wrapped her legs around him and practically rubbed his crotch. Why didn't you tell me that ballet is sex in leotards?*

Her mother removed her father's arms and turned the music off.

'Come back here, Lo. We're having some fun for a change.'

Her mother looked at her watch and stared out into the night. 'It's half an hour past Rhett's curfew. Every time he's on that damn bike,

'I'm so nervous I could spit.'

'Looking won't make him come home any sooner, Momma. Loosen up and enjoy yourself.'

'Haywood, you're supposed to make that boy come home by ten.'

'He's eighteen, Lola. Give him some slack. He's almost grown.'

Katie's stomach rumbled. It had been protesting all night. Since Miss Chichester's visit, Katie had managed to lose twelve pounds by sticking to a diet of a thousand calories a day and doing a daily barre.

'I'm thirsty,' she said when her stomach growled again. 'Anyone want a drink?'

Her father's hand shot up. 'Buttermilk, please.'

'Coke for me,' her mother said.

Katie returned to the living room with a tray. Her father took the tumbler and her mother the red-and-white can with a straw sticking out the top.

'I forgot to tell you, sugar. While you were doing your barre, Carmel McCleary called.'

'What's she ringing me for?'

'She wants to invite you to her recital.'

Katie ripped open her Tab and tipped it to her mouth. She held the diet cola on her tongue till it burned. Having studied with Madame, she had no desire to see the revue of a Dolly Dinkle dancing school.

Her mother poked the straw. 'Have you ever thought of going back to Carmel's?'

'What for?'

'It's better than sleeping all day.'

'I don't sleep all day, *madre*. I was up at nine.'

'And I was up at six.'

'Want to help me with the crossword, sister?'

Her father jerked his head in the direction of the door. From his expression, Katie knew he was trying to stop another fight.

Her mother grabbed her wrist when she stood up to follow him. 'You're going to speak to Carmel.'

'I don't have anything to say to her. How did she know I was in town anyway?'

Her mother bobbed the straw up and down. 'Because I told her.'

'You did what?'

'If you don't have the sense to go to college, you need get out of the house from time to time.'

'How could you do this to me? I don't want to see her yucky recital!'

'Until you met that damn Madame, those recitals were the high point of your life.'

'Because I didn't know any better.'

'At least none of her students have wrecked their legs.'

The phone rang.

'That'll be Carmel,' her mother said. 'I told her to ring after ten.'

'I don't want to speak to her!'

Her mother headed toward her bedroom. 'Answer that, Katie Scarlett.' When she didn't, her mother screamed from the hallway, 'If you know what's good for you, get that phone this minute.'

She let it ring and ring and ring and ring.

Katie lay on the den floor, curled in a ball. The television was on, even though the screen was swirling with static. She was so upset she couldn't make herself crawl over to switch it off.

The recital's May 26th, Katie. Why don't you come backstage after the show? I've told the girls that you've become a real ballerina. They'll dance their socks off if I tell them you're in the audience.

'I'd love to come,' she'd mumbled into the phone but, even as she was accepting her teacher's offer, she was figuring out how she could get out of her promise. After she hung up, she tiptoed into the kitchen and ate a two-pound jar of peanut butter that her mother had hidden. It was already traveling down from her stomach to upholster her hips and thighs. She started to sniffle, first in little sobs, then in big gulps.

She didn't know how long she'd been crying when the den door squeaked. She sat up, afraid it was her mother who yelled at her whenever she found her blubbering. She fell on her side and rolled into a ball.

'Katie,' she heard her father say behind her. 'Tell your old pop what's wrong.'

She wanted to shout, I'm not a ballerina. I'm a buffalo. I weigh a hundred and seventy-eight pounds! 'Oh, Daddy,' she said. 'I try so hard to lose weight and I can't see any difference, even when I starve myself.'

'But you are losing weight, honey.'

'I am?'

'Sure you are. The last few days you've had a pear-drop smell on your breath. It's ketone. A byproduct of body fat breaking down.'

She thought about the empty jar of Peter Pan and started to sob again.

'What's up, sweetheart? Tell me what's on your mind.'

'I told Carmel . . . I told her I'd come see her recital next month. But I can't. I can't! I'd rather die than have her see me the way I am now.'

Her father was silent a long time. 'Carrying a few extra pounds is something you can change. All you have to do is burn more calories than you eat. You can do anything you set your mind to. Remember the necklace I gave you? "If ye have the faith as a grain of mustard seed, nothing shall be impossible unto you."'

She wanted to throw her arms around him, but she continued to lie on her side, afraid he'd smell the peanuts on her breath. 'Daddy.'

'What, honey?'

'Do you think my knee's going to be okay?'

'It's late, sweetie pie. Things will look a lot brighter in the morning. What do you say to getting some shut-eye?'

'Do you think it will be okay?'

'Of course, Katiekins. Didn't I get you the orthopedic surgeon for the US ski team?'

Haywood closed the door behind his daughter and walked back to his Barcalounger. He was thinking about what she had just asked him. He had lied, but what else could he do?

He should head back to bed, but there was too much going on for him to sleep. He'd been to his wife's room before he heard Katie crying. When he'd tried to lift the bedclothes to slide in beside her, she'd pushed him away. *That son of yours came in at one o'clock in the morning. No mattress mambo for you, bud, unless you make Rhett stick to his curfew.*

He turned the light off and buried his face in his hands. He had never been unfaithful, but he was thinking more and more about his new bridge partner. When Maggie Hubbard walked into the Acey Deucey Bridge Club, men's heads turned. Maggie was around Lola's age, but had an hourglass figure, wore classy clothes and was stacked like Sophia Loren.

Maggie was married, but lately she'd been giving him signals. Flirtatious looks when they were bidding, touching his foot under the table and not moving it, holding his glance a little too long. After a year and a half of sleeping apart from Lola, he was daydreaming about his bridge partner more and more.

He pictured Maggie unzipping a slinky dress. He was reaching to unhook an ice-cream-white bra when the den light snapped on.

Lola was standing in the doorway in pajamas and night hat, her face smeared with Vaseline. She tapped her watch. 'Haywood, do you know what time it is?'

'I know what the goddamn time is,' he said. 'Turn that light off.'

'Why are you sitting in the dark at two fifteen in the morning?'

'Because I goddamn like it.'

Carmel McCleary's School of The Dance

In the back of her mother's closet were stacks of Fifties shoes. Katie opened the lid of every box until she found her favorite pair. Open-toed Brazilian shoes with glass fruit stitched to the vamp. She slipped on the wooden heels and, for the first time in her life, they fit.

Tiny glass cherries, oranges and bananas clicked against each other as she teetered to the mirror. Even standing still, the Carmen Miranda shoes threw her off-balance. Madame had forbidden her to wear high heels because they shortened the Achilles tendon, but Katie would make an exception tonight because she hoped the extra inches the heels gave her would make her look thinner.

She held onto the door frame as she stepped into her mother's largest skirt. She tugged and pulled but, even when she held her breath, the straining zipper would only go halfway up. She was about to rifle through her mother's drawers for a girdle when Katie saw her in the mirror, a laundry basket pressed against one hip.

'What are you doing, sugar?'

Katie felt her cheeks get hot so she pretended to admire her borrowed shoes. 'Trying to put an outfit together for tonight.'

'Why don't you try my Stork-A-Lures? They'd look good with that red Garibaldi blouse.'

'What are storkerlewers?'

'My old maternity skirts. Wedge yourself against those clothes and I'll see if I can find them.'

Katie threw herself against the packed dresses hanging on the sagging pole. Normally, she would have been furious at her mother for suggesting she wear a maternity skirt, but since her father had told her he believed she could lose weight, she'd stuck to her diet. She was down to a hundred and sixty-seven, a loss of eleven pounds since her peanut butter binge last month.

Her mother found the Stork-A-Lures flattened against the back wall. One was red with large white tulips and the other was black flared gabardine, both with a huge U of cream-colored elastic sewn into the front.

'Which one, sugar?'

Katie chose the black one. She stepped into it and stood in front of the mirror. She stared at herself, wondering what she could do to hide the embarrassing panel. Then she remembered the shawl Joe had bought for her in Juarez. She wrapped the bird-covered *rebozo* around her shoulders and smiled. Beginning to feel more hopeful, she twisted her hair into a corkscrew and secured it with two beaded chopsticks.

Her mother glanced up from folding a pile of laundry. 'I hope nobody we know sees you looking like a TV aerial.'

'This is the latest fashion.'

Her mother gave her a sour look. 'Anybody would think you're a hippy from Eight Hashbury.'

Katie adjusted her hair. 'Wearing chopsticks in your hair doesn't make you a hippy. And it's Haight Ashbury.'

'You have to worry what other people think when your father's a well-known dentist.'

'This is a one-horse town. Fortuna wouldn't recognize originality if it was bitten on the neck.' Katie rummaged through the earrings her mother kept in the bottom of a Brach's Cherry Cordials' box. She chose a pair in the shape of red chilis. They looked perfect with the parrot-covered shawl. She was admiring her ethnic look when she saw her mother pick up a sheet of paper on the bed.

'"The 1958 dance revue will be held at the Fortuna High School Auditorium on the 29th, 30th and 31st of May. Make-up: red lipstick, blue eye shadow, black eye pencil. No panties under leotard. No gum or socks. No mammas backstage during the show except those who have been asked to help. Please do not present me with gifts—a single bouquet of flowers is sufficient, though not necessary."' Her mother glanced up from the mimeographed sheet. 'Where'd you find this old thing?'

'In my ballet scrapbook.'

Her mother laid the paper in her lap. 'Know what I remember most about your recitals? All the mothers used to club together to buy Carmel a big wicker basket of roses.'

'Momma, can I wear Aunt Delta's coat tonight?'
Her mother shook her head.
'You let me wear it to graduation last year.'
'May's too hot to gallivant around in a sealskin coat.'
'It was May then too. And I'm not gallivanting. I'm going to the dance revue you tricked me into.'
For once, her mother didn't say anything. She kept folding sheets.
'Let me wear it tonight. You owe it to me for telling Carmel I was in town.'
Her mother looked at her and sighed. 'Oh all right, but anyone who sees you will think you're crazy as a box of frogs.'

Katie parked the Oldsmobile in the school parking lot. Despite not wanting to see her teacher, her heart lifted to see the trailers lined up outside the stage door like a mini wagon train. Every spring, Carmel and her mother transformed three cotton trailers into portable dressing rooms because the ones at Fortuna High were crammed with sets from senior plays. The high-sided carts were converted by stapling black plastic sheeting over the widely-spaced slats. Then Carmel and Olive laced on tarpaulin roofs, strung clotheslines to hang costumes and rigged a power supply for lights.

Katie got out of the car as two butterflies flapped past, their spotted wings attached to their wrists with elastic. A half-dozen other excited children followed in bug-green unitards and face paint. Katie knew how they felt. Intoxicated. When she'd been their age, the recital had been more exciting than Christmas.

She picked up the wilting bouquet of honeysuckle and larkspur her mother had left on the seat. *Take these in case Carmel doesn't get any flowers. I imagine she's lucky these days if she gets a boutonniere.*

Katie teetered around the side of the building to the front entrance. On this warm evening the double doors were thrown open for the annual recital of Carmel McCleary's School of The Dance. Even though her stomach was in knots, Katie made herself as tall as possible and stepped into the lobby of the only theater in town.

For the first time in four years, she was in the hall she had once considered Fortuna's own Maryinsky Theater. The high-school auditorium did not have a box for the Tzar, blue velvet seats or crystal chandeliers but, as a young ballet dancer, this auditorium had been the most magical place on earth.

She was disappointed to see spit balls on the ceiling and dried gum stuck to the upturned plywood seats. The proscenium arch that had once seemed wide as the Grand Canyon looked disappointingly small. For the first time in her life, the dragon-red curtains looked dirty and threadbare.

Hoping no one would recognize her, she pulled her aunt's coat around her and walked toward a card table piled with programs. She picked one up. Once the recital had lasted three evenings to give all of Carmel's students a chance to perform. This year's one-night stand probably had less than fifty girls.

She sat in the front row so only her back could be seen. She put the bouquet under her seat and fanned herself with the program. The curtain was jumping and she knew why. Little girls were peering through holes in the velveteen to see where their parents were sitting.

Two minutes to eight. Almost time to curtains up. She turned to look for Olive's silhouette in the lighting booth, but she couldn't see her as the house lights were already starting to fade.

The chattering in the audience stopped as tinny speakers started to play the Chopin nocturne for the overture of 'Living Picture'. Katie had performed this ballet many times and knew what was happening backstage: the giant picture frame had been flown in and the older girls in their long tulle skirts were taking their positions marked on the floor with Xs of white paint.

The curtains jerked open, revealing the crudely-painted Degas backdrop. The dancers, greased with Vaseline and dusted with baby powder, looked unearthly, their arms and faces the color of their white skirts. They held their poses: yawning, scratching, tying a shoe. Suddenly, they dropped their bored expressions and grinned big American grins. The dancers stepped through the frame and the picture molding jerked upward, leaving the stage bare for the first routine.

Carmel's students were well-drilled and energetic; they smiled and kept good time, but they were poorly turned out, their feet didn't point and their arms looked like twigs. When the corps de ballet and soloists took each new formation, their lines were so ragged that it made Katie wince.

Four variations followed. The most distressing girl to watch was a dancer Katie remembered when she'd been Carmel's student. Tracy Scotchbrook had a perfectly-proportioned body and beautifully-arched feet, but she had no idea of line and didn't stretch her knees in the air. She was gifted with natural grace and good elevation, but aimlessly flitted around the stage from one unconnected step to another which made her look like a light-crazed moth.

The solos ended, the corps de ballet clumped off. The picture frame flew back in and the dancers took their original positions. The music faded and they froze in a *tableau vivant*. Katie applauded politely, but the parents behind her were clapping wildly. 'Living Picture' always brought down the house.

Fourteen toe, tap and fire-baton routines followed before 'I Could Have Danced All Night' blared through the auditorium's loudspeakers. Then the entire cast assembled on stage in stair-step formation: little girls in front, older girls at the back. They joined hands and lifted their arms over their heads like prizefighters before they bowed.

Tracy broke away from the back row and led out Carmel, who was waiting in the wings. Before she reached center stage, the applause was beginning to die away. Carmel bowed quickly and exited without having been presented with a bouquet.

Katie remembered the standing ovation and the flowers that had always greeted Madame. How commandingly she had taken curtain calls: raising her hand to her heart and lowering her chin, then lifting her gaze as she extended her upturned hand, sweeping from one side of the auditorium to the other, seeming to acknowledge the applause of every person sitting in the darkness beyond the cage of light.

Katie didn't want to bump into any students or parents so she sat in her seat, nose buried in the program, until the auditorium was almost empty. When it was safe, she pulled her coat around her and went outside to find Carmel. The parking lot was deserted except for a half-dozen cars. Katie was heading toward the line of cotton trailers when she noticed a shadow: a hulking figure holding a megaphone of flowers. Horrified, she pressed herself against the side of the auditorium. There was no way she could see Carmel if she looked that enormous.

She hugged the wall until it ran out, then tiptoed in the open across the asphalt. She neared the Oldsmobile, her heart pounding so loudly she was sure it was audible above the clack of her heels. She fumbled for her keys and, as she took them out of her bag, they fell. She scooped them up, opened the car door and was about to step inside when she heard a voice behind her.

'Katie?' Then louder, 'Katie Rivers, is that you?'

She closed the car door and slowly clopped toward the end trailer where Carmel was standing in the doorway in blue jeans and a T-shirt. As Katie came toward her, her teacher continued to smile, even though she had seen her trying to sneak away.

Katie held the edges of her fur coat together, fifty pounds heavier than when Carmel had last seen her. She climbed the trailer's cinderblock steps and sheepishly held out her mother's drooping bouquet.

Carmel took the flowers and leaned forward to hug her, but Katie backed away.

Her teacher looked bewildered and hurt. 'They're beautiful.' With the flowers crooked in her arm, Carmel picked a net skirt off the floor. 'So tell me what you thought of the show tonight.'

Katie glanced in the direction of the car. 'I should be getting back.'

Carmel removed the paper toweling around the stems before putting them in water. 'Your mother knows you're here. She won't mind if you stay a few hours. We've got years of news to catch up on.'

Katie sat on the trailer floor and pulled her hair around her face.

Carmel held up a bottle with a bat on the label. 'Nightcap?'

'Sure,' she said, praying the Bacardi would loosen the knot in her stomach. She wasn't sure how many calories rum had; she'd have to look it up and deduct them from her calorie intake tomorrow.

Her teacher splashed generous portions of rum into two tumblers with ballerinas on them. Carmel topped them up with Coke and handed Katie her drink. 'Tell me what you thought of my girls.'

Katie stared at her glass, lost for words.

Carmel said, 'Your honest opinion.'

'I thought a couple of them had promise.'

'None of them are half as good as you. Even at five, you were a natural. You lit up the stage like an arc light.'

Katie didn't say anything. The only thing she'd lit up for the last year had been the refrigerator.

Carmel asked, 'What did you think of Tracy?'

'She's got . . .' She searched for a kind word. 'Potential.'

Carmel reached for the Bacardi and added another slug to her own glass. 'I thought Tracy was different. I thought she was like you. She didn't come to half her classes this year. She's more interested in going to football games and dating.'

Katie stared at Carmel's legs. From the waist down, she looked more like a weightlifter than a ballet teacher. Her overdeveloped quadriceps were due to the inappropriate exercises she'd devised to strengthen her students' legs. Katie was glad to have escaped before she'd started to look like Jack LaLanne.

Carmel lifted her glass and drained it in a few swallows. 'I divide my year in half. BR and AR. Before Recital and After Recital. Now I can finally relax.'

Katie said, 'How's your side?' Before the last recital Katie had appeared in, Carmel had been gored by one of her bulls. Rather than cancel the show and disappoint her students, Carmel had dosed herself up with aspirin and brandy, coughing blood into a handkerchief as she'd herded children in and out of the wings.

Carmel flicked her hand. 'I'm lucky to be here. Dr Gandy said the horn just missed my liver. Hey, speaking about doctors, your mother told me you'd had a knee operation a year or so ago. How's it doing?'

Katie threw back the rest of her drink and glanced at her watch. 'I should be getting home.'

'Tell me how your knee is. I want to know.'

'I've got the full range of movement back. It doesn't hurt me, but it's still weak.'

'What are you doing to keep in shape, Katie?'

'I give myself a barre every day.'

'That's not enough. You need to dance more. Three or four hours a day, minimum.'

Katie squirmed inside her coat. What Carmel had said was true, but there were no other dance teachers in town and Madame had forbidden her to come back.

'I've got a proposition for you. Why don't you come to the studio and teach the advanced class? My girls could learn so much from you.'

Katie looked at her empty glass, flattered and horrified at the same time. The challenge of teaching appealed to her, but the thought of Carmel seeing her in a leotard made her want to run.

'Ballet's what you were born to do. You have to honor the gift you've been given. You can't just throw it away.' Carmel gestured toward her empty tumbler. 'Another shot?'

Katie stared at the enameled ballerina awkwardly balancing on her glass. 'Sure. I mean about the drink. Not about the teaching.'

'Think about it.' Carmel took her glass, filled it, splashed in a cherry. 'The teaching, not the drink.'

Desperate to change the subject Katie said, 'Where's Olive? I haven't seen her tonight.'

'She can't help me anymore. Olive had a bad stroke six months ago.'

Katie felt her stomach drop. They were the closest mother and daughter she had ever known. Carmel and Olive were like sisters because they always called each other by their first names.

'Olive has to be turned every few hours so she doesn't get bedsores. I'd have to close the studio if it wasn't for our maid who stays with her at the farm when I'm teaching.' Carmel attempted a smile, though her eyes were brimming with tears.

'If you'd like,' Katie said, 'I could drive out to see her.'

Carmel shook her head. 'Olive's a proud woman. She would want you to remember her the way she was, not the wreck she is now.'

Katie picked at some raw cotton trapped in the splintery floor. She was thinking about Olive who resembled nothing so much as an old Russian ballerina with her ramrod-straight back, eagle eyes and hair the color of iron filings. Katie wanted to say something consoling, but the only thing she could think of was, 'Please give her my love.'

'I'll tell her, but she doesn't know who I am half the time.' Carmel turned away, pretending to admire the costumes hanging the length of the trailer. Fluorescent wings for the 'The Ugly Bug Ball', Grecian tunics for 'Delphic Dances', orange harem pants for 'Kismet', clouds of white tulle for 'Living Picture'. Olive had made every one, creating miracles with cheesecloth, cardboard and net. Cheap everyday materials that could be transformed into something more than they were under the magic of stage lights.

Katie raised her glass. 'Here's to Olive getting better.' She knew it wouldn't happen, but she said it anyway.

Her teacher lifted her tumbler, fingering the bouquet beside her. 'I love this time of year. Reminds me of the spring Olive took me to see Pavlova.'

Katie almost choked on her drink. 'You saw Pavlova?'

Her teacher smiled sadly and ran her hand over her bun. 'When I was ten. It ruined me for a normal life.'

'You never told me that before.'

'I must have told you I saw her do "The Dying Swan".'

Katie shook her head. 'I would have remembered if you had.'

'Maybe you were sick that day.'

Katie was confused. She had never missed one of Carmel's classes, not even when she'd had a broken arm.

'Olive had read in the paper that Pavlova's feet were insured for $50,000. A fortune in those days. She wanted to know what all the fuss was about so we piled in the Model T and drove out to Los Angeles.'

'You're kidding.'

'Nope. We saw her at the Alhambra Theater in 1924. The "Incomparable Pavlova" danced between a juggling act and a Chinese contortionist. The audience sat there eating popcorn like it was a circus.'

'Did she dance anything besides "The Dying Swan"?'

'The announcer came on to say she wasn't well, but that she refused to cancel. Her company danced two numbers without her, I can't remember what they were, but I remember everything about the "The Dying Swan".' Carmel half-closed her eyes. 'This tiny woman dressed in white floated in from the wings. She had her back to the audience as she rippled her arms. She looked like a human who'd been turned into a swan. She wasn't what you'd call beautiful, but you couldn't take your eyes off her. I cried through most of it, especially when she was shot and she sank to one knee. Her arms fluttered and her movements got slower and slower. She folded herself over her leg and her hands were still. There was silence for a second, then the house went wild. Absolutely wild. I don't think there was a dry eye in the house. Before you could say Jack Robinson, the stage was carpeted knee-deep in flowers.'

'I still don't understand why I didn't know you saw Pavlova dance.'

Carmel waved her hand. 'The other girls didn't know who she was. They didn't care.'

Her teacher was staring at the floor, weaving as she talked. Katie was starting to wonder if Carmel really had seen Pavlova or if she was telling her something she'd read in a book.

'Anyway, after her performance was over, I begged Olive to go to the stage door so I could get her autograph. There was a huge crowd that stretched halfway down the block. While we were waiting in line, I tried to dance like a swan. The next thing I knew, she was standing beside me.'

'Olive?'

'Pavlova. She bent over me, holding a big bouquet of flowers. "You want be ballet dancer, little one? I give advice. Nothing matter but dance. Nothing higher. Only God." She kissed me. Right there.' She pointed to her temple. 'Me. Little Carmel McCleary. I was so stunned I forgot to get her autograph, but I didn't care. Pavlova had kissed me. I didn't wash my face for a month.'

Carmel picked up the bottle of rum by its neck and took a swig. 'When we got home, I tried to dance around the farm like I'd seen her do. I put my shoes in tin cans I'd cut the tops off, pretending I was on *pointe*. Olive realized I was serious and asked around for a teacher. She found Reba Dean in El Paso and drove me once a week to her studio. I couldn't get to lessons often enough to be a pro so I decided to teach. Teach in the hope that, one day, a student of mine might move people the way Pavlova did.'

Katie watched her set the empty Bacardi bottle on the floor.

'We'll pay for that tomorrow, kid. Delayed after-effects.' Carmel slapped the floor. 'Listen to me blabbing. I haven't let you get a word in edgeways. What are you doing, hanging around Fortuna? You're like a rainbow trout. If you're out of the water too long, those beautiful stripes of yours will disappear.'

Katie reached into her coat pocket for the brochure she carried everywhere. 'I want to go to New York. I want to audition for a company.' As she was speaking, she noticed her voice was as slurred as Carmel's. 'But first I want to study at the School of American Ballet to get back into shape.'

'Can you afford to fly the coop?'

She shook her head. 'Daddy would pay for me, but Mom wouldn't let him. She's determined to make me to go to college. I'm going nuts here, Carmel. Nuts.'

'How much would it take? To go to New York.'
'I don't know. Never added it up.'
Carmel put her glasses on. 'Tuition's a hundred and three a month. And you'll need to live on top of that.' She started scribbling on the back of a program. 'The plane'll cost about eighty and fifty or so for expenses. A couple of hundred dollars for food and rent. You could get a job at Woolworths for pocket money.' She drew a line under the numbers and totaled them. 'I figure it'd take five hundred bucks to keep you going for a couple of months. In the meantime, you could dance and teach every day at the studio till you leave.'

Katie left the cotton trailer at one in the morning. She let out an Indian whoop as she wove down Main Street at ten miles an hour, hoping the police were on patrol in another part of town.
Nothing matters except dancing, Katie. Remember. Nothing matters except dancing.
In her mind's eye she saw Carmel hold up a pink check, all the lines filled in except the date.
You lose thirty-five pounds and this is yours. New York's a tough town. No point going till you're thin enough for them to spot what a great dancer you are.
But even if I drop the weight, Carmel, I don't have any way to pay you back.
I'm not interested in being paid back. You teach my girls and when you get down to your fighting weight, you'll make it in the Big Apple. I feel it in my bones. And when you do, it'll be the best five hundred bucks I've ever spent.

The Honeymoon Inn

Katie pushed her sunglasses on as she watched Joe disappear into the office. The Honeymoon Inn was so old it didn't even have a neon sign. Painted on either side of the door were faint pink hearts. Underneath one was *DOUBLE ROOMS $7.50*. Underneath the another, *FREE MORNING COFFEE*. A long time ago the *FREE* had been crossed out. She couldn't believe he'd driven straight from her house to a motel. She stared at the picnic basket on her lap, desperately trying to think of some way to stall him. She stabbed her hand with a plastic fork. She had wanted tonight to be special. She had wanted to do it in the moonlight with the river rushing past, not in this flea-pit on the ass-end of town.

The screen door swung open and Joe came out of the office, grinning. He jumped into the Jag and tossed a heart-shaped key ring onto her lap. 'The guy at the desk didn't even ask if we were married.'

She held up the plastic heart. 'But thirteen's an unlucky number.'

'It was the only vacancy he had.'

She lifted a drumstick wrapped in tinfoil. 'My Mom's made all this food. Why don't we go down to the Rio Grande first and have a picnic?'

'Are you loco? How can you think about chow at a time like this?'

She felt like he had slapped her. She wasn't even hungry; she was only suggesting a picnic because she was scared. She returned the drumstick to the basket, remembering this afternoon at the kitchen table, rolling chicken pieces in flour before her mother had fried them.

Men are not like women, Katie Scarlett. They're not happy unless their organ's happy. You enjoy your picnic, but keep both feet on the ground at all times. Don't let Joe try anything. Aunt Delta's first husband talked her into swimming naked with him in the clay pit. She was so naïve she eloped at seventeen because he told her that was how women got PG.

'Pee-jee? What's pee-jee?'

Pregnant. You may be an Honor Scholar, but you're piccaninny backwards as far as men are concerned.

174

THE DOUBLE HAPPINESS COMPANY

'What about a movie?' Katie blurted out. 'We're right next to the drive-in.'

'I'm not messing around in a back seat when I've just paid for a bed.'

He turned the key in the ignition and raced across the courtyard, the car throwing up a cloud of dust. He parked badly, then jumped out to unlock the motel door. 'Bring some Dixie cups,' he said before he disappeared inside.

She stayed where she was.

A minute later he came out. 'What are you sitting out there for? You're the one who suggested this.'

She didn't need him to remind her that she'd set tonight in motion. After Miss Chichester's visit, Katie had gone to see *Butch Cassidy and the Sundance Kid*. She'd sat in the Rio Grande Theater and watched Etta Place return to her farm house. Hiding in the shadows of her bedroom was the Sundance Kid, who forced her to undress at gunpoint. Katie had discovered at the end of the scene that he and Etta were lovers and it had all been a thrilling sexual game.

She'd come back from the movie, heart knocking, daisy aching, and immediately started a letter to Joe. *I don't know why I've been holding onto my virginity for so long. If you still want to go all the way, write and let me know.*

She'd walked straight to the mailbox before she'd had a chance to change her mind, but then Karolak had been a safe two thousand miles away.

When she entered the motel room, Joe was already half naked. He flashed his hairy chest at her and she looked away, embarrassed. She didn't know what to do. She'd never held hands with a boy, never even been kissed. She put the paper cups on the nightstand and picked up the Gideon Bible.

He jerked the curtains shut. 'Forget the Bible studies. I've driven fifty miles to see you, Katie. Won't be long till I have to get you home.'

She perched on the end of the bed. She watched as he unscrewed a bottle and handed her a cup of clear liquid. 'This isn't mescal, is it?'

He smiled his dazzling smile. 'It's gin.'

She took a sip. She hadn't eaten anything for two days and immediately felt the alcohol in her bloodstream. She threw back the rest. If she couldn't have moonlight and the river, then at least she could feel floaty with booze.

'Last time I saw you in bed,' he said, 'you showed me your leg.' He lifted her skirt and started to run his hand up her knee.

She dreaded him seeing the silvery stretch marks swimming up her thighs, the elastic panel in the Stork-A-Lure skirt. She pointed at the bedside lamp. 'Can we have that off?'

He clicked off the switch and unzipped his jeans. It was dusk, but there was still enough light to see his erection. She closed her eyes so she didn't have to see it poking at the ceiling, completely out of proportion to the rest of his body.

His jeans dropped to the floor. 'Let me see you naked.'

She felt ashamed, confused. Maybe all men made you take your clothes off in front of them, but it made her feel like a prostitute. She started to unbutton her blouse, slower than she'd ever unfastened one in her life.

'I'm waiting to see those beautiful breasts.'

'Could I have another drink first?'

'Sure, baby.'

Baby. He said it so tenderly. No one had ever called her that before. She was starting to feel a little more desirable as she unzipped her skirt. Underneath were the cobweb-lace panties she'd found in her mother's drawer. She'd been so nervous sneaking them out of the house, she'd forgotten to remove the sales tag. She was pulling it off the waistband when Joe snapped the light back on. That was when she noticed his pubic hair for the first time: a triangular, curly fan above his genitals, not growing out of his balls.

Joe walked over with a Dixie cup, his thing bobbing and nodding. She tried not to look at it and grabbed the cup from him to take a big sip. 'It's my first time,' she said.

He took her hand and kissed it. 'Believe me, popping a cherry's no big deal.' He pressed his cock against her and moaned a little. 'I'm gonna make a woman of you before midnight. How'd you like that?'

Having seen the size of his penis, she didn't like the idea at all, but she didn't want Joe to think she was a prude. 'Did you—' The words dried on her tongue. 'Did you . . . you know.'

'What?'

'Bring them.' She was hoping he hadn't remembered the condoms so she'd have an excuse to go home early.

He leaned over to pick up his jeans on the floor. She stared at his buttocks, the scooped-out muscles at the side as hard, if not as beautiful, as Nureyev's. He pulled a packet out of his back pocket, took the Trojan out of the foil. 'Putting on the rubber glove.'

She tried to cover herself with her arms. 'I'm not ready yet—'

He pushed her onto the mattress.

She lay in bed, listening to the cars clank across the metal plates of the drive-in. Wake up, she wanted to shout. Wake up and take me home! But at the same time afraid to go. Afraid she would walk differently, afraid her parents would know.

She put a hand at the delta of her thighs. She was still bleeding. He was hardly inside her when he came, moaning and pushing until she felt like she was tearing.

Lying next to her, he looked angelic, almost innocent. She inched out from under his thigh, praying he wouldn't wake up. She tiptoed to the basin, blood trickling down her thighs. For seven-and-a-half dollars the Honeymoon Inn didn't provide towels or paper-wrapped bars of soap. No bathtub or shower either, just a rust-stained sink. She felt dirty as she washed. Cheap. Last week when he had unexpectedly called to take her up on her offer, she should have been brave enough to tell him she'd changed her mind.

She went through his pockets, wondering why he'd thrown her onto the bed, why he hadn't stopped pushing into her when she'd told him it hurt. She took his car keys, then dug around inside her bag for a pen. She didn't have one, just a tube of Tangee lipstick. She wrote a message in orange letters on the mirror: *TOOK JAG. FIND IT, U BASTARD.*

She was in the middle of a barre when there was a knock on her door. Her mother shouted over the music, 'Sugar, Joe Karolak's here.'

She was so shocked she couldn't speak.

More knocking, impatient this time. 'Turn that record player off and let me in.'

'Tell him I'll call him sometime.'

'Unlock that door.'

'Can't stop now, *madre*. Say I'm practicing.'

Her mother's voice went up an octave. 'That boy's driven fifty miles to see you. Now unlock that door this instant.'

She punched a pillow before she walked over to let her mother in.

'He didn't exactly make an appointment.'

'What appointment are you talking about? He's here, Katie Scarlett, and you should be falling down on your knees.'

'For what?'

'He writes you from medical school. He took you on a picnic last week, not to mention that expensive box of chocolates he brought you when you were in Hotel Dieu.'

'I don't owe him anything just because he bought me some candy. I have to be out of here in an hour to teach at Carmel's.'

'He sent you that brochure you pore over night and day. He's more considerate of you than that damn Madame ever was. Now you throw a robe on and get out here. I want you to entertain him like the lady I brought you up to be.'

Vlad the Impaler was sitting in the living room in cutoffs and a T-shirt. Katie stood in the doorway, trying to figure out why he was here. He flashed his smile at her as though the night they'd spent together had been a success.

Her mother came in from the kitchen with a plate of Fritos and a bowl of dip the color of baby poo. 'It sure is nice of you to visit Katie so soon after your picnic.' Her mother put the dip and the bag of chips on the coffee table and grinned as he scooped a glob of sour cream laced with dried onion soup mix.

She's grateful to him, Katie thought. Grateful he took her fat daughter on a first date.

Her mother was signaling her to sit down. 'Don't stand way over there, sugar. With your faint little voice, you'll have to shout.'

Katie jerked her terry-cloth robe around her and fell onto the sofa, as far away from Karolak as possible.

'I was saying to Joe it sure is good to see him again.' Her mother girlishly tucked her hair behind her ear. 'I told him he was welcome here any time.'

He stood up and bowed like a Southern gentleman.

Katie wanted to puke.

'Next time you come courting, young man, visit the barber first. You look like a spaniel with that hair hanging down to your shoulders.'

He smiled. 'I've been meaning to do that for a few weeks, Mrs Rivers.'

'Well, I've got yard work to do. I'll leave you two young people alone. Hope I'll see more of you this summer, Joe.'

Having her mother around embarrassed her, but she felt even worse when the back door slammed and they were alone. They sat in silence for a long time, Vlad periodically trying his movie-star smile. When it didn't work, he slid closer.

'Get away from me, you jerk.'

'This is the age of Aquarius, Katie. You weren't expecting a marriage proposal, were you?'

'All I expected was you'd be gentle with someone who'd never done it before.'

He drew circles on the coffee table with his finger. She could see the shine of sweat above his lip.

'I didn't think you were interested in moonlight and roses and all that crap.'

'You never asked what I wanted. Did you think I was so desperate that all I deserved was a flophouse?'

'You said everyone in town knew your dad.'

'So?'

'At a place like that they wouldn't.'

She chewed her fingernail, considering what he'd just said.

'You really think I'm that stingy, Katie?'

'After the way you behaved, I don't know who you are anymore.'

A look of pain passed over his face. 'You didn't have to steal my car.'

'I didn't steal it, Karolak. I told you to find it.'

'You left the key in the ignition. Someone could have stolen it.'

'I wanted to get home.'

'I'd have brought you home any time you liked. Any time you asked.'

'You didn't stop when I asked.'

He ran his fingers through his hair. 'I'd waited years to go to bed with you. Once I was fired up, I couldn't find the brake. I like you,

Rivers. Liked you better than all the other girls I've ever met.' He dropped his head. 'I saw blood on the car seat and knew I owed you an apology. Sorry it's taken me a week to come see you.'

She looked at her feet and pointed them as hard as she could. 'You thought you were doing a fat girl a favor.'

'Katie, you're one of the most beautiful girls I've ever known. You've just got a warped idea of what you think your body should look like.' He slid a hand into his pocket and jingled his change just like her dad did when he was nervous. 'When you get to New York, you'll need someone to show you the ropes. Give me a call.'

'I wouldn't call you, Karolak, if you were the last man on earth.'

'Guess there's no chance of another date this summer?'

He looked so desperate, she suspected he must have been a virgin, just like her. She threw her head back and laughed. 'For another screw? Not on your sweet bippy.'

He scooped a handful of Fritos. 'If that's the way you feel, I'd better get going. Tell your mom I said goodbye. She's a nice lady.'

She stood at the door, watching him go. She didn't think Karolak would turn around, but when he got to his Jag, he waved. To her surprise, she found herself waving back.

She thought about the cobweb panties she'd had to burn, the basket of picnic food she'd had to dump. The potato salad, coleslaw and fried chicken had sunk without trace, but the Moon Pies had bobbed and floated, dancing in the dark, muddy water of the Rio Grande.

The hoop is broken

Lola watched her husband study the tango sheets taped to the living-room door. Following the complex footwork with his finger, he snaked from one footprint to the next. 'Can't make heads or tails of this diagram. It's busier than a cat trying to cover crap on a marble floor.'
Lola knew the sequence backward, but was pretending she didn't. She'd been nagging Haywood to learn ballroom dancing for years. He was a perfectionist like Katie. Lola had to make him think he outshone her on the dance floor or he'd give up.
'To hell with it,' he said. 'I don't care how we get back to promenade position. Put the platter on, Lo. Let's burn up the rug.'
She lowered the needle and curved one hand around her husband's neck. The introduction to 'Fernando's Hideaway' crackled through the console speakers. 'Push me where I'm supposed to go, hon,' she said. 'I'll do the best I can.'
She tried to follow his lead as he tangoed awkwardly across the floor, but she couldn't. 'Haywood Amory Rivers, you're supposed to dance on the beat, not in between the cracks.'
'Hang the damn beat, Lo. Dip's coming up.'
He tipped her backward till her head almost touched the floor. Giggling, she pulled herself up and flicked her leg around his, imitating a picture she'd seen in a women's magazine.
Last week at the hairdressers she'd read an article she wouldn't normally have given a second glance to. She wasn't the kind of woman who tore pages out of beauty-parlor magazines, but she'd brought home '12 Hints To Keep Your Husband From Straying' and hidden it in her Kotex box.

1. Write your mother-in-law for your husband's favorite recipes.
2. Apply face creams AFTER your husband has gone to work.
3. Greet your spouse with his slippers and a highball on the rocks.
4. Take up the tango to inject passion into a listless love life.

She'd always been afraid of losing her husband to someone with smaller hips, a bigger bust. Someone with a college degree and no shameful Indian blood. Maggie Hubbard and Hay were to compete in a Duplicate Bridge tournament in Albany in the spring. The number of times he'd been mentioning his partner lately, Lola knew she'd better pull her socks up. Hay and Maggie were competitive Life Masters so Lola didn't think any mattress mambo was going on, but last night when he'd come back from the office, she'd given him a glass of Mogen David. Instead of racing off to do the crossword after dinner, Haywood had crept into her bed for the first time in months.

Katie stood in the doorway, watching her parents dance cheek-to-cheek like teenagers. They looked so happy she dreaded telling them about the ticket to LaGuardia hidden in her purse. She cleared her throat and mumbled over the scratchy music, 'I'm going on a trip.'

Her mother stopped dancing immediately. 'What?'

Katie dropped her eyes. 'I'm going to New York City tomorrow.'

'For how long?'

'Maybe for good.'

Her father's hand fell from her mother's waist. He sat on the piano bench, arms crossed over his stomach as if someone had punched him in the guts.

Her mother marched to the console. The needle skidded across the record twice before she managed to snap it into its cradle. 'And what do you think you're going to live on, young lady?'

'I've got five hundred dollars.'

Her mother looked at her as if she'd stolen her 'mad money', a wad of bills she'd buried in a jar in the back yard for emergencies. 'How did you manage to save that on your allowance?'

'That's my business.'

Her mother jabbed a finger at her father. 'You gave her money so she can run away.'

'No,' Katie said. 'Daddy didn't know anything about it. I'm doing this on my own.'

'How long do you think five hundred dollars will last?'

'I've worked out it will last three months, Daddy. By that time I'll be in a ballet company.'

'Three weeks is more like it,' her mother said, 'then you'll crawl back home with your tail tucked between your legs.'

'I won't.'

'You'll have to, young lady,' her mother said, 'because you're a piddly high-school graduate not trained to do a damn thing.'

'I've been training since I was five years old!'

The front door swung open and her brother stepped into the living room. 'What's all the yelling about?' he said. 'I could hear you guys halfway down the block.'

'Your sister's leaving home.' Her father's voice was wobbling.

Her mother stamped her foot. 'Over my dead body she is.'

'Lo, shouting doesn't do any good.'

'Then talk some sense into her. She's gumptionless. She'll never make it in a big city like New York.'

'Cool down, *madre*,' Rhett said. 'If she'd been drafted, you'd be sending her off with a brass band.'

Her mother raised her hand like she was going to slap him. 'Shut your mouth. Your sister does not have to go to New York.'

'I do too,' Katie said. 'It's the dance capital of the world.'

Her mother whipped around, a look of jubilation on her face. 'How will you compete with girls who don't have anything wrong with their knees?'

Katie covered her ears, shaking. 'Stop it. Stop it!'

Her father stepped between them. 'Lola, that wasn't necessary.'

'Nineteen-year-olds don't leave home unless they're going to college!'

She watched as her father pulled her mother into the den and shut the door. Katie ran over and pressed her ear against the wood. She could hear her mother shouting.

'Somebody has to make her see sense. For once in your life, Hay, back me up!'

Her father said something she couldn't hear, then her mother said, 'She has no business being in New York. The only place she's fit for is Podunk Creek.'

'She's not going to change her mind, Lola, so I suggest we go out there and make the most of the time that's left. Come on.'

'I'll never forgive you for being a coward, Haywood. Not as long as I live!'

Katie ran into the living room where her brother was flicking through a comic. A few seconds later her father came in, followed by her mother.

'You walk out that door tomorrow, Katie Scarlett, and you'll pay your own way. You'll starve before you get one red cent from us.'

Her father put a hand on her arm. 'Lo, don't say something you'll regret.'

'I hope you're proud of yourselves,' her mother screamed. 'I hope you're proud of busting this family in two!'

Katie sat on the garage floor, rearranging the contents of her crammed suitcase. She wished she hadn't said anything. She should have left a note on the table and hitchhiked to the airport, rather than have a fight which had made her so upset she'd thrown up twice.

The door creaked and she froze, certain it was her mother coming to yell at her, but it was Rhett holding a Twinkie. He took a bite, swallowed and said, 'Want to spend your last night driving around?'

He went down Main Street, past Alameda Elementary and Pioneer Park and the County Court House. Past Thomas Branigan Memorial Library, the Carver Building and the Fashion Shoe Store whose slogan was WE GIVE YOU FITS. Past Merry-Go-Round, Dutch's Meat Market, Monsimer's Bakery, the Music Box. Past Price's Dairy with the huge plaster milk bottle sitting on the roof and the asparagus-green building opposite it, Carmel McCleary's School of The Dance. Rhett didn't say what he was doing, but he was showing her landmarks so she could take them away in her head.

They drove past the pink palm of Orbalee's sign and Katie rolled down the window to feel the night air rush past her arm. She was thinking what her mother had said before her father had pulled her out of the living room. *I hope you're proud of busting this family in two.*

'Want me to do a U, sis?' her brother asked.

'What for?'

'So you can get a prediction before you fly off into the wild blue yonder.'

Their laughter spilled out the open windows. She didn't need

Orbalee to tell her this would be the last night they'd spend together for a long, long time.

They drove down Picacho Boulevard lined with flashing neon: Sands Motel, Apache Motel, Del Prado Motel. Just before they crossed the Rio Grande, they passed the last motel before the desert, the only one without a neon sign. After what had happened at the Honeymoon Inn, she still couldn't find it in her heart to forgive Karolak, but she had to give him credit for driving a hundred miles to apologize.

Rhett speeded up when he passed the rusty sign marking the city limits. A few miles later they were at the iron arch of Comanche Creek Ranch. Her brother swung off the highway under its huge curve and drove down an unpaved road, throwing up dust.

'Where are we going, Rhett?'

'Doesn't matter.'

They drove another mile or so in silence before her brother parked near an old windmill. She looked at the four ladder-like legs below the metal blades. The old Zephyr reminded her of a huge pinwheel.

Rhett got out of the truck first and she followed, clapping wildly. He looked at her like she was crazy. 'Where do you think you are? A recital?'

'Daddy told me noise frightens rattlesnakes.'

'It's December first, Katie. The diamondbacks are hibernating.' He knelt at the base of the windmill and made a circle in the dirt as big as a hula hoop.

'What are you doing?' she asked.

'Nanna told me the power of the world is in a circle. Everything in nature is round. When you break a circle, it becomes a line with a beginning and an end.'

He suddenly kicked the hoop and she had to cover her eyes. 'Jesus, Rhett. I wear contacts.'

He stuck his tongue out like he used to when he was little.

'You're mad at me, aren't you?' she said. 'For leaving.'

His eyes returned to the sand ring before he headed off into the desert with a flashlight.

'Hey,' she said, 'where are you off to?'

'I'm going to make a fire. Find some tinder.'

He disappeared into the hip-high forest of creosote. The bushes were so evenly spaced they looked like a man-made orchard. She listened to the lonely squeak of the windmill's blades as she looked around for something to start the fire. She didn't want to walk into the *bajada* and stumble into a cactus because she didn't have any light.

She noticed some big tumbleweeds caught in the base of the Zephyr. She pulled them out of the struts and started to snap their branches into pencil-sized pieces.

By the time she had finished, her brother was back, carrying an armload of wood. He put the broken-up tumbleweeds into the middle of the hoop, then broke up some creosote branches to stick in the sand to form a teepee of twigs. He lit them and added more wood until there was a blaze. 'Do you remember the redheaded guy who used to come by on a chopper?'

'The one with a pigtail?'

Rhett nodded. 'DD Striker. He's dead.'

'Oh my God. DD's dead?'

He kept staring into the fire. 'He was about to come home from Nam.'

'Rhett, I'm so sorry.'

He shot up and walked back to the pickup. She watched him lift a coat hanger from the gun rack and start tearing it apart. There wasn't any point in trying to get him to talk about DD. Her brother liked to keep his cards close to his chest.

She watched him lean over and pull something out of the bed of the truck. 'Catch,' he said and threw a package at her. Holding the bag of Kraft marshmallows, she now knew why he'd told her to stay in the cab when they'd stopped at the grocery. He knew how much she loved toasting them. This was his little surprise.

He passed the straightened hanger to her and she speared a marshmallow onto the end. She turned the white pillow of sugar over the flames, watching it darken and melt. She was touched by his kindness toward her when he'd just found out about his friend's death. 'Remember how we used to pretend we were Apaches?'

'It was the only thing we ever did together,' he said.

She took out her wallet to show him a photograph she'd added this afternoon. Rhett in his Superman costume, standing next to the huge box their Frigidaire refrigerator had been delivered in, a makeshift nose cone taped to the top. 'Remember how I teased you for thinking you could fly to the moon in that?'

'Took me hours to cover it in ten layers of tinfoil. Didn't want to be burned up on re-entry.'

She smiled as she tucked her wallet into her purse.

'Know something, Katie? Even though you were always a weirdnik, we both wanted the same thing.'

'And what's that?'

'To fly. Me as an astronaut and you as a dancer.'

It was one of the nicest things he'd ever said to her. She could feel tears coming and was thankful for the dark.

Her brother pointed above his head. 'Over there is the Buffalo and that's the Horse. Nanatasis said they travel across the heavens and leave footprints in the sky.'

Nibbling her marshmallow to make it last as long as possible, she walked to the windmill. She gazed at the Mesilla Valley, trying to picture how huge New York must be if her pint-sized hometown looked so big at night.

Her brother aimed his flashlight at her, making loops in the air. 'You know the first thing I'm going to do when you're gone? Move into your room. I've been sleeping on that shitty Hide-A-Bed for almost two years.'

He swept his arm across the horizon, taking in the sagebrush and yuccas of the *bajada*, the ridges of the mountains that looked like organ pipes. 'What is out there is in you. How can you leave, Katie? The desert is so goddamn beautiful.'

She said, 'I can't wait to get out of here.'

'I'll bet a hundred bucks you love it without even knowing it.'

She said, 'Quit talking crap.'

'Nanatasis told me if you know where home is, you know everything.'

Mutual of Omaha

Lola had been awake all night. Through the wall she heard Haywood snoring. Katie is leaving home because of your gutlessness, she thought, and you're sleeping like a knot on a log. She jerked the quilt off the bed and wrapped it around her as she moved down the hallway.

At the end of the corridor she cracked open her daughter's door. She'd done this hundreds of times. This would be the last. Stop it, she told herself. Stop it. You can cry when she is gone.

She picked up an old music box on the bookshelf and took it into the kitchen. She held it in her lap, remembering how she'd come to own the one box she hardly ever played.

Her eldest sister, Gertrude, had been ill with typhoid fever the time her father had come home from town with a dollhouse that had different wallpaper in every room. Lola had never owned anything nicer than a corncob doll and she'd cried and cried when the dollhouse had disappeared into Gertrude's sickroom.

Lola remembered telling her cat that she wanted to take the fever too so she would get a present like that. She prayed and prayed and, in a few days, her wish came true. She caught the typhoid and became so ill her hair fell out.

One day everyone started to tiptoe around the house and speak in whispers. Lola didn't understand what was happening until her father lifted her out of bed. 'I want to show you something.'

He carried her into the room where her sister was sleeping. A sheet was over Gertrude's face. He pulled it back. Her sister was lying very still, pretending to be a statue. She was wearing her white Easter dress and white patent-leather shoes. She had pennies over her eyes. Lola thought it was part of a game. Any minute she expected her to sit up and shout 'Boo!'

Her father wiped his face. 'The owl hooted last night, Lola Mae. He came for little Gertrude. She was nine years, nine months and twenty-three days old.'

Lola was confused. She had no idea that her sister was so sick or that typhoid fever could kill you or that her father had bought Gertrude the dollhouse because he was afraid she was dying.

A few days later the dollhouse disappeared, and her father came home from town with a music box. *Gertrude was so sick, Lola Mae, and we were so busy we missed your seventh birthday.*
She wound up the old music box and listened to the sad, tinkly music. She didn't have any memories of Gertrude except what she had looked like under that sheet. She'd never wept for her sister; she'd been too young, but in grieving for her daughter's leaving, it was as if she was losing Gertrude for the first time.

Katie wore a red knit midi-skirt, yellow leg-of-mutton blouse and a paisley bolero to the airport. She'd made it herself from a *Vogue* pattern. Even though the under-bust waistband was too tight, she felt elegant now that she could squeeze into a size 10 again.
She picked up the new suitcase she'd bought with her graduation money, KR in curly decals on each catch. Staggering, she headed toward a gift shop where her brother was window-shopping. 'Where's *madre y padre?*' she asked.
'He's checking if he locked the car. She's putting quarters into a Mutual of Omaha machine to insure your life in case of a crash.'
She rolled her eyes. 'Why does she try to turn everything into a disaster?'
'Because she lies on the bottom of the ocean and twitches. Ma's a nervous—'
'Wreck. Very funny.' She looked at her watch. 'It's almost two. It'll be time to board soon.'
'You and Mom go to the gate. I'll wait for Dad here. He's probably bawling in the parking lot.'

Katie sat in her seat, looking out the plane window as the crew prepared for take-off. She was thinking about the drive to the airport. In fifty miles, no one had said anything. She didn't know what was worse, the screaming or the silence.
A steward bolted the cabin door. As the jet taxied to the runway, it suddenly hit her that she was leaving. Leaving her family, Burrito, Carmel, Jack and Rosalia. Everyone she had ever known or loved. She strained to see her family standing in the window of the departure lounge. Crying, she flattened her hand against the pane, thinking if they could see anything, she wanted them to see that.

NEW YORK, 1971

The city seen for the first time, in its first wild promise of all the mystery and beauty in the world.

F SCOTT FITZGERALD

Dymphna's, W 14th Street

It was an austere building, sandwiched between a driving school and the red-gloss façade of the Ace Chop Suey House. It had two entrances: an ornate door on the first floor and a plain, narrow one at basement level. Katie chose the grander of the two and struggled up the steps with her suitcases to rap the lion-headed knocker.

A tiny nun cracked open the door. Seeing her luggage, the nun jabbed a finger toward the basement. 'If you want accommodation, go to the other entrance. This one is for the sisters.' The door slammed in her face.

Katie staggered down with her bags and pressed the bell. The name on the paper she'd been given was Dymphna's, but on the lintel it said *ST DYMPHNA'S HOME FOR FRIENDLESS WOMEN*. She felt like a homeless puppy, but seeing the real name carved above her head made her laugh out loud.

Her first two nights she'd stayed at the Barbizon Hotel on 63rd Street and Lexington Avenue but, at twenty dollars a day, she had to find somewhere cheaper if Carmel's money was going to last. She was about to press the bell again when a hunchbacked woman appeared at the door. *BERLA* was embroidered in clumsy letters above her left breast.

'What do youse want?'

'I'm looking for a place to live,' Katie said.

'Sister Augustine is who youse need to talk to. She's handing out pills on the other side.'

Berla abandoned her to flop into a pumpkin-colored chair at the far end of the room, her scowling face inches from the TV.

Wondering what the 'other side' was, Katie picked up her her bags and went inside. The waiting area was furnished with sagging chairs, religious magazines and some miserable-looking ferns. Beyond the half-wall was a dining hall which smelled of cabbage and boiled meat.

Seeing how devoted Berla was to *As The World Turns*, Katie decided to wait for a commercial break to speak to her again. When a housewife appeared pinning up laundry, Katie asked politely, 'How much does it cost to live here?'

'Don't pay no rent,' the woman said.
'Pardon?'
'I just told youse. I don't pay no rent.'
'How long have you lived here?'
'I been at St Dymphna's twenty-one years.' She picked up the hem of her dress and held it in front of her, a curved sail of blue polyester knit. 'Sister Virginella made me this. It was the color of Mother Mary's robe when she was assumpted into heaven.'

Panting from the weight of her suitcases, Katie followed Sister Augustine's manlike shoes up three flights of stairs. The nun opened a door off a gloomy landing. Katie's stomach dropped when she looked inside. Four of everything: beds, wardrobes, nightstands.

'Rent is $18 a week, payable in advance. It includes breakfast which is served at seven thirty. Cornflakes and toast every day, boiled eggs every other day and bacon on Sundays. Father Patrick says Mass at seven, except on Sundays and holy days when he starts at eight.' Sister Augustine folded her arms, impatient for an answer.

Katie looked at the hospital-like beds hugging the sides of the long room. The space in the middle between them was long enough to practice in. 'I'll take it.'

The sister carefully counted the dollar bills Katie handed to her, then pointed at the bare mattress closest to the door. 'You're expected to make your bed every morning and keep your part of the dormitory tidy. If you bring food into the building, it must be eaten in the basement dining room. Absolutely no food or visitors upstairs. Cooking and smoking is strictly forbidden. It's against city fire regulations. St Dymphna's is a women's residence, not a post office. You can receive letters, but not parcels. All washing must be done off the premises, including hose and underwear. There are no sink plugs so don't ask for any. Lights out at eleven o'clock. Is that understood?'

Katie nodded. This bleak room wasn't a place she'd choose to live unless she had to, but it would do. It was better than spending the night on a bench in Grand Central Station. 'What about keys?'

'There are no internal locks.'

'But how do I get inside the building?'

'Berla's on the basement door till ten o'clock.'

'But what if I need to come in later?'

Sister Augustine gave her a look of scarcely-concealed disgust. 'A nun always sleeps by the convent door entrance. In our order, no one is refused admittance at any hour.' She flicked a hand in the direction of Katie's suitcases. 'Mother Superior expects her rent on time. You'll get one warning if you're late. If the arrears aren't paid within a day, your belongings will be put on the street.' Her lips parted in a half-smile, as if the thought of an eviction cheered her. She headed for the door, skirts swirling. 'And no undressing unless the blinds are drawn. There's been a peeping Tom on the fire escape.'

The first thing Katie did after Sister Augustine left was raise the blinds. Filmy windows looked onto brick walls and clotheslines hung with nuns' habits and flapping sheets.

She sat on the bed and opened her purse. Inside was a bubble-wrapped cactus in a plastic pot. Rhett had pushed it into her hands at the departure gate. *This is to remind you of where you're from.* She put it on her bedside table, along with her icon. In new territory you needed to have landmarks.

She picked up the old cardboard suitcase her father had insisted on giving her at the airport. He'd made her promise she wouldn't open it until she'd found a place to live. Katie took the key he'd given her and fitted it into the catch. Inside was her Aunt Delta's sealskin fur. She lifted it out and twirled around the room. The cuffs and hem were balding, but she loved it because it made her feel like a ballerina. She stroked the collar, still fragrant from the perfume her aunt had always worn. The smell of Chanel No. 5 made her want to cry.

She ran her hands down the front of the coat and felt something crackle inside the breast pocket. Sealed in an envelope were two one-hundred-dollar bills and a note from her father. *Momma said to give you the coat because it's cold in New York, but don't tell her about the money.*

'Thank you, Daddy. Thank you!' She put the coat on and galloped the length of the dorm. A hundred and forty-seven dollars of Carmel's money was gone, but the extra cash would mean she could concentrate on taking classes and getting into shape. Not have to worry about a part-time job, at least not for a couple of months. With any luck, she'd be in a ballet company by then anyway.

Thrilled by the coat and the cash, she opened her Samsonite suitcase and took out a dozen pairs of satin *pointe* shoes. She'd never owned so many new ones all at once. She held one against her cheek, drinking in its smell. She felt like Pavlova who'd buy a hundred pairs at a time. When a shipment arrived, Pavlova would be as excited as a child, her dressing room littered with slippers while she tried on every pair. Some would fit perfectly, others she'd toss aside as unwearable. Every one was different because they were all handmade, just like the ones on her dormitory bed.

She pounded a pair on the floor to break in the vamps before she sewed on the ribbons. The boxes were like coffins to dance in until they were properly softened. She cut the ribbons and folded over the edges twice, stitching the shiny fabric at an angle so the grosgrain would remain flat when they were tied around her ankle.

She was attaching the last ribbon when she jabbed her finger. A drop of blood blossomed on the tip. She smiled, pressing it into the back of her slipper, making a small red flower on the canvas. Ballerinas believed it was good luck to prick yourself while preparing new *pointe* shoes.

She walked around the dorm on half toe, letting the slippers soften and mold themselves to her feet. When the soles were pliable enough, she switched on her tape recorder. She held onto the bottom of her bed and gave herself a barre: *pliés, tendus, dégagés, ronds de jambe, grands battements*. After half an hour she was dripping with sweat, muscles ready to rehearse her favorite variation which began with a whirlwind of spinning hops. The Act II solo from *Giselle* was the one she intended to perform as her audition piece for American Ballet Theater.

She made the sign of the cross and took the opening pose. The manic music began and she started whirling for twelve counts in a series of *temps levé sur place*. She loved this step: her leg waist-high in arabesque, her arms extended like wings and, what was even better, it was on her good leg so she could throw herself into the spin without fear of falling. The *glissades* and *sissonnes* didn't push her knee too much and, like most solos, it was short, only a minute long.

She did the *piqué* arabesque at the end of the variation and stayed on *pointe* for what felt like forever. Coming out of the pose, she was startled to hear clapping. A woman with a badly-bruised face was standing in the doorway. '*Que bailen, que bailen!*'

Katie picked up a towel to wipe herself, honored the stranger had asked her to keep dancing.

The woman put her hands on her heart and shivered. 'When I see you, you are like ghost. I feel I can put my fingers through you, even when I see you with my own eyes. You dance and I feel I see your soul.' She opened her purse, pulled out some cigarettes and tapped two from the pack. *'Bailarina, bienvenida a San Dymphna.* I am Constanza. My bed beside you.'

'Katie.' She smiled nervously, remembering Sister Augustine's rant about fire regulations. 'Thanks, but I'm not a smoker.'

Constanza walked across the room and opened the window. She lit her cigarette and fanned the smoke with her hand.

Katie held onto the wall as she sprang onto the tips of her toes a dozen times to cool down. 'What do you do?'

'I cleaner at Macy's. My shift start early. Today when I come back and hear music, I think spy must be in *dormitorio*. Sisters look for wet laundry and cigarettes when people no here.'

'The nuns go through people's closets?'

'*Si*. But we take turn hiding things on different floors so they cannot find so easy.'

'Is that the "other side"?'

Constanza shook her head. 'Is where ladies live who have babies with no father.'

Katie was only half listening to what her roommate was saying because she'd just noticed blood on her *pointe* shoes.

'Aieeee,' Constanza said when she saw the stains. 'Why that happen? You dance so nice on your toes.'

Katie unlaced her shoes to inspect her blisters. 'I'll have to soak my feet in salt water to toughen them up, but the nun said there weren't any plugs.'

Constanza smiled and opened her wardrobe. Covered by a jumble of sweaters was a large pot and a Sterno stove. 'Every night I cook. Is too 'spensive to eat out.'

Constanza left the dormitory with the pan, returning with it half filled with warm water. She handed Katie a canister of salt hidden in a boot. 'For your toes.'

Katie wanted to hug her. 'You're really sweet, Constanza, but won't you get into trouble?'

She took a long pull on her cigarette and blew smoke out the side of her mouth. '*Es verdad*, but life she is trouble, no?'

Katie tipped a stream of salt into the water, then dipped in her finger to taste.

Constanza cocked her head to one side. 'How many years have you, *bailarina*?'

She hesitated for a second before putting her feet into the water. 'Eighteen.' She'd have to get used to lying about her age if she was going to join a ballet company, subtracting the year and a half she'd lost with her knee.

Katie chose an empty table at the far end of the dining room for her first breakfast at St Dymphna's. She would have liked to eat with Constanza, but she'd left for work at six. Except for Berla, Katie didn't know anyone else at the residence; the other two beds in her dorm weren't occupied.

She was pouring milk on her cornflakes when she noticed an elderly woman in a jade-green turban leave the line with her tray. The woman's head was jiggling like she was listening to some music playing inside her head.

'You must be new here,' the woman said, banging her tray down. She lowered the plastic bag she was carrying and groaned as she eased herself into the chair.

Katie nodded, hoping the old lady would take the hint that she wanted to eat in silence.

'Mary Doyle's the name. Where are you from?'

'New Mexico,' she mumbled.

'What'd you say?'

'New Mexico.'

The woman squinted at her. 'You don't look dark enough for a Mexican.'

'I'm from New Mexico.'

'Do they have houses out there?'

Katie stared at the woman's dirty turban. 'Of course they do.'

'And here's me thinking they lived in little dugouts in the sand. What brings you to St Dymphna's?'

'I'm a ballet dancer.'

Mary lifted her nose in the air. 'Not the first ballerina we've had here and you won't be the last.'

Katie looked at her wilting cornflakes and picked up her spoon.

'I didn't see you at Mass this morning.'

'I'm not a Catholic.'

'Then why'd you come to St Dymphna's?'

'It's all I can afford.'

Mary Doyle reached down beside her chair and took a cookie tin out of the plastic bag. She hit it like a drum. 'Know what's in here? Newspaper clippings of rapes and murders, some of them not two blocks from here. I keep them to show greenhorns like you.'

Katie pushed her chair away as the old woman pointed to the untouched food on her tray. 'You're not having that then?'

'I'm not hungry.'

Mary swooped on Katie's egg and toast. 'Think of all those black babies starving in Biafra.'

Lightning

The fourth floor studio was as spare and plain as a Shaker church: bare, high windows, unadorned walls and a baby grand piano. So different from Carmel McCleary's School of The Dance with its rag rug, Bogen record player and cheesecloth curtains.

Morelli's Ballet Studios was a walk-up on the corner of West 14th Street and 6th Avenue, only minutes from St Dymphna's. Morelli's had three studios and what surprised Katie most was the size of the biggest one, only a third as large as Carmel's barnlike space in the desert. Seventeen dancers had already squeezed into the long, narrow room and more were arriving.

She was still cold from pacing outside for the last half hour, trying to find the courage to go upstairs. She was fifteen pounds overweight and scared of reinjuring her weak knee. She stood in the corner, as far away as possible from the mirrors that ran the length of one wall. The last three months she'd been taking daily lessons at Carmel's, but she hadn't been to a professional class for almost two years.

As she warmed up, she realized she was surrounded by dancers from some of the biggest companies in New York. She knew who they were because she read *Dance Magazine* every month. Compared to these paper dolls, she felt enormous in her bulky sweater and baggy sweat pants. Her lone attempt at glamor was the wire spray of cut-glass chips she'd pinned in her hair.

A man with a body that looked like a Michelangelo sculpture pushed in front of her at the barre. He gave her a look as if to say, This is my spot, fat girl. Find somewhere else. She nearly fainted when she recognized him: Jan Koenig, principal dancer from the Harkness Ballet.

Just before class was due to start, Madame Demidenkova walked into the room, a wooden stick in one hand and a watering can in the other. She was old and plump and one of the most famous teachers in New York. Madame moved around the packed room, sprinkling the planks so their feet wouldn't slip.

She walked to the grand piano when she'd finished wetting the floor and clapped her hands twice. 'Boys and girls, we do *plié*. First and second position *demi, demi,* two *grands*. Second same with *cambré* to barre. Fourth with *cambré derrière*. Fifth same with *cambré* away from barre and take pose like so.' She demonstrated how she wanted the arms positioned in the balance, then turned toward the pianist to set the tempo. 'Eee one, eee two—'

The pianist played an introduction. Katie quickly made the sign of the cross as the other dancers moved their arms from fifth *en bas* to second. Katie knew her bad knee would be okay at the barre; it was the jumping in the center she was worried about.

'Push heel forward more,' Madame said as she walked past. 'Perfect turnout for perfect *plié*.'

The professionals treated the class as a workout, but to Katie it was a chance to perform. The pianist was playing soaring music: Brahms, Bach, Schubert, Prokofiev. Though she felt cowed by the presence of so many company members, she let the music move through her, phrasing every movement as if she were on center stage.

Exercise followed exercise. Condensation fogged the mirrors and cried down the glass. After *grands battements,* sweating dancers moved the portable barres to the sides of the room. Madame stood at the front and took fifth position. She called out the steps, her elegant hands dancing the combination. 'For *adage,* boys and girls, we do *grand plié, développé* left *à la seconde, demi rond de jambe en dedans* to *croisé devant. Promenade en dedans in tour lent* to end facing 1. *Relevé* on supporting leg and close *croisé. Développé* right *à la seconde* and *promenade en dedans* to face front. *Fondu* on left, *pas de bourrée en tournant* to fourth. Finish with pirouette *en dehors,* double pirouette *en dedans,* arms fifth high.'

The teacher's falcon eyes swept the room. The few dancers wearing sweat pants removed them; Katie was the only one who kept hers on. She prayed that Madame wouldn't ask her to take them off or she'd have the humiliation of looking at her piano legs for the next forty minutes.

Madame divided the students: principals in the first row, soloists in the second and open class members in the third. The first group did the *adage* while the others waited at the back. They moved off to the sides when they finished, followed by the second and third groups.

Madame stood at the front of the classroom, calling out corrections.

'Hip over foot in *promenade*. *Développé écarté derrière* eee *plié*. Use mirror to check line.'

They did *battements tendus, battements fondus* at 90 degrees, a *grand adagio* and several combinations of *petit allegro*. Katie performed the smaller jumps, but when everyone started to do steps landing on one leg, she hid at the back. She could do jumps from two feet to two feet and many of the ones from two feet to one foot. It was the big jumps, the ones that turned in the air or landed on her bad knee that terrified her. It depressed her to watch the other dancers moving with abandon when she was forced to hold back.

Madame Demidenkova set a grand allegro of *sissonnes, glissades* and *grands jetés en tournant*. Before the first group started she said, 'When you jump, do not sit in *plié*. Spend more time in air and less on floor. Be like great Nijinsky who go up and stay like bird. What is ballet without jumping? Nothing. Ballet dancer is creature of air.'

Katie's group moved forward to perform, but she stood at the back. She had once been daring, wild, her jumps almost as high as a man's. Jealously, she watched a young principal from the New York City Ballet, her body arcing upward in breathtaking jumps, Madame banging her stick on the floor and shouting, 'Up, up, Gelsey, maximum high!'

After all three groups had completed the *enchaînement*, Madame talked them through a combination that ended with a multiple turn. Koenig did five pirouettes, throwing off perspiration like a soaked dog. He landed in a perfect fourth, his hands turning up as if to say how easy it was.

Madame saw him admiring his reflection and clicked her tongue. 'Open soul, Jan,' she said, beating her chest. 'Dancing comes from God. Give yourself to something higher, otherwise better to be weightlifter.'

At the end of the class, Madame indicated a series of turns from the corner, ending in a pose in *piqué* arabesque. The air was rank with sweat as the class lined up, two by two, to do the exercise diagonally across the floor.

Katie stood behind her partner. It was her first chance in the center to dance full out. She could throw herself into the combination because there wasn't any jumping. Exhilarated, she spun across the floor, giving the exercise two hundred percent. She and her partner had reached the corner when she heard Madame Demidenkova call out, 'Your name?'

Thinking she meant her partner, Katie didn't turn around.
'Girl in rubber shower curtains. Show them how to do, not just with legs, but with *sirtsa*.' She beat her chest with her fist. 'With heart.'

She ran all the way back to St Dymphna's. She felt like screaming to everyone she passed, Madame Demidenkova singled me out! She singled me out to demonstrate!

She skipped down the basement steps, rang the bell and waited to be let in. When Berla opened the door, Katie kissed her on both cheeks, whooped and bolted up the stairs. She reached her landing and heard someone crying in her dorm. Katie slowly opened the door. In the middle of the floor was a sobbing girl, an open suitcase and a bouquet of peacock feathers. She lifted her head and they stared at each other for a few seconds. The girl's shocked face looked half familiar, but Katie couldn't place her.

She started to howl even louder.

It didn't seem right to intrude on someone who was so upset so Katie backed out again. She didn't feel like a walk or watching soap operas in the basement with Berla. The only place left for her to go was the bathroom.

Katie took a pen and crumpled letterhead out of her purse and sat on the toilet lid. Long-distance calls were expensive and she was too proud to call home collect.

December 8, 1971

Dear Mom, Dad and Rhett,

A note from the Big Apple to let you know I arrived safely. Flying into LaGuardia saw the Statue of Liberty from the air! Despite the note paper I'm not staying at 'New York's Most Exclusive Hotel Residence for Young Women'. I've found a place on West 14th Street which is only $18 a week and includes breakfast.

Katie could hear the new girl making weird squealing sounds. If she didn't stop making so much noise, Sister Augustine would stomp up the stairs and scream at her to stop.

Had my first class today at Morelli Studios. Even though the room was full of stars from Harkness and NYC Ballet, Madame Demidenkova asked me to demonstrate! That's a good sign so I'm planning to audition for ABT before too long.

Katie heard someone come in. She jumped when the handle of her toilet door was rattled.

'Come out,' a voice pleaded. 'I'm Nadia. I heard you come in here. One of the nuns told me you're a dancer. I need to talk to someone before I go nuts.'

Katie took her to Sutter's on Greenwich Avenue, a mom-and-pop place where you could sit and drink pots of lemon tea without having to order a meal.

Nadia lit a cigarette, tipped her chin up and blew a smoke ring. 'I've only been in that residence a few hours and already I hate the place.'

Katie looked at her new roommate. She coveted the flat-topped Russian hat she was wearing. It made her look like a ballerina, incredibly glamorous and chic.

'It's grody compared to where I used to live. St Dymphna's like the crap school I went to in Seattle full of bitter, old nuns.' Nadia ground out her cigarette. Little gulping sobs started to escape from her mouth.

Katie pulled a napkin out of the dispenser and offered it to her. 'Want to tell me what happened?'

'God, I wish I hadn't been so stupid.' She took the napkin and blew her nose. 'I had a scholarship for the last two years at the School of American Ballet and they dumped me yesterday.'

Katie felt her jaw fall open. Remembering where she'd seen Nadia before, she unzipped her bag and took out her SAB brochure. On the cover were three lean girls in leotards. 'That's you in the middle, isn't it?'

A tearful look crossed Nadia's face. 'That's last year's. What are you carrying that around for?'

'I want to try and get in.'

Nadia looked her up and down as if she were undressing her. 'No guy could lift you, honey, and make it look effortless.'

Katie felt her cheeks get hot. This girl had guessed her secret, even though she'd never taken off her coat.

Nadia stabbed the brochure with her finger. 'I never even had a weight problem till Mr B told my teacher he wanted me for the company.'
'Mr B . . . George Balanchine?'
She nodded. 'I was only a couple of pounds overweight, but he told me I had to lose ten because stage lights make you look heavier. Madame Doubrovska kept saying, "Eat nothing, Nadia, eat nothing. Live on music and air. Mr B has picked you." I got so freaked out I wouldn't eat for days and then I'd pig out. I ended up putting on weight instead of losing it.'
Nadia looked as if she might start crying again so Katie said, 'You must be a fantastic dancer if Balanchine wanted you for the New York City Ballet.'
'Didn't stop the school putting me on probation. Yesterday they threw me out because I was fourteen pounds overweight.' Nadia jabbed another cigarette into her mouth. 'I can't even tell my mom what's happened. She works in a fish cannery to pay for what my scholarship doesn't cover.' She flicked ash into her saucer. 'Didn't cover.' Her eyes started to fill and she turned away to look at the glass case filled with desserts. 'Want to split an éclair with me?'
Katie laced her fingers around her cup. 'No thanks.'
'Come on. Just half.'
Katie shook her head.
'You'd like one, wouldn't you?'
'No.'
Nadia walked to the counter and came back carrying a tray with four pastries. 'Know the meaning of éclair?'
Katie shook her head. She'd studied French, but pastries hadn't been included in the vocabulary.
'Lightning.' Nadia picked up one and started to eat it. 'They call them that because they're gone in a flash.' She gestured to the plate. 'Have one.'
'No thanks.'
'One bite's not going to kill you.'
'No.'
'Just a little taste. To keep me company.'
She shook her head again.
'Dare you or you won't be my friend.'

Katie looked at the pastry, took a tiny bite off the end and returned it to the plate with the other éclairs.

Nadia picked it up and dropped it onto Katie's saucer. 'It's yours. Your germs are all over it.'

'But you made me!'

'You were dying to eat it. I could see it in your eyes.'

Katie picked up the éclair and ran her tongue slowly along the shiny brown icing. If she was going to eat it, she might as well enjoy it. She'd treat herself to just this one pastry and not eat anything else for the rest of the day. She bit into the end. Cream squirted onto her tongue. It tasted delicious after being on a strict diet for three months. She decided she'd chew each bite twenty times to make it last.

Nadia picked up the last éclair. 'I'm going to eat whatever I want till the end of the year. On the first of January I'm going on a diet. I don't have to dance for Balanchine. ABT has a better repertoire and don't expect their dancers to look like skeletons. Besides,' she said, before she tucked half into her mouth, 'I can always take Ex-Lax.'

Swallowing stars

On Christmas Eve Nadia jumped onto the wall of the fountain in Washington Square. Ballerina elegant in her long coat and *ushanka* hat, she teetered on the rim, her arms waving like a tightrope walker's. Katie stood on the pavement, looking over Nadia's head at the decorations marching down Fifth Avenue. It was the first time she hadn't been home for the holidays. She was feeling more than a little homesick which was why she was glad to have made a friend in the last few weeks. It was the reason she'd let Nadia talk her into sharing a bag of iced doughnuts rather than go to class this morning. *We need to do something to cheer ourselves up, Rivers. This is the worst time of the year for suicides.*

Her roommate lifted her leg in a perfect *attitude*. 'Know any rep, Rivers?'

Katie blew on her fingers; they were stinging from the cold. 'Sure.'

'"Little Swans"?'

'Performed it a few years ago in El Paso.'

Nadia hopped down from the fountain. 'Let's dance to warm ourselves up.'

Katie looked around the park. 'Where?'

'Here.' Nadia threw her hair over her shoulder. 'This is where the musicians busk on Sundays. Let's give the Square some culture. Besides, I'm five dollars shy on my rent.'

'But you just got that hatcheck job—'

'Had to shell out fifteen bucks for my uniform.'

Katie looked at the pavement covered with frost. 'I don't think so, Nadia.'

'It's only a minute long. There aren't any big jumps.'

'My knee gave out on me last week just walking down the street.'

'You'll never join a ballet company if you're scared to dance.'

Katie bit the inside of her cheek. Nadia had a way of always making her feel like a coward. 'Only if we do it half-time.'

'Deal.'

They started to warm up and a crowd of shoppers stopped to watch. After ten minutes of stretching, *pliés* and *tendus*, Nadia shouted, 'A dance from *Swan Lake* will be performed as a special Christmas Eve treat. All contributions welcome.' She put her hat on the ground and they linked hands, Nadia singing the Tchaikovsky melody in her clear soprano.

They managed all the steps, substituting simpler jumps for the ones with beats that couldn't be performed in boots. On the last two counts they released hands and finished on one knee. The crowd clapped enthusiastically as they stood up, panting, their breath making clouds in the air.

Nadia made a sweeping bow and elbowed Katie to join her. The shoppers threw bills and coins into the hat. Nadia blew kisses to a middle-aged man in a camel-colored scarf who was shouting, 'Encore!'

The crowd started to move off with their packages, everyone except the man who had applauded. 'You two are good,' he said, walking over to the patch of pavement they'd used as a stage.

Katie bent over to count their takings. Nadia seemed to have forgotten about her rent money.

The man tapped out a cigarette. He was wearing a wedding ring.

Nadia said, 'Mind if I join you?'

'Not at all.' He handed her a cigarette and lit it with his own. 'What's your name?'

'I'm Nadia and that's Katie.'

'We should get back to the convent, Nikitovich.'

Nadia shot her a look. 'I don't want to go back to that stiff.'

'Stiff?' the man said.

'An old nun dropped dead at our residence. They laid her out in the chapel. We have to pass a corpse if we want breakfast.'

Stop talking, Katie thought. Please stop talking.

'Why don't you two join me for lunch?' the man said.

Katie hoped Nadia would refuse, but she batted her eyelashes and blew a perfect smoke ring. 'That sounds groovy.'

Katie said, 'Excuse us for a moment.' She pulled Nadia out of earshot and tucked five one-dollar bills and a handful of change into her pocket. 'There's your rent. Let's head back to St Dymphna's. We've been gone for hours.'

'I don't want to go back to that mausoleum. Neither do you.'

'He's married. You don't know anything about him. He could be a weirdo.'

'Weirdo or not, Rivers, I'm cold and hungry. The only way I'll get rid of him is if you treat me to lunch.'

Nadia tapped her fingernail on the menu in the window of the Ace Chop Suey House. 'I'm having wonton.'

'One ton of what?' Katie looked inside her wallet. She was half-listening, wondering if she had enough money to pay the bill.

Nadia said, 'Haven't you ever eaten Chinese food?'

'Fortuna only had Mexican restaurants.'

'Wonton's my favorite. Means "swallowing clouds".'

She showed Nadia the ten-dollar bill. 'This is all I've got.'

'Wonton's only seventy-five cents. It'll cost four bucks each, max, if we order beef and rice. Stop pulling that face, Rivers. With a fucking corpse in the basement we need something to cheer us up.' She opened the door and waved her inside.

Katie chose a red plastic-covered booth at the back. She would have preferred to fast for the rest of the day, but she was looking forward to what would be her first hot meal in weeks.

A Chinese waitress came to their table. 'You ready order?'

Nadia opened the menu. 'We'll have one No. 10 soup, one plate of fried noodles and two No. 59s.'

'Soup first?'

'All at the same time.'

The waitress hurried back to the kitchen, shouting in Chinese as she went.

Nadia fanned herself. 'It's boiling in here, Rivers. Take your coat off.'

Katie pretended she hadn't heard her. If she took off the sealskin, she felt every customer could see the doughnuts she'd had for breakfast sitting in her stomach.

Nadia brushed the curtain away from Katie's face. 'You like to hide behind your hair, don't you?'

Katie pretended to look at the winking lights on the tree in the window, thinking about what her family would be doing tonight: her mother stuffing the turkey, her father reading *'Twas the Night Before Christmas* out loud to her brother and sniffling because she wasn't there.

'I wish I'd gone to Seattle for Christmas,' Nadia said. 'My mother's all alone this year.'

'Why didn't you go?'

'I couldn't let her see how fat I am or she'd know I lost my scholarship.'

The waitress wheeled their food to the table. Katie stared at the rice, wondering how she was supposed to pick up those little grains when there wasn't a fork in sight. The only chopsticks she'd ever used were those beaded ones she'd stuck in her hair.

Nadia picked up a flat-bottomed spoon to eat one of the little pillows floating in broth. 'Why don't you come to the club tonight? I'll try to sneak you in so you won't have to pay the cover charge.'

Katie stared at her roommate. The last place she wanted to spend Christmas Eve was Trude Heller's. 'I need to sew some ribbons on my *pointe* shoes.'

'Come to the nightclub and have some fun. You don't have to sit in the convent like those miserable old nuns. Trude's looking for a cigarette girl.' Nadia blew on a steaming pillow and popped it into her mouth.

The thought of working in a nightclub scared her. Katie loved hearing the gossip about the drag queens who used the women's toilets and the go-go dancer who wiggled on a ledge while holding to a handle bolted to the wall, but she had no desire to see the Village's most famous discotheque for herself.

'I'll put in a good word for you with Trude. You could still take Demidenkova's morning class. You can make lots of tips if you flirt with the straight customers.'

Katie shook her head.

'You sit in that dump, dreaming you'll be the next Pavlova. Grow up.' Nadia pushed a plate of fried noodles at her.

Katie was suddenly aware that it was eating, not ballet, that had sealed their friendship. 'Shut up and leave me alone.' She shoved the plate back.

'What's wrong with you? You've been grumpy all day.'

'I've put on three pounds since you came to St Dymphna's. Even Madame's noticed. She's been ignoring me.'

'Why didn't you say something? I know a laxative that's dynamite. You can eat all you want, take a pill and the food blows straight through.'

'I can't take laxatives,' Katie said. 'They give me terrible cramps.'

'When we get back to the convent, I'll show you a little trick I learned. It's called riding the porcelain pony.'

Katie stared into the dormitory toilet and took a deep breath. She hated throwing up, but sitting in her stomach were thousands of calories. She stuck a teaspoon down her throat and retched, but nothing came up. She wiped her eyes, thinking about the latest letter from Fortuna. It was sitting with the others in a shoe box under her bed.

I'm so proud of you for getting into American Ballet Theater! All the girls are thrilled for you, especially Tracy. Write and tell us what it's like dancing with Natalia Makarova and Mikhail Baryshnikov. Can't wait to hear from you. Love, Carmel

She took another deep breath before forcing the spoon into her mouth. She was determined to have eighteen-inch thighs and hipbones like the wing mirrors on Karolak's sports car. She gagged as she edged the teaspoon down. She thought she was going to choke when a stream of vomit finally exploded from her mouth.

She stared at the lumps of partially-digested food. It was disgusting, but at least it was out of her body. She lowered the lid and leaned her forehead against her hands. It would have been more hygienic to throw up in a sink, but she didn't want to risk being caught by Sister Augustine.

Katie wiped the spots off the seat and the floor, then left the cubicle to brush her teeth. They felt furry and horrible, like they were covered in little sweaters.

After she'd cleaned herself up, she walked back to the dorm. She held her nose so she wouldn't breathe the cooking odors from the restaurant's ventilator shaft. Usually she found the smells comforting, but not when she'd just puked her guts out.

She pulled the scales from under Nadia's bed. Purged of three doughnuts, eight shrimp crackers, fried noodles, a plate of beef and rice, a pot of jasmine tea and a fortune cookie, she was exactly the same weight she'd been this morning.

She walked to the window, wanting to find the constellations Rhett had shown her the night before she left. She knew she'd feel better if she could find the Buffalo and the Horse. She looked for them, but they had disappeared. It seemed impossible, but the lights of the city had swallowed the stars.

Throwing away the past

Katie watched a small heap form in the middle of the dormitory on New Year's Eve: old clothes, pantyhose, a stuffed turtle, a pair of gold-lamé shoes, one missing a heel.

Nadia flicked her hand in the direction of the pile. 'What gives, Constanza?'

'Is custom in Peru on New Year's Eve to build bonfire. We burn things what we no want to start New Year right. You *bailarinas* find things so you have good luck next year.'

Nadia took out her compact. 'Can't light a fire in the convent, Connie.'

'I take to incinerator. Same thing.'

'Yeah, right.' Nadia was gazing into the mirror, applying sapphire glitter to her lids.

'Better hurry, *bailarinas*.' Constanza tapped her watch. 'Is only a few more hours till midnight.'

Katie went through everything she owned: clothes, cosmetic bag, cassettes, *Dance Magazines*, but she couldn't come up with anything she didn't want. 'I've only been here since the beginning of the month. I can't find anything to throw away.'

'And I only been here since Thanksgiving. Is very bad luck not to get rid of something before midnight you no want no more.'

Nadia pointed at Katie's nightstand. 'Do me a favor, Rivers. Get rid of that icon. It creeps me out.'

Katie stared at her Virgin of Vladimir, trying to see what it was that her roommate hated so much. She had to find something to throw away, but it wouldn't be that. She dug through her purse and saw her mother's latest letter. She dropped it on top of the pile. Receiving it had upset her so much she'd skipped class and gone to Sutter's to stuff herself.

'What'd you just throw away, Rivers?'

'Nothing.'

'Yes, you did. I saw you.' Nadia snapped her compact shut and grabbed the aerogram before Katie could stop her.

'Mommy says, "Stop living in a dream world."'

Katie tried to snatch it back. 'That's private, Nikitovich.'
Nadia leapt onto her bed and started bouncing. '"Quit that durn ballet and find yourself a new career. You can type ninety words a minute so stop wasting your life. Don't be like Ashley Wilkes, pining away for what might have been."'
'Nadia, give me that!'
'No wonder you pig out whenever you get a letter from your mother.'
'Give me that or you'll be sorry!'
'What's wrong with you, Rivers? Can't take a joke?' Nadia smirked and dropped the aerogram.
Katie ripped it into little pieces, then walked to the pile and let the scraps flutter like confetti.
Constanza picked up the picture on her bedside table and ceremoniously laid it on top of the things to be burned. 'I never let you mash me up again, Hernándo. Next time you see me will be in the court of divorce.'
Katie looked at her roommate's husband, grinning stupidly at the ceiling, his last smile of the year. 'Anyone who breaks your nose, Constanza, deserves to be incinerated.'
Nadia raised her fist. 'Right on, sister.'
'So what you throw away, Nadia?'
'Nothing, Constanza. I'm not superstitious.'
The sound of stomping on the stairs. Katie froze. She prayed the shoes would continue upstairs, but the dormitory door burst open. Katie held her breath as Sister Augustine went straight to Nadia's closet and started to raid it.
Nadia yanked the nun's rosary. 'What the hell are you doing? I didn't give you permission to search my things!'
The nun jerked her beads back, grim lipped with rage. 'I don't need your permission.'
Sister Augustine bent down and pulled out a tangle of clothes. Hidden in them was a bag from Dunkin' Donuts and a greasy box. *FAMOUS RAY'S PIZZA.*
'There are rules here, Nikitovich. Under no circumstances is food to be brought upstairs. Where you have food, you have mice and where you have mice, you have disease. Mother Superior told me that you owe this week's rent. You're on the street if eighteen dollars isn't in her office by three o'clock tomorrow.'

'And a Happy New Year to you too, bitch.'
'What did you say, Nikitovich?'
'I said you'll have your rent.'
'Yes,' she said. 'We will have our rent.' Sister Augustine marched toward the door and slammed it.

Nadia threw the pizza box across the room. 'Miserable old crone. They sent you to St Dymphna's because no other convent would have you.'

Constanza was shaking her head. 'I tell you, Nadia, is very bad luck not to get rid of old things on New Year's Eve.'

'That's bullshit.' Nadia bent down to shove her clothes back. 'You don't get rid of the past by throwing it away.'

Constanza took a carton of eggs from under her pillow and handed Katie one. 'Before you sleep, fill glass with water. Break egg and put white in only. I tell your fortune for the New Year of what shape that grows.'

Nadia plucked an egg for herself. 'Just because I don't believe in bonfires doesn't mean I don't want my fortune told.' She put it on top of her nightstand before she started to dress for work. She pulled on black stockings, hatcheck uniform and coat. 'Bye, girls,' she said. 'Some people have to earn a living.'

Constanza stood looking at Hernándo after Nadia had gone. 'We have to make party, Katie.'

'With what?'

Constanza lifted the large plaster statue of Jesus at the end of the dorm. Inside was a bottle of wine. 'I have a salami in *la* Virgin on third floor. I also sneak in Ritz crackers, cookies and a piece of Swiss cheese.'

They made canapés, sipped Rioja from toothpaste cups, danced to the top one hundred hits of 1971: 'Brown Sugar', 'Wild World', 'Me and Bobby McGee'. On the stroke of midnight they sang 'Auld Lang Syne', but not before Katie had put her egg white into a glass of water.

Before lights out, she watched Constanza leave out crackers and cheese for the mice that scrabbled across their floor at night. Though Katie was frightened of them, she was glad her roommate fed them with food smuggled in under the snitchy nose of Sister Augustine.

On the first of January, Nadia woke at noon. Katie heard her moan before she swung her legs over the side of the bed.

'Happy 1972, Nikitovich.'

Nadia grabbed her temples. 'Keep it down, Rivers. I've got a splitting headache.'

She whispered, 'What time you get in?'

'After five. I bribed Berla to stay up and let me in. Didn't want one of the old hags giving me a lecture.' Nadia rubbed her eyes, still sparkly with patches of glitter. 'Tell me my fortune, Connie.'

Constanza walked to Nadia's nightstand and peered inside her mug. 'I don't see nothing.'

'What do you mean you don't see anything?'

'You will never be dancer. Your dreams, they are all gone.'

'What did hers have?' Nadia asked.

Constanza showed her the floating egg white shaped like a tutu. 'For her is very, very good year. She get into ballet company soon.'

Nadia looked at Katie. 'You switched cups in the middle of the night.'

'I did not.'

'Yes, you did.'

'Why would I do that, Nadia?'

'Because you're jealous George Balanchine wanted me for the New York City Ballet.'

Katie looked at her, dumbfounded, then burst into tears.

'Why you so nasty?' Constanza said.

'I'm not,' Nadia said. 'It's the truth.'

'You make your best *amiga* upset. Now you pay the price. I tell you is very, very bad luck not to throw away things, but you no listen.'

'Shut up,' Nadia said. 'Shut up about your stupid Indian superstitions.'

On the first of January it was an unseasonable sixty-three degrees. Katie wandered the streets of the Village. Greenwich Avenue, Bleecker Street, Bedford Street. On Christopher Street she passed the Oscar Wilde Bookshop and the Stonewall Inn and the crumbling Northern Dispensary where Edgar Allan Poe went for his cures.

She headed down the Avenue of the Americas, past the Women's House of Detention, Greenwich Library and Jefferson's Market. She turned onto West 13th Street that reminded her of Paris, even though she'd never been there. Past elegant brownstones with gingerbread-glass windows and the art deco Evangeline Residence and the Bells of Hell jazz club.

She continued to Sheridan Square with its birdshit-stained statue and sat on a bench, composing New Year's resolutions in her head. *I will make myself go to class every day, even though I've put on weight. I will get down to 117. I will find a way to leave St Dymphna's. I will laugh more. I will answer Carmel's letters. I won't worry so much. I will never eat another éclair.*

A way to do this right

Rhett was alone in the house the Saturday morning the registered letter came. He knew what was inside the government envelope before he opened it. The letter said the date of his birth had been drawn in the Federal draft lottery and he was to report to Fort Bliss in El Paso, Texas, in a month's time. If he met Army medical requirements, he would be inducted and classified. He hit the table with his fist. He knew what this meant. He was fresh meat for Vietnam.

Hollis needed to know he wouldn't be going into work today. There was too much he had to figure out. Rhett took his notebook out of his jacket. To find his boss's number, he had to flip through pages of notes. He glanced through information on financing, percentages, slang he'd had to memorize so customers wouldn't know what was being said under their noses. $500: *nickel*. Vinyl roof: *sun/moon*. Tires: *shoes*. He finally found what he was looking for in the back of the notepad. He dialed and waited for Archie Hollis to answer.

Ten, fifteen, twenty rings. He slammed down the receiver. The old bastard was probably sleeping off a hangover. Drunk or sober, one thing was for sure. Hollis didn't like him and he didn't like Hollis.

Rhett started to pace the kitchen. He needed to call in sick so his pay wouldn't be docked. He had to save as much money as he could in case he needed to leave town quickly. He read the draft board letter again before he picked up the receiver to dial.

Not long after he'd joined Sierra Motors, Hollis had decided that every customer would get a free *BOMB HANOI* bumper sticker. Rhett was the only employee who had refused to hand them out. That's when Hollis had started calling him 'Arnold', short for Benedict Arnold. Even though Hollis hated his guts, Rhett had been kept on the payroll because he was the firm's top salesman, flipping the lookie Lou's into buying the trash trade-ins they called irons. He could bird dog as successfully as his boss and Hollis knew it.

Archie finally picked up after thirteen rings. 'Hollis residence.' His voice was rough, unused. He didn't sound happy.

'Rhett, sir. Sorry to call you so early, but I can't open up at the lot.'
'This some kind of joke?'
'No, sir. I've got a migraine.'
'Take some aspirin, Arnold.'
'Already done that, sir. Hasn't done any good.'
'First thing I want you to do today is call the cockroach who wants the blue '69 Chevy. Tell him not to bother coming in. The mouse house said his credit's shit.'
'I could hardly read your phone number, sir. I'm seeing double which is why I can't come in today.'
'You've got to come to work if you're going to make a low ball on commission this month.'
'I'd come in if I could, sir, but I can't.'
'I'll open up for you today, Arnold, but you'd better get yourself down to the lot on Monday morning, nine o'clock sharp, or you're fired.'

Rhett unlocked the gun cabinet. He checked the barrel of his father's Colt revolver. Empty. He picked up a handful of bullets from the cartridge box. His father had always said how much he hated the Army, but that he'd been proud to serve his country when it had needed him.

Rhett put the pistol and loose bullets in his jacket and went to the garage. He strapped on his helmet and lowered himself onto the Kawasaki, felt himself sink down further than he should. He slammed his fist on the flat tire. 'Goddamn fucking Jap piece of shit!'

He kicked the garage door and limped down the driveway toward his father's truck. He drove to the supermarket where he picked up two cans of Coors. He slipped them inside his jacket when the cashier wasn't looking. At nineteen, he was old enough to be sent to war, but too young to buy alcohol. All he had to do now was stop by Lota-Burger for a chili cheeseburger and a double order of fries.

Rhett saw the windmill long before he got there, eagle-feather-shaped fins against the turquoise sky. He got out of the pickup and walked toward it, at its base the remains of the fire he and Katie had made the night before she left. He picked up the rusty coat hanger. It felt like a lifetime since they'd been here toasting marshmallows and it had only been four months.

He listened to the sound of the blades creaking in the wind as he took out the revolver. The war he'd been drafted for was insane. Before DD was due to be shipped home, he'd been blown to pieces by a GI who'd cracked up and booby-trapped a latrine.

Rhett swung out the barrel, loaded all six chambers with bullets and clicked it back into place. He raised the pistol, shooting five times at the windmill's spinning blades.

He counted as he fired, thinking about Striker's mother who had climbed into his grave. Everyone could read the sticker on DD's casket once she'd ripped off the flag. *REMAINS NOT SUITABLE FOR VIEWING.*

He lowered his arm and spun the barrel. He could say he was messing around, shooting beer bottles in the desert. An accident. Nobody would think otherwise, not even his dad.

He pointed the hot muzzle at his kneecap. Sweat rolled down his back as he fingered the trigger. A bullet from a .38 was slow. If the last cartridge was in the chamber, it would take everything with it: muscle, tendon, bone. Just one squeeze and he'd no longer be combat material.

His arm started to shake uncontrollably. Rhett held his breath and pulled the trigger. Empty chamber. He jerked the trigger again. Another snap. Unable to make himself fire again, he threw the gun in the sand. What would he do now? What the hell would he do now? He fell on his knees and stayed that way for a long time.

He finally stood up and stumbled back to the truck for the hamburger he'd left on the seat. He jumped onto the hood and peeled away the waxy paper. It was soggy with catsup the consistency of thickened blood. He leaned over the side of the Ford and threw up. He rolled back, emptier and more frightened than he'd ever been in his life.

He closed his eyes and fitted his back against the curve of the windshield. He was panting so hard he could barely get the words out, but he was praying. He was praying for an answer. Praying for a way to do this thing right.

'Good day at the lot?'

His mother was standing at the stove, mashing potatoes. She hadn't noticed he wasn't wearing his business suit. He flopped down in a chair, aware of the draft-board envelope crackling in front of his heart. 'Pops?'

His father glanced up from the evening paper.

'You know the bridge convention in Albany you're playing in next month?'

'What about it?'

'Booked your plane ticket yet?'

'I'm planning to in the next few days. Need to speak to Maggie Hubbard about it first.'

'Ever thought of driving up?'

His mother pulled a pan of meat loaf out of the oven. 'Course he's not thought about driving up. It's thousands of miles.'

'You could go to your Duplicate convention while I bum around Albany. We could drive over and see Katie when it's over.'

His mother turned the pan upside and started to shake it onto a plate. 'Mr Hollis wouldn't let you have the time off.'

'Archie wants to take his vacation the first two weeks of June. He told me to take mine at the beginning of May.'

His mother started to saw the brick of shiny hamburger. 'If you hadn't been a fool and mooned half of Fortuna, you could be in college now instead of working for a man who runs a used-car lot.'

His father closed the paper. 'Now that you mention it, buckeroo, driving to New York isn't such a bad idea.'

'I can hardly get you to take me to El Paso, Haywood, but you're willing to drive to New York with Rhett.'

'Come with us, Momma,' his father said.

'New York City is Sodom and Gomorrah as far as I'm concerned. Why on earth would I go to a place that's got one of the highest crime rates in the world?'

'Now, Momma. Stop exaggerating.'

'I am not exaggerating. People get shot and stabbed there all the time.'

Rhett spooned some potatoes onto his plate. 'Mom, don't you want to see Katie?'

'There's no one to take care of Burrito or the yard.'

His father put a slab of meat on his plate. 'Flying would be a lot faster.'

'It'd cost more, *padre*. Besides, it's better driving. You get to see more of the country that way.'

His mother said, 'While your daddy foots the bill for motels and gas.'

Christopher Street

Katie glanced at the nameplate screwed to the desk. *MISS DELAPORTE.* The old lady sitting behind it was wearing a feathered hat and crêpe de Chine dress patterned with blue flamingos. On this chilly spring day she looked like she was going to an Easter parade.

Miss Delaporte tipped up her glasses. 'Have a seat.'

Katie dragged her chair closer to Nadia's. 'I'm Miss Rivers and this is Miss Nikitovich. We're here about the unfurnished apartment.'

The old lady put out a gnarled hand studded with rings. A walnut-sized sapphire glinted on her index finger. 'Dixie Delaporte. Pleased to meet you.'

They shook hands. Katie couldn't help staring at the ruby-eyed gold serpent coiled around her wrist. It looked like something Queen Nefertiti would have worn.

'I can tell you like it, dear,' Miss Delaporte said. 'It's a *grigri*. Protects my dicky heart.'

She was about to ask Miss Delaporte about the apartment listed in the *Voice* when Nadia pointed to a painting. The bare-shouldered, bare-legged woman was holding an enormous feathered fan.

'That's you,' Nadia said.

Miss Delaporte fluttered her false eyelashes. 'I was a Bohemian artiste. I was almost as well known as Sally Rand.'

Nadia leaned forward like she were going to whisper a secret in the old lady's ear. 'You were a foxy lady. You must have had lots of lovers.'

Miss Delaporte laughed. 'That's how I got into real estate.' She rested her elbows on the desk. 'I'll bet you two are ballerinas.'

'Until we get into a ballet company,' Nadia said, 'she's temping and I'm hatchecking at Trude Heller's.'

'Which of my properties did you come to see?'

Katie held out the classified ad, ringed in red.

Miss Delaporte lowered her glasses. 'That's on the top floor of what used to be Romany Marie's Tavern.' She bent forward to speak into an intercom. 'Benny, I need you to take two young ladies on a tour of the garret.'

Just above Miss Delaporte's office was 20 Christopher Street, a three-story building covered with white stucco and a tangle of wisteria vines. Benny, a big man with an Afro like a dandelion head, unlocked the mint-green door to take them to the garret. He led them up creaking stairs to the third floor landing where there were two apartments, one with an orange eviction notice tacked to the door. Katie expected him to unlock the one without anything on it, but she was wrong.

In the evictee's apartment the galley kitchen was the first thing she saw. An ancient refrigerator, grease-caked stove and rusty sink. The floor was covered in garbage. When Benny turned on the light bulb, a herd of cockroaches stampeded for cover.

He opened the dormer windows in the living room and stood, arms folded, as they looked around the unrenovated apartment. The front room had a small closet and sealed-up fireplace. A recess with two shelves served as a book case. The black gloss floorboards, where they were visible, were speckled with globs of dried paint. So many colors had been drizzled together it looked like the floor had been used as a canvas.

The whitewashed bedroom had a cast-iron radiator and the curtain-less windows made the place feel faintly Parisian, the sort of cold-water walk-up where Hemingway might have lived as a young man.

They'd visited a dozen apartments and none of them was half as good as this one, right in the middle of the West Village, only a five-minute walk to Morelli's Studios. Breathless with excitement, Katie poked her head into the bathroom, where Nadia was inspecting the medicine cabinet. 'What do you think, Nikitovich?'

'Someone's dumped gloss paint in the bath.'

'So what?' Katie said. 'All this place needs is a little elbow grease.'

'They've done the same thing to the sink.'

'What's wrong with you? I thought you'd jump at this. The other places we've seen were tenements with no heat. We could cook food without having to hide Constanza's burner. We can wash our leotards and tights without worrying about raging nuns. We could have guests.'

Nadia kicked a gin bottle. 'It's not that, Rivers.'

'Then what is it?'

'I only have a hundred for the deposit.'
'What?'
'Things came up.'
'What came up? You told me you've been putting money aside. I've been temping for three whole months so we can move out of the convent.'
'Cover me for a hundred, Rivers. I'll wire my mother to repay you.'

Miss Delaporte said, 'The deposit is two twenty-five, plus a month's rent in advance. Total, four fifty.'

Nadia handed over a hundred in cash and Katie took out her checkbook for the rest. She had written out the date when she felt Nadia's hand on her arm.

'Miss Delaporte,' Nadia said, 'there's something I need to talk to you about.'

The old lady looked up. 'What is it, dear?'

'Have you seen the apartment upstairs recently?'

Miss Delaporte nodded, the plumes on her hat swaying. 'The tenant was a crazy artist.'

Nadia said, 'We're going to have to do a lot of cleaning and repainting if we're going to live there. Think you could knock fifty off the total for decoration?'

The old lady turned to look at Benny, who nodded.

'Four even it is.' The old lady put a piece of paper on the desk and made two Xs. 'The lease is for twelve months. No subletting, otherwise you girls can do what you want with the place.'

Benny said, 'What about references, Miss D?'

Miss Delaporte took off her glasses. 'They seem like good girls to me. Hell, Benny, if you can't trust people when you're my age, you might as well stick your head in a noose and swing.'

Bertha Samaniego for 1972 L.U.L.A.C. Queen

Rhett stood in the driveway, waxing his father's Camaro, polishing it until he could see his reflection in the shine. In less than twenty-four hours they'd be driving up Interstate-25. He dipped the chamois in Turtle Wax and rubbed it in big circles on the hood. After what had happened to DD, Rhett had only one choice: to split. He wasn't good at languages so Mexico and Sweden were out. That left Canada. He hated snow, but at least there they spoke English.

His mother had always said northerners were peculiar. *They're like their weather. Cold and unfriendly.* It was certainly true of their next-door neighbors. The Langstroms were from North Dakota and not once in seventeen years had they asked his family over for a barbecue or a swim in their pool.

Even if northerners were standoffish, Rhett knew he wouldn't have trouble finding a job. A good used-car salesman would be at a premium in Canada, where there was hardly any public transportation and you had to have a car to get around. He knew too that, with luck, he could slip across the border without any trouble. With a face like his, people would mistake him for a native.

He picked up a clean polishing rag. He swung his arm and the cloth slipped from his hand, landing where he and his sister had scratched their names in the concrete over a decade ago. He looked at their childish writing, wondering if he'd tell her what he was planning to do. He had no idea if she would understand, or if she'd think he was a traitor. He'd get her alone when he got to New York and sound her out. If he couldn't say goodbye to his parents, it was important for him to be able to say goodbye to someone.

On his last night in town he went to a bar in Old Mesilla and ordered a pitcher of sangria. He didn't like wine with floating fruit, but he figured they'd sell it to him and not ask for an ID. He looked around the cantina for someone to talk to, but most of the kids he'd hung around with in high school were away at college. Only he and DD had been unlucky enough to be drafted.

Cherokees believe the dead rise up and become stars. It is from stars that spirits return to earth to be reborn as children. He hoped that what Nanatasis had told him was true, that DD was up there somewhere in the Milky Way, riding his souped-up Tiger, his pigtail flying out behind him like an Indian brave.

He looked around the bar again. On the counter was a pickle jar filled almost to the top with coins. A picture of a girl in a beehive hairdo and prom dress was taped to the outside. *BERTHA SAMANIEGO FOR 1972 L.U.L.A.C. QUEEN.* Every spring there were jars like this all over town, promoting candidates for the League of United Latin American Citizens. The nominees whose photographs collected the most money were crowned King and Queen in an annual festival that raised money for the Catholic church.

Rhett took a dollar bill out of his wallet, folded it and pushed it into the slot. He'd known Bertha since grade school. She was pretty and he wanted her to win.

He finished off his glass of sangria and poured another. And another. He hadn't even packed. Not that it would take a lot of time. He didn't want to look suspicious so he'd take things that would fit into a small suitcase and holdall. A couple of sweaters and jeans, shirts, Y-fronts, a pair of tennis shoes, his high-school yearbook and battery-powered wool socks. For sentimental reasons, he wanted the arrowheads he had dug up in the desert and a New Mexico state road map.

He picked up the menu on the counter from the restaurant next door and flipped through it. He was planning to order enough chili rellenos, sour cream enchiladas, refried beans and sopaipillas to last him for years.

He paid his tab. He lifted the pickle jar when the bartender's back was turned and slid it inside his denim jacket. His heart was thumping as he walked through the swinging doors. If someone caught him now, he'd never be able to explain that he wasn't stealing Bertha Samaniego's L.U.L.A.C. jar for the money.

Crayola flowers

Katie unlocked the apartment and tiptoed inside. Her shoes made a soft sucking sound as she walked through the kitchen. The floorboards still weren't dry a week after she'd painted them. She hadn't mixed the gloss properly, or it was a faulty can, because the floor was like flypaper. Instead of an obsidian finish, it was covered with dusty footprints like the diagrams in her parents' ballroom dancing course.

She opened her bag and took out a newspaper. All she had left after paying most of the deposit was a dollar, a nickel and two pennies. To leave St Dymphna's, she'd temped solidly from January to March. A week here, three days there, an unwelcome employee tolerated by office managers and staff until the real receptionist, invoice typist or filing clerk returned to work. She hadn't been to Morelli's once since moving to Christopher Street and she was desperate for a permanent job in the Village so she'd be free to take Madame Demidenkova's five o'clock class and start to lose weight again.

Katie leafed through the classifieds without seeing a single job that was suitable. The ads were all for full-time employees and she only wanted part-time work. She was about to throw the paper away when an ad at the bottom of the page caught her eye.

> **Typing.** 10.00AM - 4.00PM. $5.00
> per hour. No shorthand. Jeans OK.
> Tel: (212) 243-9188

She looked at her watch. Noon. Hoping the job hadn't gone, she ran to the phone and dialed.

'Wolfsheim's Import Export.'

She tried not to sound too desperate. It she got this job, it would be perfect; she could walk to work and wouldn't need to buy a new wardrobe she couldn't afford. 'I'm calling about the secretarial spot advertised in the *Village Voice*.'

'How fast can you type?' The man on the phone sounded like he'd slam the receiver down if she didn't give him the right number.

'Ninety words a minute.'
'Great. Name?'
'Katie Rivers.'
'How long would it take to get to 360 West 16th Street?'
She looked at her watch. 'Quarter of an hour?'
'Wolfsheim's. Fourth floor.'

The old warehouse was two blocks from St Dymphna's. Mr Wolfsheim met her at the elevator, a fat man in a baggy suit and candy-cane tie. He led her to the section of the floor that had been partitioned into an office. 'I want you to take some dictation.'

She looked at the stenographer's pad he held out and felt sick. She'd had two years of shorthand in high school, but she was slow. She always got hopelessly behind after a few sentences. 'But the ad said no shorthand.'

He waved away her protest with a flip of his hand. 'Just write fast.'

Smiled on by pictures of his children, grandchildren and blue-rinsed wife, she struggled to keep up with his Gatling-gun dictation. From the moment she started, she knew she wouldn't be able to transcribe her squiggly loops and lines. Unable to take the pressure of rapid-fire letters and a dozen purchase orders, her skin broke out in hives.

Mr Wolfsheim looked up to see her clawing her polka-dotted arm. 'First-day nerves,' she said.

'Take a break, kid. Stretch your legs. I'll give you a tour of the warehouse.'

He made her a coffee and took her up and down rows of shelving, pointing out the different kinds of cloth he traded: moleskin, sharkskin, Bamberg cotton, Virginia satin, cretonne, lace. She was in front of him as he reeled off the names of the bolts, completely off guard when his hand reached from behind to squeeze her breast.

She pulled away, terrified. It never occurred to her that a man old enough to be her grandfather would be a pervert. Then she remembered what her mother had said before her date with Karolak. *You may be nineteen, Katie Scarlett, but you're piccaninny backwards as far as men are concerned.*

She didn't know what to do, except pretend it hadn't happened. She walked back to her desk and barricaded herself behind it. Because she needed this job so badly, she did her best to make sense of the hieroglyphics on her pad.

At four o'clock she handed Mr Wolfsheim a stack of papers to be signed. She stood over him, filled with anger that he had tricked her. She watched the hand that had groped her scribbling his name, hating him for taking advantage of her, hating herself even more for not having the presence of mind to leave. Not waiting for him to finish signing she said, 'Could I have my money now, please?'

'You can have it on payday.'

'But I need the money now.'

'No employee gets money up front. What planet are you on?'

'I want my sixteen dollars now, Mr Wolfsheim. I have rent to pay.'

'So do I. See you tomorrow at ten.'

She wanted to bite his lecherous fingers. 'I won't be here tomorrow.'

She stood by his desk for five whole minutes, hoping to shame him into paying. Empty-handed and embarrassed, she picked up her purse and headed out the door.

With her last dollar, she bought a bag of hot crullers at Dunkin' Donuts. She'd worry about money tomorrow; she needed some comfort now.

She timed the doughnuts to last until she got home. While she was eating, she didn't worry about how much weight she'd put on or that she didn't have a job or she hadn't been to class in weeks. She ate the crullers slowly, savoring every buttery morsel, chewing them until they were a thick, sweet soup on her tongue.

She'd just finished the last doughnut when she put the key in the door. Inside, the first thing she noticed were sheets of paper taped around the walls, each one decorated with bright Crayola flowers. The one in the hallway said, *Haven't been to class lately, Katie. You're supposed to be auditioning for ABT! Proceed to mirror in bathroom to put up your hair. Love, Nadia*

Taped on the medicine cabinet was a lemon tea bag and a note. *Fill your stomach with this, then put on your leotard and tights. Proceed to print of* La Goulue.

Attached to the Toulouse-Lautrec reproduction was another note. *Make yourself feel beautiful for class. Put something sparkly in your hair. Proceed to bedroom. That's an order. Your new old roommate, Nadia*

Stuck to the closet door was, *You need to get in shape, Rivers, so no excuses!!! Madame's Intermediate class starts at 5.00.* Last note on bookshelf. Rolled up in the neck of a Mateus Rosé bottle was, *Ballet is fun, so is sex. Sorry about last night. The banker I picked up gave me this because we 'don't have any furniture'!!! Pay for class with this Benjamin and put the rest toward my rent.*

She looked at the hundred-dollar bill and then at the foam rubber mattress Nadia had stolen from a sun lounger in a furniture store. She and Nadia alternated: one night on the daisy-covered pad, the next on the sticky floorboards. Not only had Katie been forced to give up the foam mattress last night when it had been her turn, she'd lost sleep listening to Nadia screwing her latest conquest.

What Katie didn't know was what she was going to do the next time she saw Nadia: hug her or shake her. She still owed her over a hundred bucks.

Rollins' Running Indian

Rhett had seen nothing from the car window for hours but cactus, creosote and the occasional roadkill. The reflector sign ahead said it was twelve miles to the Colorado border. Twelve miles of not knowing if he'd ever set foot in his home state again.

Rhett started to choke up so he reached for his silver wraparound shades, one-way mirrors he could hide behind. He read the blurred words on billboards as they flashed past: Lazy Z Mobile Homes. Jako's Dirty Shorts Laundry. New Crop Pinto Beans!! The one coming up was a sprinting cartoon redskin. *6 MILES TO THE LAST NAVAJO TRADING POST IN NEW MEXICO • PLAN TO STOP FOR BARGAIN BULL WHIPS, CACTUS JELLY, TOMAHAWKS & CONCHO BELTS.*

His father had an arm slung over the steering wheel as he sang along to the cowboy on the radio. They hadn't said a word since lunch when they'd stopped for hamburgers and a shake. Rhett was grateful he didn't have to make small talk when so much was weighing on his mind.

He watched his father's head sway to a song about a man in a cheap motel, looking at the bottom of a whiskey glass, but Rhett knew why he was smiling. In a few days he'd be seeing Katie. It was the first time he'd seen his father look so happy in months.

With only two of them in the car, it reminded him of all the trips they'd made to pick up his sister when she'd lived in El Paso. At the time, he'd hated sitting around until Katie finished her class or rehearsal, then the long, monotonous drive back to Fortuna in the dark. Now he'd give anything to have that time again, to be on that road home.

In front of them was another yellow billboard, ticking off the miles to the next state like an odometer in reverse. *4 MILES TO ROLLINS' RUNNING INDIAN.*

His father snapped off the radio and started to drum his fingers on the steering wheel. 'That billboard Indian reminds me of a joke. What ailment do constipated Eskimos get?'

'Don't know, Pops. What?'

'Polarrhoids.'

His father laughed and Rhett made an attempt to join him. He'd always been embarrassed by his dad's sense of humor, but embarrassment wasn't what he felt today. Just a tremendous knot of love in his gut he couldn't begin to express.

'You okay, buckeroo?'

Rhett wondered if he'd somehow found the draft board letter hidden in his holdall. 'What makes you ask?'

'You've been looking worried since we left home. Forget something?'

'Naw,' he said, looking out the window. 'I've got a headache.'

'There's aspirin in the glove compartment.'

'I'll tough it.' He picked up the map on the dashboard. 'Looking forward to playing bridge with the big guns?'

His father's eyes left the road to look at him in the rearview. 'I've been doing some thinking. I'm going to skip the bridge tournament. Giving Albany a miss will mean two more days in Manhattan with your sister.'

Rhett's palms started to sweat. He'd worked out everything: when and where he'd cross the Canadian border, how he'd get his father to lend him the car to drive to Niagara Falls. 'What about your partner?'

'I'll call Maggie and tell her to find someone else.'

'But you love Duplicate. It's a chance for you to win more masterpoints.'

'To tell you the truth, buckeroo, after Katie left I realized I should've spent more time with you two when you were growing up. I was too damn busy trying to earn a living.'

Rhett remembered his dad coming home from work, collapsing in front of the TV, watching one football game and listening to another on his transistor radio.

'I keep seeing Katie's hand on the window of the plane. Hell, before you know it, you'll be cutting loose too.'

Rhett turned to look at the next billboard. *LAST TRADING POST IN NEW MEXICO • BLACK HILLS GOLD • TRUCKERS DISCOUNT • EXIT 1/2 MILE.* He knew he should be worrying about slipping into Canada without being caught, but all he could think about was that he didn't have anything from his home state except some Indian arrowheads and that L.U.L.A.C. jar. If he was going to be able to face leaving the country, he'd need more than a few pieces of flint and a picture of a girl with a beehive. He saw the corrugated roof of the trading post glinting in the distance. 'Can we stop there, Dad?'

His father eyed the gas gauge. 'We've got two-thirds of a tank.'

Once he was on the road, Rhett knew his dad didn't brake unless someone needed to eat or use the john. 'You're gonna have to stop at the post. I need to drop a twinkie.'

They parked behind a plywood sign that said WHOAAA . . . YOU'RE HERE. A black mongrel puppy lay in the shade of the porch, its tail beating them a welcome.

Rhett held the screen open, trying to hurry his father inside. Dogs reminded him of Burrito. He'd totally lost it when he'd said goodbye to her this morning. Look after the folks because I don't know when I'll be back. When this war's over. Whenever the fuck that is.

His father leaned over to pat the dog. 'You look like you could use a friend.' The puppy's tail thumped harder when he scratched her belly, but she couldn't be bothered to lift her head.

Rhett followed his father into the coolness of the trading post. Normally, he'd take his shades off inside, but he didn't because he already felt like an outlaw.

A young Navajo was sitting behind the counter, his hair in a long braid. He was wearing a turquoise sweatshirt with pink letters. *DRAFT BEER, NOT INDIANS.*

His father put his hand up in greeting, palm out. 'How.'

The teenager didn't say anything, just looked like he wanted to scalp him. Rhett felt his cheeks burn as he asked the Indian where the restroom was.

The Navajo looked straight through him and thumbed behind him.

Rhett whispered, 'My dad says outrageous things to start conversations. He doesn't mean any harm.'

'Anything else?'

Rhett was tempted to say that his grandmother was a full-blooded Cherokee, but there wasn't any point. 'Two boxes of Kodak 400, thirty-six exposures.'

'Prints or slides?'

'Prints.'

His father walked over. 'You must be planning on taking lots of pictures.'

Rhett pulled a five-dollar bill out of his wallet, slid it across the counter. 'I want to take some of you in front of the trading post.'

'You want a picture of an old guy with a Mount Rushmore-sized nose?'

'I want to remember how happy you look today, *padre*. Double happy.'

His father watched the grim-faced Navajo put the film in a sack. 'Looks like you could use some cheering up, buddy.'

Rhett took the bag. He knew what was coming and didn't want to be around. As he walked towards the can he heard his father say, 'An Irishman, an Italian and a Polack are in this bar—'

Rhett went into the toilet and cracked open the door. He wanted to hear what trouble his father was getting into. At least it wasn't the one about the Indian who'd named his kid after the first thing he saw after his wife had given birth. Two Dogs Fucking.

'. . . and they're having a good ol' time drinking when the Irishman says, "Back in Dublin, there's a bar called McGonigle's where you buy a drink, then you buy another drink and McGonigle himself buys your third round." Then the Eyetie says, "At Rico's, you buy a drink, Rico buys you a drink. You buy another drink, Rico buys you another drink." Then the Polack says—'

Rhett flushed the toilet. The water drowned out what his father was saying, but he'd heard this joke so many times he had it memorized. *In Chicago there's this place called Warshawski's where they buy your first drink, they buy your second drink, they buy your third drink, then they take you to the back and you get laid.*

Rhett came out of the john, pretending to zip up his fly.

'"Is that what happened to you?" his father was saying, "and the Polack says, "No, but it happened to my sister."'

His father waited for the laugh and looked disappointed when the stony-faced Indian kept staring at him. Defeated, his father jerked his head in the direction of the door.

Rhett said, 'I'd like to get a housewarming present for Katie.'

'Hey, buckeroo, that's a good idea. While you're doing that, I'll call Maggie and let her know the change of plan.'

They moved in the direction of the pay phone and his father said under his breath, 'That kid shouldn't be allowed to wear a T-shirt like that to work.'

'Maybe he just got his draft notice.' Rhett felt his face flush. He wished he could take the words back, but they'd come flying out of his mouth.

His father cuffed him on the shoulder. 'You'd do your duty if you were called up. Military service makes any man a prouder man, a better man, able to look anyone in the eye.'

Rhett sifted through barrels of souvenirs: wooden tomahawks with fake feathers, jars of pebble candy made to look like rocks, boxes of piñon incense, scorpions and hairy tarantulas encased in cubes of lucite. Nothing he saw spoke to him of the desert with all its majesty and beauty.

He wandered to the back of the trading post where the shelves were stocked with Indian pottery and kachina dolls with strange names: *Talavai, Wuköqotö, Kwikwilyaqa*. The statues of these supernatural beings were brightly-painted, each with a different head. Most of them looked like creatures from outer space. He studied the shelves lined with dolls and picked up one painted the color of red-brown clay. It had a duck mouth, square eyes and feathered nose cone on the crown of its head. On the base was the name of the kachina, the Indian who'd made it and a price sticker. Rhett's heart dropped. He had no idea kachinas cost so much.

His father came over to see what he was looking at. 'Find anything?'

'Not anything Katie might like, but I saw this.' He held out the Mudhead kachina carrying a baby Mudhead on its back. 'The tag says these are clowns. I wouldn't mind owning these guys.'

His father looked at the half-naked statue that was wearing a kilt. 'Ninety bucks for this? You're kidding me, right?'

Rhett turned the statue in his hands, trying to see it as his father might: miniature aliens from the set of *Star Trek*. 'It was made at Zuñi Pueblo.'

'Trading posts in the middle of nowhere are gyp joints.'

Rhett put the kachina back. His dad was right. He didn't have almost a hundred bucks for a doll, no matter how much it reminded him of New Mexico. He was going to need every penny he had to make a new life up north.

His father opened the screen door. Rhett dragged his feet across the porch before following him down the steps.

'You can get a kachina on our way back,' his father was saying. 'We're sure to see a cheaper one.' His father unlocked the car. 'What do you say to a cold beer before we hit the road?'

I could do with more than a beer, he thought. I could do with getting hammered. 'Sure, Pops.'

'I'll get a six-pack to set us up. Momma's not around to keep her beady eye on us.'

His father came out of the trading post. In one arm was a brown paper sack with the beer and, in the other, a cardboard box. 'Here's something for you.'

In packing peanuts was the Mudhead kachina. His dad could be tight with money for things he didn't consider necessities; a cottonwood doll was definitely off his radar. Rhett was too choked to say thank you. He'd lose it if he did. He shook the paper bag the film was in. 'Camera's empty, Pops. Have to load.'

Rhett sat in the back seat and pulled his denim jacket over his head. By the time he finished, he hoped he didn't look like he'd been crying. He sat for a moment to compose himself before opening the car door. 'Stand in front of the trading post for me, Pops.'

His father held the kachina next to his face and grinned. 'We'll have an ugly contest. You've got to judge who's got the ugliest nose cone, me or the Mudheads.'

Rhett wished he had the courage to ask the Navajo to take a photo of them. It would have been an excuse to put an arm around his dad's shoulder, but after that 'how' joke, he didn't dare ask the Indian for anything. He took aim, took two shots and swung the camera down.

'Let me take one of you, son.'

Rhett handed him the Kodak and stood next to the plywood cutout of the running Indian. *LAST CHANCE FOR CHILI DOGS, BLOCK ICE, FILM.* Last chance for a lot of things. He blurted out, 'There's something I have to tell you.'

'What, buckeroo?'

Rhett realized he couldn't ruin this trip just to ease his own conscience. He and his dad might never have this time together again. 'I had this spooky dream about DD.'

His father squeezed Rhett's left ear where the cartilage had melted together like two pieces of cheese. 'I lost a lot of friends during the war. You can take comfort in the fact that DD died for his country.'

Rhett started to shake. He didn't die for his country, he wanted to say. He was blown up by a GI who booby-trapped a shithouse.

His father pulled two beers out of the sack, lifted the pop-tops and handed him one. 'Tell me your dream.'

'DD and I were in this old house and he was stuffing a glass suitcase with clothes. I tried to take the bag away from him and he said, "People die, Rhett. You just have to accept it." Then he lifted the case and went up in the air. I tried to grab him, but by that time he was flying.'

They got into the Camaro in silence and pulled out of the parking lot. A few miles past the trading post they came to a signpost shaped like a headboard. *YOU ARE NOW LEAVING NEW MEXICO. HASTA LA VISTA!*

His father let out a cowboy whoop. 'New York City, here we come!'

Rhett turned to look out the window so he could wipe his face. He pictured the photograph he would carry across Canada. In the foreground, his father pulling a face at the Mudheads. In the background, a mongrel puppy in the shade of a tin-roofed porch.

The Cactus Club

Katie was sitting in the old lion-footed tub, fully clothed, hacking at the gloss the former tenant had tipped down the side. She'd been here over an hour and her arms felt like she was trying to strip an acre, not a few feet, of paint. She dropped her hands in her lap, exhausted. While she was resting, the front door creaked open.

'Anyone here besides the cockroaches?'

Katie leaned over the side of the bath, glad to have company, maybe even a little help. 'I'm chipping off paint.'

Nadia tiptoed past in espadrilles, the soles of her shoes sticking to the floor. 'Speaking of paint, if your floor ever dries, I'm going to get a real mattress. That sun bed is as wide as a stick of gum.'

Katie stared at the water blisters on her palm. 'How are you going to afford a mattress? You've been telling me you're broke for weeks.'

'I'm not going to buy one. I'll get one off the street. You wouldn't believe what people in brownstones think is junk.' Nadia walked into the bathroom and sat on the toilet. 'Why the home improvement at eight o'clock at night?'

Katie pointed at the aerogram lying on the sink. She ducked her eyes and returned to work.

Nadia lit a cigarette. 'Let's see what the *Rivers' Weekly* has to report. "Dear Katie, Went to see a play this week, *Three Sisters*, with the setting in Russia."' Her roommate's eyebrows shot up. 'From what you've told me about Lola, she doesn't strike me as a Russian literature fan.'

Katie kept scraping.

'"If you get a chance to see it, don't bother. No one is happy in it and all the characters are a bit strange and most of them not likable at all so it was a waste of time and money."'

Nadia read on in silence while Katie braced herself for what was coming.

'"The biggest news of the week is that Daddy and Rhett are driving up—"' Nadia stopped reading. 'Your family is coming to New York?'

'I didn't invite them,' Katie said quietly. 'They invited themselves.'

'They're not staying here.'

'Of course they're not staying here. We've only got one mattress which, incidentally, I have to give up all the time for your one-night stands.'

Nadia pointed at the living room with her cigarette. 'The goddamn floor would be dry by now if you hadn't bought such cheap paint.'

'And if you'd pitched in with some cash, I could have afforded to.'

Nadia took a long drag on her cigarette and blew smoke from the side of her mouth. 'You'll get your precious money back.'

'Are you going to give me a hand to get this paint off or not?'

'Personally, Rivers, I don't give a damn. If you want to make the apartment nice for Daddy-O, you go ahead. We've lived with that paint for weeks.'

'You got your salary the other day. What'd you spend it on?'

'None of your fucking business.'

'It is when you owe me a hundred and thirty-six dollars.'

Nadia stared at her sitting in the tub. 'Know what you remind me of in that dress, Rivers? Ten pounds of shit in a five-pound bag.'

With one leap, Katie was out of the bath. 'You're as fat as I am, Nikitovich. You're the one who drags me off for éclairs all the time.'

'You never need much convincing.'

Katie slapped her roommate so hard she stumbled into the radiator. Nadia cupped her face as Katie stared at the handprint she'd made.

'We may both be fat,' Nadia said, 'but I have perfect knees.'

Katie lunged to slap her again, but Nadia dodged. 'Don't try that again, bitch.'

'When are you going to repay me, Nikitovich?'

'When I'm good and ready.'

'You'll pay me my money. Now.'

'Want my answer to that?'

Nadia slammed Katie's head against the sloping roof.

Dazed, she put her hand up to see if she was bleeding.

Nadia started to laugh.

Katie picked up the scraper and held it in front of her. 'Get out before I throw you out.'

'I live here, you fat cunt.'

'I want my money in twenty-four hours, Nikitovich. I'm not bankrolling you anymore.'

Nadia grabbed her purse. 'You won't get away with this, bitch.'
'Piss off till you find the money you owe me.'
Nadia clopped down the stairs. 'You're a fucking bitch.'
Katie called after her, 'You're the bitch who does all the fucking around here.'
She slammed the door and went straight to the bathroom mirror. The skin on her temple was the color of an eggplant, but the bruise had been worth it. If she was lucky, Nadia would find a half-dozen guys to shack up with while her father and brother were in town.

Rhett wandered up and down the grassy slopes of the Gettysburg National Cemetery. He'd been here an hour, but he hadn't had any luck finding his great-grandfather's marker. Rhett had tried to get his father to come and pay his respects, but he'd been in a hurry to get to New York. *Go if you want to go, buckeroo. I'd rather take the train and spend the time with Katie.*

Even though Rhett would have loved to have seen Gettysburg with his dad, he was relieved he hadn't come. His father had kept asking why he wanted to visit a graveyard and he hadn't been able to give him an answer. He couldn't admit that DD had come to him in a dream and told him he had to find his great-grandfather's bones.

He walked from one grave marker to the next. They were laid out in semicircles around an ugly stone monument. The burials seemed to be by states, but all the dead from Tennessee were missing.

The monument's statue cast a long shadow on the small tablets of stones set into the grass. *CHARLES LOOMIS. SIDNEY PROUTY. RUEL WHITTIER.* He couldn't understand why these markers were cutting him up so much. Maybe because he wasn't having any luck finding his great-grandfather. Maybe because he'd be in Canada soon and had no right to stand on ground where the blood of so many fathers, brothers and sons had been spilled.

Katie hurried toward the platform where her father was arriving, twenty-one pounds heavier than when she'd left Fortuna. Her weight had ballooned to a hundred and fifty-three since she and Nadia had signed the lease.

She pushed her way through the crowd, thinking about her father's phone call last night. *The buckeroo wants to see Gettysburg. He's dropping me off in Harrisburg tomorrow so I can have more time with you. Meet me at Penn Station at 12.15. Rhett'll be in New York in time for dinner.*

She moved slowly towards his train, worried what her father would say when he saw her, but when she spotted his familiar tweed jacket, she forgot her wobbly thighs and belly and ran. 'Daddy,' she shouted. 'Daddy!' He sprinted toward her, his suitcase banging against his leg. He dropped his bag and swung her around. She was so glad to smell his Wildroot Hair Oil that she wanted to cry.

He held her away from him, looking choked. 'What on earth happened to your eye, sister?'

She pulled her hair around her face. 'I bumped into a door.'

'We'll have to buy a beefsteak to put on that, honey.' He squeezed her against his side and wiped his cheek. 'I can't tell you how great it is to see you again.'

'Same here, Daddy. Have a good trip?'

'You bet. Haven't been on an iron horse in years. Your brother was hell bent on seeing Gettysburg for some reason.' He let go of her shoulder and picked up his suitcase. 'Hey, I've got a joke for you.'

'I've been doing just great without those corny jokes of yours.'

'This one's a little risqué, but I think you're old enough. Why do mice have small balls?'

'I give up.'

'Because not many of them know how to dance.'

'Your jokes haven't gotten any better,' she said.

She looked up at her father as they made their way through Penn Station, wanting to say how much she loved him. Missed him. She hung onto his golf-brown arm, trying to match his giant steps.

Rhett walked into the Visitors' Center and headed straight for the information desk. 'Excuse me, but could you tell me where the Seventh Tennessee Infantry is buried?'

The ranger leaned forward. 'You won't find any Confederate dead here.'

'But I've been told my great-grandfather is buried here.'

'Gettysburg National Cemetery contains only Union soldiers, son.'

'What?'

'The remains of Confederate soldiers were reburied in the South.'

'Did they do that recently?'

The ranger shook his head. 'Re-internment started in 1870 and was completed seven years later.'

Rhett ran a hand through his hair. He felt confused, upset. 'Do you have a record of all the infantrymen who fought here?'

The ranger opened a book with a Confederate flag on the cover. 'What's your great-grandfather's name?'

'Rivers. Elijah Rivers.'

The ranger flipped the pages until he came to the Rs. He traced down a long column. 'Sorry,' he said. 'No one by that name listed.'

'That's impossible.'

'This book records every known Confederate soldier that fought here. No Elijah Rivers.'

'Would you check again?'

'I could look in the other book if you want me to.' The ranger pointed to one with Stars and Stripes on the cover.

'My great-grandfather wasn't a Yankee.'

'I don't know how familiar you are with Civil War history, son, but Tennessee was the last state to join the Confederacy. A lot of men found they were facing a brother or a father on the battlefield. A lot of them switched sides.'

Her father followed her up the sagging stairs to her garret. She couldn't wait for him to see her first home. She'd stayed up until two o'clock in the morning, trying to get the apartment shipshape. She proudly turned on the kitchen light. A hundred cockroaches ran for cover. Hoping he hadn't seen them she said, 'Why don't you have a look around, Daddy? I'll make some almond coffee.'

He set his suitcase down and pointed at the naked light bulb hanging from a cord. 'Tennessee chandelier.'

She watched him push open the bedroom door. Nadia called it the 'monk's cell' because it was empty except for a mattress, some Toulouse Lautrec prints and a wine bottle with a rainbow drip candle sticking out of its neck.

'That a bit narrow,' he said, pointing to the mattress.

'It used to be on a sun lounger.'

'Where's your roommate's bed?'

'That is our bed. Nadia and I take turns.'
'You sleep on the bare floor, Katie?'
'It's not so bad, Daddy. Dancers are supposed to suffer for their art.'
He stood in front of the dormer windows, jingling the coins in his pockets. 'No curtains yet.'
'I like the light. Even if I had the money to buy them, I wouldn't. It doesn't matter if people look in. We're two flights up.'
He made a tour of the apartment and asked if it had a fire escape. She shook her head. 'My landlady said this is one of the oldest buildings in Greenwich Village. It used to be an inn called Romany Marie's Tavern.'
Her father stared at the wisteria whose blooms framed the crooked windows. 'Dad would get me up every morning to haul the hay and milk the cows before I rode a horse into town. Course I smelled. Didn't have any way to wash except an old rag and lye soap. I hit the books to get off the farm.'
She saw his shoulders moving and knew why he had turned his back to her. He didn't want her to see that he was crying.

Rhett sat on the porch of the Visitors' Center, looking across the neatly-clipped lawns and dogwood trees in bloom. He was remembering what the park ranger had told him. *The Union had to bury over 28,000 Confederate dead in the space of a few days. There were newspaper accounts of limbs and heads sticking out of the ground because hogs were rooting up bodies to eat.* Perhaps somewhere out there, in what had once been fields and pastures, were Elijah Rivers' bones, unless pigs had found him first.

Katie took a sip of coffee. 'Anything unusual happen on your trip, Daddy?'
'We ran into some communists in Pennsylvania.'
She looked at the floor, trying not to laugh. 'What made you think they were communists?'
'Some hippies took issue with my bumper sticker. The bastards grabbed the fenders and started bouncing the car. "One, two, three, four. We don't want your fucking war."'
'What time do you think Rhett will get in?' With only a few days together, the last thing she wanted was to waste time talking politics.
'I told him to be here around seven.'
'How is my baby brother?'

'To tell you the truth, Katie, I'm kind of worried about him. Poor kid had diarrhea the last few days. When he was a little guy, he'd get the Hershey squirts when he was upset.'
'Probably something he ate.'
'Yep. Probably.' Her father opened his suitcase and took out a cardboard box. 'You'll never guess what this is.' He lifted a kachina out of the packing peanuts. 'I wanted to show you this before your brother gets here. Isn't it the ugliest thing you ever saw?'
She turned the exquisitely carved and painted statue in her hands. She had always wanted a kachina, but her mother wouldn't let her have one because she wasn't keen on anything Indian.
'I got it for Rhett,' he said. He moved the kachina up and down like it was dancing. 'The buckeroo wanted this so I bought it, even though the kid at the trading post was robbing me blind.'

In the last few hours Rhett had drunk a quart of Jack Daniels stolen from a liquor store. He stared at Bertha Samaniego in her prom dress and beehive hairdo, her grinning photograph still stuck to the empty L.U.L.A.C. jar. He had planned to go straight to Manhattan from Gettysburg. One minute he'd been in the lane for New York City, the next he'd cut across four lanes of traffic for the Buffalo exit.

He peeled a banana and threw the skin in Bertha's direction. Katie and his dad were expecting him. If he didn't turn up, the cops would be on the lookout for a white Camaro with Doña Ana plates. 'Bertha, tell me this. If I told my old man I was going to Canada, would he rat me out to the fuzz?'

The paper girl smiled sweetly at his crotch.
'Should I call them or not?'
Bertha wasn't cooperating so he decided to flip a coin. He checked the pockets of his jeans. No silver. He'd used all his change to buy bananas. His eyes searched the room to find something else. He spotted the empty whiskey bottle. He'd spin that. If the neck pointed at him, he'd call to say he was leaving the country. If it didn't, he'd head across the border without telling anyone.

The bottle turned, slowed, stopped. He picked up the phone, but slammed down the receiver when someone in reception answered. His father was a hawk. If Rhett were to admit where he was going, his father would tell the police. So close to the border he couldn't afford to blow it now. Even Canada was preferable to spending a stretch in the New Mexico Federal Penitentiary.

Rhett threw his bags into the car before going by the office to pay his bill. He stood in the lobby of the Blue Falls Motel, dripping with sweat, even though the air conditioning was on. If he stayed, he couldn't trust himself not to call his family so he decided to drive into Buffalo before heading across the border.

He hadn't eaten anything for hours so he stopped at a café on the highway with a sign that said *BOTTOMLESS COFFEE. ALL YOU CAN DRINK 50¢.* Inside, Mississippi mud pie and Manhattan clam chowder were on the menu. He didn't want to see foods he wouldn't be eating in Canada. When the waitress came over, he pointed at the blackboard. 'I'll have today's special.'

'Okeydokey,' she said. 'One plate of catfish and hush puppies coming up.'

He liked catfish, but he'd never been fond of fried balls of mush. He remembered fish fries at his grandmother's house, his father throwing them to the dogs to stop them from barking. The memory came from a long way off and made him feel sad.

In a few minutes the waitress came out with his meal. She looked at him funny as she put it on the table. She must know the signs. He can't have been the first scared kid who'd pulled in here with out-of-state plates, soon to disappear up north.

Rhett was driving around downtown Buffalo, trying to find a bar, when he saw a neon cactus hanging outside a run-down club. Attracted by the sign, he took in the wino sitting on the steps with a bottle and figured the bartender wasn't going to be too worried about a kid who was underage and already half-cut.

He parked the Camaro and went inside the Cactus Club. The first thing he saw was a black girl perched on a bar stool. She waved him over to where she was sitting and patted the seat beside her.

What the hell? he thought. In for a penny, in for a pound. He sat down. 'Want a drink?'

'Sure,' she said. 'What's your name?'

'Rhett.'
'Like *Gone With the Wind?*'
He nodded.
'Rhett. That's a nice name. Your momma fall in love with Clark Gable?'
'Maybe.'
'You don't sound like you're from around here. You sound like you're a long way from home.'
'I am.'
The girl opened the sequined bag on her lap and took out a quarter. Pushing up her teased hair she said, 'Like the Supremes?'
'Sure.'
She dropped the coin in the jukebox and strutted back, snapping her fingers to 'Baby Love'. She tugged at his belt. 'Dance with you for a dollar.'
'My sister's the dancer in the family.'
She pulled him to his feet and put her arms around his neck. 'I'm not asking to dance with your sister. I'm asking to dance with you.'
She rubbed her crotch against his and it was only then he realized this was a cathouse.

After a couple more dances and a couple more drinks, he climbed the stairs behind her. *TRAVANA* was painted in nail polish on a piece of cardboard tacked to the door. Rhett watched her take a key from her purse and push it into the lock. He stumbled inside, a ten-dollar bill crumpled in his fist. He'd never been to a whorehouse so he asked her how much he could expect for ten bucks.

'Not much, lamb chop.'
'I thought there'd be cactus here. You know, the Cactus Club. Fuck, I'm drunk.'

He watched Travana step out of her dress, throw it on a chair. All she had on underneath was a white bra. He stared at her shaved bush and realized he was having trouble keeping his eyes open. He wondered if she'd slipped him a mickey like he heard they did in Juarez.

She flung out her hand and he pressed the wadded-up note into it.
'They take American money in Canada?'
'We ain't in Canada, lamb chop. We in Buffalo.'

He staggered toward the open window. He leaned over the sill, trying to see the prickly pear sign two floors below. He felt his belt being grabbed, being hauled backwards.

'Last thing I need is some dead honky on the sidewalk and pigs crawlin' around. You got fifteen minutes to do your business and git outta here.'

When Rhett hadn't arrived by midnight, Katie and her father went to the 6th Precinct. The policeman on duty said if he hadn't appeared in forty-eight hours to come back when he'd be considered a missing person.

Seventy-two hours later, the NYPD called Katie's apartment to say the abandoned Camaro had been traced to the Bala Motel in St Catharines, Ontario. There was nothing inside the car except banana skins and a pair of mirrored sunglasses. According to the register, Rhett had checked out the day before. They had no motive, no leads, no suspects.

The day after that a letter arrived at Katie's apartment.

May 7, 1972

Dear Mom, Dad and Katie,

You guys don't know it, but I was drafted in April. Getting the letter totally freaked me because I knew I couldn't put on a uniform and kill people I didn't have any quarrel with. I didn't want to go to war and didn't want to go to jail so I went to Canada instead. It's been a tough decision, but it's the only thing I could do to be able to live with my conscience.

I'd have liked to say goodbye, but knowing how you feel about the war meant we only would have fought. I hope you can understand why I had to do it this way. I don't know where I'll be for a while, but I'll write when I get settled. I hope you can find it in your hearts to forgive me.

Your loving son and brother, Rhett

Before her father left for St Catharines to drive the car back to New Mexico, he asked where the nearest Woolworths was.

'East 14th Street, Daddy.'

'Walk over with me. I need some razor blades.'

He pushed a cart up and down the aisles, filling it with what she needed. Garbage can, shower curtain, dish drainer, toilet brush. At the checkout he filled the bin with everything he'd bought and carried it back to her apartment. She felt so grateful and tongue-tied and grieving that she couldn't say a word.

She waved her father off at the bus station and came home to find five fifty-dollar bills and a note on the bookcase. *Sorry for falling apart on you. My subconscious must have been telling me the umbilical cord had been cut the second time. Promise me you'll buy a new leotard and something you want for your new apartment (but not curtains). Miss you with all my heart. Love, Daddy*

Katie came home from work four days after her father had left to find the apartment ransacked. She thought she'd been burgled until she realized that Nadia had cleaned her out. Her roommate had taken almost everything, including Rhett's kachina and the cash her father had given her, hidden inside a copy of *A Moveable Feast.*

She went downstairs to ask for the locks to be changed. Miss Delaporte offered to accept half of June's rent until she could come up with the balance. Katie looked at the jeweled snake on her landlady's wrist and realized that, if she didn't want to crawl back home with her tail between her legs, she needed money and she needed it fast. She'd have to give up temping and classes to find a full-time job, at least for a few months.

The day the locks were changed a huge package arrived in the mail. Inside were a dozen roach hives, a rope ladder and the round lime-oak top from her parents' coffee table. *I haven't been able to sleep worrying that your building doesn't have a fire escape. Tie this to the radiator so if you need to get out in an emergency you can. Mom and I wanted to send some furniture from home. Couldn't get the legs in the box so they've been sent separately.*

Katie waited and waited for the screw-in legs to arrive, but they didn't come. Six months went by and she realized they never would. She took the three-foot disk downstairs and left it on the street outside her apartment. Before she went upstairs, she half-closed her eyes as she stared at the upended table top. It looked like the setting sun.

Miss Lite Steps

December 8, 1972
Box 118, R.R. #1
Oshawa, Ontario

Dear Sis,

Apologies for not being in touch. Know you haven't heard from me since I left, but I just couldn't get it together to write. You know me. Never been much with a pen.

I've been in this godforsaken country for 7 months. I'm so crazy homesick it feels like 7 years. I've moved a lot. Since July I've been living outside Oshawa in a converted garage. It's hot in summer and cold in winter. Right now it's a big deep freeze. Oshawa is close to Lake Ontario so we don't get a lot of snow, but the latest storm has dumped a foot.

I'm selling used cars and that's about it. Since I've been living up here you wouldn't recognize me—hair past my shoulders and face whiter than a Canuck's. It's 4 in the morning and I'm writing because I can't sleep. Every letter I mail home gets sent back with red marks all over it. When I get one of those RETURN TO SENDERs I'll be going along okay, then all of a sudden I'm bawling my eyes out.

Hope the 3 of you will be together this Christmas. Kissinger keeps saying that 'peace is at hand'. Maybe I'll be with you next year if it ever manages to break out.

Love, Rhett

PS: If you have my kachina, please send it. There's fuck all here to remind me of home.

Katie had started to read her brother's letter again when Mr Giuliano peered around the door of Studio 1. 'Hi, Sal. Make yourself a coffee. I'll be with you in a minute.'

She stood in front of the mirror at Zanetti's School of Ballroom and forced herself to look at her reflection. She turned sideways and sucked in her stomach. This morning the scale had nudged a hundred and eighty pounds. For the next two hours, she could forget she was putting on weight, forget her parents were behaving so stupidly, forget she hadn't been to a ballet class in over six months.

She wet two strands of hair with spit and wound them around her index finger. She pressed them to her cheek, holding them until they fell in loose corkscrews. She was about to put on fresh lipstick when Sal came into the room. Even before she saw him, she could smell him. He doused himself with musk aftershave whenever he came for his lesson.

She smiled at him in the mirror, dressed in his ruffled shirt and bell-bottom trousers, his long hair side-combed to hide his shiny head. He went straight to the barre and started to do the *pliés* she'd taught him as a warm-up so his legs wouldn't cramp during the lesson.

She put her brother's letter in her purse and adjusted her shawl. 'Before we start our first session today on the tango, Mr G, I want to tell you a little about its history. It originated in Buenos Aires where it was first danced in brothels.'

Stifling a giggle, Mr Giuliano slid a gloved hand over his mouth. He had a withered hand that he kept covered when he danced.

'Millions of men came to Argentina at the turn of the century. Most were too poor to marry so the tango was a means of expressing their passion.'

She walked toward the record player wearing the shoes he had given her. Each step she took produced a flash of light generated by the AA batteries in the heels. She'd found them in front of her locker with a card. *From your loving student, Sal G.* She wore the Lite Steps for all her private classes, but when she taught Sal, she had the uncomfortable feeling that he was hugging her feet.

She wore a different costume for each of the ballroom dances she taught: a flapper's outfit for the foxtrot, Carmen Miranda turban and a ruffled dress for the cha-cha and Oxford pumps and a poodle skirt for the swing. Her outfits were old clothes she'd found in thrift shops and decorated with costume jewelry and accessories. Today she was wearing her black slit skirt, parrot-covered shawl and fishnet tights. To complete her tango outfit, she wore an enormous cloth rose pinned above her ear.

She looked up to see Mr Zanetti grinning at her through the studio window. She laced her fingers into Mr Giuliano's and cupped one hand around his neck. Mr Zanetti used to teach the introductory classes, but when he saw how successful she was with the beginners, he'd turned them all over to her.

'In the tango, there should be the illusion of two bodies moving as one, so the man has to be strong when he leads. They say that to dance tango properly you need four legs, but one heart.'

She took the man's position and fitted herself against Mr Giuliano. 'The man guides his partner with slight pressure from the whole of his right side like this.' Katie pressed against him to demonstrate, her face touching his cheek. 'The tango's classic step is a gliding figure of eight. I'll show you the simplified walk, or *paseo*, first so you can get the hang of it. The line of dance is counterclockwise like a horse race.'

'I like the ponies,' he said. 'Especially fillies.'

She smiled at him, but not too much. 'You step forward on your left foot, leaving the right in place while you count 1 - 2 to yourself. Then you step forward on the right, leaving the left in place, counting 3 - 4. Then you step forward with the left on count 5, then step to the side with the right foot on count 6. On counts 7 and 8, you close your left foot to the right without taking any weight on it.'

'Show me again, Katie.'

She demonstrated the pattern again slowly, but Mr Giuliano put his hands to his head. 'You're going too fast for this old brain.'

'Don't get caught up in the steps. Think of the *paseo* as a stylized walk.'

She pushed and prodded him around the studio floor, feeling his heart pump as her fingers held his wrinkled neck. 'Slow . . . slow, quick, quick, slow. Slow . . . slow, quick, quick, slow. That's it. You're doing great, Mr G.'

Over and over, she made him repeat the *paseo* with the music. He swayed with the rhythm as he became more confident. A lock of hair became unplastered and hung stiffly by his ear.

'With tango, the ankles come together quickly on each step. There's a little delay in the movement of the feet which gives the dance a staccato feeling.' She showed him one of her favorite moves, a running form of the walk, causing her shoes to shoot off sparks of light.

'*Brava*,' he said, clapping his hands. '*Brava*, Miss Lite Steps.'

She got into position to try it with him. Sal started to stroke the inside of her palm. She couldn't let him get away with that, but she didn't want to hurt his feelings either. She walked to the front of the studio and lifted the needle off the record. Though her back was to him, she could feel his lonely heart sail after her.

'Mr G, it's important to keep your focus.' She pointed to the chair she had her male students use when they got too amorous. 'Pick up that chair and pretend it's your partner. Keep your body straight and tall and your knees bent, like you're trying to sneak up on someone without being seen.'

Sal picked up the chair. Looking unhappy, he started to tango across the worn floorboards with swaying and jerking movements, watched by the smiling eyes of Ginger Rogers and Fred Astaire.

After Sal's private lesson ended and she'd taken the five-dollar tip he insisted on pressing into her palm, she stood in Mr Zanetti's doorway. She cleared her throat. Her feet were killing her. She'd been here since ten and it was almost four.

'Hey, kid,' Mr Zanetti said, looking up from his paperwork. 'That was some lesson. You dance tango like you're on fire. No wonder all the old guys from Little Italy want to take private lessons. They go straight from you to dance with the widows at Roseland.'

'Mr Zanetti—'

'Tony. How many times do I have to tell you?'

'Tony, this week could I have my salary check early? My brother's going through a tough time. I'd like to buy him some presents so he'll have them before Christmas.'

Zanetti opened a drawer and took out a checkbook. She watched the loops he made as he wrote. It amazed her that his handwriting looked Italian, even though he'd been born in Newark.

'I ain't trying to be funny or nothing, Katie, but you look kinda lonely.'

'I'm not lonely, Mr Zanetti. That's just the shape of my mouth.'

'Tony,' he said, handing her the check. 'Tone. What gives with you, kid? You been here six months and I still don't know nothing about you except your address and Social Security number.'

Want to know about me, Mr Zanetti? she thought. My brother is in Canada and can't ever come home. My parents think he's a traitor and refuse to have anything to do with him. I'm sixty-three pounds overweight and my parents think I'm a soloist in a big ballet company. Anything else you want to know?

She looked at the waltzing figurines on his desk. 'Save the whales,' she said. 'Collect the whole set.' She smiled and backed toward the door.

She was loaded with presents for her brother when she passed an old diner near Times Square. In the dark it looked like a huge illuminated fish tank with a hot-water samovar in the corner. Hunched over the counter was a young man in a leather jacket, hair hanging past his shoulders. From the back he looked just like Rhett. She leaned against the plate glass, heart slamming against her ribs. Surely he wouldn't have taken the chance of crossing the border and getting arrested.

She pushed open the heavy glass door to smells of roast coffee and old grease. She sat a few stools away to try and catch a glimpse of his face. *You wouldn't recognize me. Hair past my shoulders and face whiter than a Canuck's.*

She was suddenly aware of a voice saying to her, 'Wanna order, fatso?'

Katie glared at the ponytailed woman in a white uniform. 'What did you say?' She'd been staring so hard at the young man she hadn't noticed her.

'Wanna order or go?'

Katie pulled her hair in front of her face. 'I'll have a black coffee.'

'Why didn't you say so the first time?' The waitress snapped her gum and turned toward the silver urn in the corner.

Katie stole one last glance at the man bent over the counter and started to pick up her packages. Even if he was her brother, there was no way she could let him see her like this. Not when she'd told him she was dancing with American Ballet Theater. She couldn't let him see her now, any more than she could tell him that as far as their parents were concerned, he was dead.

WHITEHORSE, 1977

It is better to be a coward for a minute
than dead the rest of your life.

IRISH PROVERB

Sweetgrass

Rhett stood outside the cabin, waiting for his trapping partner to return from Whitehorse. Yas wouldn't be back for hours, but still Rhett searched the snow-covered clearing for the team of panting huskies. He was grateful he didn't have to make the long journey to Whitehorse today; he'd woken up with the Hershey squirts. Making a dogsled trip with the runs was not something he was looking forward to. He felt relieved when Yas had volunteered to go in his place, even though it hadn't been his turn to pick up supplies and hit the post office.

He had a feeling there was going to be a letter from Katie today. He'd seen a magpie when he hadn't seen one for months. There was going to be news all right; he'd just have to wait until Yas came back. That might not be for hours because Yas was an Athapaskan who lived according to the sun, moon and seasons, not a piece of ticking metal strapped to his arm.

Rhett had tried to contact his parents a half-dozen times since he'd heard about the presidential pardon last month, but all his envelopes had came back, unopened. Katie's last letter had sounded like she was going to do something. Something to pave the way for him to go home. *Ever since you went to Canada, Rhett, our family has been broken. Now that the amnesty has been announced, I see it as my duty to try to pull it together again. I'll write and let you know when I'm going back to New Mexico.*

He looked at the sky. From where the sun was, he guessed it must be eleven. He decided to play a game of *huachas* against himself before he checked the traps. He'd taught Yas the game to help get through the long Yukon summers when there was sun twenty-four hours a day and it was so bright at night it was almost impossible to sleep. During those white nights they'd have an ongoing tournament with aggregate scores, but today's game would be a match of solitaire with winter rules because the *huacha* pitch was knee-high in snow.

He picked up a jar full of washers and shook some into his glove. He threw one, aiming it at one of Yas' circular footprints. Four points to sink a washer and one point for the washer closest to the hole.

He had trouble controlling his hand because of the cold. The washer curved to the left, hit on its rim and rolled. He shook his head, glad that Yas wasn't here to tease him about his aim. He pitched three more to finish his round. He'd just started another game against himself when he felt a gurgle in his bowels.

Not wanting to be caught short, he started in the direction of the shithouse, stepping into the racket-shaped patterns he'd made earlier. All he'd done since he'd moved to Canada was make tracks, leaving little evidence of where he'd been, moving westwards from one little town to the next.

He opened the door to the privy. It had been almost five years since he'd had a crap on American soil. The only time he'd been back was when he'd visited the Vista, the stretch of tree-bare land that created a visible border between the United States and Canada.

He'd been staying at a shelter an ex-GI had set up to help conscientious objectors when they first crossed over. The house was packed and he had to sleep on a camp bed in the hall. All he did the first week was lay in his cot, slug Coke and eat Fritos. Every few days he called home but, as soon as his parents heard his voice, they would slam down the phone. When calling didn't work, he tried letters. The first envelope he received in St Catharines with *SENDER UNKNOWN* messed him up so much he went to every bar in town until they refused to serve him. Somehow he made his way into the woods outside town. He staggered into a hunters' blind on the US side, even though his paranoid brain believed the Feds were behind every tree. He'd spent a long night there, puking and crying, watching moose and caribou move freely from one side of the Vista to the other.

He looked at the sun through a knot hole in the door. He wondered if Yas had reached the post office yet, standing at the counter in mukluks and furs. He and Yas had teamed up eight months ago. Yas' offer of employment had come at a good time. Rhett had moved around Canada so much he'd been glad to stay in one place for a while. Since leaving the States he'd had all kinds of go-nowhere, shit jobs: gas station attendant, silo worker, bus boy, turkey sexer, fruit picker, janitor.

Rhett had never let himself get close to anyone up north except Yas and Marie Devereaux. He'd met her last summer in Saskatchewan while he was working on her father's wheat farm. They'd spent the summer together, sneaking out into the high grass of the prairie, making love under the stars. He'd never told her he was an American. Yankees were indistinguishable from Canadians. The surest way of telling the difference was to say that to a Canuck and watch them get mad.

He'd done something he wasn't proud of when he'd found himself falling for Marie. He'd cut and run without even saying goodbye. Marie was a Catholic who didn't believe in birth control. He knew that if he didn't leave town, there'd be a shotgun wedding and he and Marie would end up with a passel of kids like everyone else in her family. Not that that was so bad, but if the opportunity ever came to return to New Mexico, Marie would want to stay in Saskatchewan and he'd never get to cross that Vista for good, that twenty feet of dirt that kept him from going home.

He unrolled a fistful of paper, cleaned himself and trudged back to the cabin. The traps could wait. He needed some food to heat him up.

He hung his snowshoes on a nail and went inside. He pulled off his gloves to pick a big potato out of the vegetable bin. He was going to make one of his specials: baked spud with tuna fish. He pierced the King Edward with an eight-inch nail to make it cook faster, wrapped it in foil and put it in the embers of the stove.

He sat back in his chair, staring at his map of New Mexico. The corners had been chewed off by thumbtacks he'd used to pin it to the wall of every room he'd lived in since he left. Next to it was a map of Canada. He looked at the place names he'd circled one drunken night: Come By Chance, Bummers Roost, Deadman's Bay, Head-Smashed-In Buffalo Jump.

He moved his finger from St Catharines, the town where he'd first crossed over, to Oshawa, where he'd lived in a converted garage. Moose Jaw, where he'd left in the middle of the night because he couldn't pay his rent. Medicine Hat, where he'd worked in the gas fields. Fairy Glen, where he'd met Marie. He hadn't been able to put down roots in any of those places because he had a big ache in his heart for home.

He put his finger on Coutts, Alberta, then on its sister city just across the border. When there hadn't been a hope in hell of going back, he'd promised himself that if the chance ever came, he'd enter the States from Sweetgrass, Montana, because from there, home was fifteen hundred miles straight down.

FORTUNA, 1977

No matter what happens in your life,
nobody can take away your dance.

SPANISH PROVERB

Four diamond chips

Katie went straight to her bedroom with the box of skin she'd brought back from Dr Bouchard's. She locked the door and started to lift things out of her trunk. Tubes of old lipstick and greasepaint. A stencil with a dozen eyebrow patterns. Chignons. Artificial flowers. Pink leg warmers. A plug-in make-up mirror with a dozen small lights around the sides.

She picked up a scrapbook bulging with souvenir programs, recital photographs and newspaper clippings. On the first page was a yellowed article from the *Fortuna Sun-News*.

> **Dec 15, 1967.** For ten of her fifteen years, Katie Rivers has been a student at Carmel McCleary's School of The Dance. Her dedication to the art of ballet has finally paid off.
> Since September, Katie has been commuting to El Paso to take lessons with Madame Yekaterina Feodorova and attend rehearsals for her forthcoming début in *The Nutcracker* ballet. Dr and Mrs Haywood Rivers have taken it in turn to drive her to her workouts, clocking up almost 5000 miles in the last few months. Dr Rivers, a well-known local dentist, was quoted by this reporter as saying, 'You can put in your article that I wore a car out taking her to El Paso.'

She smiled as she read what her father had said. She looked at the black-and-white picture accompanying the article. She was standing in the wings wearing a long tulle skirt, a Leko lantern on the opposite side of the stage, shining on her like a miniature sun.

Katie looked at the box of skin. If she was going to make a ceremony of this, she was going to do it right. She opened her old make-up kit and picked up a small bar of soap. She spit on it and rubbed it on her eyebrows to cake them flat. She coated her face with greasepaint, applying the Panstick from hair- to chin-line, sealing it with face powder. She pressed a plastic stencil against her forehead, drawing in brows that were boldly-arched, higher and thicker than her own. She glued on a set of upper and lower lashes and applied eye shadow, mascara, rouge and lipstick which she outlined with a fine border of black. She crowned herself with a circle of cloth flowers.

She poured the parings from Dr Bouchard's box into an ashtray. She tried to think of the right words to say, but they didn't come. She didn't want to be like her student, Mr Aiello, whose dream of being a pitcher for the Yankees had ended when he'd dislocated his shoulder. He was in his fifties now, still bitter about the career he felt he had deserved. He never had a good word to say about anyone, not even his beautiful Jamaican girlfriend who met him at the studio after his weekly lessons with homemade jerk chicken.

She lit a candle and held the flame in the dead skin until the flakes caught fire. Katerina Gorbanyevskaya was gone. Those years of ballet may have come to nothing, but they had made her who she was. Wiser, kinder, deeper. She was rich in ways that could never be counted, that could never taken away. And if she had to do it all over again, she wouldn't change a thing.

She caught a glimpse of herself in the mirror, the wreath of flowers sitting cockeyed on her head. She started laughing as she opened a jar of cold cream to clean off her make-up. She was wiping away the last of the Panstick when she heard a knock at her door.

'My back's hurting, sugar. I need some help changing the linens.'

Her mother was standing in the hallway, holding an armload of sheets.

'What's that stink, Katie?'

'Just some incense.'

Her mother reached into the pocket of her smock. 'This just came. It's from Weeslaw. There's a kiss on the flap.'

Katie slid the letter into her purse, an envelope she'd typed herself and had a friend mail after she'd left New York.

'Aren't you going to open it, sugar?'

'Later.'

'You tell that fiancé of yours we're going to need a list of who he wants to invite to the wedding. I need to let the printer know.'

Katie glanced at the zircon chip on her left hand. A fake diamond for a fake wedding. 'While I strip the beds, Momma, why don't you look at these?' She opened a drawer and handed her mother some magazines she'd grabbed at LaGuardia. 'You can help me choose a dress.'

Her mother flicked through *Elegant Bride* as Katie lifted the mattress to remove the fitted sheet.

'What do you think about this dress, sugar?' Her mother pointed at a tulip-shaped gown with puff sleeves and bows on the skirt.

'I'd like something a little more classic.' Katie flicked the pages until she found an ivory empire dress with a square neck and long train. 'What do you think of this one, Momma?'

Her mother looked horrified. 'If you wear something like that, sugar, people will think you're PG.'

She laughed and sat down on the vanity stool next to the mother. 'I can assure you I'm not PG. Now I want you to tell me what your wedding was like.'

'What do you want to know about that for?'

'Because I'm curious.'

Her mother closed the magazine. 'The only planning we did was a trip to the jeweler. I didn't like the engagement rings they had in McKenzie so I made Haywood drive me to Paris. When we got to the jeweler there, he wanted to buy a ring that cost fifteen dollars. I held out for the twenty-dollar one because it had four little chips.' Her mother sighed. 'I sure loved that ring.'

Katie looked for the familiar band on her mother's finger. It wasn't there.

Her mother stared wistfully at her bare hand. 'It washed down the sink a few years ago. I'm still upset about losing that ring. I always thought of the four stones as you, me, Daddy and Rhett.'

Her mother's face drained of color. It was the first time since her brother had left the country that Katie had heard her mother say his name. But it wasn't the time to argue for Rhett's return. She still hadn't figured out how she was going to talk her parents into letting him come back. 'Tell me more about the day you got married, Momma.'

Her mother cleared her throat. She looked relieved to have something else to talk about. 'Daddy had been wanting to get married for a while, but I didn't want to until we'd both graduated from college.

Then Pearl Harbor happened and we knew he could be sent overseas any time.'

'Did Granddaddy Baker give you away?'

Her mother shook her head. 'My family didn't want Daddy and I to tie the knot until the war was over.'

'You never told me that.'

'There are some things you don't want your children to know.'

'Where were you married?'

'At the preacher's house. Reverend Wheeler worked at the U-Tote-Em Grocery and had to do the ceremony between shifts. Delta and I were secretly getting ready to go to the ceremony when Aunt Jertie came over to try and talk me out of it. She kept saying Hay and I were too young to get married and I had my hair cranked up under a turban, getting ready to elope.'

'What'd you wear?'

'An old gray dress I already had. It was the stingiest wedding you've ever seen. No music or flowers. Not even punch or a pound cake.' Her mother twisted her mouth. 'I would have given anything if we'd married at Liberty Chapel. We could have decorated the church with holly and invited friends so they could throw rice. We didn't know any better than to run off and get married, but we were young and foolish and thought we had the world by the tail.'

Katie felt a rush of sadness, picturing the young bride her mother had been. Nothing had turned out the way her mother had imagined it: her marriage, her children, her dreams of college, her expectations as remote as the stars.

Burrito wandered into the room, claws clattering on the hardwood floor. Katie picked her up to stroke her.

'That dog's never been the same since you left,' her mother said. She stiffly stood up. 'So what are you going to wear?'

Katie looked at her, confused. 'You know I haven't bought a wedding dress yet.'

'To the New Year's Eve Ball. Remember I wrote we've finally been accepted as members of the Country Club? They're having a big dinner dance with live music. You'll love it.'

'If you don't mind, Momma, I'd rather stay home. I've never been one for ballroom.'

'We've already bought your ticket, sugar. Besides, you know how much your Daddy loves to dance. He's been looking forward for months to showing you off.'

She thought of the only dress she'd packed. She'd bought it at Bloomingdale's the day after her last Weight Watcher's meeting. When she'd reached her goal of a hundred and seventeen pounds, she purchased a thigh-high backless dress to celebrate. Katie knew her mother would spit nails before she'd let her wear something like that to a function at the Country Club. 'I don't have anything to wear.'

Her mother's mouth tightened into a determined line. She went to the closet and pulled out a lime-green chiffon ball dress, a fat flower on the front. 'The New Year's Eve dance is all your Daddy's been talking about. Now try this on and see if it fits.'

The magician disappears

Katie looked at the clock on the nicotine-yellow wall of the Greyhound station. Still a quarter of an hour till her bus left. She pulled out a stick of Juicy Fruit and shoved it into her mouth.

'Hey, sweetheart. Where you goin'?'

The cowboy opposite her was wearing a ten-gallon hat, sheepskin jacket, jeans and a T-shirt that said PUT SOME RAWHIDE BETWEEN YOUR LEGS.

Katie pretended she hadn't heard him. There was something desperate about him: bitten nails, cardboard boxes stacked beside him tied with greasy string.

'Hey,' he said. 'I asked you where you was goin'.' When she didn't answer, he sat down beside her to read her ticket. 'We're goin' the same way. How about some company?'

She said in her best French accent, *'Je ne parle pas anglais.'*

His lip curled into a sneer as he slid his hand inside his jacket. She thought for a second he might be reaching for a gun or knife, but the only thing his fingers held was a crumpled pack of Lucky Strikes.

'You think you're something special,' he said, waving a bent cigarette at her. 'You think you're too high an' mighty to talk to a stomp.'

She pushed her way through the crowded lobby to the bathroom. For half a minute she patted the wall, trying to find the light switch in the dark. The tube groaned, crackled, flickered into life.

Katie looked at herself in the mirror and put on some foundation to try and hide the patch of hives that had just erupted on her neck.

The bus didn't take I-10 like she expected. It turned onto the old two-lane highway south of town. She checked to see if the cowboy was still sitting at the back. She saw him near the toilet, stetson tipped over his face. With half a bus between them, she hoped she wouldn't have to dredge up her high-school French again.

She stared out the window. Outside the city limits ranch-style houses disappeared, replaced by fields of cotton stalks waiting to be plowed under for the winter. Katie leaned her neck against the cold window to cool her burning hives. She took out two sticks of Juicy Fruit and rammed them both into her mouth while the tires whispered, *Madame... Madame... Madame... Madame.*

She saw the familiar Citroën outside the stage door and her palms started to sweat. She looked at the ten-dollar bill in her wallet and then the meter. She was afraid that if she waited for change she'd chicken out and tell the cabbie to go back to the Greyhound station.

'Sure you got the right time for the matinee? Everyone's leaving the auditorium.'

Katie leaned over the seat and handed him the bill for her $6.30 fare. 'Happy New Year.'

He gave her a big grin as she got out. 'And a happy New Year to you, too, lady.'

She walked over to the Citroën to run her hand along the frog-shaped body, so unlike the boxy American ones pulling out of the parking lot. She made a roof for her eyes to look inside. Tutus were piled on the leather seat where she'd once sat to be driven to costume fittings. She'd loved it when Madame turned the ignition on and the hydraulics had lifted the chassis. It always made her think of a ballerina going *en pointe.*

She tiptoed past the noisy dressing rooms toward the rehearsal studio. Madame would arrive soon to say a prayer in front of her icon as she always did after a performance.

A program was on the grand piano. Katie picked it up.

Alejandra Castillo............................ Cinderella

It didn't surprise her that the little girl with carnations in her hair was now dancing a leading role.

Kevin Self............................ Prince Charming
(Guest Artist, American Ballet Theater)
Lauren van Patten .... Fairy Godmother

Her eye swept down the list of credits as she heard footsteps in the corridor. She threw the program down and turned so that her face couldn't be seen from the door.

The shoes stopped. Silence for what seemed forever and then, 'Katyusha.'

A chill ran up her spine. She felt Madame's eyes boring into her back, stunned she had recognized her from behind after not having seen her for eight years.

Madame looked exactly the same, except that her make-up was thicker. She was wearing a chiffon dress cinched at the waist and had an orchid pinned in her hair. Her teacher leaned forward to kiss her. She did it cooly, politely, three times.

'So you've come back to see me,' Madame said. 'What are you doing with yourself these days?'

'I'm . . . I'm—' Before she could stop herself she blurted out, 'I'm teaching ballet in New York.'

Madame walked over to her icon and made the sign of the cross. 'You should come back to El Paso and teach with me.' She kissed the tips of her fingers and pressed them to the Virgin's mouth, smiling in a way that Katie couldn't read.

'Don't look shocked, Katya. I always knew you'd be a teacher. You were too intelligent to be a dancer. The cast party is starting. Join us.'

She was reeling, completely stunned by what her teacher had just said. Katie wanted to speak to Madame alone to get her to explain what she'd meant, but she'd already left the room. Katie had no choice except to share her with a crowd of teenagers, high on post-performance adrenaline.

She rushed out of the rehearsal room to follow Madame down the maze of corridors to a room decorated with balloons. By the couch was a buffet table covered with chips, dips and a large rectangle of cake iced with HAPPY NEW YEAR.

Madame touched her arm, grinning like an alligator. 'Tell me exactly what you're doing in New York.'

She was desperately trying to think of a convincing lie when Alejandra appeared in the doorway. The last time Katie had seen her, she had been one of the rats in *The Nutcracker*. That little girl was now a stunning eighteen-year-old.

'*Golubchik*,' Madame called out, 'there's someone I want you to see.'

Katie felt a stab of jealousy hearing the Russian nickname she'd never heard Madame use with anyone else. She realized now how other members of the company must have felt when Katie used to be her 'little dove'.

Madame stroked Alejandra's waist-long hair. 'She's just been accepted by the New York City Ballet. She'll be joining the company after she graduates from high school.' She smiled at her protégée. 'Do you remember Katya?'

'She used to take the beginners' class with us. She was twice as old as everyone else.'

'That's right,' Madame said. 'She had a lot to unlearn.' She glanced over her shoulder at the buffet table. 'Alejandra's tired after her performance. She needs to put her feet up. Why don't you get her a little piece of cake?'

Katie went to the table and picked up the knife. She cut two pieces: a huge slab for the *golubchik* and a sliver for herself. She handed Alejandra the paper plate bending with cake and mashed her own thin piece into crumbs as she watched her teacher and Alejandra talking, their heads bent toward each other like lovers.

Madame looked at her watch and suddenly stood up. She walked to the center of the room beneath a frilly paper-covered donkey suspended from the ceiling. 'Boys and girls,' she said, clapping her hands. 'Time to break open the *piñata*. Everyone gets three tries. Cinderella first.'

Alejandra stepped forward. Madame blindfolded her with a bandana. She handed the girl a sawn-off broom stick and spun her a half-dozen times. Alejandra staggered coming out of the spin, took a swing at the *piñata*, then another and another. Katie smiled to herself, glad the *golubchik* had struck out.

Alejandra blindfolded Lauren van Patten and spun her around. Lauren broke the donkey's leg on her first try. The crack was so like the one her knee had made that Katie shivered. Wanting to see what effect the sound had had on her teacher, she looked for Madame, but she wasn't there. Katie frantically searched the room. The bus for Fortuna left in an hour. This would be her last chance if she was going to speak to her.

Katie headed backstage, even though she didn't know where her teacher had gone. She rushed in and out of the flats, asking every stagehand if they'd seen Madame Feodorova. Finally, one thumbed toward a flight of stairs leading to the catwalk.

Katie ran to where he'd pointed and stood in the shadows. It took a few seconds for her to catch her breath, for her eyes to adjust from the bright work lights of the stage to the darkness in the wings. It was then she saw her teacher sitting at the bottom of the catwalk stairs.

She watched Madame put her hands behind her. She started to lift herself up backward, riser by riser, her face twisted in pain. She was a third of the way up the stairs before Katie asked, 'What are you doing?'

Madame's chin snapped up. She gazed into the darkness, her mouth open. 'Who's there?'

Katie waited a few seconds before she stepped from the shadows.

'Why are you spying on me?'

'I'm not spying on you, Madame. I wanted to see you alone.'

'What are you doing here?'

'Why have you been avoiding me?'

'I don't know what you're talking about, Katya.'

Katie looked upstage, remembering exactly where she'd fallen, how Madame had pulled her twisted leg out from behind her and forced her to do *pliés*. 'As a teacher, you had a responsibility toward me.'

'What do you mean?'

'You told me not to see a doctor.' She searched Madame's face, hoping to see some remorse, but it was as impassive as the icon's face she'd watched her teacher kiss.

'I told you that if you saw a surgeon he'd stick a knife in you and you'd never dance again.'

'And I was told I needed surgery if I wanted to dance.'

'It was your fate, Katya.'

'It wasn't my fate. I'd been rehearsing a principal role for six hours without a break.'

'I couldn't have judged how tired you were. Only you could have done that.'

'I wanted to please you. I worshipped you.'

Madame gave a little bark of a laugh, carefully studying her face to see if she had drawn blood. 'Dancers are expendable, Katya. I couldn't waste my energy on someone who was broken.'

'Did someone say that to you, Madame?'

The faintest of smiles passed over her face. 'We have the life of our dreams, Katya, and our real life. When you fell, your dream was already behind you. You just refused to acknowledge the truth.' Madame straightened her back; her face became hard again. 'If it will make you feel better, call the others. Have your revenge. Show them I am a cripple.'

She stared at her teacher's hands, resting in the folds of chiffon, old hands covered with liver spots. She shook her head, loving and hating her at the same time.

'You who had the possibility of being a star in the true meaning of the word. Not of this earth.'

Katie watched in astonishment as her teacher started to beat her neck with her fists. She wrapped her arms around herself, then put her hands to her heart and with jerky, demented movements gave it away.

The skin on Katie's arms rose in goosebumps. Was Madame trying to say that she was angry? That she was sorry? Or only showing her how Petrouchka was meant to be danced?

Katie was trying to figure it out when she heard a crash. She turned around and saw a ladder had fallen but, by the time she looked back, Madame Feodorova had vanished into thin air.

One last little white lie

At 303 South Main her mother turned the Lincoln into a unpaved driveway. 'This car has been here so many times, I don't even have to steer it.'

Her mother left the motor running as Katie opened the passenger door. 'It's nice you're going to surprise Carmel. She hasn't been that good lately. A new ballet teacher's moved to town and Carmel's only teaching part time now.'

Blushing, Katie thought about the last letter her teacher had sent. *The studio roof is leaking and the well at my farm has gone out. I've had to borrow six grand and the well still isn't worth a hoot. If that wasn't bad enough, I'm down to thirty-seven students. What they pay for their lessons hardly covers my rent.*

Katie leaned forward to gave her mother a peck. 'Thanks for the ride.'

'Give me a call when you're ready to come home. We're leaving for the New Year's Eve ball at eight sharp.'

The car pulled away and Katie remembered how, even after receiving that letter, she hadn't tried to get in touch with Carmel. She'd been meaning to write, but since she'd told Carmel she'd joined American Ballet Theater, her teacher's letters had long lists of questions. Like what roles was she performing and what cities had she been to on tour. In the last six years, she'd only written a half-dozen letters. It had been easier to put Carmel's letters into a shoe box rather than make up complicated lies she wouldn't remember.

Katie saw her engagement ring sparkling on her finger. She slipped it off and put it in her purse. One less lie to have to worry about. Before knocking on the peeling door she read a dozen times the dates the Carmel McCleary School of The Dance would be closed for Christmas.

Carmel stood in the doorway, hands clapped to her face. 'I can't believe it's you. I can't believe it's you and not a mirage!'

Katie bashfully kissed her, the familiar scent of Evening in Paris on her teacher's wrinkled neck.

Carmel stepped back to admire her. 'Don't you look fabulous.'

'You're the one who looks fabulous. You haven't changed in years.' In her red leotard and fishnet tights her teacher was lean and flat-stomached, even though she was in her mid-sixties. 'I wanted to give you a surprise. Hope you don't mind.'

'Mind?' Carmel said. 'Seeing you, kid, is the best thing that's happened to me in years. This calls for a celebration.' Her teacher draped a towel around her shoulders as she headed toward the back room.

Katie wandered around the huge studio. It was exactly as it had always been: the lamp with a cardboard circle taped to it for spotting, the rag rug in the lobby, the record player that could speed up or slow down LPs without distorting the sound.

Over the large windows were curling silhouettes of dancers, each in an awkward cardboard pose. Above the wall of mirrors at the front were four bas-relief ballerinas in nylon-net tutus. The grinning girls who'd witnessed Katie's first *plié* hadn't aged in twenty years.

She walked over to the bulletin board covered with a dozen orange squares pinned with thumbtacks. *CINDY SCHAEFER, JOSIE TELLES, WAVA SUE BIRKETT.* Katie took down the name of a girl she had danced with as a child. A 1964 bill for two months of dance classes. Carmel's vain attempt to shame her parents into paying a $24.72 debt.

Carmel came out holding two tumblers wrapped in napkins. 'I made us a Volga Boatman. Two parts vodka, one part brandy and a squirt of OJ.' She raised her glass filled with ice. 'Chin-chin.'

Katie looked at her tall drink. It was just what she needed to give her the courage to confess.

Her teacher took a long sip. 'When did you blow into town?'

'A few days ago.'

'How long's it been since you were back?'

'Six years.'

Neither of them said anything, then Carmel finally looked up. 'Know what I was thinking when I was mixing our drinks? When you were five and first came to the studio, I called you my happy little puppy because you were always at my heels. I could never get you to look at my feet when I was demonstrating, no matter what I did.'

'Know why that was, Carmel? You were the most glamorous woman

I'd ever seen. You were always in a leotard and tights and wore your hair in a ballerina net. I wanted to be like you, even at five.'

Her eyes filling, Carmel turned to face the picture of Pavlova that hung above the couch.

'I'd like to propose a toast, Carmel. May 1978 be a great year for you, your studio and your farm.' Katie reached inside her purse to take out five hundred dollars in cash. 'I can't tell you how guilty I feel about not repaying you sooner.' She tried to give Carmel the money, but her hand was pushed away. 'Please take it. I don't know what would have happened to me without your help.'

'I don't want to hear any more about it.'

'I'd never have been able to leave Fortuna if it hadn't been for you. I might have given up.' She tried to give her the money again, but Carmel waved it away.

'Case is closed.'

'It would make me feel better if you'd take it.'

'I'll never take it, kid.'

You need it, she wanted to say, more than I do. 'Why not?'

Carmel took a long slug of her drink. 'Because you're what keeps me going. The number of kids that have trooped through that door and the only one who ever made a success is you. When I'm on the verge of strangling the preschoolers, you're what keeps me going. When the first to sixth graders horse around, I think of you. When I'm screaming at boy-crazy teenagers who go backwards instead of forwards, I keep telling myself that maybe one of these kids will turn out to be a ballerina like you.'

Katie looked at the hook rug Carmel's mother had crocheted out of old dresses. 'Didn't you ever wonder why I never sent any programs or press cuttings?'

'I know how hard professional dancers work. Every spare minute you're sewing ribbons on toe shoes or washing tights. Writing letters is for people who have spare time on their hands.' Carmel smiled and threw back what was left of her drink.

Katie didn't know where to begin. She stared at the floor and glimpsed a vodka bottle lying beneath the couch. Remembering what had happened before she left for New York, she gently nudged it out of sight with her foot. One evening she'd rung Carmel to ask if she could come to the studio on Sunday to practice. A little girl had picked up the phone. Katie asked to speak to Carmel. There was a long silence. She thought she'd dialed a wrong number and was about to hang up when a sliding voice said, 'Katie, is that you?' The voice was Carmel's: ashamed, sad, desperately trying to sound sober. That was when Katie had put the receiver down and cried.

She looked up into her teacher's wrinkled face, knowing that Carmel had devoted her life to this school. Carmel who had never married or had children, her only companions a pair of fierce Dobermans who grew old and died and were replaced by big-footed, dock-tailed puppies. For more than two decades, she'd lived in a room added to the back of her studio, working for half the year to put on a recital so that little girls in Fortuna could have the thrill of performing on stage, experience the magic of ballet.

Katie smiled sadly as she cupped her teacher's hand. She had come here not just to repay Carmel, but to confess the only dancing she'd done for the last six years had been at a school that taught ballroom. But she realized that sometimes—sometimes—one little white lie can be a far greater gift than the truth.

The Double Happiness Company

Her father was planning to wear his white boat Oxfords to the New Year's Eve party, huge leather hulls he'd moored on the floor of his closet for more than twenty years. He sat by the toaster polishing them. They were being given a new paint job, the laces stiff as vermicelli.

'The tickets were only thirty bucks for everything, Katie. Dancing, party favors, champagne at midnight. You'll love it. The Down Beats are playing. They're the best band in town.'

'Bet they took a long time to come up with that name,' she teased. 'People are so short on imagination around here.'

A dribble of white polish ran down his arm. 'You used to like it before you left.'

'Can't keep 'em down on the farm once they've seen Paree.' She adjusted the straps of the black dress she'd worn in spite of her mother's objections: V-necked, a vast expanse of back.

'I hope you're not wearing those old clodhoppers to the dance,' her mother called from the bathroom. 'Wear a pair of my pumps. Nobody wears things like that at the Club.'

She meant the Country Club. There were two now in Fortuna: a new glass palace with a postcard view of the mountains and the old one off Elks Drive. Her parents had joined the cinderblock club with its peeling paint and mangy fairways, cast off by the well-to-do like last season's coat.

Her father started lacing up his Oxfords. 'Hurry up, Momma. We need to get this show on the road.'

'Hold your horses, Haywood. I need to put on my war paint.'

Katie leaned around the bathroom door. Her mother was squinting into the mirror, prodding her once-dark hair with her teasing comb. She drew on the arch of her eyebrows, rouged her cheeks, then massaged cornflower-blue eye shadow onto her lids. She put her glasses back on and opened her mouth for a swipe of Orchid Pink.

They slid into the Lincoln, the front seat wide enough for three not to touch. As her father backed out of the driveway, their breath plumed in the unheated air. Her mother dabbed Jungle Gardenia behind her ears and warned her husband to watch out for the drunks.

The car's headlights beamed down the highway past Perla's Upholstery, Smitty's Auto, the Lota-Burger drive-in. On the hill in front of the Country Club were three tall crosses in memory of the Spanish friars murdered by Apaches. The giant iron Ts had been there for years, but it was the first time Katie had seen them blinking with Christmas lights.

'I have some new groaners for you, Katie. What song did Dracula's gondolier sing?'

'I give up. What did Dracula's gondolier sing?'

'"Drained wops keep falling on my head."'

'Oh, Daddy, that's terrible.'

'Why don't Baptists make love standing up?'

'I give up.'

'Because people might think they're dancing.'

Her mother slapped his arm. 'Haywood, I'll never get you polished.'

'It's your patients I pity,' Katie said. 'They're a captive audience.' She was thinking of the poster in his treatment room. 'I'll bet you're the only dentist in the world who's got a picture of real pigs who look like they're kissing.'

Her father grinned from ear to ear. 'Not everyone can be sophisticated.'

They walked toward the clubhouse. Her mother kept looking at her clogs. Katie knew she was embarrassed by them, the same way Katie was ashamed of her father's old Oxfords. The two of them made the same big noise walking across the parking lot.

The Country Club ceiling was decorated with twisted crepe paper. Banqueting tables herringboned the room, on each one funny hats, paper horns, silver sparklers. Stuck to the plate-glass windows overlooking the golf course were foil-covered stars left over from Christmas.

They moved toward their table and her father said, 'What's wrong with you, Momma? You're walking like an old woman.'

'You know it's my back, Hay. It's been bad since I decorated the living room.'

'I told you not to do it,' her father said.

'And I told you to mind your own beeswax.'

Two Hispanic women floated past in identical fiesta dresses with gold-lamé shoes and belts. Katie smiled to herself. When her parents had moved to town, membership in the Country Club had been restricted. No Mexicans, Jews or half-breeds. Only Fortuna's top-drawer Protestants.

They sat at their table and drank bourbon and Seven in tall glasses with golfers enameled on them. Her father swirled his drink with a miniature nine iron. 'I'm sure glad you could come home this Christmas, Katie. I know how busy you are, but we sure appreciate it.' His giant feet on the dirty avocado carpet, the toe-cap of one shoe already scuffed.

He thumbed behind him at the Down Beats, four old men wearing vests with gold notes embroidered across their chests. 'Great band, aren't they?'

Her mother elbowed her to remind her of the conversation they'd had last night. Katie had gone to her mother's room where she'd been propped up in bed with a heating pad. 'I expect you to dance with your father when we go to the Country Club. It's his first chance in six years to show you off.'

'I don't want to be shown off. Why can't you dance with him?'

'I can't dance when my back's like this.'

'I don't know how to dance.'

'I don't know how you don't know how to dance, Katie Scarlett, after the thousands of dollars we spent on ballet lessons.'

She looked at her father, leaning in the direction of the dance floor, beating out the tango rhythm on the table with his ring. Her mother sitting next to him, swirling her ice cubes. *I can't dance when my back's like this.* Three wallflowers at the long table. Her mother nursed her back, her drink. Her father looked out the window into the rough.

'Made any New Year's resolutions, Daddy?'

Her father continued to drum his ring in time to the music. 'At my age, there's nothing to resolve.'

She pictured Rhett in Canada, sitting by the phone. There's an awful lot to resolve, she thought, even though you don't know it yet. She picked up a book of matches and struck one after another, watching the flames lick toward her fingers. 'How about a spin around the ballroom?'

'You know I'm a no-hoper as a dancer. I don't mind sitting out tonight.'

'No,' she said, leading him toward the dance floor. 'Won't take no-hoper for an answer. Besides,' she said, 'we've got to get our thirty dollars' worth.'

They got into promenade position and he said, 'I've got a joke you haven't heard.'

'Hit me, Daddy.'

'Mickey Mouse was in front of a judge who was looking over his divorce petition. "Mr Mouse," the judge said, "I can't grant you a divorce from your wife just because you think she's crazy." "Your honor," Mickey says, "I didn't say Minnie was crazy. I said she was fucking Goofy."'

'Oh, Daddy,' she groaned, batting his arm.

Dance after dance, they bobbed up and down in silence, uneasy together, yet perfectly at ease. In a voice that tore at her heart he finally said, 'This holiday has just flown by. In a couple of days you'll be flying off into the wild blue yonder.'

An attractive woman in stiletto heels and a floor-length ruby dress polkaed past. She hiked up her gown and flashed her father a big grin. One, two, three and a one, two, three, dancing past an enormous woman with hollyhocks on her skirt.

Her father said, 'See that woman over there in the red dress and high heels? That's Maggie Hubbard. She's got a butterfly tattooed on her hip.'

She wondered how he knew, but was too shocked to ask.

'When you're young,' he said, looking out the window, 'your eyes are blue and your pecker's red. When you're old, it's the other way around.'

She glanced at her mother's feet as they polkaed past their table. She remembered hearing a podiatrist on the radio say that high heels were the greatest aphrodisiac known to man. With her bad back, her mother could never wear them, her closet stacked with a dozen pairs of ballerina pumps.

Her father's friends ask her to dance. She dances with men with silver hair. As she sails past, she sees her parents sitting together, turned away from each other like the two faces of Janus.

Before midnight, a last dance with her father. They tango past the rows of tables. Her mother is sitting alone and sad, staring at the foil-wrapped stars.

Champagne is poured at the stroke of midnight. Her father points to the label on the Jacques Bonet bottle. 'It's a good thing that old guy's last name wasn't Strap.'

They light sparklers, blow noise-makers made by the Double Happiness Company. She stares at the Chinese characters above MADE IN HONG KONG. The Down Beats play 'Auld Lang Syne'. She will be leaving in a few days and still doesn't know what to say, or do, to bring her family together.

Her father lifts a foil horn. He crosses his eyes as his cheeks swell with air, reminding her of the statue she was given this Christmas. 'It's from Florence,' her mother blurted out when she removed the paper. The foot-high plaster statue was pocked with air bubbles, the seams of the mold visible. *David's* eyes were crossed as if he were mocking the poor imitation.

'Don't you like it?' her mother asked.

She didn't say anything, but her face must have said it all.

'And I thought I'd finally managed to get you something you'd really like. You've always admired naked statues, Katie. When I saw it in the catalogue, I thought you'd just love it.'

Nothing more was said about the *David* until tonight, when she was getting dressed to come to the Country Club. Her mother came into her room and said she didn't have to take the statue if she didn't want to; her suitcase was already pretty full. Her mother's back was to her but, in the mirror, Katie could see she was crying, her stoic mother who never cried, the fifty-percent Indian.

Her mother had walked to the bookcase and wound up one music box after another, their melodies melting together: 'Lara's Theme' from *Dr Zhivago*, 'I'm Dreaming of a White Christmas', 'Strangers in the Night'.

Katie watched her father pick up a noise-maker as she remembered that painful music. His cheeks filled with air and she thought, How helpless we all are. We can never say what we mean to say; we can never love the way we want to love. We can only signal each other in the dark, like revelers who sound their paper horns as they pass in the night.

Don't give me that baloney

On New Year's Day her parents were in the den reading the paper. Katie marched into the room in her pajamas and stood in front of her father's chair. She held out a letter. 'I got this eight months ago from Rhett.'

Her father's head jerked backward as if she'd slapped him. 'I don't know any Rhett.'

'Don't give me that baloney, Daddy.' She tried to hand him the envelope, but he knocked it away, as if touching it would scorch his fingers.

'There is nothing in that I want to read.' He stood up to leave and her mother grabbed his hand as he went past.

'It won't hurt to hear what he's got to say, Hay.'

'You listen to that crap if you want to, Momma, but I won't.'

'Haywood Amory Rivers,' her mother said, 'put your butt in that chair and hear your daughter out.'

Her father looked disgusted, but Katie was relieved to see him sit down. She cleared her throat, started to read out loud.

'"I discovered something interesting when I passed through Saskatoon. In every new town I go to, I do what Dad does. Look through the phone directory to see if we have any relatives we don't know about. An Abe Rivers was listed so I called him. When I asked if he had any American relatives, he said his great-grandfather, Elijah Rivers, was from Union Grove, Tennessee."'

'That's a crock of shit,' her father said.

'Go on, sugar. Don't mind your father.'

'"Elijah didn't believe that one man should own another. When his brothers joined the Confederate Army, he went to Canada."'

'My grandfather would never have done that.'

'Shush, Haywood.' Her mother put a hand on his leg.

'"Elijah was disinherited for being a Union sympathizer so he stayed in Canada after the war. Abe said that when Elijah's son, our Grandpa Amory, decided to move back to Tennessee around 1890, he invented the story about his father dying at Gettysburg. Thought you'd be interested to know that Great-granddaddy Rivers was a Civil War draft dodger."' Katie folded the letter and looked at her father.

'If you think I'm going to accept a lie from a yellow-bellied coward,' he said, 'you've got another think coming.'

Something made Katie go to the gun cabinet. Last night she had dreamed about a tree. In the dream her brother had told her that for him to come back, she had to show their father a tree. But what tree?

'What the hell do you want in there?' her father said.

Hidden under some boxes of ammunition she found an old leather-bound Bible. She opened it to a page of names filled out in faded blue ink. She wanted to jump up and down when she saw that an entry had been cut out of the family tree. She held it out so her father could see for himself.

'Doesn't mean a damn thing.'

'Rhett met Abe, Daddy. He has the Rivers' trademark. The cartilage is fused together at the top of Abe's left ear, just like yours and his and mine.'

Her father was staring at the book, jingling his change.

'Haywood,' her mother said, 'our son wants to come home.'

'I have no son.'

'Then it's okay with you that our boy spends the rest of his life in Canada?'

'That chickenshit can rot for all I care.'

Katie said, 'Daddy, he's been pardoned.'

'Not by me he hasn't.'

'How can you be like that?' she said. 'Rhett is my brother. I want him at my wedding. I told him I'd call today to let him know what you said. If he can come home.'

'Tell him he can go to hell.'

'Haywood,' her mother said, 'it's time to turn the other cheek.'

Her father was quiet for a moment, then he started jingling his coins again. 'That damn traitor practically had me drive him across the border. He even tricked me into buying him a kachina.'

Katie picked up her brother's letter, flicking through the pages to find the paragraph she wanted. '"I was wrong to leave the way I did, but I'd thought about the alternatives. There was Canada and there was the slammer and Canada won hands down. Looking back, I wish

I'd done things differently—"'
'Then why the hell didn't he?'
'He was brave enough to refuse to be drafted, Daddy.'
Her father stood up to leave. 'I don't have to listen to your liberal bullshit.'
'Let me read you just one more paragraph.'
'That's not going to make one iota of difference, Katie.'
'One paragraph,' she said. 'That's all I ask.'
He slouched in the doorway, half-in the room, half-out. 'Well, read if you're going to.'
' "Please tell Mom and Dad I don't blame them. They were only being true to themselves and what they believed in. If I could speak to them right now, the question I would ask them is this. If Jimmy Carter can pardon a hundred thousand draft dodgers, can't they find it in their hearts to forgive just one?"'
Her mother bolted off the couch. 'I'm calling Rhett right now.'
Her father stepped in front of her. 'The neighbors spat at us when he ran away. We lost patients we'd had for twenty years.'
'That was over five and a half years ago, Haywood. I couldn't afford to want Rhett home before now because he couldn't come, but he's been pardoned. I don't know about you, but I'd rather have a son some people think is a coward rather than one who's six feet under.'

Merry-go-round

Katie sat in her mother's bedroom, trying to get through to Whitehorse. It was the third time she'd called in the last few minutes.

'Still no luck, sugar?'

Katie looked up to see her mother chewing her lip in the doorway. She was holding a lime-oak picture frame, the image toward her.

'No answer yet, Mom.'

Her mother carried the frame into the room and leaned it against the wall. Katie was curious what it was. All she could see was one badly-burned edge. She was about to ask her mother about it when she heard a crackly voice on the line.

'What's he saying, sugar?' her mother said. 'What's he saying?'

She hung up. 'Recorded message. "The international lines are busy. Try again later."'

Her mother sighed and replaced the picture above her bed with the scorched one. Katie wanted to cry when she saw what it was. In the black-and-white portrait they all looked happy. Katie's arm was hugging her father's neck. Rhett was in her mother's lap grinning, holding a jack-o'-lantern her father had carved to match her brother's gap-toothed mouth.

Her mother wiped the frame with a rag. 'This is the only thing I pulled out of the fire that wasn't burned to a cinder.'

She stared at her mother, felt her jaw fall open. 'So you didn't go along with Daddy when he burned everything.'

'I didn't go along with anything. I kept thinking I'd be able to make Hay see the light, but he'd clam up whenever I mentioned Rhett's name.' Her mother straightened the picture. 'I don't want you to think your father's not a fine man. He is. He's just like the rest of us, a little blind and stubborn.' She lifted the bottom corner. 'Why don't you try again, sugar? This infernal waiting is driving me crazy.'

Katie redialed the number. The phone rang a dozen times. She was on the verge of hanging up when she heard her brother's voice. Her heart started to race like she was on the back of Rhett's Kawasaki, flying along at a ninety miles an hour.

'Rhett. Yeah, it's me . . . Happy New Year to you too. Been a long time. Too long.' She gave her mother a thumbs up. 'I read your letter to them. Yeah. All of it . . . This morning . . . The Abe part he had a little trouble with. What? The line's breaking up . . . We didn't think it would be. Sure. I'll talk to you after Mom.'

She held the phone out. Her mother grabbed the receiver and as she spoke, Katie watched her mother trace something on the bedside table, then rub it out with her finger, then draw it again in the dust.

Her mother's face was tense when Katie came into the den. She'd never seen her look so scared.

'You've been with Daddy over twenty minutes, sugar. Did you manage to get him to call—'

'He's talking to Rhett right now.'

Her mother's hand went to her heart. 'Thank the Lord and Jesus Christ.' She quickly wiped her eyes. 'Your hair's all knotted, sugar. Sit on the floor. I'll comb you out with my fingers like I used to when you were little.'

Her mother had just started raking her fingers through the ends when Katie heard shouting coming from her father's bedroom.

Without breaking rhythm her mother said, 'At least they're speaking.'

They both burst out laughing, then fell silent.

'Momma,' she said finally, 'there's something I have to tell you. I'm not engaged to Wieslaw and never have been.' She turned around, surprised to see the hint of a smile on her mother's mouth.

'Don't give it another thought, sugar.'

'You're not angry with me?'

'You might have fooled your Daddy, but you didn't fool me.'

She was relieved her mother wasn't upset, but felt a little annoyed her story hadn't been believed. 'How did you know I wasn't telling the truth?'

'Whenever I brought up your wedding, you never seemed that excited about it. Those magazines you brought almost had me fooled, but I had my suspicions. I don't hold with lying, but if you had to say you wanted your brother at your wedding to get round Daddy, well, bully for you.'

'There's something else I have to tell you. I'm not a soloist with American Ballet Theater and never have been.' She braced herself, but her mother's fingers continued to scratch gently down her neck.

'I'm sorry, sugar, your career didn't turn out the way you wanted it to. I know how hard you worked to make it happen.'

Katie sat in silence as she thought of the dozens of excuses she'd given the last six years for not coming home. 'How can you forgive me?'

'I know how much ballet meant to you. You must have had your reasons for doing what you did. That doesn't mean I don't want to put you over my knee and give you a good hiding.'

She looked at her mother's calf where there was a green-black spot the size of a fifty-cent piece. Her mother had always bruised easily. She was always rushing around in a world that was too small, running up against the edges.

Her mother was saying, 'Remember that lavender chiffon dress you wore to your first Cotillion?'

'The one we bought at Merry-Go-Round?'

Her mother nodded. 'You wanted to keep it perfect so you begged to borrow my dress shields. You were twelve and hadn't even started to sweat, but I let you wear them, even though you didn't need them. We all need our little illusions to help us get through life.' Her mother gently stroked her hair. 'There. Your fairy locks are all combed out.'

The love she felt for her mother was so enormous that she reached back to touch her leg. Realizing that wasn't enough, she turned around to hug her, but her mother pulled away. She lifted the hem of her housecoat like a ball gown, wheeling and spinning and turning as she pirouetted across the floor.

ACKNOWLEDGMENTS

Like any novel that has evolved over a period of years, this book has benefited from the generous input of friends, family and strangers. John Steinbeck created a word for chunks of prose that readers skip. Hooptedoodle. If you don't want to read a list of names, stop here. You have been warned.

Thanks to Kieran McCloskey, first reader of the first draft, who supported me in every way throughout the book's long infancy.

The Double Happiness Company had its first public outing with The Group, to whom I am deeply indebted. *Besos y amor* to fellow writers and friends Cecily Bomberg, Hume Cronyn, Candyce Lange, Keith New, Wendy Perriam and David Spencer.

Very special thanks to three people whose enthusiasm for this book made me think I might salvage it after seven years in the bottom drawer: Danijel Lozancic, Eugene Skeef and especially to Dr Ian Douglas-Wilson who motivated me to deliver weekly installments.

Namaste to the writers' group at the North London Buddhist Centre: Za Ball, Anne Ballard, Neil Devlin, Jackie McGarry and Anna Meryt. A second *namaste* to Anne Ballard for reading the complete manuscript.

I owe an enormous debt to ZenAzzurrians Aimee Hansen, Roger Levy, Steve Mullins, Annemarie Neary, Sally Ratcliffe, Richard Simmons and Elise Valmorbida. Double thanks to Steve, Annemarie and Elise who read the complete MS and made illuminating comments. *Compadres, siempre os llevaré en mi corazón.*

I am blessed to have three incredible friends on the other side of the pond, Nancy Wright Hardy and Kathleen O'Neill who read the book in e-mail chunks and John Claassen who acted as my Manhattan courier. You all have big pieces of my heart.

There have been other friends who have read the book in manuscript long before it was ripe: Tippy Ackerman, Sebastian and Gráinne Balfour, Mary Boyle, Thomas Dormandy, Jane Geerts, Jane Glitre, Susan Hinchsliffe, Sue Lacey, Fiona Passantino, Beverlie Manson and

Katie Mitchell. A big *abrazo* to Rachel Sanger, a fan of my first novel who arranged for her book group to read my second. I would like to acknowledge the help of Rena Boucher, Van Pittsenbargar, John Pittsenbargar, Scott Williams and the late Jackie Mann Williams who provided me with information on subjects as diverse as police procedure, the effects of Demerol and what it's like to enter a Viet Cong machine-gun nest.

Very special thanks are due to Anthea Eno who, before I had an agent, liked this book so much she took it personally to Faber and Faber. To Jenny Parrott at Bloomsbury for finding me an agent. To Fiona Jakobi whose keen interest in the book was responsible for getting me my US agent. To Kathleen Tiernan who was an enthusiastic and loyal supporter at St Martin's Press. Biggest thanks to Uli Rushby-Smith and Eugene Ludlow who, at a time of seismic upheavals in publishing, worked hard and long to place this novel.

Special thanks to Jonny of Eclectic Method who mixed the book's trailer and to Tom Platten who directed the promotional recording, 'Acrobat of God'.

To my first ballet teacher, the late Marion McGuire, who generously taught me all she knew. A standing ovation to Christian Holder who read the 375-page manuscript of a stranger, to master teachers Finis Jhung and Rosanna Seravalli for agreeing to read the typescript. Extra bow for Naomi Sorkin, former soloist at ABT, who generously read the manuscript twice and introduced me to Christian.

Thanks to Gary Chryst, the late Enrique Martínez and Kevin Self for allowing me to use their names fictitiously in this book. Also to my god-sister, Marilyn Heathman, for permitting me to use her name as a character. *Mil gracias* to ace photographers Kurt Nimmo and Marcus Bastel/Millennium Pictures for allowing me to use their work, to Robin Beste for help in reformatting the manuscript, to Sandra Tena and Christian Martí-Menzel for correcting my Spanish, to Niki Natarajan for being my palmistry advisor and to Dr Carl Chang for his medical expertise. 'Home is so Sad' by Philip Larkin is reprinted by permission of Faber and Faber Ltd.

I have been the beneficiary in cyberspace of what Tennessee Williams called 'the kindness of strangers'. The following people took the time and trouble to answer my e-mails: Laura Cruz and Leon Metz of the *El Paso Times*; Dr Ronald B Frankum, Jr, Vietnam expert and historian; Padraig Houlahan, Lowell Observatory; Julie Nixon, City Manager's Office, City of Oshawa, Ontario, and 'Craig' for information on vintage Ford pickups.

Thanks to my editor, Charles Boyle. For making a ream of paper into a beautiful book, thanks to word-design.co.uk. Gratitude and thanks to Ian Gollan, the IT wizard of Judd Street, who has come to my aid more times than I can count.

Last, but certainly not least, my family needs to be thanked for their incalculable support. To my late father, John E Aylor, who set this book in motion with a chance remark about flowers. To my mother, Alice Aylor, who has blessed me with her stories, her wisdom, her generosity and her love. To my brother, John K Aylor, who patiently provided information about subjects as diverse as Kawasakis and mouse houses. To my nephew, Keaton, whom I adore. (Here I must apologize to my long-suffering cats: first Nambé, then Tiva, who had to hear the manuscript a thousand times out loud.)

But most of all, thanks to my husband, David, who has been amanuensis, cheerleader, critic, cook, chauffeur, life coach, proofreader and sounding board. He has tolerated this book for as long as I have known him. It would never have been finished without his encouragement, tireless support and enthusiasm. *Pequeño, te amo con todo mi corazón.*

Finally, this book would never have been published had it not been for Geraldine Godfrey, my own personal angel. *Nada puede quitarme su danza.*